FALLING NIGHT

Falling Night by Phil Clarke was a hard read. The difficulty in consuming Clarke's book was that it was a stark retelling of the myriad of experiences our family and team members had throughout the Horn of Africa, especially during the famine and civil war in Somalia. His book dredged up memories of starving children, abused women, and skeletons that pointed the way to remote villages–where not one soul was left alive.

Falling Night is startlingly real as it recalls the dangerously shifting sands of tribal alliances, western political agendas, and brutality that have characterised Africa's recent wars. Shockingly honest, it reveals how hairline cracks in human relationships become insurmountable ravines as they're tossed into the crucible of life. Yet astoundingly, faith, and love can somehow be grasped where hope goes to die. Humankind at their worse are overshadowed by faith in God and His love.

Though this book is not light, bedtime reading, it's a surprising book. For all the evidence to the contrary, light and love conquer the darkness and hatred. This book sings, rather than moans, in regard to what plagues this world. It encourages the reader to choose Light when that choice makes little sense. It challenges us to attempt the impossible when life takes on its most ugliest forms. Clarke dares to suggest that inside the worst that the world has to offer, love wins.

DR. NIK RIPKEN
FOUNDER AND CEO NIK RIPKEN MINISTRIES
AUTHOR OF *THE INSANITY OF GOD*

PHIL CLARKE

FALLING NIGHT

An unlikely aid worker in a horrific war zone that hides a greater evil

AMBASSADOR INTERNATIONAL
GREENVILLE, SOUTH CAROLINA & BELFAST, NORTHERN IRELAND

www.ambassador-international.com

Falling Night

ISBN: 978-1-64960-344-9
eISBN: 978-1-64960-361-6

Cover design by Hannah Linder Designs
Interior typesetting by Dentelle Design

AMBASSADOR INTERNATIONAL
Emerald House Group, Inc.
411 University Ridge, Suite B14
Greenville, SC 29601
United States
www.ambassador-international.com

AMBASSADOR BOOKS
The Mount
2 Woodstock Link
Belfast, BT6 8DD
Northern Ireland, United Kingdom
www.ambassadormedia.co.uk

The colophon is a trademark of Ambassador, a Christian publishing company.

DEDICATION

This novel is dedicated to Africa's countless unnamed victims of war.

Blood and destruction shall be so in use

And dreadful objects so familiar

That mothers shall but smile when they behold

Their infants quartered with the hands of war.

Julius Caesar, Act III, Scene 1

AUTHOR'S NOTE

I started this novel in 1994 during my first posting as an aid worker to the civil war in Somalia. I soon abandoned the project, as I was overwhelmed by experiences that required time and distance to process.

When I went to Côte d'Ivoire to work with Liberian refugees in late 1997, I picked up my pen/computer again as an outlet to deal with post-traumatic stress from five difficult months in Rwanda and Zaire (now the Democratic Republic of the Congo). Straightaway, the plot of this book fell into place, but for many reasons, it has taken me over twenty years to complete the tale that I envisioned back then.

Kugombwala mixes elements of the African conflicts in which I have worked as an aid worker—Somalia, Rwanda, Congo/Zaire, Liberia, and Sudan—with a little bit of Sierra Leone, where I have not been. My aim has been to create a realistic yet fictional African civil war set in the 1990s, based on actual experiences by me or by others I have met. However, I have deliberately toned down the brutality and atrocities because the story would have become sado-pornographic and unreadable. Africa's wars during that unhappy decade were far worse than I describe in the novel, except that each conflict contained only some of the mentioned elements, rather than all.

MedRelief is inspired by my many years with Médecins Sans Frontières, an organization that does sterling medical work throughout the world, while the London office described in the novel echoes that of a British environmental organisation I worked for prior to becoming an aid worker. I have used poetic licence to create a situation where the same MedRelief international team is present throughout Alan's stay in Kugombwala. In reality, most aid agencies have a regular turnover of international staff, such that expat teams are constantly changing in composition and dynamic.

I have avoided telling the stories of the countless victims of Africa's civil wars, since the novel is predominantly recounted through the eyes of an international aid worker—the lens through which I experienced some of these conflicts. These wars can be described from other angles, including the accounts of the perpetrators who have been forced by their superiors to kill fellow citizens. Their stories—as well as those of the victims—are for more appropriate and better-experienced people to write.

PROLOGUE

Ambushed. Underfoot. By discarded belongings—the detritus of hunted humanity, littering the path. Before them lay the evidence of an attack on a group of fleeing refugees—a necklace, family photos, a blanket, cooking pots, food. Personal treasures and essential possessions, all jettisoned in the haste to escape imminent death.

The team continued along the trail, softly treading the soil to avoid being snared by additional human refuse. A kilometre further, the rank stench of rotting flesh forewarned them of what was to come.

First on the path was the carcass of a small child, its porcelain-white skull smashed by a blunt object and its body stripped to a skeleton by ants.

At last, he had found the evidence he sought.

CLACK-CLACK-CLACK.

A rattle of gunfire. He hit the ground face-down, covering his head with his hands as bullets whistled past. The shooting stopped and was followed by distant shouting from the road behind him. Nearby, a colleague moaned.

Heavy footfalls reverberated on the ground, accompanied by the flop, flop of wellington boots slapping alternately against calves and shins.

Another burst of fire. Loud and close. The smell of gunpowder smoke. Angry shouting near where he lay.

And then his spinal radar told him that guns were pointed at his back.

His turn now.

CHAPTER 1

KUGOMBWALA, AFRICA

END OF THE SECOND MILLENNIUM AD

Thud. Reality hit Alan Swales when the Hercules cargo plane struck the crater-scarred tarmac of Ndombazu International Airport after a steep descent to evade enemy gunfire. The hard touchdown sent a jolt up his spine, followed by violent vibrations from the rattling airframe as the plane rapidly decelerated down the runway. *I'm about to die!* Alan braced himself for the fuselage to break apart.

After the shaking and emotional shock subsided, his attention was drawn to the window. An array of military assets scrolled past his view as the aircraft traversed the airfield, presenting a world apart from safe, little Britain: armoured personnel carriers patrolling the perimeter, ground-attack helicopters readied for action, and battle tanks guarding the terminal. The runway was surrounded by a rampart of fresh soil, topped by rolls of razor wire, and interspersed with sandbag towers and foxhole emplacements. From these, soldiers in blue helmets peered out over heavy machine guns.

Alan was aware the United Nations had sent a peacekeeping force to the Democratic Republic of Kugombwala yet had assumed this would be limited to a few soldiers slouching in the sun, separating opposing sides that welcomed the excuse not to fight each other. But it was clear this was not the case here. Why would the U.N. need so much firepower to oversee a simple ceasefire?

"Stay away from that window, or you'll get a bullet in your face!" his fellow passenger yelled above the roar of the engines.

Alan jerked his head back as the reason for the arsenal of heavy weaponry struck him—Kugombwala was extremely dangerous. Which meant the locals were hostile and willing to kill. Would they also shoot at him? Until then, he had not considered that possibility because there was no risk of taking a hit when watching action movies. That was the closest he had hitherto been to war.

By contrast, his current circumstance was far from the fantasy of film—a noxious feeling of fear mixed with disappointment—for his arrival in the combat zone of an African civil war lacked cinematic drama. There were no explosions, no triumphant background music, and no cool comrades carrying big guns. Instead, he was deafened by the drone of aircraft engines and sitting beside someone with the machismo of a mouse.

"Welcome to body-bag land," his travelling companion squeaked after the plane had come to a halt. "Did you remember to bring yours? I tell ya, it's mighty hot out there, and I ain't talking Fahrenheit."

The American accent made Alan momentarily wonder whether he might nonetheless be in a Hollywood film. No, that was impossible, as their heroes always made it to the end. So, this was not theatre, for he already doubted whether he would leave Kugombwala alive. Had the humanitarian agency fooled him into thinking it was safe to volunteer without combat experience as an aid worker in a war zone? Would that ill-informed decision that had plunged him into the jaws of death turn out to be the biggest mistake of his life?

The jackal bit into the maggot-infested corpse. Carrion was now plentiful on the plateau, but the scavenging predator still looked up in alarm as a plane passed overhead.

Colonel MacEdwin Mfaume-Simbwa scanned the surrounding bush as the aircraft eased down onto the airstrip. He did not want company in this remote corner of Kugombwala, for he had no intention of sharing the incoming cargo.

"Wait here," he commanded his subordinates before marching off to meet the pilot.

A rugged, tanned face accosted him as he approached the cockpit. "Hey, you, who's in charge here?"

"I am." The colonel took an instant dislike to the pilot for his disrespect, but decided to not display it. He might become a useful acquaintance: a courier to his contact at the embassy, a smuggler for future illegal shipments, or a source of intelligence. "Are you Rhodesian?" the colonel guessed from the accent, using that country's pre-independence name to provoke a reaction.

"Yes, and proud of it."

Typical white Zimbabwean—the colonel frowned—*thinks he owns this continent because of his skin colour.* He feigned a smile to appear affirmative before getting down to business. "Let me have the cargo manifest."

It was amazing how easy it had been, he reflected, as he checked the list. All it had required was a visit to an embassy in one of Europe's capitals, where he had presented his credentials and asked to meet the military attaché. After a long interview he was advised to return the following week, when he was promised support on strict condition the deal was kept to himself. The weapons and ammunition were Soviet-made, he noted, and had been flown in from another African country to conceal their origin and source of funding.

Pfffffttttttt. He whistled his troops over. "Careful with those crates," he barked. "You will all get a bullet if any are missing or damaged."

The pilot laughed. "Proper discipline; thet's what I like to see."

The colonel suppressed a chuckle at his ruse that had started their bonding. *White people are so easy to dupe,* he confirmed to himself. "Tell me," he could now ask, "what's your take on Kugombwala?"

"Can't say I'd heard of the country until the civil war hit the news a few months ago."

That had coincided with a lack of juicy stories for the media to report on, the colonel recalled. Africa only got mentioned when there was a lull in the West's political spats, sex scandals, or sporting events.

The pilot continued, "There was talk about rebel groups controlling large parts of the country." He laughed. "Sounds like this place is going to the dogs."

The colonel churned the soil with his boot heel. African chaos. A favourite narrative peddled by editors to feed their public's insatiable appetite for horror. "Western media tend to exaggerate—they described Kugombwala as degenerate and dangerous to entertain their punters, rather than to inform them of the facts." He referred to the time before the war had worsened.

"Ag, you can't trust reporters." The pilot spat. "They're all communists."

The colonel ignored that allegation as the Cold War was over, but otherwise agreed. He recalled the period before he had defected from the army to instigate his own insurgency, when he had been tasked with monitoring the war correspondents who had descended on Kugombwala's capital, Ndombazu, to cover the outbreak of hostilities.

Those parasites, he huffed to himself, *earning a living by spreading bad news about foreign countries, while playing and partying there as if the lights were about to be switched off.* They had occupied the best hotel where they had set up their satellite phones before heading for the poolside bar to catch up with colleagues and swap stories from the other combat zones of the 1990s. Their egofest had been enhanced by Kugombwala's lively music as well as the attentions of Ndombazu's bucks and beauties—most of whom reported to the colonel.

His government had been concerned about the presence of foreign journalists, as bad press could trigger a withdrawal of international support. All areas beyond the capital were therefore designated off-limits to non-nationals to prevent them witnessing the government's military setbacks. A stringer who had attempted to evade the restrictions was roughed up and imprisoned for espionage by the colonel's unit, which had kept the other newshounds at bay.

By hindering access to fresh news, the Kugombwalan government had temporarily curtailed overseas interest in the civil war, even though the fighting had continued. But it had been unable to prevent access to rebel-held areas, where an adventurous film crew had stumbled upon starving women and children covered in flies, providing shocking images to sell to newspapers and TV.

The pilot interrupted his recollections. "A few weeks ago, the story shifted to the famine and the resulting U.N. intervention after the military coup. Kugombwala's now making headlines—even on CNN." He laughed again. "Perfect timing for Christmas, huh?"

Ignoring the sarcasm, the colonel conceded his point about the great festival of consumerism. The tragedy allowed editors to pander to the public's subconscious desire to savour other people's sufferings in order to intensify the smug pleasure of spoiling oneself when others could not. Such feelings would be enhanced during the season of goodwill by a delectable dose of hidden guilt over their selfishness. He thought about the busy shoppers who would boost this gratification by easing their troubled consciences through the token sacrifice of a pound coin into a collecting tin after spending a hundred times more on food and presents.

"Let me guess"—the colonel seethed at how the media would be marketing the possibility to augment Christmas cheer by purchasing indulgences—"the papers and telly are now full of wide-eyed, starving children—and the message that money is needed to feed them."

"You got it, bro." The pilot grinned. "Same, same story—corrupt African government, nasty rebels, civil war, famine, and hapless kids caught in the middle."

"You must be doing lots of flights into Kugombwala," the colonel probed for real intelligence.

"For sure, three or four times a day."

"Food for the famine?"

"Not only, my friend."

"Guns?"

"My client's business is confidential." The pilot winked.

Ah, that's what I need to know. The colonel watched his men load the last crates onto a truck. The arms deal with the foreign government was not exclusive—they were supporting all rebel groups to ensure they backed the eventual winner. The amount he received in future would accord with his ability to outmanoeuvre his rivals.

"It was good to meet you," he told the pilot. "Hope to see you again." *With more weapons,* he continued in his mind.

"Ya, man, it's been a pleasure. Keep up the good discipline."

That's only part of the equation to achieve military victory, the colonel reflected as the plane taxied to take off. He also now had an overseas backer supplying weapons and ammunition. But he lacked additional funds as well as a force of loyal soldiers who would fight to the death for him. Given the competition over Kugombwala's meagre resources, he would have to find alternative sources of cash and gullible recruits.

NDOMBAZU AIRPORT, KUGOMBWALA

Alan unclipped his seatbelt. The Hercules had come to a halt, and the engines had been switched off. Relief from the overpowering noise was quickly reversed by the mounting heat in the cargo hold. Rivulets of sweat dribbled down his neck and flowed from his armpits.

The passenger door was opened from outside, revealing an Indian soldier wearing a blue U.N. helmet.

"Time to go, Greenhorn," the American chirped.

Alan followed him into the bright sunlight. He was first struck by the stifling heat. It was just as hot as inside the aeroplane and even hotter in the direct sun that scorched his freckled skin. His next impression was of vivid, verdant, jungle greenery, with plants sprouting everywhere. Weeds pushed through cracks in the runway tarmac, while bushes burst out of the fresh earthworks, and a wall of great trees loomed all around. Nature's vigour contrasted with human decay. A dilapidated cluster of concrete buildings bore the words *Ndombazu International Airport,* while nearby, a pile of crashed planes made an interesting sculpture, though Alan doubted they had anything to do with art.

He followed the other passengers towards the airport terminal, where the pale blue U.N. flag hung limply from a pole.

"So, what brings you to this circus?" A fellow traveller appeared alongside him.

"I'm an aid worker."

"Oh, yeah? Saving up for a villa in the South of France with your Red Cross salary?"

"No, I'm a volunteer with MedRelief."

"Never heard of 'em. What do they do?"

"Feeding programmes for starving kids, plus running the General Hospital."

"Oh, that lot. They're those mad idealists trying to save the world. Good luck to you, mate. Everyone else is here to make money. Take him, for example." He pointed to the American ahead of them who had sat beside Alan on the plane. "He's a hairdresser working for a U.S. multinational corporation that services the United Nations—and he's clearing four thousand bucks a month."

"You're joking!" Instant envy reminded Alan that he was an unsalaried volunteer.

"No, I'm not. Even the Indian, Pakistani, and Bangladeshi soldiers are getting an extra nine hundred dollars per month in danger pay for being here."

The U.N.'s limitless wealth was not evident at the terminal, which had been stripped by looters of everything that could be sold, right down to its electrical fittings, leaving bare wires that sprouted out of walls and ceilings. Rather than renovate the building, the peacekeepers had partitioned off a billet using cheap plywood for screens and sackcloth for doors.

The foreign troops were the likely tormentors of a distressed monkey that was tethered by its neck to a concrete pillar.

"Stay away, sir. It's vicious," a female official at the reception desk warned Alan as he approached it. She then addressed the newly arrived passengers. "Register here, please, for your passes. The military convoy to town will depart from the front of the building."

"When's it leaving?" Alan was disappointed that no one had come to meet him, heightening the discomfort of being alone in an alien environment.

"As soon as it gets here from town, sir. I can see from my list that your agency is sending a vehicle with it."

Relieved he had not been forgotten, Alan exited by the main entrance, detouring around a wall of sandbags to reach the forecourt. More sandbags screened the windows, making the building look like a bunker.

A white-painted battle tank was parked in front of the terminal, with *U.N.* emblazoned in large letters on the turret. Its barrel was aimed at a gap in the razor-wire perimeter fence between sandbag towers guarded by peacekeeping soldiers. Beyond, an empty road stretched into gloomy rainforest, where unknown dangers lurked.

Alan noticed the airport personnel had adopted two contrasting strategies to cope with the surrounding threat—pretentious disregard or aggressive posturing. Some tried to look cool and casual in t-shirt, shorts, flip-flops, and shades; others were armed and armoured, ready to repulse a surprise attack. One of these individuals stood by the tank having a smoke—a hard-looking man with a crew cut, clad in a flak jacket, with a handgun holstered under his armpit and an automatic rifle slung over his shoulder.

"Got a light, mate?" Alan's inquisitive personality motivated him to make conversation.

"Sure, pal."

"You working here?" Obvious question, but what else to ask?

"Yeah, I'm the U.N. security officer."

"How did you get into that?"

"Done twelve years with Special Forces."

At last, someone who could give a professional opinion about the situation. "So, what's it like here?"

"Mayhem, pal. Total anarchy out there. Kugombwalans are bandits—the lot of them. They've all got guns and are willing to use them. You just arrived?"

"Aye."

"Glad I'm not you. My contract finishes next week, and I'm not staying a minute longer than I have to."

"What makes it so bad?"

"Haven't you heard? They killed three peacekeeping soldiers last week."

"I must have missed that story." Why hadn't MedRelief told him?

"It happened down that road where you are about to go. Ambushed a U.N. vehicle . . . "

Alan's attention was diverted by an increasingly urgent whine from across the tarmac, where a ground-attack helicopter revved its engines in preparation for take-off. The rotor blades started to spin, rotating ever faster until they became a blur.

"So, they're sending that chopper to cover the military convoy coming from the city," the man continued. "We keep having to increase our security measures here. Latest intel is one of the armed gangs wants to take an aid worker hostage to score a hundred thousand dollars in ransom money. My advice, pal—get out as soon as you can. Kugombwalans hate foreigners and will kill to chase us out. Even the women and children throw rocks at us."

Alan shuddered. The irritating American had not been joking about the need to bring a body-bag; being personally targeted put the hazards on a much higher level than being accidentally caught in crossfire.

Why had he risked his life and liberty coming here, instead of staying in the safety and comfort of home?

CHAPTER 2

YORKSHIRE, BRITAIN

ONE MONTH EARLIER

Life's great, Alan acknowledged as he placed the trophy from the day's football tournament on the mantelpiece. He then flopped onto the sofa to admire his collection of cups and medals from further away, but the day's exertions combined with padded comfort caused him to doze off into sweet, well-deserved sleep.

Vvvoooooommmm. He was awoken by the oppressive sound of the vacuum cleaner that filled the house.

Alan cursed. Why did his girlfriend insist on hoovering three times a week? He faced an imminent attack by the fast-moving nozzle, a command to shift his feet, plus criticism for lazing around. He had to get out. But he needed an excuse that would not be construed as shirking his share of the housework.

"Mandy?" he shouted to make himself heard above the din.

The motor stopped. "Aye?"

"I'm going to the allotment to scrounge some vegetables from my old folks."

"All right, Al. See ya later."

Spared confrontation, Alan bounded out of the door and up the hill towards the edge of town. Relief gave way to reflection along the way, for the disruption to his peace roused a recurring worry, which had plagued him over the previous months with the awareness that something was wrong with his otherwise successful existence.

It seemed a perfect life from the outside, for he and Mandy had it all—a modern, three-bedroom house on a quiet cul-de-sac in their hometown in the north of England; two brand new cars; and enough money for an overseas holiday every year. Alan could congratulate himself on how much he had achieved, for already at the age of twenty-eight, he had an attractive partner plus many friends, had reached junior management, and was captain of the town football team. His needs for companionship, sex, money, success, and respect were all being satisfied.

Yet it was not enough. Something was missing from his life—and it was not children, as confirmed by his experience of coaching the junior soccer squad. Nor was it a lack of optimism, for the end of the Cold War and the economic upturn of the 1990s promised an unprecedented time of global peace and prosperity.

Alan had first assumed his deep inner dissatisfaction was caused by not getting enough of what he already had, but a decent pay rise, plus his team's promotion in the local football leagues, had not dissipated the unidentified desire. The feeling baffled him, as he was the only person he knew who was affected in this way.

The success-driven culture of Alan's peers made it socially unacceptable to discuss such personal problems with his friends. Likewise, it seemed sensible to avoid sharing the subject with Mandy, in case it exposed a weakness she might exploit. He was thus forced to ponder his troubles alone, but was unable to diagnose his problem.

At the top of the slope, he pushed open a gate and approached a hunched figure tending a patch of potatoes. "Ay-up, how's our dad doing today?" he called out.

"Not too bad," came the grudging reply. "Just a few aches from this digging. Me back's playing up again."

"Sorry to hear that."

"I got no reason to complain." His father was quick to brush off any sympathy before adding, "And nor have you, lad."

"Right." Alan only half-agreed but decided not to voice his opinion. "You got any cauliflowers going spare?"

"You can take two, but leave the big one. It's for the show."

"Thanks, Dad." He cut off a couple of heads, but his mind refused to let go of his predicament. It was now or never. "By the way, what's wrong with moaning once in a while?"

"What do you mean?" His father sounded suspicious of the subject.

"You were saying we got nowt to complain about. But wouldn't that be hiding the truth if something weren't right? I mean, are you totally happy with your life?"

"Now, don't get philosophical with me." His father punched the ground with his spade. "I've sweated and toiled for nigh on half a century and got plenty to be proud about. Not like you youngsters. You're all the same; you've had it too easy, and you're never satisfied with what you've got. You always want more because you've got no appreciation of good, honest graft."

"That's not fair. Me and my mates have all got jobs."

"None of that is real work, lad. When I were your age, I was doing twelve-hour shifts down the mine to put dinner on the table. It was right hard labour, and I went months in the winter without seeing daylight, 'cept on Sundays, which were me only day off . . ."

Alan stopped listening, as he had heard the lecture many times before. The dire struggle to raise the family out of the gutter and their exodus from the dingy back-to-backs of Arkwright Row to the Victorian, semi-detached villa in Wellington Avenue. It was his father's favourite subject—revelling in past miseries as a subtle way to celebrate later accomplishments.

Alan had already achieved a lifestyle that had taken his father fifty hardworking years to attain and was still young, so he should have had greater cause for satisfaction. But he hated to admit to himself, there was some truth in his father's words. His life was too easy. Success and comfort came at the price of the crippling boredom of a routine and unchallenging existence.

Having now understood his problem, Alan failed to find an obvious solution, for he was faced with a conundrum: why make life hard for yourself when it can be easy? Only a fool would do that.

"Watch out, you idiot." Mandy screeched as Alan knocked a glass onto the carpeted floor.

"Calm down," he retorted. "It was empty and didn't break."

"Okay, but be more careful, Al."

"It was an accident, Mandy."

"Sorry." She tried to mollify his obvious irritation. "Can I get you a cup of tea?"

"Aye, love, a brew would be great. Thanks."

Mandy stood up from the soft sofa where they had been watching their favourite soap opera. Alan cast an admiring glance over her fine form; she was the prettiest girl in their group of friends, and he took regular pleasure in observing the way the other lads looked at her. Take Barry, for example. No one envied him for being lumbered with slug-faced Sharon. What did he see in her?

"Shall I turn off the telly?" Mandy interrupted his musings. The soap opera credits had given way to the theme tune of a boring history programme.

"No, thanks. I want to see how United did against City. Can you change it over to the news and sports?" The TV's remote control had mysteriously disappeared a few days earlier, though he suspected she had hidden it to stop his annoying habit of flicking through the channels.

She stepped over to the television and crouched down to reach the buttons underneath the screen, causing her skirt to stretch under the increased tension. A loud tearing sound announced the separation of zip from fabric.

"What's up, love? You putting on weight?"

"*Famine in Kugombwala . . .* " The news headlines were being announced on the TV.

"I don't think so." Mandy's face reddened in embarrassment.

"Well, what do you weigh now?" Alan was alarmed at the prospect that she might have started the irreversible process of weight gain.

" *. . . more and more children are dying of hunger.*"

"Oh, about eight stone, I suppose."

"Eight stone? That's half a stone more than last year."

"Strong gains for the pound today . . ."

To Alan, it was the thin end of an ever-widening wedge of insulation, which would steadily smother Mandy's feminine figure and transform her from a buxom belle to a broadening balloon.

"Better lay off the chocolates, love, or you'll look like Sharon," he added, only half joking.

"Oh, shut up, Al," she snapped. "I hate how you keep tabs on my weight. It's my body, and it's up to me what I eat. So, mind your own business."

"Calm down; no need to get stroppy. Anyway, it is my business because I love you for who you are. I don't want you to change."

"Well, women's bodies do change, Al. You can't live in the past. Just accept it." With that, she stormed off, slamming the door. Loud footfalls declared she had stomped upstairs to bed.

Their argument made him think about change. He did not want her to change, and yet she, by contrast, was trying to mould him into her image of who he should be. It annoyed him to think about the new habits he was forced to adopt since they had moved in together. Like tidying his football boots away from the hall. Or putting down the loo seat and cover after he had been to the toilet plus washing his hands. She even insisted that he take a shower and wear fresh underwear every day.

There was often subtle criticism from Mandy aimed at his trivial misdeeds or minor aspects of himself that she wanted to alter. Bothered by that line of thought, he turned his attention to the TV.

The headlines had given way to the main stories, which meant there was still a short wait for the sports results. Crowds of emaciated Africans filled the screen, and he guessed it was about yet another famine in that unhappy continent. He knew little about the place, except that it was full of elephants, lions, and other wild animals, as well as people who went hungry. He had never held any desire to go there.

"Aid workers are confident they can make a difference . . ."

Why bother? Let Africa solve its own problems. Alan's opinions echoed those of his favourite tabloid.

"We need help," an aid worker told the cameraman.

Sure, but charity began at home, he dismissed the appeal by invoking the oft-quoted proverb. Which was hypocritical, as he had never given anything to good causes apart from some used postage stamps during his primary school years that had cost him nothing.

"We need money for food and medicine; and we need doctors, nurses, administrators, engineers . . ."

Engineers? Alan shook his head. Not him in a million years.

"Relief supplies are getting through; but for many people, it may be too little, too late . . ."

The words were narrated over a scene of a plane arriving at a bush landing strip, where two young Europeans stood waiting with their crew of African colleagues, who then unloaded sacks of food from the aircraft. The aid workers stood out in their gleaming white t-shirts, like modern knights in shining armour. They were obviously enjoying themselves.

Looks like a laugh, Alan noted with a touch of envy, recalling the crushing boredom of his own life. Their work did not seem particularly difficult, handing out a few orders to the willing locals.

He imagined himself in front of the cameras amidst all the chaos, bringing succour to the miserable masses. He would be the local hero, going out to battle the twin-headed dragon of famine and disease before returning to share stories with his mates in the pub, who would be impressed by his courage and noble character. Alan smiled; a short stint as an aid worker would inject some adventure into his life and elevate his standing with his acquaintances.

"Al, are you coming up to bed?" Mandy's call from upstairs interrupted his thoughts.

"Aye, I'll be right there, love." He smiled again, seeing an additional advantage to this sudden new career option. It would be a way of introducing positive change into his relationship with his lass, which, for once, would be initiated by him.

Alan appreciated her affections but felt threatened by her intrusion into his personal space. Mandy had chosen a car of the same colour and brand as his, albeit a smaller model; she had decorated the walls of their house with an abundance of photos of them together at parties or on holiday; and she had bought matching sweatshirts for their joint shopping trips to town. *Her* obsession with *them* becoming the perfect couple filled *him* with angst over losing his precious individuality.

"Al, come and join me!" she called again.

"Aye, as I told you, love, I'll be right there."

"But you said that five minutes ago. What are you waiting for?"

Alan had been flattered by Mandy's attentions when their teenage romance had begun because it had confirmed his hunch that he was a great bloke. But the surfeit of her presence in his life now irked, especially her obvious effort to get on with his mates' wives and girlfriends to ensure their social life revolved around the couples they knew together. That left Bobsy, his best mate and team goalie, as his one Mandy-free outlet. She was unable to connect with the sweaty chauvinist, whose sole interests, apart from football, were girlie magazines and vintage diesel motors.

"Al! Now!"

The command startled him—it was like hearing Mandy's mother haranguing her father. Alan disliked Mrs. Carter, and the sentiment had been mutual ever since he had started dating Mandy, when her mother had resented the spotty teenager who was the first to seduce her daughter. As his complexion and financial prospects improved, so did Mrs. Carter's outward attitude—though Alan suspected it was a façade to mask her ongoing disapproval. Mandy confided almost everything about him to her mother, which fomented the paranoia that they were plotting how best to tame him.

The conclusion was clear—he needed a temporary break from the two Carter women, and distant Kugombwala would be a good place to achieve that. They would then realise that it was *he* who made the big decisions in *his* life.

However, Alan soon encountered a serious setback with his Great Escape. He phoned the big-name charities from the privacy of his office to prevent Mandy from hearing of his intentions. As he was an engineer, the organisations showed some interest in employing him, but this evaporated on discovering his utter lack of previous aid-work experience.

"I'm totally trapped here." Alan swore to himself as he pulled into the drive. It had been a bad week, with rejection after rejection diminishing his hope of breaking out of his golden cage.

The light was on, indicating Mandy was home, cooking their dinner. He slammed the car door and started towards the house, when an eruption of yapping caused him to freeze. A familiar, furry shape hurled itself against the frosted-glass front door. Mrs. Carter's demanding dog. Just what he did not need.

"Hi, Al, we've got Arthur with us for the week." Mandy emerged from the kitchen to give him a kiss. "Mum's got workmen in to fix the extension roof."

"Ay-up, love." He gave her a tight squeeze. "Get down, Arthur!" Alan had to manoeuvre his hands to avoid the eager, slobbering tongue. A trying time now lay ahead—yelping at the TV whenever he watched football, howling by the front door to demand walks, plus being followed every step around the home. Added to that was the unpleasant task of locating and removing dollops of dog dung from the overgrown lawn.

"By the way, don't forget it's Mum's birthday on Saturday."

That confirmed the old superstition that bad luck comes in threes. First, the rejections from the aid agencies. Then, Arthur to stay. And now, the forced ritual of polite pretence with Mrs. Carter's old-fogey friends, when he would rather have a laugh with his mates down the pub.

He silently cursed his situation, just as the telephone rang.

Alan picked up the receiver. "Al here."

"All right, mate," said a familiar voice.

"Hey, Bobsy, how are you doing?"

"Not too bad. I've been thinking, maybe you want to come with me to the Yorkshire Industrial Engine Society Christmas show? I'm sure you'd like it. I'll be displaying me three-horsepower motor."

Alan sighed. "I need to think about it, Bobsy." He tried to think of a suitable excuse. "When is it and where?"

"This Saturday, mate, over in the city. It's for a favour, like. Got no wheels at the moment."

So, he needed transport. "Sure, Bobsy, I'd be happy to help," Alan said, relieved to now have an excuse for missing Mrs. Carter's birthday party.

"Mate, can you turn down the volume? I can't hear myself think."

Alan had to shout to be heard above Bobsy's favourite pop album, which thumped out of the car's quadrophonic stereo system while they cruised down the motorway.

"So, how did you write off your motor?" he continued after the din had subsided.

"Blow out." Bobsy grunted, unhappy to be reminded of the incident that had cost him his beloved vehicle with its go-faster stripes, wide wheels, and souped-up engine. "Swerved to avoid an idiot on a bike and then hit the kerb."

"How come you didn't you see him in time?"

"Didn't see him?" Bobsy cursed. "He got in my way, didn't he?"

Alan smiled, for he had already heard another version of the story from a mutual acquaintance. Bobsy had been showing off a high-speed handbrake turn that involved a sharp swing into a side street but had been distracted by the oncoming cyclist, causing him to lose control of both the car and his tongue.

On arrival at the exhibition venue, Bobsy's engine was unloaded and carried to a big hall where an array of motors were being admired by a throng of male enthusiasts. Alan spent a few minutes pacing the hall but soon accepted defeat in trying to understand the fascination with ancient machinery. That prompted him to wander off in search of refreshment.

He did not have to go far, as there was a pub opposite the hall, which at eleven in the morning was empty, except for an old man propping up the bar while chewing his own spit. Alan ordered a drink and then went to explore the place to avoid the stares of the strange, old man. Unfortunately, it turned out to be a cheerless watering hole without a fruit machine, telly, or pool table. That meant there was nothing to do except study the Victorian decor. He then spotted a broadsheet newspaper, which someone had left on a windowsill.

He usually avoided such papers, as they were crammed with tedious text rather than the attractive images that adorned his favourite tabloid. He flicked through to the supplement in search of the horoscope and cartoons, only to find pages of job adverts. Some of these were for aid work, including the agencies he had called that week, so he skipped angrily past, still smarting from the repeated rejections. But at the end of the supplement, he noticed a tiny advertisement for an organisation he had not previously encountered.

MedRelief

Kugombwala Famine Programme

Volunteers needed for immediate departure

No previous aid-work experience necessary

The last line electrified Alan, for he sensed an opportunity. He tore out the advert and slipped it into his wallet, with the intention of contacting the agency the following week.

Piiiiiifffffft.

The half-time whistle brought the game to a temporary halt, permitting Alan to enter the pitch.

"Gather round, lads," he shouted, to make himself heard and to vent his frustration at the ineptitude of the junior team, who were three goals down. "You lot are playing like a bunch of losers. The ball won't come to you by itself; you've got to run after it."

"That's what we're doing," the big-mouth among them countered. "You don't need to tell us how to play football."

"But you're not running hard enough. As soon as the other side gets close to the ball, you give up. Keep going for it and snatch it from them. You have to fight for it."

"Aye," they answered half-heartedly.

Alan wondered why he wasted a precious evening each week coaching the brats. Their lethargy and inability had dashed his original ambition to train them into future football stars, while their rudeness and ingratitude often caused him to question his commitment to them.

Such thoughts struggled with stirred memories of his early childhood, when he was the poor kid in the class. His schoolmates had teased him for his cheap clothes and homemade skateboard, which his dad had built because he couldn't afford to buy one. The lingering scars from that repeated humiliation drove Alan's determination to avoid poverty like the plague, which meant earning a decent wage while shunning unsuccessful people, in case their failure was infectious.

Yet contrary to his vow, he could not give up on the lads from the council estate, recognising in them the underdog he had been. They needed someone to believe in them, he realised, to mobilise them to make something of their lives. They were unlikely to become high-fliers, but he hoped to instil enough self-motivation in them to drag themselves out of the gutter.

That reminded him of the job advert in the newspaper. Despite his initial excitement, he had semi-forgotten, semi-ignored it, demotivated by his earlier failure with the other aid agencies to make the necessary effort to call the number.

I must do that tomorrow, he promised himself.

"MedRelief, Isabella speaking," declared the plummy voice at the other end of the line, with a tone that suggested the call had rudely interrupted whatever she had been doing.

"Al Swales h-here," he stuttered, conscious of his Yorkshire accent. "I saw your advert in Saturday's *Guardian* about needing workers for the famine in Kugombwala."

"Are you a doctor or nurse?"

"No, I'm—"

"Well, I'm awfully sorry." Her voice was empty of apology. "We are only employing medics at the moment."

"But that's not what your advert said."

"No, but the newspaper unfortunately left out a line of text . . . Just a moment, my colleague is saying something . . . "

Yet another rejection. Alan felt deflated.

"You're not a mechanic by any chance?" Isabella then asked in a friendlier tone.

"Well, kind of. I'm an automotive engineer," Alan stated with rediscovered pride.

"An automotive engineer," Isabella repeated. "Oh, Fiona, he is," he heard her screech to her colleague before addressing him again. "Can you fax your CV right away?"

"Sure."

"Thanks. I'll get back to you."

She phoned a few minutes after he had sent it.

"Hi, Al," she purred, now pronouncing his name with the familiarity of an old friend. "Listen, darling, we love your resumé. You are just the person we want, and we need you pronto in Kugombwala, as our mechanic recently left us. You don't need a visa; but you must get vaccinations against yellow fever, cholera, dysentery, tetanus, polio, hepatitis, and meningitis. And start your malaria prophylaxis pills straightaway."

"Okay. I'll call the hospital near work." Alan winced at the prospect of so many jabs.

"Excellent. I'll post a list of what you need to pack. Come to our office in the city at eleven on Friday morning next week, so we can do your contract and brief you about what you are going to do. You will be taking the six o'clock night flight to Nairobi; our office there will arrange your onward travel to Ndombazu."

"Eleven o'clock next Friday," Alan repeated, bewildered by Isabella's assumption that he had already agreed to work for MedRelief.

"Yes, and don't be late. Ciao for now."

Alan stared at the blank wall ahead of him. Weeks of frustration when no one had shown any interest in employing him had given way to a job offer that he had tacitly accepted without thinking to ask the usual questions about pay and conditions or requesting time to consider the terms. He decided to be optimistic. MedRelief was a charity, so that would mean they treated their staff well.

His mind then turned to Mandy and his current employer. He would need their blessings for a decision he had already made, but which—he now realised—they were unlikely to approve.

That would require some creative thinking—and a good deal of fast talking.

Alan's pulse rate increased as he eased his car beside Mandy's on the drive. She always arrived home before him; it was one of her many admirable traits that she put his needs before those of her employers once the five o'clock threshold was reached. He found her ironing his shirts, whilst watching a TV chat show.

"All right, love? Had a good day at the office?" He gave her a hug, hoping that a few lines of normal conversation would reduce the impact of what he was about to tell her.

"Not too bad. Mary in sales has just had a baby."

Alan suspected this was a subconscious hint from his broody bird, but to avoid aggravating the imminent storm, he refrained from making jokes about vomiting infants, as was his habit on such occasions. He was not ready for the encumbrance of kids; he wanted the freedom to live life to the fullest while he was still young.

"Mandy," he deliberated, "I've got something to tell you. I'll be going away for a bit."

"Oh, are ya?" Her face revealed a mix of surprise and sadness. "Will you be going to Germany again? And for how long?"

"Well, it's going to be a while." His heart was pounding. "You see, I'm off to Kugombwala."

"Kugombwala?" Mandy looked puzzled. "Where's that?"

"You know, that country in Africa where the United Nations has gone in."

"What are you going there for?" she almost shouted.

"To help the starving kids." He could smell stress-induced odour emanating from his armpits. "I've been asked to go, so I thought I might take a little break from the job. My boss has said it's okay and will pay a retaining salary while I'm gone—"

Then it happened: the volcano exploded. Yet it wasn't the expected eruption of tears, but rather, the red-hot lava of rage.

"Taking a break from work? Just to pretend you're the Good Samaritan?" Her scolding shifted to screaming. "But . . . but . . . it's *Christmas,* Al! Didn't you think about asking me first?"

"That's what I'm doing," he lied, desperate to reclaim some common ground of acceptance.

"No, it isn't. You've already made up your mind. I know you, Alan Swales; you only ever think about yourself."

"Now, that's not fair—"

"Yes, it is. I do all the housework here. I cook every meal and always do the washing up, plus the shopping—as well as your ironing! And I *never* get any thanks."

"Love, I mow the lawn—"

"And what's more, you're really inconsiderate to live with."

"In what way?"

"You're often late for meals, and you never tidy up after yourself. It's always me that has to do it."

"But that's because you criticise me when I put things in the wrong place."

"Well, how about trying to learn where things go, Al? But you don't because you can't be bothered. And now you have the cheek to blame me for it." She was livid with rage. "I'm sick of living in your mess and being your household slave, Alan Swales—you can iron your own clothes and get your own supper!" She stormed off, slamming the front door so hard that the net curtains of one of the neighbouring houses parted moments later.

As Alan lay alone in bed that night, a wave of guilt washed over him for his selfish behaviour and for the separation and loneliness he was going to inflict on Mandy. He imagined her now crying on her mother's shoulder. Was he doing the right thing?

Just a few feet away, the bedroom walls hemmed him in, suffocating him with claustrophobia. He had to break out.

Mandy was back at the house when he returned from work the next day.

"Ay-up, love!" He hoped his joviality would be reciprocated.

"Hiya, Al," she said, looking away.

An awkward silence followed. Realising she was still upset, Alan resigned himself to an inevitable sanction that evening. Why did their relationship have to be so difficult?

"Have you had a good day, love?" he tried again.

"Not really." She sniffled, holding back tears. "But that doesn't matter."

Another awkward silence.

What to say next?

"Anything you want to do tonight?" He hoped that pretending nothing was amiss would make the problem go away.

"No." Sniff. "Don't mind me. You do what you want." Sniff.

Trial by ordeal—one of the punishments he dreaded most. Hours of self-deprecation would follow to intensify any feelings of anguish in him. It was a strategy that usually worked—she enacting the role of wounded waif abused by Alan the Unkind until sufficient levels of guilt and fatigue built up to make him relent to whatever demand she was making.

He had to hold out against this siege of his own free choice, or he'd buckle under the onslaught. Normally, he would have made a tactical retreat to the sports club. But on this occasion, it would make matters worse, as it would double her perceived feeling of rejection from him deciding to go to Kugombwala and for spending one of his few pre-departure evenings away from her.

"Wanna watch something on the telly?" An excellent alternative, which would combine being together while minimising the need to interact.

"You go ahead without me." Sniff. "There's nothing I want to see."

Alan's assaulted psyche reacted in self-defence to her manipulation. "Right, then. I'll watch the video of England's 1966 World Cup victory that Bobsy lent me."

Yet the excitement of the game, combined with patriotic pride, failed to stifle his awareness of her sobbing in the kitchen.

She joined him on the settee once the match was over. "Al, are you really going out to Africa?"

"Aye, love, like I told you yesterday, they need me to sort out the famine." He would counter the renewed attack on his conscience by playing the humanitarian trump card. How could anyone accuse him of doing wrong when he was off to do good?

"But I don't want you to leave; I don't want to be left alone. Especially over Christmas. Everyone will think we're breaking up, and they'll say you've gone because we've had a row. You don't know what it will be like with all the gossip . . . "

It was painfully true, and Alan felt genuine pity for Mandy. He had not previously fathomed the depth of her insecurity, and he felt an instinctive urge to protect her from the dark void of loneliness and social shame. Perhaps it would have been easier if they had children . . . But that thought caused more guilt to gnaw at him for withholding kids from her. He sensed she might become the ultimate victim of his inexplicable inner turmoil, yet Alan the Selfish nonetheless put his needs above hers, overcoming guilt with guile.

"I know it's going to be hard for you, love; but there're kids out there starving, and I want to do my bit to help them. I'd . . . I'd never be able to live with myself if I didn't go."

Mandy's response was more tears, though this time they were the genuine tears of dejection and defeat.

Yvonne Carter's gaze retreated to the blurred window. Instinctively, she wiped away the condensation. Cold spatters of November rain dribbled down outside, distorting the houses opposite: number twenty-six with the fake flowers and number twenty-eight with the curtains always drawn. *If only they could be happy*—her thoughts dwelled on Mandy and Al.

His announced departure troubled her, for it required her to meet Mandy's expectations of how she should think and act—with an implicit threat of retribution should she fail. To avoid yet another indictment for being a bad mother, she would concur with her daughter that Al was being unreasonable and attempt to persuade him to change his mind, whilst unhappily aware that her intervention would poison their already awkward relationship.

Her eyes focused on the tawdry, grey street that constrained her view, an ever-present reminder that Brickdale had become her unchosen cage. It was the inevitable consequence of marrying Bert Carter, a decision forced by an unwanted pregnancy. The shame from that time still made her shudder, as did the resentment for the lost lifestyle that could have been: ambitions of becoming an airline hostess, marrying a handsome pilot, and living it up in London had been dashed . . . but never forgotten. Oh, the years she had yearned to rewind the clock and escape her current circumstance.

Maybe Al felt the same need? A momentary glow of empathy arose within her, though she knew Mandy would never forgive her if she were to air such a rebellious thought. The last thing Yvonne Carter needed was a difficult relationship with her only daughter to cap a failed life.

The window had fogged up again—as it always did, no matter how much she wiped it.

"Hello, Al. It's so nice to see you."

Alan braced himself for the inevitable. He was unable to guess what form the confrontation would take, as he barely knew Mrs. Carter, even after thirteen years' acquaintance. Beyond the over-familiar greetings and probing questions about his friends and work—which he regarded as espionage rather than interest—they rarely spoke. He was usually ignored during the long lunches while Mandy and her mother nattered about neighbours, dogs, and soap operas.

The presence of Mr. Carter did little to ameliorate the event, for he rarely spoke, except when addressed to obtain moral support for his wife's opinions. To which he always gave her the standard reply of "Of course, dear," though it was impossible to determine from his monotone whether he genuinely agreed.

"Al," Mrs. Carter started as soon as she had served the meal, "you don't know how I've been losing nights of sleep, worried sick about you. I think it's great that people are going out to help the suffering in Africa, but you've got to ask whether it is right for you. You know, somebody's got to pay the taxes, support the community, and run the country; and with all your abilities, that must be where you fit in . . . " And so, her speech went on, a mixture of flattery and well-crafted arguments as to why he should stay.

Alan had been so determined to go that he had never properly weighed the pros and cons of his proposed venture, but now, as he listened, he felt his decision wilting under the onslaught of Mrs. Carter's formidable logic. She was right: he might die from a nasty tropical disease, and what good would that do for the world? The football club was unlikely to win the cup without his exemplary leadership; plus, his family and friends needed him to be there for them. Perhaps he should stay. It wasn't too late—he hadn't signed a contract, and he could save face by telling his boss that the cars he was going out to fix had been stolen, so there was no need for him after all.

Once the final arguments had been delivered, Mrs. Carter turned to her husband out of habit to obtain his usual words of support. "Isn't that right, Bert?"

"No, not at all."

She blinked in surprise.

But Mr. Carter's soft voice was now edged with conviction. "I say, good on you, Alan, for getting off your back. Hunger and poverty won't be stopped if we all find clever excuses for staying here and pushing the task onto other people. The world needs young folks like you to solve those problems."

The uncharacteristic outburst brought Alan back to his senses, reminding him that the shackles of social conformity were the real motive for his desire to escape. Such chains, he realised, had imprisoned Mr. Carter in a lacklustre life and were now being used to punish him, for his outburst shifted the focus of his wife's attention away from Alan. Her lunchtime discourse thereafter degenerated to a diatribe against her husband, in which all his faults were exposed in minute detail, and ended only when he found an excuse to depart for the gentler company of his pet ferrets.

"Al, come and see. There's a cute bunny in the garden!"

Alan dragged himself up from the sofa, where he had been sprawled, starfish-like, to watch snooker on TV. "I can't see any rabbits," he said, ambling over to the window.

"Look, in the middle of the lawn."

"There's nowt there, love." Was Mandy affected by the fumes from her cooking?

"Oh, yes, there is. Look closely."

He turned towards her, perplexed, and then noticed that special Mandy smile, indicating a tease.

"But it's difficult to see it, as the grass is so long." She giggled.

He would miss her quirky sense of humour. How would the coming separation affect their relationship? Would she forgive his flight, or would it poison their future?

Alan woke with his neck damp with sweat. He could remember little of the nightmare, except the sense that something horrible had happened, linked to some vague images on his mental retina. In one of these, Mandy was berating him for not noticing the rabbits around him in the garden. In another, they stood in the middle of a wide plain scattered with corpses that she was unable to see.

Tomorrow, he would leave all safety and security behind. He would say goodbye to his loved ones and venture alone into the unknown. Would he cope? Would he enjoy the experience? Would he come back in one piece?

Half of him wanted to go, and half wanted to stay; but the outcome of that struggle was inevitable: it was already too late to turn back.

"You will come back, won't you, Al?"

Mandy's tears wetted his shoulder as they embraced through the open window of the waiting train to London. The departing express pulled them apart, leaving him sorrowfully aware of the event's symbolism.

Alan's knowledge of London was limited to the area around the Wembley football stadium, so he did not know the address that Isabella had labelled as being in "the city." All seemed well on exiting Liverpool Street station, but after a few minutes' walk, he realised her description was an exaggeration. The finance houses of corporate London soon gave way to the litter-filled slums of Smithfield and Brick Lane, where the MedRelief office was located above a betting shop. He manoeuvred himself over a sleeping tramp to press the buzzer, which responded with a tinny, female voice.

"Who's that?"

"Alan Swales. I'm going to Kugombwala tonight."

"Is that smelly tramp still there?"

"Aye."

"Don't let him in," commanded the voice as the electric catch on the door lock was released. Alan entered a dingy hall and climbed an even gloomier flight of concrete steps. On the second floor, he found the MedRelief logo on a battered door that had suffered many break-ins. He knocked hard; the door was then unlocked and opened by an attractive, young brunette.

"Hi, you must be Al," she purred, confirming his guess that this was Isabella. "Come in. Our director and founder, Gordon, is dying to meet you."

In contrast to the tawdry street where it was located, the spacious MedRelief headquarters was tastefully furnished with pinewood units and abundant pot plants; but despite the pleasant surroundings, the atmosphere was far from calm. A dozen young women were engaged in frantic activity, shouting in strident voices at telephones or marching at high speed across the room, which released drum rolls of stiletto heels bashing the bare, wooden floor.

Isabella led Alan towards a loud male voice that emanated from behind a closed door, where they waited until the conversation ceased. She knocked and then opened the door, revealing an imposing man standing beside a large desk, phone in hand. Behind him was a huge map of the world, while photos of children being treated for various afflictions covered the walls.

"That was the Foreign Office on the line, Isabella," he announced, taking no notice of Alan. "Looking bad in Ndombazu—rebel forces about to attack the city. Embassy's evacuated. Good news is they have decided to fund the hospital. Hello. You must be the new mechanic?" The last word was pronounced with a dismissive tone for a trade associated with dirty hands.

"Aye, I'm Alan Swales," he responded, overawed by the man's aura of authority, which was heightened by crisp establishment features produced by generations of selective breeding.

"Gordon Blair-Campbell." He gave Alan a firm handshake. "We are relying on you to fix our Land Rovers, Alan. Don't let us down. Now, Isabella, take him to see Chas. Can't hang around; must call the United Nations."

Chas turned out to be the only other male employee in the office. Alan had not previously noticed his presence, for he had created a sanctuary out of packing cases to shield himself from the mayhem outside. They found him slouched in an easy chair with his feet on the desk, reading a report.

"Great to meet you, Alan. I'm the Africa desk officer." Over the next ten minutes, he explained his task as overall coordinator of MedRelief's field projects, finishing with a question. "Have you ever been to Kugombwala?"

"No." Alan prudently kept to himself that he had never heard of the country until the recent crisis had hit the world news.

"Not one of our old colonies, although for a brief time, there was a slave fort on the coast run by an Edinburgh-based company of merchant venturers. That's why all Kugombwalans speak English, even though it is their third or fourth language after their tribal tongues. It also explains why they have Scottish-style first names, calling themselves MacThis or MacThat, followed by an African surname." Chas flicked back a mop of hair from his forehead. "There is little other legacy of the former Scottish presence, but the Caledonian connection excites Gordon—he's from a family of lairds, so he feels a nationalistic attachment to Kugombwala. Though I can't see anything romantic about a few Scots making money out of slaves in order to live in mansions with mahogany furniture and silver cutlery . . . "

Most of what Chas then said washed over Alan, since he had no interest in culture, politics, or history. So, he was relieved when the lecture finally stopped, after which he was taken to see another Isabella-lookalike called Fiona.

"So, off to Africa then?" she asked. "I expect you're looking forward to the sunny tropics. I so envy you getting out of this miserable climate. Here"—she handed him three MedRelief t-shirts—"is your uniform. Wear one at all times. Who knows? You might get on TV. It's important for our donors to see our logo, so they know we're active in the field, which will encourage them to give us more money.

Anyway, I've got work to do, and you've got a plane to catch. Collect your flight ticket from Isabella and then take the tube to Heathrow."

Thus, on that bright December day, as Alan descended into the dark tunnels under London, he was overwhelmed by the odd feeling of knowing he was about to enter a war zone on a distant continent—a rite of passage to a destination of unforeseeable experiences and consequences.

Once the train emerged above ground, he stared at the passing rows of smog-blackened terraced houses with a foreboding fear for the future, wondering how long it would be before he would see such familiar scenes of his beloved Britain again. MedRelief had purchased a one-way ticket for him, so he had no idea when he would return.

Yet above that sense of uncertainty, he also felt the exhilaration of newfound freedom and independence, plus excitement in the expectation of imminent adventure.

CHAPTER 3

NAIROBI INTERNATIONAL AIRPORT, KENYA

Alan emerged from the arrivals area into a chaotic crowd of shouting hustlers, all wanting to carry his bags in different directions or offer him a taxi to town at over-inflated prices. Fortunately, a smiling Kenyan wearing a MedRelief t-shirt was there to rescue him.

"Hello, Alan, my name is Kahiga. Welcome to Kenya." He introduced himself as the local administrator at MedRelief's Nairobi office. He led Alan to a smart car outside the terminal building, and they drove across open grassland studded with characteristic flat-topped African acacia trees towards Nairobi looming in the distance. Huge billboards featuring lions, giraffes, and beautiful Kenyan women advertising consumer goods lined the route from the airport. Everything had a fresh and exotic look in the bright sunlight.

The road took them straight to the skyscrapers of downtown Nairobi, whereupon they continued to the western suburbs. The urban landscape morphed from tall cliffs of concrete and glass to a forest of verdant trees bearing vivid flowers that shaded large, walled compounds. Magnificent mansions peeped over high, defensive walls, providing glimpses of a flamboyant and varied architecture that exceeded the smartest areas of Alan's hometown. Uniformed guards stood outside solid, metal gates to prevent the poor from pilfering that glaring wealth or polluting it by their presence.

MedRelief occupied a smart villa located on an exclusive side street. A few downstairs rooms were used as offices, while the remainder of the house doubled as a residence for the international staff who ran the organisation's East and Central African base.

"Make yourself at home." Kahiga led him into a spacious living room. "The expats were out partying last night, so they are still asleep. They should be up soon."

A maid arrived with breakfast, which Alan ate while studying the vast array of blackwood carvings that occupied every available shelf in the room, ranging from elephants and Maasai warriors to platters and bowls. Elegant cane furniture and numerous large, native drums were scattered about on a dark, hardwood floor. The opulence of the place projected a living standard that far exceeded his cramped semi-detached house in Britain: the large, imposing residence; the exclusive walled compound with the luxuriant garden; the guard who opened the gate; the maid who cleaned the house and did the cooking. Life for those who worked for MedRelief in Nairobi was obviously comfortable. He hoped it would be the same in Kugombwala.

Alan was still munching through his meal when Kahiga returned.

"I've just spoken to the office that runs the U.N. flights into Kugombwala. There's space on a plane to Ndombazu at nine this morning, so we have to go straightaway."

Returning to Nairobi's international airport, they drove to another part of the complex marked United Nations Terminal. Back in Britain, the U.N. had been an obscure organisation that seemed, from the news, to be a well-paid talking club. Yet here, it was much more than that, with a dedicated terminal in one of the continent's busiest airports, as well as its own airline serving the region's many trouble spots.

Out on the runway stood two large Hercules cargo planes, together with a small executive jet—all painted white with *U.N.* in large black letters on the sides and on the tailplanes. One of the Hercules was starting up, producing a loud hum that brimmed with energy and restrained power, like a mighty stallion chomping at the bit.

"This is a call for flight UN238 to Ndombazu, now ready for departure," the intercom announced. "All passengers, please proceed to Gate Number Three."

Alan exited through to the departure lounge, which was packed with uniformed and civilian personnel bearing U.N. and NGO—non-governmental organisation—name tags or t-shirts. It was strange to think he was now part of this huge humanitarian operation, one of the world's noble team of aid workers and peacekeepers, who ventured to the distant corners of Africa to provide much-needed relief and security. He and the few other passengers boarded the waiting Hercules without going through security checks, and no one asked to see either identification documents or flight papers. As an aid worker, he was now a member of that international class of outstanding citizens, whose conduct was considered so exemplary as to render such checks unnecessary.

He sat with the other passengers on a row of military-specification webbed seats in the cargo hold, squeezed between the side of the aircraft and a stack of strapped-up cardboard boxes. The large cargo door at the back of the plane was closed, and the engines revved to a roar. The reins were then unleashed, causing the stallion to charge forwards and leap through the air from Kenya to Kugombwala.

Ndombazu proved to be a world apart from Nairobi—a sprawl of low-rise, dilapidated concrete blocks, boarded-up shops, and makeshift shelters. The pot-holed streets were strewn with rubbish, interspersed by burnt-out military hardware. Weapons were everywhere. Mean-eyed guys carried Kalashnikovs, while massive machine guns loomed above the flatbeds of battered pickup trucks.

Alan gazed with a shudder at the military convoy that was escorting him and his fellow passengers into the city. It signalled that the U.N. was seriously concerned about security. Two jeeploads of soldiers bristling with weapons drove ahead of the MedRelief Land Rover, followed by another jeepload of soldiers and a truck with a huge gun behind. He was glad of their presence; they made him feel much safer in this city with its sinister atmosphere of post-apocalyptic anarchy. Yet it was strange that the U.N. did nothing about all the weapons that were brazenly brandished on the street. Why did the peacekeepers not disarm the gunmen? Was that not part of their mandate?

A clatter of gunfire caused him to duck.

"Not close." The driver smiled as he looked up. "You can hear too much shooting here. We call it Kugombwalan rap. You will get used to it."

They arrived at a large, iron-clad gate, set between four-metre-high cement walls topped by rolls of razor wire and flanked on each side by a sandbag turret. The gates opened as they approached and straightaway closed behind, leaving the military escort to continue to the main U.N. headquarters at the harbour.

"This place can be MedRelief Kugombwala Base," the driver announced. "Hospital is next door."

Alan looked up at the high walls crested by barbed wire and guard towers. They were there to protect him and his colleagues from the fighters who prowled outside, but he could not escape the feeling of having entered a prison.

By the end of lunch, Alan had mastered the names of the other MedRelief expatriates with whom he was incarcerated. They were to be more than colleagues—they were the closest he would have to a family in Kugombwala and the most likely candidates for friends. He, therefore, had to make a quick assessment of them, to decide how to deal with them.

To do this, he applied his standard method of categorising strangers, starting with where they came from. They were all Brits, so they could be subdivided by region: Northerners like himself—who were all great folks, with the exception of Mrs. Carter; Southerners, who were even worse than Mrs. Carter; Scots; Welsh; and then those from the Midlands, known as Brummies, who drank bad beer and supported loser football teams.

Half of the MedRelief team hailed from southern England, which did not bode well for the coming months, given that straightforward Northerners rarely got on with two-faced Southerners. Northerners usually distinguished three sub-groups: Cockney, posh, and farmer.

From first impressions, Alan classified the team as follows:

First, Jules, the head of mission and hospital surgeon. He had a Scottish surname but was clearly a Southerner, as he belonged to the London elite. From the conversation at dinner that evening, he came across as stuck-up and self-important, so Alan immediately labelled him a posh nob. Friendship opportunity: impossible.

Next, there was Lorna, the hospital doctor dressed in a long, brown skirt that indicated a frumpy, sensible personality. She hailed from the West Country, so another Southerner. Most people from that area were farmers, yet she talked with the irritating, overly nice manner of the middle-class, so not a yokel. How to reconcile those opposing extremes? Bingo! His mind found the solution: she was a posh farmer. She had so far been pleasant to him, so he reckoned they might get along as colleagues, as long as he kept the necessary distance dictated by their differences in social status.

Then there was Megan, the hospital nurse from Wales. She wore hideous, baggy clothes and had plaited a few locks of hair on the side of her head, which he found strange. Plus, she had that bitter, pungent odour that he associated with the grunge community. He, therefore, labelled her a Welsh weirdo. He reckoned they would get along, but he did not relish the prospect of anything beyond a cordial relationship—in addition to her repugnant smell, he found her physically unattractive.

He shuddered then as he pictured Paula, the pharmacy and feeding centre nurse. From the moment they first met, he knew she had decided to hate him. Given her strong Essex accent, he characterised her as a cantankerous Cockney. Prospect of friendship: zero. Prospect of continuous conflict: inevitable.

Keith the mechanic was also easy to stereotype: boring Brummie. He had commandeered much of Alan's attention during the meal that evening, droning away about the relative merits of different off-road vehicles. It was going to be a struggle to keep some distance from him, to avoid being talked at for hours about trivial mechanical issues. Friendship: no thanks.

That left Dave, the security coordinator. He was from Lincolnshire, which was in that grey zone between the North, the South, and the Midlands. That alone made him difficult to classify. Added to that, he was neither Cockney, posh, nor farmer. Alan mulled for a moment, and then it was obvious. He was a good bloke, and someone he hoped to soon call mate.

"Get down!"

Bewildered, Alan turned to see Dave collapse below the rim of the sandbag parapet. A couple of loud cracks erupted from the street below, followed by the sound of a large insect whizzing past his face. The warm air pressure on his cheek switched his senses onto full alert; instinctively, he dropped down into a crouch. That was no beetle—that was a bullet.

More gunfire ensued, this time from the Pakistani peacekeeper in the sandbag turret on the roof, then shouting between that soldier and somebody in the street.

Silence. A few seconds of stillness.

"Probably just a warning shot." Dave had already stood up to peer over the parapet. "But you've still got to take death threats seriously out here."

Alan hardly heard him, for his ears were drowned by a staccato of loud thuds emanating from his heart. Sweat flowed from his neck and upper chest, soaking his t-shirt, and he started shaking from the massive rush of adrenaline that coursed through his veins.

"Lucky I saw him raise his gun." Dave seemed to be laughing. "Otherwise, you might have walked into that bullet!" He was now standing to full height, calmly surveying the street below like a lord overlooking his land. Dave cut an impressive figure with his muscular frame, reflective sunglasses, combat trousers, and desert boots. He was nothing like Alan's preconceived image of aid workers. Only the standard-issue MedRelief t-shirt set him apart from the stereotype of a battle-hardened soldier.

"Is it okay to get up now?" Alan was self-conscious of his inability to make that decision.

"Sure, he's gone."

Alan picked up the cigarette he had dropped during the commotion and went over to the easy chairs in the middle of the terrace. He needed nicotine to calm his nerves and was grateful for the ugly stacks of sandbags that blocked the view to the ocean. Those bullet-barriers also shielded him from the street and squatter camp that lay at the foot of the building, except when he was standing.

"Hey, Al, that was your first security incident." Dave chuckled, slapping him on the shoulder. "And you haven't even been here a day. Welcome to Kugombwala."

They had gone up to the terrace of the MedRelief base to take a break during an introductory briefing. The gunman would have been waiting for him, assuming it was the same person who had threatened to kill him a few hours earlier, which, according to Dave, was likely.

"Kugombwalans don't like to kill in cold blood," he explained. "They prefer to have a good reason to shoot you, which is why they push you to insult them. Just like you did to those guys earlier today."

A flashback of shouting Kugombwalans flooded Alan's mind. Foaming mouths, snapping teeth, flying spittle—his first meeting with some of the locals had been a disaster. They had visited in the hope that the naïve new guy in town would authorise the donation of food to a fake good cause, but Alan had refused in his normal, straightforward Yorkshire manner. No insult was intended, but among a people hoping to be offended, it was sufficient to trigger a barrage of death threats—and the bullet that had narrowly missed his face.

"Are you ready to go through radio protocol?" Dave interrupted his introspection.

"Not just yet. I need another smoke." Alan's hands were still shaking. "It's been a long day, and I need a bit of time to process me thoughts."

Alan lay awake for a long time that night, unable to fall asleep in the noisy darkness. The whistling sound of the bullet was stuck in continuous play in his acoustic memory, whilst whining mosquitoes sought holes in the defensive wall of netting around his bed. Above this was the howling of dogs, first one and then a whole cacophony, as the city's entire canine community vied for verbal territory—until a burst of machine gun fire silenced them for a while. It was a wonder any dogs were left in Kugombwala.

Alan knew he was way out of his depth. The day's disastrous meeting with the locals had shown him he lacked the essential skills for dealing with other cultures. Combine that with a cocktail of civil war, trigger-happy Kugombwalans, and a group of Brits he barely liked, it would be madness for him to stay. He had to leave. The others in the team would not be impressed, but so what? He would never see them again.

Yet there was a fatal flaw to this plan: how would he explain to his mates at home that he was back so soon after he had left? No story could ever remove the suspicion that he had chickened out, and the shame of cowardice would hang over him for the rest of his life. He was doomed if he left and doomed if he stayed.

So, which to choose?

With pounding heart, he recognised there was only one option, and that was to remain. If he left now, he was guaranteed a lifelong feeling of failure; while if he stayed, there was a good chance he would survive, thanks to the U.N. peacekeepers.

Trapped by his own pride, Alan realised he would have to stick it out until he could justify to himself that he could go—in about a month, he told himself.

"There's been a mess-up with communications between here and London HQ," Jules briefed him after breakfast. "We recruited Keith from the U.N. a few days ago, so we already have a mechanic. But we need someone to take on the tasks of our logistician-administrator, who had to leave just before you arrived. Tell me, can you do finances?"

"Aye, I've been the treasurer of my local football club for a few years, so I'm used to accounts, audits, and such tasks."

"Great show. Much appreciated if you would take that on. I see from your CV that you are also an engineer, so it should be easy for you to run the logistics—ensuring the steady supply of power and water for the hospital, food for the feeding programme, and household items for the expatriate base."

"Sure, I reckon I should manage," Alan lied through his self-doubt.

Delicious! Alan scooped up the last morsel of meat from his plate before helping himself to more. He had been a week in Kugombwala and was pleasantly surprised by the quality of food served at the MedRelief base. It countered the expected monotonous diet of the local version of baked beans on toast. Instead, he ate much as he would at home, although the ingredients were more exotic. At first, it seemed bizarre to be feasting in the midst of a famine, but Alan soon accepted the idea that aid workers needed to be well-fed to do their jobs properly.

MedRelief employed a cook at their base, who had been a chef in a restaurant before the civil war and worked wonders with the limited range of local produce that included tropical fruits as well as fish from the sea. This was supplemented by a large block of cheddar that arrived in a cool box every week by plane, along with other crucial survival items, such as cigarettes, tomato ketchup, and toilet paper.

The food distributed by MedRelief to its starving beneficiaries was far less appetising. Rations of cooking oil and a protein-enriched flour were handed out to the families of kids who were moderately undernourished. Alan's face contorted with revulsion, as he cast his mind to the dull brown powder in the sacks in the stores. They would need to be emaciated to eat that mush. Much of it was contaminated by small beetles, which, like the Kugombwalan fighters, were plundering the food for the hungry. And like the fighters, it was impossible to keep them away. Every visit to the stores revealed yet more insects crawling over the food sacks, while larvae congealed the flour inside into lumps with their cobwebs. Alan felt great shame over sending food that was unfit for human consumption to the feeding centre but had no choice, for there was no alternative.

"Al, Al for Paula?" His walkie-talkie crackled into life.

What now? Alan scowled. It was the third time she had called him since breakfast. He was considering ignoring the call when the squelch opened again.

"Al, Al for Paula? Al, Al for Paula?"

Alan cursed the walkie-talkie and its persistent demand for his attention. Paula was forever calling with urgent problems that she required him to solve.

"Aye, Paula, Al here. Over." He tried to sound as calm as possible, for radio conversations were public to anyone listening on the same channel, so he had to be careful what he said. Right now, he wanted to tell her to shut up and leave him alone. In fewer and less friendly words.

"Where are you? Over."

"In my office. Over," he lied. It would not sound good to say he was still enjoying his meal, five minutes after the official end of the lunch break.

"We need you to come to the feeding centre right now. One of the water pipes is dripping. Over."

It was typical Paula, using her position to bash him with tasks, which he suspected was primarily about grinding him down to demonstrate her comparative superiority in the MedRelief hierarchy. As the new kid on the block, he was forced to suffer her sadistic bossiness—for the time being.

"Aye, will do." Alan took a deep breath, before adding, "Over and out." If only it could be as simple as that. He felt like a mule being whipped by an overweight rider, continuously goaded to go faster.

He was not expecting all aid workers to be saints but was surprised that some acted as slave drivers, using humanitarian objectives as the justification for bullying their colleagues. It was yet another reason to leave Kugombwala.

The short trip to the feeding centre required a security escort, so he switched his walkie-talkie to the U.N. communication channel.

"Uniform Seventeen for Foxtrot Base. Over." This meant MedRelief was calling the U.N.'s NGO liaison officer. He loved this coded language; it made him feel important.

"Come in, Foxtrot Base."

"Yes, Uniform Seventeen, escort request: Foxtrot Base to Golf Sierra. Over."

"Roger that. At your location within an hour. Over."

"Well copied. Over and out."

Forty minutes later, the honking of klaxons announced the arrival of three military vehicles outside the gates to MedRelief's base, as well as their impatient demand to move on. The presence of the U.N. peacekeepers—plus their big toys—gave much-needed zest to his experience of Ndombazu.

The journey to the feeding centre involved a long detour, as the convoy also had to visit a series of fortified aid agency compounds to deliver canteens of supper for the guarding soldiers. Alan did not mind the delay. He was not looking forward to the inevitable pecking from Paula, and the long trip enabled him to see more of Ndombazu. Added to that was the benefit of a chat with MacJohn, who was his favourite among the MedRelief drivers. He was fun to talk to, unlike MacGarry who was often in a bad mood, while old MacNed rarely said anything.

"So, Alan." MacJohn's face lit up at the prospect of discussing an issue that had been troubling him for some time. "How can you expats divide the women?"

"What do you mean?"

"You can be four men and only three girls. Dr. Jules must be with Dr. Lorna. And I think Dave is with Megan. She is very much beautiful. So, who is with Paula? Is it you, or is it Keith?" He giggled.

"Definitely Keith." Alan smiled at the incredulous concept of the two of them together, causing MacJohn to erupt into laughter. "So, you find Megan attractive?" he probed, interested to find out more about MacJohn's alternative taste in women. Megan did not interest him in the slightest.

"Oh, yes, she can have such a nice face. And her shape, it is bountiful. Kugombwalan men enjoy women like her."

"Well, there might be a possibility there, MacJohn." Alan was enjoying the conversation. "I don't think Dave is with her anymore. As far as I know, none of us are with each other."

"Then you can now be very hungry!"

"Aye," he acknowledged, reminded of Mandy. It made him aware how little he had thought about her since coming to Kugombwala. *It must be because of all the new experiences and impressions,* he told himself.

"But, Alan, another question." MacJohn was now serious. "You have a girlfriend, but why did you abandon her in Britain? Another man can take her."

"No, that won't happen. We live together."

"Then why can you not be married?"

"Because I haven't yet decided it's forever." He felt uncomfortable to be reminded of Mandy's regular requests that he had rebuffed and of her tears that had followed.

"That cannot happen in Kugombwala. The families of the boy and girl would not allow them to live in sin."

"Well, we are freer in Britain. We can do what we like."

"Alan, it is not freedom. It is lawlessness. Look how that can destroy my country."

They passed the national stadium where a rabble of labourers were swarming over the unprotected building like ants on a fresh bone. They were removing bricks and tiles to barter for food at the local market.

The feeding centre was located in an abandoned school in one of the city slums. Medical tents were squeezed into the shells of buildings that had been stripped of roofs, doors, and windows and were now surrounded by rolls of razor wire to prevent thieves from taking anything more. Beside the complex stood a small fort built of sandbags for the detachment of U.N. peacekeepers, who guarded a depot of precious but tasteless food.

The Land Rover had to push through a crowd of mothers and children outside, clamouring to get in. Three local guards fought back the shouting women before opening the barricade of coiled razor wire strung across the entrance.

"What's the problem?" Alan asked MacJohn.

"They can be the mothers of the children who have not been admitted. They are angry that MedRelief is not feeding them. Sometimes, they can throw rocks at us."

Inside the feeding centre, the atmosphere was calmer. A few Kugombwalan mothers drifted about, while others sat fanning flies from their faces, seemingly oblivious to the haunting sound of wailing, which grew louder as Alan approached the main building. He stepped through a doorway and into a tent, where he was confronted by rows of bodies spread out on the plastic sheet floor. It could have been a morgue but for the moaning of miserable children. Here, too, was the same stench of poverty that reeked through the hospital wards. How could Paula and Lorna cope with it every day?

He proceeded through the enclosed space, treading carefully to avoid tripping over a body or stepping on a small head. Added to the distressing sound and rank smell, the risk of unintentionally harming a child made him uneasy. He looked forward to being outside again.

Lorna was at the far end of the tent, engrossed with her patients. It amazed him that she was so relaxed in their company, as the pitiful wretches in revolting rags terrified him. Yet she cuddled one of the kids as if the child were a teddy bear.

"Hi, Al." She looked up. "Is this your first time here? Great place, isn't it?"

"Aye." He replied only to her first question.

Then, to his horror, she offered the child to him. "Here, hold her for a minute, while I write down a few notes."

Alan had no desire to touch the emaciated toddler—an extra-terrestrial with its oversized head disproportioned by a stunted body and eyes enlarged by shrunken skin. Peer pressure alone prevented him from refusing. He took the child, trying hard to hide his reluctance. The gaunt figure felt different from any child he had previously held—unbelievably light and unpleasant to touch, with neither flesh nor fat to pad the loose, skeletal frame. British children were warm, plump, and soft, while this one was cool, bony, and hard with dry, lifeless skin that was too baggy for the contents it enveloped. Added to that was the withered, almost wizened, face.

Was it suffering that aged peoples' features? Old people naturally look their years after decades of accumulated distress, while the rich and pampered degenerate more slowly than their poorer neighbours. This child had already endured more trauma than most do in a lifetime, hence it now had the visage of a centenarian.

"How come we are only feeding kids here?" Gratefully, he returned the child to Lorna.

"Because children are the most susceptible to malnutrition, especially during their first five years, as their bodies need extra resources to feed their growing as well as living. This means only some of the food they eat is used by their bodies for survival."

"Even if they don't get enough?"

"Yes, a starving child will continue to grow, despite dying of malnutrition. Also, because they are small and weak, they are unable to stop older children or adults from stealing their food."

"And they can be too young to take from other children," a local nurse added.

"That, too. I think it explains why Western aid largely ignores adults, while being obsessed with helping little kids—because they are the only ones who are perceived to be sufficiently innocent to deserve unconditional help, which is why we don't get enough food for everybody."

"So, you have to prioritise the hungriest kids?"

"Exactly. Even though there are other children—and even adults—who are also hungry." Lorna sighed. "Many of them are wasting away from malnutrition, but there is no help for them until they almost die. By that time, it may be too late. Imagine how that feels for them, seeing this huge U.N. operation in Kugombwala—the vast amounts of money spent on logistics and supplies for the peacekeepers, while nothing is made available to them."

"No wonder they're angry."

"Yes, and it upsets me, too. Sometimes, I think we are only here to stop the dying but not to end the suffering."

"Anyway, I've got to go now, to save some more lives . . . "

Alan bristled at Megan's self-righteousness. It was the same charade every day. She was the first to leave breakfast and lunch, while regurgitating the same irritating words, with the implicit message that she was better than those who were not involved in direct life-saving activities. Her way of asserting position in the MedRelief expat pecking order.

There was an unspoken hierarchy among aid workers, Alan now realised, that overshadowed the official organogram. The medics saw themselves as superior to everyone else, so Megan was merely voicing their professional arrogance. Surgeons, who performed emergency, life-saving operations, were at the top of that order, followed by doctors, nurses, and then everybody else, with further subdivision according to mission experience.

It meant that the other expats—including Keith—all considered themselves above Alan, which riled him. The medics were also privileged to have positive human contact with their patients, while his task of controlling the finances forced him into regular confrontations with the scum of the local community—its warlords and businessmen.

"Oh, Mr. Alan, we hear you can be such a good man!"

"Thanks." *For the flattery.* He forced a smile. The two locals had been shown into his office by one of the guards.

"Please, Mr. Alan, we come because of a big problem."

"Right." Alan regarded them steadily, wary of their tricks.

"You see," the man continued, "there can be too much fighting in Kugombwala because of tribalism. That is why everybody must work against it. Especially the foreigners."

"I agree."

"But MedRelief make the situation worse."

"That surely can't be true. What do you mean?"

"When a ship or aeroplane comes and you bring the goods to your base, MedRelief always uses the same transport company."

"Yes, because they give the best price."

"Oh, Mr. Alan, you can sound too stupid, just like Mr. Toby before you . . ."

Alan felt his hackles rise at the insult but controlled his reaction while recalling Dave's advice: never offend anyone in Kugombwala, as they all have guns.

"You see," the man continued, "your organisation can be against our tribe because you never use our trucks."

"That can be how we help you," the other man added. "We have a lorry, and MedRelief can do business with us. Our tribe will then forget your insult."

Interesting way to get new customers, Alan noted, while seeking a strategy to fob them off. "How much to rent your truck for a day?"

"Three hundred dollars."

"No way! I only pay two hundred for the other lorry."

"It can be our best price, special for you, Mr. Alan," the man said before adopting a sinister tone. "If you do not hire our truck, then our tribe cannot guarantee MedRelief's security."

Alan's pulse began to race. The subtle death threat put him in a quandary, for if he acquiesced to their demand, a new problem would arise—the existing haulier would get upset at losing business and might take revenge. On him.

He was caught like a flea between two fingernails.

What to do? A possible option would be to divide the jobs between the different transport companies, but without competition, there would be no incentive for them to lower their prices. Massive inflation would follow. Somehow, he needed to control costs while limiting the security risk. He recalled further advice from Dave: pass the buck for unpopular decisions while transfering potential conflicts back to the Kugombwalans.

"My boss in London says two hundred dollars is our maximum price—"

"Okay, then, we can do all your transport," the first man jabbered, hoping to lever a rival out of business.

"Thanks, but every truck company from any tribe that accepts this amount can work for MedRelief. One at a time. And when it's their turn. I will tell our existing company why they are losing half of the work—because you are receiving the rest of the business." *As well as the blame for the loss of contracts,* he mentally continued.

The two businessmen argued with each other in their local language before one of them turned to him.

"Okay, we can agree."

"Good!" Alan smiled out of relief for having kept MedRelief out of the conflict between Kugombwala's competing tribes.

"You be careful, Mr. Alan." The other businessman turned sour, having mistaken his smile for supercilious self-congratulation. "Just remember what happened to Mr. Toby."

"MacJohn, why did Toby leave?"

"He can be getting too many death threats, so he ran away."

I'll be joining him in three weeks, Alan confirmed to himself. He couldn't wait to get out, before his bad decision to come to Kugombwala would degenerate into a disaster.

"So, Al, why did you leave Britain to become an aid worker?" Megan had lingered over lunch, captivating him with a conversation about his hometown until the others had left the table. She was showing unwanted interest, which made him uneasy. He noted that she had left the top two buttons of her blouse undone.

"And have you got a girlfriend?"

Her probing questions put Alan on the defensive. "Aye, we've been together for many years."

"Do you have kids?"

"No."

"So, you are not that close?"

"What makes you think that?" Alan blurted.

"Well, you never talk about her. I bet you haven't written to her, have you?"

Mind your own business, he mentally rebuked her, while grateful for the reminder. Later, he penned a quick postcard at the airport before handing the outgoing MedRelief mail pouch to a departing plane.

Dear Mandy,

I hope you are doing well. I'm fine, though it's really hot and sweaty here.

Ndombazu is a total pit with some nasty locals, but we've got three thousand U.N. soldiers keeping them in order. Thirty of them are protecting our house and the hospital, which is next door. It's great to have so many bodyguards.

Work is hard because I'm running the non-medical side of the 150-bed hospital and the feeding centre that is full of starving kids.

I'm eating okay, as we've got someone who makes food for us, though I've already had diarrhoea twice. So far, no malaria, touch wood.

The MedRelief crew I work with are weird, except for the security coordinator, Dave, who is cool.

Think about you every day.

Love,

Al

P.S. I reckon I'll be home in a couple of weeks.

His heart beat faster as he finished the note, due to his in-built lie detector, which he overruled as he considered it more important to ameliorate her emotions than to tell the truth. If Mandy thought he was enjoying himself, she'd be even more annoyed with him for going; she mustn't know he was in danger, or she'd worry herself sick; and she mustn't suspect he was befriending any women, or she'd assume infidelity.

A low drone announced the arrival of another aircraft—a medium-sized Soviet-built Antonov. Alan looked up to see the cargo plane corkscrewing down through the hazardous airspace above Ndombazu airport.

"Please, sir, this your plane?" a nearby Indian soldier asked.

"Yes."

"What is it bringing?"

Alan looked at the radio telex message that listed the cargo. "Forty tons of corn soya blend, high-energy milk powder, sugar, and cooking oil." The soldiers at the airport were always asking questions. Perhaps it was out of boredom. Or maybe they were trying to comprehend what the strange Westerners were doing in Kugombwala.

"For selling?"

"No, for our feeding programmes."

"No money business?"

"No, we give it free to the starving kids."

Alan's answer perplexed the soldier, as there were no free lunches in his society. "So, who is paying for this food?"

"The British government."

"Thank you, sir." The soldier was satisfied to learn that the provisions came from the Western cornucopia, from which there seemed to flow a continuous supply of goods to Kugombwala.

"What happened at the World Food Programme warehouse last week?" Alan hoped for details on a raid about which the U.N. peacekeeping command was reticent.

"Very bad business." The soldier shook his head. "Four sepoys killed. Eight soldiers wounded. Everything gone. One thousand tons of food stolen."

The U.N. had been unable to despatch their rapid response force to counter the attack, due to an angry demonstration by a group of women and children that materialised outside the gates to their base. It was clearly a set-up by the warlords. Rumours were rife that the stolen food was later loaded onto a ship and sold abroad in exchange for weapons and ammunition.

Once the Antonov had taxied to a halt, Alan walked out onto the tarmac apron to join the gang of workers and three rickety trucks he had hired for the day to unload the plane. The rear cargo door was lowered, and the labourers swarmed onto the sacks, tearing them at random from the neat piles in which they arrived and competing with each other to load them as fast as possible into the waiting trucks.

During the mayhem, Alan noticed one of the drivers taking a sack out of the back of his lorry and stashing it in the cab.

"Oi!" Alan bellowed. "Put that sack back."

The man slammed the cab door shut, shouting back in his own language.

"Thief! I want my sack back." Alan marched up to the lorry, barged past the driver, and attempted to open the cab door. A rough hand pulled him back, but he shrugged it off. The mutual shouting between them brought over the workers, as well as the two Indian soldiers who had been standing guard near the plane.

MacJohn intervened. "Boss, what can be the problem?"

"That man," Alan pointed at the driver, "is a thief. I saw him steal a sack from the back of the lorry and put it in the cab."

"No thief!" The driver was hysterical. "Me no thief!"

"If you are not a thief, then let me search the cab."

"You no can go in. My lorry. It is for me."

One of the Indian soldiers took the cue to open the cab door, revealing a fat sack on the driver's seat.

"See?" Alan pointed triumphantly at the loot. "You are a thief."

"No thief. This sack for me . . . "

His lack of shame was bizarre. Even now, when it was obvious that he had stolen food destined for starving children, he still believed he could convince everyone that he was innocent.

"Why does he feel so insulted?" Alan turned towards MacJohn. "He's the one stealing from MedRelief, not the other way around."

MacJohn smiled. "Try to understand, Alan, that stealing food from the white man or NGOs is not theft in Kugombwala. You give it away, so it can have no value for you. Also, you white people have been taking our natural resources for many years. We have too little, and you have too much; so when we take from you, we are just getting small payback."

The truck driver let out a tirade in an ugly Kugombwalan language. It sounded like abuse.

"What did he say?"

"Nothing." MacJohn studied the ground.

Another death threat. Alan was grateful the driver and the Kugombwalan workers had been disarmed before entering the airport. Although the U.N. peacekeepers were not subduing the mad gunmen of Kugombwala, at least they were protecting the aid workers from harm. It would be unimaginably dangerous to be in Kugombwala without them, so he appreciated the U.N.'s presence.

Another positive aspect of the U.N. was their parties. Every Saturday evening was celebrated in honour of one or another U.N. day, with the festivities rotating between the different agencies that laid on a bounteous buffet or barbeque. To cap it all, the U.N. provided three jeeps and two truckloads of soldiers to secure the transit of their guests.

The experience of venturing out into the dark streets of Ndombazu with fifty armed guards to attend a party gave Alan a real kick. *Shows how important I have become,* he told himself with a smile. *Not even the British prime minister warrants this level of protection.* It would make a great yarn to impress the lads back at home.

The event that night was at the UNICEF compound, an appropriate venue for the U.N.'s Day of the African Child. A local school choir had been mustered to entertain the guests and to ensure a token presence of African kids. They were then whisked away so that the party's real purpose of networking and socialising could begin. Before that, the head of the UNICEF delegation closed the formal part of the evening with a speech about how the children represented the hope and future of Kugombwala.

"Total nonsense," muttered one of the guests standing beside Alan. "This place got no government, got no hope."

The tedious speech lasted ten minutes and was followed by a round of applause—U.N. diplomacy in action. The guests then dispersed towards the tables loaded with food and cold chain boxes filled with chilled drinks. It was an awkward moment for many, stuck in a crowd of strangers, most of whom they would never see again. But for some, it meant an opportunity to act without recourse to the consequences.

"Right, Al!" Dave handed him two cans. "Time to find a bit of talent." They went over to a group of young women who were being bored by a German pilot.

"Ay-up, girls." Alan interrupted an anecdote of landing under machine gun fire in Mogadishu. "Any of you want a drink?" His brash entry caused two of the women to flee, but one stayed—an American.

"Thanks." She accepted the tin. "I'm Peggy Sue. Say, are you British? I love your accent. It's so cute." She beamed at him.

Alan gave her a quick once-over. Not bad at all, he concluded, approving of her fine form plus features that had been artificially enhanced to achieve near perfection: immaculate teeth that were a credit to her dentist; a massive mop of styled hair; and a rather obvious application of make-up—much like a Hollywood film star.

The chemistry between them was instant. "You're so funny, Al." She giggled at his inept jokes, flattering him with her undivided attention. Her vivacious and sophisticated manner further eroded any feelings of fidelity. *More attractive and interesting than Mandy.* He fantasised over this opportunity for a fling. Or even an upgrade.

"You should come and stay. I've got a great condominium on Lower Manhattan . . . "

Alan imagined his glittering future in New York, the coolest place on the planet. He would thrive in the land of freedom and prosperity, released from the shackles of being born to the wrong social class in depressed northern Britain. And all thanks to becoming an aid worker, which was the best decision he had ever made. *It is going to change my life,* he predicted.

The fairy tale evening of mutual flirting was interrupted just before midnight by the growling engines of the Indian army's lorries and jeeps, which announced their imminent departure to ferry the visitors back to their compounds. Like Cinderella, he had to leave the ball before the magic wore off.

"Hey, you," Peggy Sue greeted Alan at a U.N. coordination meeting the following afternoon, having already forgotten his name. "Great to see you again. Come 'round sometime. I'm here all week; then I gotta head back to New York."

The World Food Programme representative introduced her to the regular participants as one of their roaming experts, who wished to share an important discovery.

"I just wanna touch base with you all about the findings of our food security survey. We're getting the preliminary results right now, which show that the Kugombwalans have traditional coping strategies to overcome the annual hunger gap before the harvest. Most of the malnutrition you agencies are seeing now can be ascribed to social causes, which are an underlying phenomenon of African societies. That suggests the problem has stabilised and that we are back to normalcy."

Her talk continued for ten minutes, a string of technical jargon and buzzwords to justify the World Food Programme's announced cutback in rations for the Kugombwalan famine. In short, the U.N. had decided that the Kugombwalans no longer needed food aid because they traditionally went hungry, and that was acceptable because "Africans are used to that sort of thing. I mean, hey, what's new?" as Peggy Sue put it.

Alan thought of the child he had held in the feeding centre and the gaunt, emaciated mother who had stared on listlessly. She was about the same age as Peggy Sue, but that was the only similarity. One was on the brink of starvation, watching her child die; the other was flourishing on five thousand U.S. dollars a month for telling the rest of the world that malnourished people didn't need more food because they were used to going hungry. A wave of revulsion passed over him, displacing his earlier attraction.

Everybody was on the make out of Kugombwala's misery, he realised. The bandits and warlords outright stole aid supplies; the local staff pilfered from it; and the businessmen colluded to push up the price of their services. Meanwhile, the U.N. staff, journalists, pilots, peacekeepers, and many aid workers all took fat salaries to fill their bank accounts. For them, humanitarian aid was a resource to be milked to achieve more comfortable lives for themselves. That meant less for those to whom the aid was intended, who were too poor or weak to prevent what was destined for them from being diverted to other recipients. It was no consolation that he was getting so little out of aid himself, for he had been tricked into accepting no salary by Blair-Campbell and his henchwomen at the MedRelief headquarters, who profited from exploiting gullible people wishing to help the hungry.

Alan had hitherto assumed there was goodness in everyone, which would surface during times of hardship and suffering. That was how his father had described the way people in Britain had pulled together during the Second World War. But the opposite seemed to apply to almost everyone involved with the conflict in Kugombwala.

He resolved to be different—or, at least, to try.

Alan was back at the airport the following week to meet a new cargo of food aid, which also gave him temporary respite from the confines of the MedRelief compound.

"Anything happening around here, Major?" he asked the Indian officer in charge of the airport. They sat at his desk, sipping cups of sweet chai served by a subaltern, while he waited for the plane to arrive.

"It is quiet, thank goodness. But today, big VIP is coming. This fellow is special friend of the U.N. secretary general. Maybe you know?"

Alan shook his head, and the conversation moved on to Major Khan's favourite subjects of cricket and possible mutual acquaintances in Britain.

" . . . and you must be knowing Mr. Amar Singh in Bradford? My sister-in-law's brother's cousin. He is a merchant with a very big store . . ."

An hour and fifteen families later, their conversation was interrupted by the arrival of an executive jet landing on the runway, which taxied over to the apron in front of the airport building.

Major Khan left Alan to watch, while he led out the Indian army reception crew of ten soldiers, who lined up on either side of the aircraft door with Major Khan, ready to welcome the visitor. A tall European in an immaculate suit and tie emerged. He was accompanied to a waiting helicopter, which promptly took off towards the U.N. base.

The klaxons of the Indian Army security escort team disturbed the peace at the MedRelief base later that afternoon. Guards hurried to open the main gate in time to allow three jeeps to screech into the middle of the compound at high speed. It was a well-rehearsed routine that took place every morning when Alan and Dave were collected to attend the U.N.'s security meeting.

The sergeant major in charge of the lead jeep sprang out and presented the waiting Alan with an envelope.

"For you, Sahib, special letter." His waxed moustache was groomed into double antennae that emerged above his upper lip and pointed like the hands of a clock at ten to two. After saluting, he returned to the front jeep that then took off with the rest of the convoy, all hooting their way out through the gate.

The envelope was addressed to Jules, who was away for a week, attending meetings in London. Alan took the letter to Lorna, who was acting head of mission during Jules' absence. She pulled out a gold-edged card, causing her to frown.

"It's an invitation from the U.N. zone commander to a lunch reception tomorrow at the Indian Army HQ, in honour of the visit of Mr. Lars Holmborg, the U.N. special representative to the secretary general for Kugombwala."

"That would be the guy I saw arrive earlier today at Kugombwala airport."

"I don't have time." Lorna handed the card to him. "Do you want to go instead?"

"Sure. It could be a laugh."

The U.N. base hummed with activity. Soldiers from the different peacekeeping nations marched back and forth in their best uniforms, their boots glowing in the bright tropical sun. Fresh flags fluttered in the breeze, while a military band serenaded the convoy of aid agency vehicles as they rolled up to an abandoned warehouse that been converted to host the gala—a worthy spectacle to mark the visit of a high-level VIP as part of the U.N.'s last-ditch attempt to find a solution to the Kugombwalan civil war.

Lars Holmborg turned out to be a former Scandinavian politician, who had joined that elite circle of distinguished names whose job was to fool the world that high diplomacy actually worked.

"Madam Chairwoman. Mr. Watanabe. Colonel Patel. Excellencies. Ladies and gentlemen. Friends and colleagues," he addressed his audience during a disappointingly stodgy meal. "It is an honour to be with you today. Indeed, it is a personal privilege to bring to you direct from the secretary general his sincerest thanks for your tireless efforts to address the plight of the people of Kugombwala."

He paused to give gravitas to his speech.

"The fruitful collaboration between the United Nations and our NGO partners has created a solid partnership that has alleviated the worst suffering of the people of this country. Lives have been saved, dignity restored, and hope returned. I surely speak for us all when I say that we can be proud of a job well done . . . "

The speech flowed with more flattery for those present to acquire their support for its coming message. Meanwhile, the heavy meal, combined with alcohol and the tropical heat, began to have an effect on Alan, and he found himself dozing off. It took a great effort to stay awake, and he only caught intermittent snippets of the rest of the speech:

"Together, the leaders of the world have agreed to spare no effort in the fight against war, famine, and disease . . . The international community has, therefore, mandated the United Nations to reach all vulnerable stakeholder populations . . . through their implementing agencies, which have made a strong commitment to integrate human rights and humanitarian principles in their participatory programmes for refugees and internally displaced persons . . . with special emphasis to ensuring a gender perspective . . . that will be implemented in a coordinated manner to internationally recognised standards . . . "

The liberal use of aid jargon provided even less incentive for Alan to listen. He hoped no one was watching him as he nodded like a pigeon at the plate in front of him, in a desperate struggle to prevent his sleepy head from thudding onto the table. Apart from the embarrassing bump that would cause, there was also the unpleasant prospect of waking up with his face immersed in curry.

Holmborg was still talking. "We must not forget the immense contribution of the United Nations peacekeeping forces . . . "

The speech droned on. For there was more to come. Much more.

" . . . together with the officers of the monitoring and observation mission, who have been . . . using our combined competencies and capacities to create a sustainable environment for development . . . I have been greatly encouraged by the active promotion of peace building . . . and I am delighted to note that the warlords have unanimously agreed to unite as peace lords . . . "

Warlords as peace lords? What nonsense was this? Alan's small glimmer of wakening was soon snuffed out by the soporific struggle with his closing eyelids.

" . . . the people of Kugombwala are now in a position to help themselves once again . . . for Africa's problems call for African solutions . . . Therefore, the United Nations has decided that the time has come for this great continent to take on the mandate to foster peace in Kugombwala . . . In this regard, I am pleased to announce that the community of African nations have risen to this challenge . . . the United Nations peacekeeping forces will, therefore, be relieved, to enable them to take up duties elsewhere . . . Excellencies, ladies and gentlemen, let me then conclude . . . "

The word "conclude" caused Alan to sit up and pay attention, as if a large dose of caffeine had been injected into his veins.

" . . . the community of African nations will soon deploy their own battalion to oversee the next phase of the rebuilding of Kugombwala. In the meantime, I can assure you that the United Nations agencies will continue to deliver humanitarian assistance in proportion to the needs, and our efforts will be complemented by support to activities that will bridge the transition from emergency to development. With the full range of U.N. human rights promotion and protection instruments at our disposal, we will not relax our vigilance; we will continue in our strivings to urge all duty-bearers in Kugombwala to protect the rights and address the needs of the Kugombwalan people."

A distant rattle of machine gun fire indicated how the warlords intended to address those needs. Holmborg showed no reaction and continued to perform as the monkey that chooses to neither see, hear, nor speak of any evil.

"The war is now over; peace will bring the dividend of prosperity to Kugombwala. Let me, therefore, end my statement by wishing the peacekeeping forces every success with future missions elsewhere in our common interest of global peace and security. And let me commend the United Nations humanitarian agencies and our NGO partners with continued success in attending to the plight of the people of Kugombwala and in rebuilding this great and proud nation. Thank you."

There was a moment's stunned silence.

A burst of polite applause followed. Alan found himself clapping out of an instinctive reaction to the noise and sight of other people doing the same, like a circus sea lion responding to a cue without considering what it was clapping for.

"So, how did the lunch go, Al?" Lorna asked Alan once everyone had assembled for supper.

"Lots of U.N. blah-blah—"

"I could have told you it wasn't worth going," Paula interrupted.

"Wrong there, Paula. That VIP announced the U.N. will soon pull its troops out of Kugombwala."

"What?" Keith gasped. "We's all going to get killed. Or kidnapped . . ."

Nobody responded, as everybody had the same thought. Keith was the least likely to get killed or kidnapped, as he had, by far, the safest job among the MedRelief expats. He never left the compound, and his work kept him out of conflict with Kugombwalan staff, patients, businessmen, and gunmen.

"It's about time the U.N. left." Paula scowled. "I'll be glad to see them go. We might get some peace around here without those honking jeeps bringing chapattis three times a day for the peacekeepers."

"But don't forget that they do provide our security." Lorna often argued with Paula.

"I think they make it worse." Dave lit a cigarette for effect. "Their security officers exaggerate the threats to justify their well-paid jobs. Our local guards at the gates will be just as good at keeping away the fighters."

"I'm not scared," Megan piped up. "No one wants to harm us. Half the patients in the orthopaedic ward are wounded fighters, and their comrades like us for treating them."

"But if the warlords start fighting each other, then they will want to decide who gets treated and who doesn't," Lorna said. "We'll be seen as collaborators with the warlord who controls access to the hospital and, therefore, enemies of those who don't. Our perceived neutrality will be under threat, and our safety depends on that."

"The VIP also told us the U.N. is going to hand the responsibility for security over to an African force." Alan struggled to get a word in edgeways.

"Oh, that's really great, isn't it?" Paula sneered. "I can't see them making things better."

"I disagree," Dave argued. "It'll solve the problem with different factions fighting to control the hospital. And who knows? We might get to see some action. It's become a bit boring around here . . . "

Alan slept badly that night. The curry was working its way through his intestines, causing urgent visits to the bathroom. He was then disturbed by shouting in the street outside that made his heart pound with fear—and made worse by not understanding what was said, together with worries over earlier death threats and the uncertainty of what would happen once the U.N. peacekeepers left. He wondered if this was his cue to go. Would it be an adequate excuse to leave Kugombwala with enough integrity to be considered a hero back at home?

But his colleagues depended on him to run the logistics and keep the admin in order. He had cleared up a lot of mess from his predecessor, and without him, financial chaos would resume. That would create a security hazard. No, he couldn't abandon the team, which meant he was trapped once again, this time by loyalty and responsibility. He couldn't go unless the others also left, so a MedRelief evacuation due to deteriorating security was now the only feasible option for an honourable escape from Kugombwala. Perhaps after the U.N. peacekeepers departed . . .

A nearby burst of machine gun fire was succeeded by a second, followed by an uneasy silence. Why was there no return fire? Did that mean somebody had been killed? Snuffed out by the salvo that publicly proclaimed their death?

He lay in dark silence, filled with apprehension. And then it came, what he had been expecting—another burst of released bullets.

Silence again, occupied by a single thought: *was that another killing?*

The gunfire rendered sleep impossible. Darwin was wrong: life was not about the survival of the fittest. Instead, it was a deadly competition for scarce resources that favoured the most vicious. That was clear in Kugombwala, where the warlords, fighters, and the businessmen who backed them were the most likely to survive because they preyed on ordinary people. Was MedRelief interfering with natural selection by bringing aid? Would the efforts of his team make any difference in the long term, or were they delaying an inevitable outcome, now that the U.N. and international community had given up on Kugombwala?

Lorna had mentioned that the aid agencies were merely stopping people from dying, but not alleviating their wider suffering. Perhaps it was worse than that. Were humanitarians just keeping them alive until the TV cameras disappeared with the departing U.N. forces?

No, that hypothesis was too harsh. It required a huge effort to save those lives in the feeding centre—and at no small risk to himself or his colleagues. MedRelief and the other aid agencies were committing vast resources to stamping out starvation. They clearly wanted to help the people of Kugombwala as best as they could.

Yet most of those who got fed would still go hungry after they had been discharged because nothing was done to stop the bandits stealing from the poor. No food aid was provided for the hungry masses, only for those who were starving to death. Why was that?

The question kept him awake, his mind hunting for an explanation.

It led him to consider the situation from the donor's side. For many people, compassion for their fellow humans was first triggered when they saw them dying. This was linked to another strong feeling that would emerge at the same moment: the observer's fear of their own death. Was that why the living intervened to end severe suffering? Were they motivated by a desire to avoid having to see someone's demise? That would be enhanced during situations of mass death, which had a high chance of being reported in the news, unlike the passing of a single individual, who would less likely remind us of our inevitable mortality.

Alan thought back to the first images of the Kugombwalan crisis he had seen on British TV: the aid workers proudly tackling an African famine. Now that he was here among that misery, he sought to remind himself what had attracted him to come. Severe self-reflection revealed his subconscious enjoyment of seeing that disaster from a distance and observing the aid workers solving it.

Maybe people derived satisfaction from watching the misfortune of others because it affirmed how well they, by comparison, were living? But that theory only worked if such disasters were mitigated and death rates fell, which was perhaps why society made such an effort to combat mass mortality: to ensure that humanity could hold on to the notion that it was in control of its collective destiny.

Destiny. A word he had never thought about before. He had only a vague notion of its meaning. Something about where a person was going in their future. Where was he headed? What would happen to him?

For the first time in his life, Alan's *foreseeable* future lay before him like a blank book, with no words written on the pages—except for the lettering in the watermark that predicted trouble ahead.

CHAPTER 4

"This is London," the radio announced in a polished English accent, followed by the uplifting theme of the BBC World Service News.

Listening to the headlines had become a regular suppertime ritual at the MedRelief base. The team were bored and irritated with each other, so a daily dose of current events was required to provide alternative topics for conversation that had nothing to do with the medical programme, the war, or the local staff.

Alan had never taken any notice of the news beyond the sports results. His arrival in Kugombwala changed that, for the conflict was a major focus of media attention, and it was encouraging to hear the country's regular mention in the headlines. Were his friends back in Britain listening to the news and thinking of him? He hoped so.

But over recent weeks, there had been a drop in reports about Kugombwala, following the departure of the United Nations peacekeepers. Western media had lost interest in the incomprehensible squabble between rival clans in a faraway continent, and without the presence of U.N. troops, the conflict held little international news appeal.

Jules turned up the volume to broadcast the headlines. That night, like the previous fortnight, there was no mention of Kugombwala. He turned down the sound after the main stories had been announced but kept the radio playing so he could still hear what was said. Fifteen minutes later, he interrupted Paula's monologue about incompetent local colleagues.

"Shh," he ordered. "It's a report from Kugombwala."

They all fell silent to concentrate on the radio.

"The recent withdrawal of the United Nations from Kugombwala has caused the country to disintegrate into a multi-factional civil war that regional peacekeeping soldiers of the Organisation of African Unity's African Battle Group—known as AfriBat—have failed to contain. Kugombwala is now divided into separate territories controlled by different militia groups, who tax the local population for food and funds when they are not fighting each other. One of these factions, the Kugombwalan Patriots—or 'KP Nuts,' as they are locally called—is, however, an army with a difference. For it is an army of small boys."

There was a perceptible pause in the narration, as the reporter allowed time for his statement to resonate.

"I travelled for six hours through thick jungle to meet the leader of the Kugombwalan Patriots. Major MacAmos Buo is a young man in his early twenties and has created a remarkable rebel force comprising youngsters half his age. He is known to his troops as 'boss-brother,' and I asked him why he was using children in his liberation struggle."

"My man," broke in a slurred voice, edited to follow the narrative, "I no can make them come; they is coming by themselves. Every day, more boys come to me. They want to fight, and I make them into warriors. I teach them how to kill. I show them that small boys can be stronger than big men."

"But, Major," the reporter interrupted, "what makes these boys come to you?"

There was a slight laugh. "Them boys can want payback. They see their fathers and brothers killed, their mothers and sisters raped. I give them new family, and I give them a weapon for to get revenge."

The report then concluded. "A senior UNICEF official has expressed concern with this latest development in the Kugombwalan civil war. There are unsubstantiated reports that the KP child-soldiers kidnap young boys during their attacks on villages, who are then forced to become fellow warrior slaves. This is Mark Jeffreys in Ogugawa, Kugombwala."

Jules turned off the radio. There was a stunned silence, broken by Lorna.

"I was expecting this to happen sooner or later. We've seen this before in Africa: Mozambique, Uganda, Liberia, and Sierra Leone. Those wars have shown that kids make the bravest and most loyal soldiers—and also the most vicious."

Worphans. The orphans of war.

Kugombwala's conflict had spawned a new word for the English language to label the crazed kids who carried Kalashnikov rifles. Suddenly, they were everywhere in the upcountry areas outside Ndombazu: manning—or kidding—checkpoints and hassling the few who dared travel without an AfriBat military escort. Negotiating these roadblocks added a new trauma to the war, a series of hurdles on the major routes that led into the anarchic interior.

"Another checkpoint," MacGarry the driver announced to Alan and Megan. It was the fifteenth they had encountered that day on an exploration mission to assess the health situation in the rural area beyond Ndombazu.

Fifteen. The five brats in the distance looked a fraction of that age. Butterflies fluttered in Alan's stomach as the vehicle slowed its approach to the roadblock. A confrontation was inevitable in a game where two sides play with different rules and a loaded dice. Once again, Alan wished he were somewhere—anywhere—else.

MacGarry drew the car to a halt some thirty metres before the checkpoint. "You two can stay here. I go present our papers."

Alan was grateful to remain in his seat. His heart beat faster as he watched the tall driver walk over to the three plastic Coca-Cola crates and their miniature guards. On reaching them, the full difference in their heights became apparent: a surreal sight of five dwarfs with their machine guns surrounding an adult man. The ensuing conversation was drowned by the idling engine, giving Alan the sensation of watching an old silent movie—the exaggerated gesticulation of the kids, the pointing in his direction, and then a rifle butt rammed into MacGarry's groin, forcing him to keel over. Whereupon, more rifle butts were bashed into his body.

What now? Megan stifled a scream while Alan watched aghast as the horror unfolded before their eyes. Paralysed by helplessness and fear, they could do nothing other than stare as the worphans attacked MacGarry like a pack of hounds bringing down a stag. And just as dogs differ from deer, so, too, did the infant warriors appear to belong to a different, inhuman species.

The silent movie continued—a few more rifle butts into the defenceless driver, and then a round of kicks from over-sized wellingtons once he hit the ground. They then stopped and stood back. MacGarry got up and hobbled back to the vehicle, both hurt and humiliated.

Their reunion was awkward.

"You all right?" What else could Alan say?

The driver struggled to respond. "What can be happening to my country?" he asked, to which neither Alan nor Megan could answer.

MacGarry entered the vehicle, and they drove slowly to the checkpoint and the five brats who guarded it.

"Where you can go, white man?" a boy no more than ten years old chirped. At his age, Alan was in the Cub Scouts, enjoying the childhood innocence of those distant campfire days. Had this kid lost that innocence, or was this mere child's play for him?

"I c-c-can be going to Ngolindi village," Alan stammered, attempting a local accent in the hope of bonding with the boy.

"Get out the truck, white man," another child ordered, sticking the barrel of an AK-47 through the open car window towards Alan's face. He looked a little older, perhaps twelve, with a perceptible meanness etched into his features.

The thought of leaving the relative safety of the Land Rover filled Alan with a fresh dose of fear. What would they do to him? Subject him to the same ordeal as MacGarry? Or worse? He had no choice. The muzzle of the machine gun was pointed at him, demanding total obedience.

"My man, how can the white man be getting out of this truck when you be putting that blunderbuss through the window?" MacGarry asserted, having regained his composure.

The barrel was duly withdrawn; a psychological victory had been scored, and with it, the worphans had lost their upper hand.

MacGarry was now on the verbal offensive. "This white man can be good friend of your boss-brother. You make big palaver for him, and he come cut off your ears and fingers and eat them."

His outburst had the desired effect. The look in the worphans' eyes went from bloodthirst to blind terror. The oldest child soldier waved them on.

Alan felt a spasm run down his spine as the Land Rover moved forwards, his body shaking off some of its fear as they left the checkpoint behind, while aware there was more to come.

A few kilometres later, they ran into another roadblock.

Alan had failed to notice the length of frayed rope across the track, but MacGarry spotted it in time to slam on the brakes before it was too late. The vehicle came to an abrupt halt, with the bonnet almost touching a small cloth bag that was attached by a thread to the rope.

"What's that pouch for?" Alan asked.

"Checkpoint fetish. It can make big palaver and kill you if you touch it."

The burnt-out corpse of a vehicle lay beyond the rope to the side of the road, almost immersed in the forest—a possible victim of the fetish curse.

They waited for five tense minutes, suspecting they were being watched. MacGarry revved the engine a few times, hoping the additional sound might provoke a reaction from whomever guarded the place.

No response.

After five more minutes, he resorted to sounding the horn.

Still nothing.

It was hot in the vehicle, even with the windows open. The running motor made it worse, so MacGarry switched off the engine.

He opened his door to increase the air circulation, but that failed to prevent beads of sweat from breaking out on Alan's brow. The forest was lifeless but for the grating cacophony of cicadas, whose shrill sound concentrated his attention on the suffocating heat, which emphasised the trapped sweat that was building up over his back, under his seat, and behind his legs, where the plastic seating prevented his perspiration from escaping. He was about to open his door when MacGarry stopped him.

"My man, stay in the truck. The people here can believe the white man pollute their soil."

They waited in sticky, tropical discomfort.

"I don't like this." Alan voiced his fear after a few minutes, to which MacGarry gave an affirmative grunt.

"Well, I'm not scared," Megan piped up from the back seat. Alan had forgotten she was there. Unlike Lorna and Paula, Megan did not chatter away at every available opportunity—a positive attribute that almost made up for her strange smell and grunge attire.

"You what?" Alan turned around.

"I was saying, I'm not scared. I've got Chris with me, and he looks after me."

"Who's Chris?" There were only the three of them in the car. Was Megan hallucinating, or was she even stranger than he had hitherto reckoned?

"Chris? My pet crystal. I bring him everywhere I go."

That does it, Alan concluded, downgrading her in his mind from weirdo to witch.

Ten minutes later, a figure emerged from the forest ahead of them—a young man of about twenty, dressed in dirty combat fatigues. He ambled towards them in a relaxed gait that demonstrated his complete control of the situation. In one hand, he carried an AK-47 with the muzzle pointing downward, almost scraping the ground. In the other, he held out a grenade as if he were bringing a choice fruit offering. A handful of bullet cartridges, like a row of small horns, stuck out of his curly hair. Half-closed eyelids indicated he was sky-high on dope.

"Yes, sir, where the white man can go?" he asked MacGarry, rolling back an enormous pair of lips that revealed teeth filed into sharp points. His face was pockmarked with pustules and spots, giving him an impressively ugly appearance.

"The white man can go bring medicine to Gagawugu," MacGarry replied.

"White man." Fangface now turned his attention to Alan. "You can have present for me? I want cigaretty." The hand grenade was tapped on the sill of the car window to remind them of its presence.

Had the rebel warrior posed the same question to MacGarry, he would have received a cigarette, for the drivers kept a packet in the vehicle for such occasions. A gift could be given as a token of comradeship, a sign of solidarity with someone poor enough to need to ask. It was normal in his culture to share what little one had—the guy you gave to today might help you out tomorrow. Rich and powerful Kugombwalans were exempt from this rule, for there was no need for them to give in order to get something back because they had discovered how to get without giving.

MedRelief's regulations followed a different logic, which forbade gifts to combatants. It was a sensible rule intended to make life easier for MedRelief employees, under the supposition that once it became known that presents were never given, then the fighters would not bother asking for them. But whoever had come up with the theory had failed to realise that those asking had nothing to lose in making a demand.

Bound by those rules, Alan hesitated, not knowing how to deliver a refusal without offending. But his silence and indecision were mistaken for arrogance. Fangface became aggressive.

"Yeah, white man, I can want cigaretty." He waved two fingers in front of his face to demonstrate the action of smoking. "You give me cigaretty, or I go blow you."

Alan was about to answer when a movement caught his eye. He turned away from the cratered face that was framed in MacGarry's door window to look out through the back of the Land Rover. A small child, about ten years old, had appeared out of nowhere and was skirting the vehicle, peering through the windows to check the contents. His eyes only just reached the bottom edge, but their movement around the periphery of the cabin captivated Alan's attention. The whites of the eyes glowed in contrast to a dark face. He found himself staring at those eyes until they rotated in their orbits. Their gazes met, and Alan had to look away. A shiver shot down his spine. There was an indescribable evil in those eyes—eyes that had witnessed things that no man, let alone a child, should ever see.

Fangface had also spotted the arrival of his accomplice. His eyelids retracted as a dreadful idea appeared in his mind.

"You, boy," he addressed the child. "You can make the white man see how make chop. Start with the driver." He then let out a hideous laugh, as he raised the AK-47 assault rifle to point it at MacGarry. "Get out."

By now, the child had crossed in front of the bonnet of the vehicle and walked up to MacGarry's open door. Alan could see that he carried a machete. Megan gasped.

"My man," the child addressed MacGarry whilst lifting the machete to shoulder height. "You can want me give you long-sleeve or short-sleeve?" His face remained impassive; he was about to perform a task he had clearly carried out many times before.

MacGarry, usually so cool and composed in the face of the checkpoints, let out a howl of fear at the invitation to decide where his arms were to be amputated. "You can go chop the white man, boy," he urged, breaking into Kugombwalan bush slang. "The white man bring me here; I no want go. He force me big time; he make to kill me if I no come." He then delivered a long verbal onslaught against Alan, against MedRelief, and against all foreigners.

A cold fear filled Alan's gut. Was this the same MacGarry whom he had, until now, counted as a loyal colleague? His disbelief was immediately displaced by premonitions of excruciating pain, as he was bombarded by image upon horrific image of him, there on the ground, his arms being hacked off—one agonising chop at a time—by a kid with too little strength to do the job quickly; and then the grief of seeing his beloved hands forever parted from him and the disability that would hinder him for the rest of his life.

The sound of vehicles stopped MacGarry mid-speech. They all turned to see three jeeps screech around the corner ahead, filled with soldiers brandishing guns. Two large trucks followed them, stacked with rusting air conditioner units.

Alan exhaled the contents of his lungs. Saved by the arrival of an AfriBat convoy on its way back to Ndombazu, loaded with looted goods.

They drove back in silence. There was nothing to say, for the bond between him and MacGarry had been broken, assuming there had ever been a bond in the first place. The experience at the checkpoint had made a profound impact on Alan's impression of Kugombwalans. Were they all like MacGarry? Outwardly friendly and polite, yet deep down hating the uninvited intruders from the developed world? It was a discomforting supposition.

Then there were the Kugombwalan kids, who mutilated their fellow human beings with machetes or murdered them with machine guns. How could they do it? What drove them to commit such savagery? He was tempted to think the worphans were far more wicked than the worst young offenders back in Britain, but he had to admit that occasional horror stories did emerge in the U.K. of young children using horrendous methods to murder toddlers. Yet there was a difference: children in Britain never killed adults.

The car engine's drone temporarily deflected his thinking. He was grateful for the noise that now protected him from having to make conversation with MacGarry or Megan. Alan was also thankful for the protection provided by the soldiers of the AfriBat convoy, which they had joined on its way to Ndombazu. They now sailed through the checkpoints, and he contemplated making faces at the kids who guarded them, to spite them from the safety of AfriBat's accompanying military might. They wouldn't dare harm him now . . .

Children never murdered adults in Britain. The thought was back. Why was that, he wondered? And then he realised it was because kids in the U.K. did not have the means, the firearms, or the encouragement of other adults to kill. But that did not necessarily mean that they would not do so under other circumstances. He was aware that kids in countries where guns were abundant sometimes shot their teachers—or even their parents.

Looking at the AfriBat convoy, he suddenly understood the problem. The soldiers were only safeguarding him and the other aid workers, but not the country's children. The kids of Kugombwala had lost their much-needed protection from the adult world of war—the protection that they should have been granted as a right, which meant that even as perpetrators of the most horrific crimes, they were nonetheless victims—guilty victims—of a society that had failed to shield them from the worst elements of itself.

At last, the car arrived at the compound gate. MedRelief's base often felt like a prison, but today, Alan welcomed being shut in from the horrible world outside. Fortunately, the usual cluster of Kugombwalan elders with their endless requests was not waiting for him at the entrance. The vultures of daily hassle and occasional death threats had already flapped off home for the night.

Alan trembled as he exited the car. He felt drained from the day's confrontations, with an emotional exhaustion that far surpassed the physical tiredness that came after a Sunday morning football match. On reaching the MedRelief house, he mounted the stairs and made straight for the fridge, retrieved two cans of cold drink, and collapsed into an armchair on the terrace.

His peace was short-lived, for Paula was on the prowl, like a predator seeking prey.

"There you are! I've been looking for you all day. The hospital roof's leaking yet again, and the patients are dying of cold." Skilfully, she applied the long lever of guilt to prise apart his armour of affected indifference. "It's really not acceptable that you haven't fixed it. We are a humanitarian organisation, you know."

"Eh?" Alan struggled to speak. An altercation with Paula was the last thing he needed at this moment.

Paula spoke slowly to suggest he was stupid. "I. Said. The. Hospital. Roof. Is. Leaking. Like a sieve. It's as permeable as a teabag. I suppose it's the only way you know of providing air conditioning and running water for the patients . . . "

Sarcasm was always a red rag for Alan, especially when it came from Paula. His normal reaction would have been a caustic reply. He was about to deliver a snide remark when Lorna appeared, causing him to change tactic, as it seemed inappropriate to swear in front of the prim and proper doctor.

"I'll get MacJosiah to look at it tomorrow." There was no need to hurry; Paula was exaggerating the problem as a means to wield power.

Paula noticed his uncharacteristic backing down from a verbal battle, spurring her to re-attack. "And what about tonight?" she scolded. "It might rain again. I suppose it's all right for you to lie in your nice, warm bed while my obstetrics patients shiver to their death?"

Despite Lorna's presence, incessant criticism triggered Alan's allergy to being nagged. "Aw, give us a break, you ugly, old hag!" He forced himself out of the easy chair and stomped off, leaving behind an equally angry and temporarily speechless Paula. *Stupid, self-righteous aid workers.* He hated the lot of them.

It was raining by the time he reached his room, and he had to concede that Paula was right. Here he was, sheltered from the elements, whilst many hospital patients were getting dripped on. It disturbed him to think that there might be a deep-rooted racism in him, which somehow accepted that the Kugombwalans could take a bit of discomfort because they were poor Africans. He lay down on the mattress and looked around at his spartan room—the rough, wooden bed with its mosquito net, a crude chair, and a simple shelf unit in which he kept his clothes and sports bag with most of his personal effects. Compared to what he had at home, he owned next to nothing here; yet by Kugombwalan standards, he was living in luxury. Unlike the unfortunate souls crammed into Ndombazu's urban slums or crowded displacement camps, he had a room all to himself, with a solid roof and a flat floor, as well as both running water and electricity. Or more precisely, intermittent electricity, since Keith had yet to master the quirks of the generator.

After the long day and the spat with Paula, he fell into a fitful sleep of recurring nightmares, suffused with the image of the rotating eyes of the child wielding a machete. He tried to stir himself awake, but something heavy prevented him by pinning him down. Then, behind the eyes, he saw a face—it was that of Megan, wearing a peaked black witch's hat. She held her crystal in one hand and started to hack at his arm. Thud, thud, thud. The awful sound of stone bashing into bone . . .

Knock, knock, knock.

The sound of hard tapping on his door forced him out of sleep.

"Al, are you okay? It's half-past seven."

He had overslept.

"Thanks, Megan."

"Are you all right? You weren't at breakfast."

"Aye," he lied. He still felt drained from the encounters of the day before.

"Can I come in?"

"Well, I'm not dressed yet—"

"All the better."

That confirmed his fear: Megan fancied him, while he did not fancy her.

Back in Britain, there was a range of strategies that he could use when attraction was not mutual. He could avoid the other person; he could be nasty to repel them; or he could take advantage of the one-sided flirtation, which was what Dave would do. But none of these options was possible for him as Megan was a colleague, with whom he was forced to live and work.

It was different for Dave. Any girl who shacked up with him knew it would be temporary, for he was always bragging about his many female conquests. Megan had been one of them, so he guessed she was now in need of another relationship to compensate for the break-up. Why couldn't she go after Keith and leave him alone? They would make a good match, being both equally irritating.

Megan's crush on him was going to make life even more complicated. It was yet another reason to get out of Kugombwala, together with the deteriorating security situation and the checkpoints. It amazed him that none of the others in the MedRelief team had thrown in the towel. Were they less afraid than he was, or were they all as scared as one another but too proud to be the first to chicken out? Once the first person went, he predicted there would be a race among the others to be the second—a contest he intended to win.

A week later, MedRelief received a letter of invitation from a warlord who controlled a little-visited corner of Kugombwala. Women and children were dying in great numbers, his letter claimed, and the assistance of the international aid community was urgently required. Jules saw an opportunity to establish a new project that might attract donor funding. He decided to take Lorna, Megan, and Alan with him on an "explo mission" to assess whether the situation was as critical as the warlord claimed and to see how feasible it would be to meet the needs.

The trip demanded much preparation. Access had to be negotiated with the rebel groups that controlled the different sections of the road and permits acquired with many impressive-looking stamps to limit confrontations at checkpoints. AfriBat HQ was informed and a route selected where they conducted regular patrols. Two vehicles were to go in convoy, with a couple of expats in each, as a security measure. Supplies and vehicle spares had to be taken in the event of a breakdown. A large medical emergency kit was brought in case the humanitarian needs at the destination required immediate action.

They left at sunrise and drove for four hours along an old highway, away from the coast and up onto the soft, undulating hills of the Kugombwalan plateau. The forested slopes gave way to patches of open farmland interspersed with frequent clumps of tall trees and clusters of villages among rolling downs. It was a bucolic landscape with a fresher and cooler climate than the claustrophobic heat of the coastal plain and the hot concrete jungle of Ndombazu. But the roads on the plateau were atrocious. The vehicles hopped from bump to bump, causing the passengers to be thrown around inside and the radio antenna at the front of each car to wag like a dog's tail.

After passing the first checkpoint into the warlord's zone of control, they felt safer, calmed by the knowledge they were there by invitation. They then cleared another barrier at the entrance to an uninspiring village composed of the usual scruffy mud huts and stray chickens. MacJohn stopped the Land Rover to address a toothless, old woman.

"Auntie, how much further to Gongowa?"

"It can be here," she mumbled.

"But where can be military HQ of Kugombwalan Alliance for Reform and Democracy?"

"At the plantation house."

Following her directions, they passed two further checkpoints before reaching an avenue of ornamental trees that led up to a collection of colonial-era buildings on a low hill. A group of teenagers with wooden rifles were being drilled in the important military manoeuvre of marching in unison. Two soldiers, with real guns, came down to meet the cars.

"Colonel ready," one of them grunted. "You can come. Driver stay."

Four soldiers and two large, tripod-mounted machine guns guarded the dilapidated entrance to the largest building. The soldiers stood to attention and stamped their combat boots as they passed.

Inside, a handsome young man in his late twenties was waiting to meet them. He would have stood out from any crowd in his crisp, Italian suit and shiny new brogues, but here, he contrasted starkly with his rag-tag bodyguard of teenage youths in torn t-shirts and dirty combat gear. His smart, almost effeminate, clothing radiated power, while gold rings and a necklace signalled wealth and influence. Here was a high-flyer ascending the warlord career ladder with ambitions to reach the top, and holding a fighting chance to become president of Kugombwala if he could survive the contest for long enough.

"My dears, welcome to *glamorous* Gongowa," he announced, emphasising the adjective as if the village they had passed through was one of the favourite haunts of the international jet set. "I'm so frightfully delighted that you've come," he continued in the poshest English accent Alan had ever heard. "I'm Colonel MacEdwin Mfaume-Simbwa, but do call me Edwin, as we're friends. I just can't believe that you're all from England. I was at school there, you know, at Igglesham. Which schools did you go to? I might have played yours at rugger."

He had never played against Alan's northern comprehensive, Lorna's all-girls grammar, or Megan's village school, but he did not have the opportunity to discover that, for Jules stepped forwards.

"Are you really an Old Iggleshonian? I was at Peregrine Hall!" He held out his hand. "Julian Sinclair, head of mission for MedRelief and surgeon at Ndombazu General Hospital."

"Ah, so you are the famous doctor." The warlord seized his hand, and they exchanged a firm handshake.

Jules laughed. "Yes, that's me, old chap. Just call me Jules. Which years were you at Igglesham, Edwin?"

"I was at Iggly-Piggly from 1977 until 1985. I even did my A-levels there."

"Then you must know my cousin, Felicity Blassingford?"

"I don't believe it!" the warlord exclaimed. "I courted her in the lower sixth."

"No way! Then you must be Edwig. I've heard so much about you. I had forgotten you were Kugombwalan."

"That's me." He chuckled. "Headwig and Edwig were my nicknames at school because I had a humongous afro hairstyle during my teens. Oh, I'm totally gobsmacked that you've come! How is dear Flick doing?"

"Quite marvellous, thank you. After she came down from Oxford, she joined the FCO."

"The Foreign and Commonwealth Office? I've been talking to them! They are going to support me with weapons. Along with the Americans."

"Do you, by any chance, know Jeremy Turlington-Henry?" Jules steered the conversation away from a controversial topic. "He went to Igglesham. One of my closest chums. We were at prep school together."

"You mean Turtles? Why, he was head prefect of Kipling House when I arrived. And captain of the polo team. A jolly, decent chap. What's he up to now?"

"He's in the City, making a fortune with the Grenfield Smythe Bank. And what about Tim Tarleton-Griffiths? He was in the year below you, I think?"

"Timmy Tee-Gee? Oh, that's absolutely amazing that you also know him. I was at his wedding in Henley last year when he married Porcelana de Montselles. He's now in Angola with Anglo Imperial Petroleum. We've agreed that they will prospect in Kugombwala when the war's over."

"Small world! Porcelana and my sister Tamara hunt together with the Beaulieu hounds. She's now betrothed to Fraser MacDuffy, who you might know . . . "

"But of course, I do . . . "

The game of snob-snap continued, as upper-crust names and cosy nicknames were compared to map out their mutual network of acquaintances and to further cement a fast-growing bond.

A tide of anti-establishment resentment welled up within Alan, as he was reminded of divided Britain and his inferior social background from the slag heaps of the industrial North. No amount of ability could ever project him through the glass ceiling imposed by the country's upper-class elite, yet here was a nasty Kugombwalan warlord boasting his membership of the U.K. establishment through having been to an expensive British boarding school.

Jules and Colonel Mfaume-Simbwa's hobnobbing was interrupted by a teenage soldier, who marched in, saluted, and delivered a message in the local language. The warlord's face hardened, and he barked a series of orders in a Kugombwalan dialect. The soldier gave a short reply, saluted again, and did an about turn on his heels before marching out.

"So, how on earth did you get to be here, Edwin?" Jules attempted to ease the tension.

"Papa was the minister of mining and natural resources in the 1970s. He was a real visionary, you know, and did so much for this ungrateful *turd world* country. He was killed during a military coup while I was at Sandhurst doing my officer training. I then returned to help depose the Soviet-backed regime. After they fled, I continued the fight, this time against the savages who are now trying to get power. I simply can't understand why the U.N. doesn't recognise me as the only real representative of the former government—"

A loud squealing erupted outside, and the warlord rushed over to a window.

"Rosie! Fifi! Stop it!"

Alan joined him to see what was going on. The noise had subsided to a series of low growls, but he could not make out what had made it. Some bushes obscured the view of a small pen; through the gaps, he could make out one or two large, brown animals, about the size of a Great Dane.

"What's that you got there? Dogs?"

"Oh, *please,* they're hyenas." The warlord's tone indicated he considered Alan to be mentally subpar for raising such a stupid question.

"You know he's got a couple of pet hyenas?" Alan turned towards MacJohn as they drove off.

"Ah." The driver grinned. "So that is how he makes magic."

"What do you mean?"

"Those hyenas? They can eat everything. Even bones. It means the colonel does not need to bury the people he executes. I talk to the boys who guard him. They are very scared of him. They think he is a big witch doctor because his victims disappear without a trace."

"How come they don't know about the hyenas?"

"Those animals cannot be from here. They do not live in forest. He bring them from another African country."

"Doesn't seem like a particularly pleasant character," Megan commented from the back of the car.

"Jules seemed to get on with him." Alan made no attempt to hide his contempt for his boss.

"Edwin is clearly someone we can work with," Jules had said, before boasting. *"One of our more dangerous old boys!"*

"It's the bond of the British public school. Gives them a lot in common." Megan paused. "Doesn't say much for elite private education. The colonel has had the best schooling in the world, but look at him now—a bloodthirsty killer surrounded by boy soldiers."

"Why is Jules so keen on MedRelief starting a hospital up here?" Alan forced himself to turn around to face her, even though he was trying to avoid direct eye contact. "Lorna was saying the medical needs are not massive."

"It's about politics. I think the colonel wants a treatment facility for his worphan soldiers, and the U.K. government has an interest to help him to exercise soft power and gain influence in Kugombwala. People say there are minerals up here on the plateau, and many British mining companies would like to get their hands on that wealth."

Alan had to admit Megan was a puzzle—sometimes weird and sometimes wise. But her positive character traits would not sway him to be pleasant to her. Self-interest took priority over kindness to others.

"MacGarry, can you stop for a minute?"

They were in a poor neighbourhood of Ndombazu, where they were disinfecting the wells to prevent an outbreak of cholera. Alan opened the car door and walked over to an old man who always sat on the same street corner, wearing the same shiny, pink blouse.

"Here, this is for you." He handed him one of his sports shirts from home. He didn't need it, as he had been given three t-shirts by MedRelief, and he felt sorry for the old man who had been forced by poverty to wear whatever was available.

"Oh, thank you, thank you, thank you!" The old man shrieked in delight and ran about, holding high his cherished gift that would release him from the shame of cross-dressing.

How amazing! Alan was stunned that a tiny act of charity could have such a positive impact. It then occurred to him it was the first time he had ever acted out of selfless generosity.

He recalled what Dave had said. “In Kugombwala, always expect the unexpected.” That might even apply to him, he acknowledged, discomforted by having lost the certainty of knowing himself.

“Okay, guys, listen up.” Jules opened the weekly MedRelief team meeting. “We’ve got some important security developments. Over to you, Dave.”

“Three cars belonging to the World Food Programme were shot at yesterday on the road to the plateau, and a local driver was killed. Third attack in a week. It’s beginning to look lively up there.” Jules nodded. “That means we are putting the hospital project at Gongowa on hold for the time being, until things improve. Now, the news about AfriBat, Dave.”

“Whisper in the bars is they will stop all patrols out of town from next week.”

“Is that for security reasons, or is it because there is nothing left to loot?” Paula was her usual cynical self.

“I’d say both.” Megan relished the opportunity to show how smart she was. “You don’t see any air conditioners on their lorries any more. Now, they are only bringing low-value fans and fridges.”

“Whatever the reason,” Jules continued, “it means that up-country areas of Kugombwala are deemed unsafe. Our activities will henceforth be limited to running Ndombazu hospital. Anything more, Dave?”

"Yeah. I had a chat with the money-changers in the market this morning. The exchange rate has fallen, which is usually a sign people are getting nervous as they want more foreign currency. There are rumours that one of the rebel groups is employing white mercenaries from South Africa, Serbia, and the Ukraine to train their fighters in more advanced combat techniques. Some say that the mercenaries are taking part in the battles themselves."

"Any confirmation from your AfriBat sources?"

"Not as yet, but I called a mate in Antwerp who works for a military magazine. Apparently, huge quantities of weapons are being airlifted to one of the rebel groups here. They are circumventing the U.N. embargo by being disguised as arms consignments for other countries."

"So, who is supporting them?"

"I've got my theories, but for the moment, let's say it's anybody's guess."

The following week's team meeting brought more bad news when Dave relayed that all frontline AfriBat troops had been pulled back to Ndombazu.

"Just as well we did the same." Jules liked to compliment his own decisions.

"The AfriBat guys I meet in the bars are getting jittery. They're taking a lot of hits at their outposts around the city. Seems like worphans are being infiltrated to attack them and draw their fire—"

"What do you mean by the worphans being infiltrated?" Lorna interrupted.

"They are easy to disguise as ordinary children, which enables them to get close to the AfriBat posts. Just imagine what it is like for the soldiers at the small bases in the bush, unexpectedly being attacked by innocent-looking kids or being ambushed by a hail of bullets that seems to come from the ground."

"Sounds horrible!"

"It gets worse, for when the AfriBat soldiers then get in position to respond to that threat, they are taken out by sniper fire from another direction. Those attacks are well-coordinated, probably the work of white mercenaries. Rumour is that isolated groups of AfriBat soldiers have been annihilated. The remainder are getting spooked, and some believe the rebels are using witchcraft. Their morale is at rock bottom."

"I must say, that is a worrying development." Jules looked serious. "Given the deteriorating security situation, I think it would be wise to temporarily reduce the team. I want to get our complement down to the capacity of a single four-passenger plane in case we have to do a sudden evacuation. So, that means sending some of you to Nairobi."

Alan remembered the house he had visited on the way out. A spell of calm luxury would be most welcome and might also become a stepping stone to going home.

"Which means we need to get you, Keith, out on a flight as soon as possible . . . "

Alan frowned. It was a good thing that Nairobi was a big city. He did not fancy being lumped together with Keith, who would attach his boring self to him like a ball and chain. It would be far more fun to hang around in the Kenyan capital with Dave.

"And then next week, Megan—"

"But I don't want to go, Jules. I'm not scared of staying here."

"And, Paula, once you've had time to hand over to Lorna . . . "

"Great to feel wanted." Paula showed no emotion.

"Look, ladies." Jules made no effort to hide his annoyance. "This isn't about what you want or being wanted. It's about maintaining flexibility in a fast-moving situation. You'll be back once things stabilise. Anyway, let me continue. I need you to stay, Dave . . . "

"Sure."

" . . . and Al to manage the finances . . . "

Alan cursed his key role in MedRelief. It anulled any excuse to leave, unless he was replaced or evacuated.

"Lorna and I will run the hospital in the meantime. I'm confident that AfriBat will reverse their losses once they get their act together or get extra support from the Americans. We can rely on Uncle Sam to keep us safe."

Zeeeezt, zeeeezt, zeeeezt. The printer was spewing out incoming text from the radiotelex system with a coded message from the Nairobi office about flights and money. Alan rushed down to the vehicle inspection pit.

"Keith, you've got a seat on a plane leaving at 13:30."

"Right, let me finish this little job with the clutch."

"No, Keith. You need to be at the airport in an hour; otherwise, you'll be bumped off. That means fifteen minutes to pack."

Alan fumed over the endless time-consuming urgencies that ate up his days, as he hurried back to his office to close the interim accounts and create a cash request to go with the outgoing mail pouch. It meant he only had a moment to pen a quick note to his parents before Keith left and no time to write a longer letter to Mandy. He hated himself for always doing things at the last minute and resolved to write to her before Megan and Paula's upcoming departure. He'd been thinking about her lately, spurred by the growing ache of absence.

Later that day, he picked up a blank airmail envelope obtained from Lorna and penned his home address onto it. The Nairobi office would add a stamp—hopefully one depicting exotic African wildlife—and post it. He imagined Mandy receiving it, her manicured fingers examining the beautiful maize-coloured paper banded by alternate red and blue lozenges around the rim. She would like it, for it oozed the romance of correspondence from faraway lands of the kind that is lovingly preserved for posterity. Therefore, this letter had better be good and say more than the brief postcards he had sent until then. He wanted her to cherish it as a symbol of his affection.

Dear Mandy,

I hope you are well, and thanks for your cards. I'm okay but in an awkward situation, which is why I'm not back yet. MedRelief can't find anyone to replace me because it's quite dangerous now in Kugombwala, as some nasty rebel groups have surrounded Ndombazu and are attacking the city. Our mechanic was evacuated to Nairobi this morning, and the nurses are leaving with this letter. That means it's just me and Dave, plus the two doctors who are left. I offered to go, but they can't run the hospital without me, so I've got to stay here for a bit longer.

He crossed out the words that might be misconstrued as cowardice—"I offered to go." An alternative explanation was needed.

Trembling from the trepidation of venturing into new emotional territory, he continued.

> *I really want to be back with you, love, but I hope you will understand why I'm stuck here. I'm truly sorry, and I'll do what I can to leave as quickly as possible.*

He then added some stories about the worphans and the kids in the feeding centre to thrill her with doses of horror and pathos. After he had finished, he wrote out the whole letter again, so that there were no mistakes or corrections.

Alan smiled as he folded the finalised sheet and slid it into the envelope. He couldn't wait to find out how she reacted, but his hopes were tempered by the realisation it would take at least three weeks for her to receive the letter and for her response to reach him. A lot could happen in that time.

Contrary to Jules's expectations, the security situation in Kugombwala continued to deteriorate. Within days of Keith's departure, it was deemed too dangerous to venture further than the centre of the city without a military escort, even during daytime. Dave learned that the rebels had penetrated the suburbs by infiltrating their well-disguised infant army. Unable to distinguish between civilian and combatant children, the AfriBat forces suffered ever-heavier losses, and their soldiers became visibly more nervous. Fortified checkpoints were set up at all the major intersections in

Ndombazu, while unsubstantiated rumours reached the MedRelief team that some AfriBat soldiers were shooting street kids in the poorer areas of the city.

A week later, AfriBat withdrew from the international airport, forcing the U.N. to suspend their daily aid flights to Kugombwala. Alan frowned as he stared at the unsent envelope still on his desk. Not only would Mandy not get this letter, but she also would receive no news from him of any kind. How would she cope with the worry and uncertainty? Would she be angry? Or would she be anxious?

The loss of the airport was also a blow to Ndombazu's citizens, for it cut a major lifeline to the outside world and raised serious doubts about whether the AfriBat troops could hold the city. Now, only one supply route remained open to them—the sea.

Alan found himself spending ever more time on the terrace, staring out over the ocean like a prisoner looking through the bars of his cell window. The crashing waves mesmerised him with their lullaby of escape, enabling him to briefly forget his predicament with the notion that Britain, safety, and freedom lay across that water and that no rebels obstructed the route in between.

Ndombazu was awash with conflicting rumours. Some spoke of the imminent arrival of massive AfriBat reinforcements to retake the airport. Others predicted the complete withdrawal of the entire peacekeeping force that had been sent by Organisation of African Unity, which would leave Ndombazu utterly abandoned by the international community. Everyone had a different opinion about the situation.

"I'm going to the AfriBat HQ to arrange a meeting with the commanding officer. We need to find out what's going on," Jules told Alan and Dave. "Can you two go to the port to see what's happening there?"

The one-kilometre journey to the harbour meant presenting permits at three successive checkpoints to proceed further. Thousands of Kugombwalans must have circumvented this formality, for they were everywhere, clogging the only access road while dodging AfriBat soldiers, who battled the unarmed civilians with their rifle butts to maintain law and order. They passed a group of soldiers beating a young man. Two of the soldiers looked up as the MedRelief Land Rover passed but soon got back to kicking and pummelling their victim. International witnesses to human rights abuses were of no concern to them.

Further on, they skirted a dirty beach, where small, traditional boats had been dragged up beyond the high-water mark. The crowd who had reached this far along the harbour peninsula were concentrated around these craft.

"Fishing port," MacJohn informed them.

"Let's stop here for a minute." Dave had already opened the passenger door. "I want to see what they are selling." Leaving the Land Rover, he was soon in his element, mingling and joking with the local people—the big man who honoured them by entering their world.

Alan was drawn to an array of bright, multi-coloured tropical fish laid out for sale in the sun. Nearby, a fisherman was chopping a dead shark into hunks of meat that he threw onto the dirty beach sand. Beside him lay a slimy octopus and a sea turtle helpless on its back. It was still alive, flapping its flippers in desperation.

The fisherman, whose gold earrings and bushy beard gave him the appearance of a pirate, walked over to the turtle. With hefty blows, he punched his machete through the weak spot in the centre of the turtle's defensive chest armour, causing it to spasm in dying agony.

At the Land Rover, Dave whistled for his attention. "Time to move on, Al!"

"Just as I expected," Dave said once Alan was back in the vehicle. "The crowd is not only here to buy fish. Some are negotiating with the boat captains to sail them out of Ndombazu."

"Where to?"

"The neighbouring countries."

"Very dangerous!" MacJohn said. "The journey can take three to five days, and there are many storms now. Wind and waves too big for small boats. Not normal to sail so far at this time of year."

"Looks like the skippers can't resist the prices being offered to them," Dave continued. "People were offering them wads of cash to outbid their rival refugees."

"It can be expensive," MacJohn agreed. "Because some captains drown on the way. With everyone else on their boat—"

"Shows how desperate those people are to flee Ndombazu," Dave concluded.

They must know something we don't, Alan thought.

"The crowd's thinning," Dave remarked as they continued through the port system towards the container terminal. The Kugombwalans who had reached this far into the harbour complex were carrying luxury goods, such as televisions and refrigerators.

"Looks like these guys want to stay cool on their travels," Alan joked, as they passed a young man with two air conditioners balanced on his head.

MacJohn corrected him. "They can bring looted goods for AfriBat to buy, for sending to their own country by ship. Soon, there will be nothing left in Kugombwala to steal. Maybe then, we will have peace."

A little further on, they came to the stolen goods market, where AfriBat soldiers were bartering down the prices of the items on offer. Beyond, a fence cordoned off the customs-bonded area of the port, followed at a distance by a double-height row of containers, strategically placed to shield the view of the cargo ships that were moored on the other side.

"That's where we want to get to." Dave nodded towards the funnels of two ships, visible above the barrier. "But it won't be easy. I don't see any Kugombwalans between here and the container wall, so it seems that only AfriBat soldiers are allowed in there. We're going to need some friends to let us in. MacJohn"—he turned to the driver—"take us over to the gate."

They drove along the fence until they reached the fortified entrance, where four AfriBat soldiers lounged behind a barbican of fresh sandbags. A fifth soldier was taking his duty more seriously, machine gun at the ready. Behind them, a parked battle tank pointed its barrel at all who dared enter.

"We need a story," Dave said as the Land Rover pulled up at the official parking place. "Stay here, MacJohn, while you come with me, Al. We'll say that we've come to meet a boat that has been sent for us. Let's call it the *Cuba Spirit* because this is a rum story. When they say it hasn't come, we'll try to get in on the pretext of needing information about when it is due."

"Very good!" MacJohn laughed in delight at the attempt to trick AfriBat. Dave was popular with MedRelief's local staff, both male and female, though for different reasons.

They walked over to the gun emplacement and its complement of five curious guards.

"Hey, guys," Dave addressed them. "Who's in charge here?"

"That is me." One of the soldiers stepped forwards. His uniform bore the triple stripes of a sergeant.

"Okay, Boss Man, my name is Dave. I work for MedRelief, and we are running the hospital for the people of Ndombazu. I've come to meet my boat, which is bringing important medicines for the children in this town. Can you find out if a ship called the *Cuba Spirit* has arrived?"

"I am sorry, Doctor," the sergeant answered, holding the common belief in Kugombwala that all foreign aid workers were medics. "Our ships are the only ones here."

Dave deliberately pulled out his packet of cigarettes, took one for himself, and then offered the others to five eager hands. The bonding was beginning. "Are you sure it is not one of those behind there?" He pointed to the funnels of the vessels looming above the container wall. "It should have arrived last night."

"No, those are AfriBat ships."

Dave blew out a puff of smoke. "That makes me very worried. Our ship was meant to arrive yesterday, but we lost contact with her two days ago. I need to find out if anyone knows where it is or when it was last seen. Without the medicine that it is bringing"—he looked into each of the soldiers' eyes—"many children are going to die."

"Let me ask the harbour office if it has come." The sergeant pulled out a walkie-talkie and spoke to it in his own language, then translated the reply. "They say your ship is not here."

"Oh, no, that is a very serious problem." Dave applied the necessary mix of emotion and agitation to make his plea sound realistic without being too pushy. "Can you ask if they know where it is?"

The sergeant spoke again to the walkie-talkie and relayed the response. "I am sorry; they know nothing."

Dave repeated his demand slowly to massage his message into the soldier. "This means we are facing a humanitarian disaster. I have a hundred sick children in the hospital who will be dead in a week if they don't get medicine. So, I must know what has happened to my ship. Your harbour office does not know anything. But the captains or crew of the big boats in the port might have some information. Maybe they have seen my ship? Can I go and talk to them?"

"I am sorry, Doctor. Only AfriBat soldiers are allowed on those ships. I have orders not to let civilians come near them."

"Then let me go and talk to your commander at the harbour office to ask for his permission to speak to the captains and crew. We can go in my vehicle, and you can send one of your soldiers to accompany us. Please help us. We are facing an emergency."

The emotional pressure was beginning to work because the sergeant now looked worried. He clearly didn't know what to do. "Okay." He buckled under Dave's persistence. "Let us go."

Dave beckoned to MacJohn to bring the Land Rover. Together with the soldier, they drove through the gate to the inner harbour area, bypassing the battle tank on the way in. They continued to a gap in the wall of containers and then went through, where Dave's subterfuge was rewarded by the sight of a line of tanks and heavy field guns in the process of being loaded onto a ship. Nearby, rows of looted four-wheel drive vehicles also awaited embarkation.

The conclusion was clear: AfriBat forces were not receiving reinforcements to retake the airport. Instead, they were pulling out of Kugombwala, after having stripped Ndombazu of everything worth removing.

"Al, do you mind waiting outside while I talk to the commander?" Dave gave him a wink as he entered the harbour master's office. Alan understood the message: watch what is going on at the boats.

He gazed at the field guns being winched up into the hold of a ship. The action reminded him of a nursery rhyme, which he adapted in his mind:

Five little guns

Parked along the shore,

A crane took one away,

And then there were four.

Four little guns

On the harbour quay,

A crane took one away,

And then there were three.

Three little guns

Lined up in a queue . . .

Like in the verse, the sight of the departing guns, one by one, pointed to an inevitable outcome:

One little gun

Standing in the sun,

A crane took it away,

And then there were none.

The activity unfolding before him would continue until there were no Afribat soldiers left in Ndombazu to protect him and the others from the advance of the rebels.

The fall of the city was now a mere matter of time.

The slow drive back from the harbour contrasted Dave's chatter with MacJohn and Alan's silence. Watching the withdrawal of the heavy guns had removed all hope that Ndombazu would somehow avoid a rebel invasion. With that loss of hope went the last of his optimism, replaced by a deep melancholy, which even Dave's bonhomie could not dispel.

They returned the way they had come, dropping off the soldier at the tank-guarded gate before proceeding through the crowd of hawkers. The access road into the port had become even busier, and they were forced to drive at a crawl. They passed three soldiers hassling a street urchin, accusing him of being a rebel. The child, who would have been no more than twelve years old, argued back vociferously, delivering a determined defence like a high-court barrister, punctuated by minor breakdowns to relieve himself of a few tears.

It is amazing how quickly children grow up when placed under stress, Alan noted while slouched in his seat, like he did back at home on the sofa when watching television, only here it was he who was in a box, looking out. Emotional numbness had set in, and he found himself a passive spectator, without any wish to intervene—partly due to fatigue but also because he sympathised with the soldiers, for he was aware the rebels had recruited numerous worphans who had killed many of their comrades. Even if the child were a mere street kid rather than a juvenile combatant, it did him no harm to learn a bit of respect for adults. Besides, the AfriBat troops were armed and would not appreciate the intervention of a foreign do-gooder.

Having finished his defence, the child was pushed out of the circle of soldiers in which he had formed the centre of attention. Then, one of them gave him a few more shoves to move him on. The youngster took the hint, half-running, half-skipping towards freedom. He had probably been in many similar situations—run-ins with the police, in which verbal abuse and a few slaps were the usual order of the day. Alan's attention wandered as he remembered his own childhood experiences of getting caught by the cops in the disused factories that littered his hometown.

I was once like that lad, he mused.

CLACK!

The crack of a rifle shot shocked Alan out of his reminiscence, while the crowd fell silent. The soldier who had pushed the boy had lowered his upheld rifle and taken a pot shot at the child, who had been in the middle of a small jump when the bullet had gone through him. The effect was instantaneous. His body dropped out of the air, collapsing into a lifeless heap on the ground. A split second earlier, he had been skipping with youthful vitality; but in that instant, he had become an inert corpse, hitting the dirt hard, like a sack of falling cement.

Seeing that it was only a street kid being killed, the crowd returned to their business of shouting at each other. But Alan was left speechless by the image of the child murdered in mid-air, now etched into his memory. Although he had seen plenty of people getting shot in films, he recognised that the screen was unable to relay the harshness of reality. No matter how good the actors and stunt performers were, they could not simulate the suddenness with which a living being becomes lifeless in death. Like a pricked balloon that in a moment is transformed into a rag of rubber, so, too, was that once-active human straightaway reduced to dead flesh and bones.

And yet a punctured balloon was the same as an inflated one, except the air had been let out. Was life as ephemeral as the air in a balloon? The corpse of that boy matched its living echo, consisting of the same grouping of the same cells and yet so different. Diverging by a factor called life, which in spite of its all-importance was still not understood by scientists.

Life. For the last twenty-eight years, Alan had taken his existence for granted. But that had changed. Life was precious, he realised. And now he was determined to keep hold of it, to protect it, at whatever cost—which meant getting out of Ndombazu as fast as he could.

CHAPTER 5

"Al, I want you in my office in five minutes."

Alan turned to see Jules standing behind him. He got up from where he had been inspecting the hospital gate, which was being strengthened to withstand being rammed by a heavy truck. MacKevin, the foreman, and his construction crew were hard at work, applying further fortifications and reinforcements to the compound in anticipation of the rebel attack—extra sandbags stacked on the terrace and in front of windows, additional layers of steel welded onto the gates, and masking tape applied to window glass.

"Aye, I'll be there."

"Good. Don't be late." Jules was unsmiling.

Alan watched his boss march off. He loathed Jules' stern management style. It exacerbated the stress of being snared in the tightening noose of a city under siege, from which there seemed little hope of escape. The strain of their situation was showing on all members of the team: Jules had become more authoritarian, Paula pricklier, Lorna more distant, and Megan extra irritating. Dave followed the trend in his own way—by appearing calmer than ever. Did he relish the imminent prospect of an invasion, or was it bluster?

Alan finished his discussion with MacKevin on how to brace the gate and then walked over to the MedRelief base. He could sense disaster looming. What a fool he'd been to come to Ndombazu. He needed to find someone to blame for his current predicament, but his efforts were always in vain, for the conclusion was ever the same. It was his decision and, therefore, his fault. All thanks to being bored and wanting to impress his mates. He now realised what a pointless thing heroism was, luring people into difficult situations that were to their detriment.

He found Jules at his desk, talking to someone on the satellite phone. Dave lounged in an easy chair, smoking a cigarette.

"Close the door behind you, Al." Jules covered the mouthpiece of the satphone, before continuing his conversation. "As I was saying, we are hemmed in by at least three rebel groups that have already reached the outskirts of the city. AfriBat are struggling to hold them off while they prepare to abandon Ndombazu. It is going to be a big mess when they leave because the different factions will fight each other to get overall control."

"Total anarchy, for sure," Dave muttered to Alan with a grin. "We're going to see an amazing firework show!"

Jules ignored them while listening to the person on the phone, so Alan focussed his attention on the background noise. The usual clatter of gunfire was supplemented by the distant crash of mortars—ominous booms that portended the bombardment that would soon reach the city centre. How he envied Keith, who had been sent out before the airport had fallen into rebel hands.

"There are only ten U.N. staff left here," Jules told the person on the telephone. "They are trying to get out by negotiating with one of the rebel groups for a safe passage through the frontline."

"That'll be expensive," Dave murmured. "But peanuts for the U.N. monkeys with their limitless pot of money."

"No, staying is not an option," Jules continued his conversation. "Chas and Kahiga have been unable to get guarantees for our security from the foreign representatives of two of the rebel groups, and they failed to make contact with another. Without an assurance that we won't be harmed, we risk being wounded in the fighting; we will likely be taken hostage; and Lorna, Paula, and Megan are sure to be raped."

"Hey, Al, how about being worth a hundred thousand dollars?" Dave joked, but Alan did not answer. His heart was hammering from imagining what would happen once AfriBat left Ndombazu. Jules had voiced what they all feared—that there would be no mercy from the approaching rebels.

"Word is that the Americans won't get involved," Jules spoke again. "There aren't any here, as they closed their embassy when the war started. Anyway, let me call you back, as I've got Dave and Al with me in the office for a meeting."

He put down the receiver. "Okay, chaps, as you know, the situation here is serious. Very serious. The rebels are closing in, and we need to get out before they arrive."

At last, the decision Alan had desired for many months. He could now leave Kugombwala without shame and without letting the team down.

"We have little time and even less options," Jules added. "That was Gordon on the satphone. He can't do anything for us. He's tried his U.K. government contacts, but the Foreign Office aren't going anywhere near this hole." He paused to allow his words to sink in. "Gordon has authorised us to use all the means at our disposal to evacuate. But we have to act fast. The rebel fighters could reach this part of town any day, and I don't want to be around when they do. Rumour has it at least one group don't like whiteys—"

There was a knock on the door, which opened to reveal the young house assistant, MacZak, bearing a thermos and cups on a tray.

"Tea, Boss Man."

He barged in before making a clumsy attempt to place the tray on Jules's desk while studying what was on there. He then dribbled tea into the cups, using the time to make frequent glances around, clearly gaining intelligence about what was in the room.

"That's all right; we can do that ourselves," Dave growled. "Now get out. And close the door," he barked after MacZak had deliberately left it open. "The walls don't need ears here with the local crew spying on us."

"Exactly." Jules swiped a fly from his teacup. "We've got to be careful how we handle this. Because if the national staff realise we are leaving, they could panic and do something stupid. Some of them have this crazy idea that nothing is going to happen to them as long as we are around—"

"They're right," Dave interrupted, "because we'll be gone before that something does happen to them."

"Well, let's make sure of that," Jules continued. "Now, in order for this to succeed, we need to keep our plans within the expat team. I'll have a quiet word with the others tonight. But don't tell anyone else what we are up to, not even the drivers."

"When you said the local staff might panic, what do you think they might do?" Alan asked.

"They could take us hostage. As soon as they hear that we plan to go, they will demand severance pay and maybe a couple of months' advance salary, which is understandable, as they will need all the dollars they can get to survive the next few weeks. But we don't have enough money here for that—they think we hold a lot more cash than we do. They will, therefore, be angry with us for leaving without giving them what they think is rightfully theirs. That might unleash some harboured grudges against us. I don't, for a moment, think they all love us, and it will be made worse if they see us as symbols of the West abandoning their country during its hour of need."

"So, we need to give the local crew the impression that we intend to stay," Dave said. "Secretly pack our bags but leave a jumble of non-essential items around our rooms so it doesn't look like that we can go at a moment's notice."

"Exactly, Dave. Everyone should be ready to leave by tonight."

"We also need codewords, which we can communicate over the walkie-talkies to inform each other what to do if things get serious, so that everyone in the team can react quickly before the national staff know what is happening."

Jules nodded. "Good thinking."

"Thanks. What thoughts have you had for our exit?"

"We need to get on one of the AfriBat container ships that are being piled high with guns and looted goods."

Dave swore. "It will be no luxury cruise. There'll be hundreds of soldiers on board with few facilities. We might have to sleep outside on the crowded quarterdeck of a rusty, old hulk for up to a week, where we will be exposed to the sun, as well as rain and storms. We'll have to take enough food, water, and sunscreen to cover that time, plus tarpaulins and bog roll. And it will be a security nightmare if the boat is piled high with desperate Kugombwalan refugees. We'll all have to carry machetes—and be prepared to use them."

"We don't have any other choice, at least as far as I can see."

"What about a chopper? There's space in the middle of our compound for one to land."

"I looked into that when I last went to Nairobi. It would cost a fortune, which we don't have; and besides, their range is too low to get here and back without refuelling on the way."

"How about a seaplane?"

"Very few of them in Africa. If we were in the States or Canada, there'd be hundreds to choose from. But there aren't any on this coast. I've already checked."

"Okay, let's go back to the ship option. How much money have we got?"

"Almost thirteen thousand dollars," Alan chipped in. "The closure of the airport blocked the usual consignment of cash that comes at the start of the month, so we don't even have enough to pay all the staff their wages in three weeks' time."

"Well, we had better get out before payday then," Jules said. "There's six of us, which makes a bit more than two thousand dollars each. We'll need to keep a wad of cash for contingency bribes during the journey, plus paying our way out of whichever port we end up in. Two thousand dollars per person won't go far."

"We could trade the Land Rovers for places on the AfriBat boat," Dave suggested. "Our vehicles are going to be stolen, anyway, by the first rebel group to reach the hospital, so why not make use of them ourselves?"

"Good idea, but we won't hand them over to AfriBat until we are all on board. We can also take our walkie-talkies. Sell them on the way, or use them to bribe our way past obstacles. Go down to the port and see what can be done, you two," Jules ordered.

"Right-o, Boss." Dave sprang out of the couch with enthusiasm. "Let's go, Al."

"Harbour's busy today," Dave remarked, as the vehicle nosed through the crowd crammed around the entrance to the port.

"Dave!" A hand reached out to touch his arm resting on the sill of the open window.

"Hey, MacLisa, how are you doing?"

"Small, small." This was a standard Kugombwalan reply, meaning, "Sort of okay, but things could be better."

"What are you doing here?"

She lowered her eyes. "I can be with the lieutenant. That man make me his wife. He take me to his country." She pointed with her chin towards one of the AfriBat ships.

It was the same story with three other girls Dave knew. The lovers of the AfriBat soldiers were promised places on the container vessels that had become the last hope of escape from a city about to go under.

"Talk about rats leaving a sinking ship." Dave laughed after they had parted from the crowd. "There won't be a prostitute left in Ndombazu once those boats go. Definitely time for us to get out, Al."

Dave's regular visits to the AfriBat HQ ensured the soldiers let them through without question. That made it easy to speak to the officer in charge of loading the ships. Negotiations opened with the gift of a bottle of whisky; within a few minutes, they struck a deal. The officer would receive two Land Rovers in exchange for two cabins and a passage out.

"We are leaving soon," he told them. "It can be tomorrow, or it can be the next day. Or the day after. Maybe even next week. Please come every day to check. Then I can tell you when you must bring all your people. And the cars," he added with a wide grin.

It seemed sensible to wait until the day of departure, given the mayhem in the port, which was not a safe place to hang around. People and activity were everywhere, from the loading of looted goods onto the container ships to the frantic scramble of refugees trying to get places on overcrowded fishing canoes.

"I wouldn't fancy my luck in one of those," Dave echoed Alan's thoughts. "Stuck for days with no space to move and so overloaded they could easily capsize. It might be safer to stay in the city."

"Shows how frightened they are." Alan sympathised with the dilemma of choosing between shrapnel wounds or shark bites. He felt intensely grateful for the places they had negotiated on the AfriBat ship.

"Hey, Al, check this out." Dave whistled as they drove past the fishing port. "Isn't that a whitey coming in on that canoe?"

Alan looked over to where he was pointing. Sure enough, there was a lone European in the prow of a motorised dugout, which had just arrived to load up with refugees fleeing the besieged city. He sat imperious in splendid isolation as the boat's only passenger, conjuring an archaic image of the colonial past. The man wore a white Panama hat over long, curly, blond locks; his khaki waistcoat loaded with pockets indicated he was a journalist.

"Crazy fool." Dave laughed. "Coming in when everybody else is trying to get out. Let's go and meet him."

They went down to the dirty beach and waited for the man to force his way through the crowd that was fighting to get the few places on the fishing boat. He emerged from the mayhem clutching a briefcase plus carry bag and raised his hat once he caught sight of them.

"Ah, Dr. Livingstone, I presume. Good of you to be here to meet me. My name is Stanley Bradshaw of the BBC." He cited a well-rehearsed line. "What a marvellous mess this place is in! Looks like I got here just in time for the fun." He smiled as he surveyed the chaos around him. "We're in for a terrific party, don't you think?"

He was in his mid-fifties, with a lined and reddened face that had seen plenty of action, yet still radiated joviality and humour. After doing introductions, Dave invited him to come by the MedRelief base to see if Jules would allow him to stay.

"But bear in mind," Dave warned, "we're trying to get out of here ourselves, so we'll leave you the keys when we go."

"That's quite all right. You can rely on me to feed the pets and water the plants."

Alan frowned. A wacko with a big ego, who thought he was funny. An additional burden they did not need.

"Dave, are you sure we'll get on that AfriBat boat?" he asked quietly on the drive back to the base. It had been too easy. Something was bound to go wrong. The local staff might prevent them from leaving. The route to the harbour might be blocked. AfriBat could refuse to take them after all.

"Yeah, no problem. The AfriBat colonel is a good mate."

For the first time, Dave's eternal optimism was a cause for concern. Over-confidence could create a false sense of security. But Alan was aware they didn't have other options. Dave was right to be positive. Worrying would not help anyone.

Not until he was on board that ship and watching it glide into a safe harbour would he relinquish the deep disquiet that gripped him.

"Anyone know where Dave is?" Paula asked at supper that night.

"Out chasing a bit of skirt, I expect." Jules looked exhausted, worn down by overwork and the worries of responsibility.

"Well, some of that skirt was in our bathroom this morning. I'm not in favour of strangers using our sanitary facilities as if it was a public convenience. I find it rather dirty."

"You mean, you don't want Kugombwalan women using our bathroom." Jules sighed. The last thing he needed was a Paula conflict.

"Now, don't you try that one on me." Paula raised her voice to stamp out the suggestion that she might be racist. "What I am saying is I don't like sharing my home, and especially my bathroom, with prostitutes. And I think you, as the boss, should be setting a much firmer line on Dave bringing back the trophies from his hunting expeditions."

"Calm down, Paula. You can't assume that they're prostitutes just because they're Kugombwalans. Can you prove he is paying them?"

"Doesn't matter whether he is paying them or not. A prostitute is a prostitute."

"Oh, come, come," Bradshaw chipped in. "I've enjoyed the intimate company of many an African lady during my thirty years on this continent. Mutual passion was the sole currency of our exchanges."

"So, it was always true love between you?" Paula's voice became shrill. "Get real, Mr. Casanova; I can guarantee they weren't attracted to your pale, overweight body or your wrinkled face. The only things they would fancy about you are your wallet and your passport."

"So, what if they are opportunists? You can't blame them, given that they're poor. But that doesn't mean that every girl who gets together with a man without physically fancying him is a prostitute. By your way of thinking, every secretary bedded by her boss back in Britain could be considered a whore . . . "

Alan pushed back his chair. He felt uncomfortable about the topic, as he suspected some of the others did. He was not alone in holding a deep loyalty towards Dave—with the imminent threat of an invasion they all realised that their lives depended on his resourcefulness, contacts, and cool head. It felt unreasonable to be gossiping about his sexual habits when he was working hard for their safety and well-being.

The AfriBat soldier waved the MedRelief truck through the crowded checkpoint near the main market in Ndombazu, where Alan and MacJohn had bought materials to build staff shelters in the hospital compound.

"AfriBat can be leaving soon," MacJohn said. "Maybe tonight."

"You think so? Where did you hear that?" Alan was taken aback. He had been to the harbour that morning with Dave, but the embarkation officer had told them to check again the following day.

"It is what the people can be saying," MacJohn replied. "Are you going on their ship?"

"I'm not allowed to comment." Alan could not suppress a slight grin; it was impossible to keep secrets from the national staff, whose eyes and ears were everywhere.

MacJohn giggled, having acquired his desired answer, but then became serious. "Alan, I can think you are right to go. Ndombazu will soon be too dangerous. You chose to come to my country to help us, so you can be free to leave. But it will difficult for us who stay."

"Why don't you flee? Get out before it is too late?"

"The children can be small, and my mother and father are old. Too weak for travelling."

"So, what will you do?" Alan felt for MacJohn; it was hard enough trying to survive a warzone as a single person, without having the added burden of dependents. It made him realise how selfish he was, only thinking about his own survival and escape.

"It can depend on the fighting. Maybe I take my family to the hospital compound. I think it will be one of the safest places in the city."

Dave had said the same, Alan recalled. It was his idea to build shelters for the local staff and their families, who were forced to flee their homes on the outskirts of the city. More and more were setting up camp in the hospital compound.

"Why don't you move in now, before the place fills up?"

"My house can be emptied if my family go too soon. This city has too many thieves."

"Looters!"

MacNed pointed to a gang of youths sauntering down the street with huge bundles of goods balanced on their heads. The imminent fall of Ndombazu was fuelling a crime explosion among its citizens, as AfriBat no longer maintained law and order. Signs of wanton plundering were becoming ever more widespread, from broken windows to damaged articles spewing out of gaping storefronts. An epidemic of anarchy had infected the people in their desperate need to obtain, stockpile, and consume before the invasion that would lead to the almost inevitable loss of what little they had, which might include their lives.

The pillaging would start with a gang of youths casting the first stone or prising shutters apart. This attracted nearby bystanders, who then descended in swarms onto the hapless shop, like wasps into an open pot of jam.

After passing one group emptying the contents of a store, Alan and MacNed caught up with another mob massed in the middle of the street. The rabble ran down the road, continuously augmented by new members who sprinted over to join it. They all shouted a single word in the local language, which Alan did not understand. Then the crowd stopped moving and became wild with hysteria.

"What's going on?" Alan asked the driver. He sensed that something nasty was about to happen.

"Thieves." MacNed's face lit up. "They have caught one, and now they kill him." After a pause, he gleefully added, "Jungle justice!"

The crowd tightened as people fought to get into the middle, whooping with excitement. Alan was paralysed by the mounting horror, his mind absent of any pre-prepared strategy to respond to such a situation, except to wind up the window in an attempt to cocoon himself from what was going on outside. But the glass could not shut out the view of the frenzy, and he felt compelled to watch, partly out of macabre curiosity but also out of self-protection to monitor possible threats to his life.

The glass also failed to silence the shrieks of at least one individual that he knew did not originate from pleasure. For after those agonised howls had stopped came a comparative silence. The crowd dispersed soon afterwards, slinking away to disassociate themselves from their own guilt. And as they separated, they left behind a small group of children, scarcely older than toddlers, dancing over a pile of something that he preferred not to look at. But he had no choice, for a little girl in a dirty, pink dress came running towards the Land Rover where he sat, carrying a hacked-off hand. She was giggling as she tried to escape three other squabbling children who ran after her, jealous of her trophy. Alan gasped. Even the smallest children here had human blood on their hands.

That observation triggered a memory, long suppressed, of when he and Bobsy had shot a cat with an airgun and then stamped on its head as it lay dying. Then a morning when he and another friend had pulled the legs off garden insects and left them to expire in a bucket, writhing in agony. Alan wiped his face, struggling between remorse and his wish to avoid becoming engulfed by the horror of his own self. For he recognised that if he had been a child in Kugombwala, he might have been there, defiling that corpse. He was no better or worse than that kid; he was just fortunate not to have been brought up in an environment where he could have acquired human blood on his hands.

What a horrible place this was, and it was only going to get worse. What more would it do to those who stayed?

"Are you okay, Lorna?" Jules asked.

She had arrived halfway through lunch and looked harassed. "It's been a hard morning—chaos at the gynaecological ward. We are now receiving many women with medical complications from sexual violence. It's all rather overwhelming."

"Men are scum." Paula injected potential bait for a vicious gender-polarising debate. "They should all be castrated."

Ignoring her, Jules turned towards Lorna. "Are these women coming from thc frontline?"

"Yes, most are from the outskirts where the fighting is taking place. But there are also many from downtown and at much higher levels than we used to receive before. It is now really risky for females in this city."

"How peculiar," Bradshaw chipped in. "I had always thought that rape during war was about soldiers conquering the women of their enemies. Why is there so much in areas that are not yet under rebel control?"

Jules answered, "Could be because of gang turf wars. Law and order are breaking down with AfriBat pulling out."

"Yes," Lorna agreed, "but I don't think it's only about domination. Rape is also a nasty way for some men to cope with themselves being victims of violence."

"Compensating pain with pleasure?" Bradshaw queried.

"No, it's more complex than that. I think some have a twisted logic that they can rid themselves of their pent-up feelings of humiliation and hatred by transferring those emotions onto others who are physically weaker than themselves through subjecting them to the same suffering. It makes me, as a woman, worried about walking over to the hospital at night on my own."

Shouting from the street below interrupted their conversation. Megan was first up, hurrying over to the parapet to see what was happening outside the entrance to the compound. Alan joined her.

Below, five women stood in front of the gate, gesticulating and shouting at the guards in a local language. The word "Dave" was repeated often. Moments later, a flustered guard appeared on the terrace.

"Dave, there can be women here to see you—bad women, who say they know you."

"So." Paula smirked as Dave left, the predator scenting potential prey. "I wonder what all this is about." She went over to the edge of the terrace to get a full view of the proceedings. It soon became obvious that some of Dave's former girlfriends had arrived to demand help to escape the country. The connection he thought had been dissolved by subsequent relationships, absence, and time was still present—at least in their minds.

The shouting intensified once Dave arrived, which brought the whole team out to watch the scene below, privileged to have access to the royal box above the stage that was their compound.

"With that many tarts in here, we should open a baker's shop." Jules snorted with laughter, watching the spectacle below.

For a moment, Alan felt inclined to add his own comment to support Jules, in a bid to forge some bond of friendship with his boss. But his loyalty to Dave swayed him to silence. Besides, those women were manipulating the situation to their advantage, coming to squeeze what they could out of Dave before he left.

Megan thought out aloud. "Notice how Dave has no problem leaving his girlfriends behind, while the AfriBat soldiers are willing to take their women with them."

"Don't go thinking those AfriBat guys are saints," Paula said. "They'll probably make those women into their personal sex slaves once they get back home."

They watched while Dave offered money to his ex-girlfriends.

"Typical white male behaviour," Paula spat. "Trying to pay his way out of the problems he creates by bribing his victims to accept his abuse."

The women took the cash but with nothing to lose, pressed for more. The shouting became hysterical.

"And you can go leave my baby hungry . . . "

"Oh, Dave, you can say you want to marry me . . . "

"Where money for me to buy house? You can promise to help me . . . "

Alan smiled. They were good actresses, these Kugombwalan women, even if they were overdoing the melodrama. There were plenty of crocodile tears between the talk.

"Your baby, he can go sick. You kill little baby . . . "

"Oh, Dave, my heart can break now. You say you love me, but you no better than African man . . . "

"I never can leave slum town now; you not help me . . . "

Dave hid his emotions behind his sunglasses. He turned to leave, causing the women's complaints to rise to shouts:

"I no wanted your baby!"

"You can lie to me!"

"You can owe me for all my affection!"

Dave then lost his temper and started shouting back, pushing the Valkyries out through the gate. It was an ugly sight, and Alan felt for those women, subdued by superior male muscle.

Paula interrupted his thoughts. "I don't think it's right that Dave is allowed to exploit those women. You're his boss, Jules, and you're condoning his behaviour by doing nothing to stop it. What would our donors think if they heard on the news that a MedRelief expat had beaten up defenceless African prostitutes while the head of mission looked on? It wouldn't be great for our fundraising, would it?"

Jules looked irritated at being forced into the conflict. "He's hardly beating them up, Paula. Look, one moment you accuse Dave's girlfriends of being prostitutes because they aren't with him out of love; and the next minute, you accuse him of exploiting them. Be consistent!"

"Of course, he's exploiting them, even if they think they are getting something out of him, because there's an uneven balance of power between them. He's abusing their vulnerability—"

"Dave's no better than a rapist," Megan took over, "using economic rather than physical power to get what he wants from those disadvantaged women—"

"Cut it out, ladies." Jules straightened up to emphasise his authority. "I don't want to hear any more from either of you on this subject. We are all under a lot of stress, but we have to hold together to get through this crisis. Our security depends on it. So let this matter rest."

Doooooot . . . doooooot.

What was that noise? Alan had just settled into bed. It sounded like a ship's siren. Intuition told him something was wrong.

Alan threw on some clothes, then rushed upstairs and out onto the terrace. Above him, a full moon lit up a cloudless night. The sea was calm, and a gentle breeze cooled the air. There was surprisingly little background gunfire to disturb the tranquillity.

Doooooot . . . doooooot. Definitely a ship.

His heart beat faster as he imagined what might be happening. What he had most feared.

Out at sea, silhouetted against the bright moonlit night, a container ship was coming into full view after rounding the promontory that hid the harbour. He watched as it was followed by another and then by a third. AfriBat had weighed anchor without them, sailing away with their last hope for evacuation.

Now, they were in deep trouble.

"We need guns."

"What do you mean?" For the first time, Jules's face was fraught with fear and indecision.

"With AfriBat gone, we've lost the last of our protection." Dave was stern. "It's only a matter of time before we get robbed . . . or worse."

"Can't we pay a local gang to guard us?"

"Which gang, Jules? There'll be loads of militia groups fighting over the city, plus the rebels who are already trying to take over from outside. We don't have the money to pay them all off, and even if we did, there'd still be nothing to stop them coming in to loot us."

"But we can't arm ourselves; we are a neutral humanitarian organisation, not an army. What will the media say when they hear?"

Dave ignored the question by asking another. "So, are you going to stand back and watch while the girls get raped in front of your eyes?"

"I can't make that decision." Jules appeared more concerned about the consequences of his choice on his career than about the welfare of the team. "I'll have to ask Gordon."

"Forget him and the London office," Dave snapped. "They'll say no because they are only interested in covering their backs and don't care about what happens to us. Anyway, I'm going to the market now to buy an AK-47 before it's too late—whether you like it or not. Are you coming, Al?"

"Aye." For once, Alan faced an easy choice: Jules or Dave.

"Looks like the ladies have taken over town," Dave muttered from the front passenger seat. "This is going to be interesting."

All eyes focussed on two figures in flowery dresses, who guarded the checkpoint at the end of the street. One of them had long, blonde hair and pale purple lipstick that contrasted with her dark skin. She brandished a crude club studded with nails, whose points poked out in all directions. The other was armed with a machete and a machine gun; she was adorned by a mass of jewellery, while her colleague wore a simple necklace of string with a severed scrotum as a pendant.

"It must be the Girl's Brigade," Bradshaw quipped. "African women empowering themselves against rapists. Great story for the evening news. Could we stop to do an interview?"

"Not girls," MacJohn giggled. "Those ones can be men."

Alan studied the transvestite thugs. This place got weirder by the day. They had ventured out of the MedRelief base into a curiously calm city to find out what was going on in the wake of AfriBat's departure.

"Hey, Doctor," the queen in the blonde wig addressed Dave as the vehicle drew to a halt. "Give us your girl." He pointed his club at Bradshaw in the back seat.

"Sorry, Boss Man," Dave answered. "Goldilocks is a boy."

The man poked his head through the window to get a closer look and then grunted. "Okay, you can go," he said, with a touch of disappointment.

"So, you think I'm ugly, do you?" Bradshaw continued an imaginary conversation with the combatant, after the car had left the checkpoint. "You don't know what you're missing."

"Lucky you didn't shave this morning," Dave retorted. "Otherwise, you would have been in a sticky situation. Grow a beard or get a haircut if you want to stay out of trouble."

"Who were those guys?" Alan asked. "Rebels?"

"No," MacJohn answered. "Rebels not here. Those youths can be from a local gang. They are wearing looted clothes."

Alan then understood their strange logic of dressing up in drag. It was to disguise themselves from their victims while pretending that someone else was perpetrating their crimes.

"Strange how the rebels haven't renewed their attack on Ndombazu now that AfriBat are gone," Dave thought out aloud. "I wonder what's holding them back?"

Alan lifted the satphone receiver and dialled the number. He was unexpectedly nervous, for although he had been sending occasional letters home, he had not spoken to Mandy in many months. Jules had allowed him a two-minute call to compensate for the rupture in postal communication following the rebel capture of the airport. The expat team had to reassure their families they were still alive.

But what to say in such a short time?

Click. The telephone was picked up at her end. "Hello?" she said in her usual chirpy voice.

"Hi, love, it's me."

"Oh, hi, Terry."

Terry? Who was Terry? "It's not Terry. It's Al."

"Al? Oh, Al! Oh, hiya. You sound really distant. Where are you?"

"In Ndombazu."

"Where's that?"

"You know, where I'm working."

"Oh, you mean Africa? I haven't heard from you in ages, Al. Why haven't you written?" She sounded annoyed.

Thanks for your concern, he thought. "The airport's been—"

"Oh, while I remember," she interrupted, "I've got a bone to pick with you, Alan Swales."

"You what?"

"I found one of your statements and saw those new wheels for your car cost a thousand pounds, not the hundred quid you said—"

"Mandy," he started. "I'll explain later, but I've only got two minutes, and you need to know that the airport—"

"Don't try to change the subject, Al. You told me that we couldn't afford a new kitchen, and there you go buying fancy aluminium hubs for more than it would have cost for the appliances. You lied to me!"

Alan realised he had only two options—contrition or counter-attack. "Tell me who Terry is, Mandy."

"No one."

"Then why did you say, 'Hi, Terry' to me when I first called?"

"I thought you said you were Terry."

"No, you didn't." He sensed he had the upper hand. "I said, 'Hi, love, it's me,' and then you answered, 'Hi, Terry.' So, who's Terry? Someone you're seeing?"

"Stop accusing me, Al!" she screamed. "I hate it when you do that."

Clunk.

Deet-deet-deet-deet.

She'd hung up.

Alan swore as he replaced the receiver. They'd blown the only opportunity in months for a decent chat. Something was seriously wrong with their relationship, he realised, for they couldn't even talk for a minute without hurting each another.

He then sighed in despair. Even if he escaped the war here, there would be another conflict waiting for him at home.

A barrage of heavy artillery fire sent everyone running for cover, bombarded by an eardrum-bursting staccato of sound and shockwaves. The street outside the MedRelief base filled with people sprinting away from the direction in which the mortar fire was coming; all running for their lives.

"Oh, what fun," Bradshaw exclaimed, watching the spectacle from the terrace above. "Nothing quite like Africa when it's collapsing. Wonderful people, marvellous spontaneity. I wouldn't want to be anywhere else!"

"It won't be such fun when the guns are turned on us," Dave growled. "That was outgoing fire. The rebels are bound to hit back soon. I'm surprised they haven't done so already."

The following morning, Dave beckoned from the edge of the parapet, where he was smoking a cigarette. "Hey, Al, come and check out these guys."

Alan got up from his breakfast and joined him. A squad of armed combatants clad in military fatigues and red wellington boots was advancing down the street. The group glided forwards in silent formation, moving like a modern mime dance, each member continuously twisting and revolving, so that some of them were always pointing guns or rifle-propelled grenades in every direction.

"Rebels?"

"Yes." Dave lowered his voice as the group moved past the compound gate below them. "Looks like a search-and-destroy squad, sent from one of the groups attacking the city. Probably on their way back from a dawn raid to take out a target. My guess is they've knocked out the heavy guns downtown."

"How come the local militias haven't attacked them?"

"They wouldn't dare. They don't stand a chance against these professionally trained guys. The checkpoint thugs will melt away once this bunch shows up."

"Who do you think is supporting them?"

"Can't say for sure." Dave was cagey again. "There's a lot more going on in this country than we are aware of."

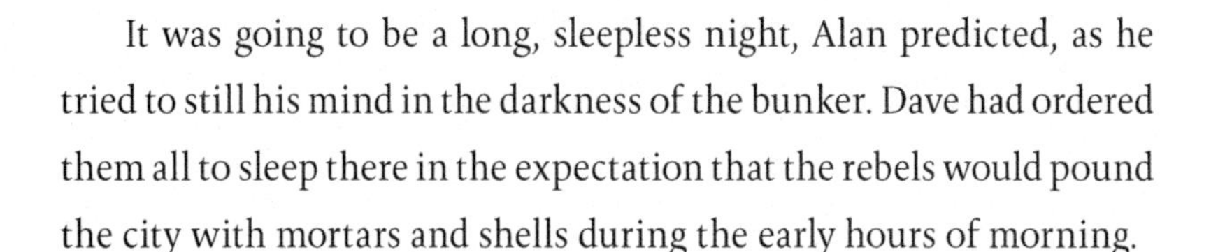

It was going to be a long, sleepless night, Alan predicted, as he tried to still his mind in the darkness of the bunker. Dave had ordered them all to sleep there in the expectation that the rebels would pound the city with mortars and shells during the early hours of morning.

The windowless room was hot and stuffy and smelled of the damp, musty sandbags lining its walls. Megan had huddled down next to Alan, adding her distinctive scent to his suffering. Yet it was not her odour that troubled him but the recognition that he no longer found it unpleasant. He was annoyed that Megan was dictating the terms of their relationship by assailing him with her attention. He could see the success of her strategy of laying siege to his sentiments, knowing that it was only a matter of time before his defences crumbled under the formidable weight of her determination to possess and control him.

He tried to focus his attention on evidence that some of the others might have slipped away into the bliss of sleep and its temporary suspension of their worries. But from all corners of the room, there was only the sound of occasional frustrated twisting and turning.

Crackle-hiss! Crackle-hiss! Burping a sequence of radio squelch, their walkie-talkies opened simultaneously from various locations in the room, interrupting their collective insomnia. Someone, somewhere, within the short radius that could be picked up by their VHF transceivers, had acquired a walkie-talkie and hacked into the MedRelief communication frequency.

"White people," came a hoarse voice in surround-sound stereo, as all of their walkie-talkies broadcasted into the blackness of the night, "we can be coming to eat you!"

Bradshaw's voice broke the subsequent silence. "How extraordinary," he murmured from somewhere in that dark room. "I thought cannibalism was a thing of the past. Sounds like these fellows are reviving ancient traditions."

Nobody spoke.

"Makes me rather worried about being overweight," he continued. "I hope they like their whiteys well-done. I would hate to be undercooked. Just think of it, they might sink their teeth into me before I was properly dead—"

"Shut up and go to sleep!" Dave barked.

Half a sleepless hour later, Megan started scratching, making it impossible once again for Alan to ignore her. Was it a deliberate ploy to conquer his attention, he wondered, bombarding his brain with a thought he could not escape: *Megan.*

Honk. Honk. Honnnk. Honk. Honk. Honnnk.

Startled, Alan looked up from his desk. He had struggled all morning to concentrate on the finances after a hot, sleepless night. Insomnia was adding to his stress and irritability, made worse by the suffocating, stuffy weather that, like Megan and the approaching rebel forces, was closing in on him. He felt his freedom and self-will being slowly strangled.

That noise had come from the street outside, over by the gate. It sounded like cars were demanding the guards to open up, beeping like the Indian army security convoys when they had wanted to enter. But both U.N. peacekeepers and AfriBat had left Ndombazu, so it could only mean one thing—the rebels had arrived.

This was the moment they had been preparing for.

He sprang up from his chair to ensure the watchmen had barricaded themselves in as instructed. His presence at the gate might be necessary to prevent unwanted visitors getting in. Without an expat there, the guards might succumb to the pressure to open up.

He had just reached the door to the corridor when the roar of vehicle engines announced it was already too late. He turned to glance through the gaps between the sandbags that partially blocked his window. A series of battered off-road cars had screeched into the compound, bristling with guns that poked out of doorless frames.

They had been let in. Now it would get nasty. He had to act fast.

He slammed the door shut behind him, in case they started firing into the windows of his office. His priority was to get upstairs and lock behind him the iron gate to the first floor, which would buy time to alert the others.

He sped up the steps, bolted the barrier at the top, rounded the corner, and almost collided with Bradshaw going in the opposite direction.

"The cavalry"—Bradshaw struggled to speak through the exertion of a short trot—"have arrived." He took a deep breath. "That will send the Indians scarpering."

"What are you talking about?" The Indian army had long gone. This was not the moment for more of Bradshaw's fantasies.

"Take a look for yourself," Bradshaw wheezed.

Alan did a running crouch out onto the terrace and then over to the edge. He bobbed his head above the sandbag parapet, intending to drop it again immediately afterwards in the expectation that he might be shot at.

Below, he saw burly figures clad in massive body armour and matching combat fatigues, helmets, and goggles. And then he noticed the flag.

It was Old Glory, the Star-Spangled Banner.

A rush of emotion overwhelmed him. It was like a scene straight out of a film, yet it was happening right in front of him. Uncle Sam's soldiers had arrived to save the country.

"Hey," he called to get their attention. "I'm coming right down."

Almost falling over himself in haste, he unlocked the iron gate and flew down the stairs to meet his liberators. Kugombwala would be safe now with the arrival of the Americans. They would do what the U.N. had failed to do—disarm the factions and introduce democratic government, ensuring a happy ending.

"How are you doing, sir?" one of the soldiers greeted Alan once he had joined them in the courtyard. "My name is Lieutenant Bradley G. Johnson of the U.S. Marine Corps. We've come to get you folks outta here. How many are you, and what are your nationalities?"

"We are six Brits."

"Seven." Bradshaw joined them, still panting. "Mind if I join you? I don't like living on my own." He took a moment to catch his breath. "You see, I prefer my meals in company, except when I'm on the menu."

"Sure thing, wise guy," the marine answered, not understanding his private joke. "You're coming with us, too." He turned to Alan. "Tell your folks to assemble here immediately. We ain't got much time."

Trembling from excitement, Alan pulled up his radio. "Al, Al, for MedRelief team. Al, Al for MedRelief team. Birthday drinks at the office in five minutes," he told them through his walkie-talkie. This was their secret code announcing that they should gather for an imminent evacuation. "Who's coming? Over."

"I am. Dave out."

"Lorna here. Well copied."

"Paula, copy."

"Megan, too."

"And Jules. Happy birthday."

"Ladies and gentlemen," the lead marine announced once they had gathered, "we're here under the orders of the President of the United States of America, to conduct a non-combatant evacuation operation—which means you folks are getting outta here, courtesy of the U.S. government. So, please do everything to cooperate. You've got ten minutes to get your essentials, and I mean *ten minutes*."

Alan returned to his room, retrieved the stash of cash from the safe, and packed it with the accounts ledgers into a bag he had earlier readied for that purpose. Then he shoved his own things into a rucksack. He was ready to go, with eight minutes to spare.

What to do with those last moments in the MedRelief base, which had been his home for six long months?

A strange thought struck him. It would be wrong to leave with all MedRelief's remaining money when his local colleagues needed it more than the expat team. Their escape was now guaranteed, while the national staff would soon face certain hardship. He did some quick thinking.

"MacJohn! MacNed! MacGarry!" he yelled through the window to the waiting drivers, summoning them to his office. "Here's your pay and a month's advance salary. Please sign the receipt and get the guards and house staff. But don't say anything to Jules or to anyone else."

"Thank you, Boss," MacJohn said, as he left the office. "We will always remember you."

Within minutes, it was over; he had managed to disperse half of MedRelief's funds. There was no time to pay the hospital staff, but there was not enough money to do that, anyway. He hoped they would be able to earn some money from their patients to get by during the difficult times ahead.

"Come on, Al, we're going now!" he heard Jules shout.

He hurried out to meet the others, who were already in the courtyard with their bags. Jules gave final instructions to MacHenry, the hospital administrator, and they exchanged a hasty round of farewells with the local staff who had gathered there, before being bundled by the U.S. soldiers into requisitioned vehicles, whose doors had been ripped off to allow a full field of fire from the marines inside.

Alan felt the deep guilt of betrayal as his vehicle sped out of the compound. It had been hard to say goodbye to his local colleagues. He tried to blot out thoughts of what might happen to them by reasoning that, as Kugombwalans, they would be able to look after themselves.

It was cramped on the back seat, sandwiched with Paula between two burly marines who rode shotgun either side, weapons readied to annihilate any attackers. They drove like banshees through a city that had disintegrated into an orgy of drunkenness, looting, and violence. Corpses festered on the pavements, while a few buildings in the city centre burned—an omen that the apocalypse was about to begin.

They raced past roadblocks that had been set up at every street corner, manned by youths who were drunk or stoned into an ulterior state of conscience. One comprised a gang of men wearing gorilla masks, who raised homemade weapons and cheered as they drove past. At another, they were stark naked, clad only with bandoliers, guns, and a token piece of string. A third group wore shades and business suits, decked out in the spoils of their looting sprees, while gyrating to aggressive American gangsta rap music from a huge ghetto-blaster. Nothing was normal anymore in Ndombazu, the city of the doomed.

They arrived to frenzied activity at the seaport, where U.S. Marines hurried about, shifting weapons and ammunition or changing guard. The MedRelief team were ordered to stay put at the harbour master's office, until given further instructions. No one minded the wait, relieved to be under military protection. They sat in silence, staring out across the rain-spattered harbour, each deep in their own thoughts.

Morning morphed into midday. A marine came by with meal packs and bottles of water, which temporarily eased the boredom of waiting.

"What's happening, Boss?" Dave asked.

"Gotta fetch a few more folks; then we'll be outta here."

A strong wind brought heavy showers of rain, and for the first time in many months, Alan felt cold. He was glad of the shelter provided by the ruined harbour master's office, where he had earlier sought refuge from the relentless sun. Today, it was from the cold and rain.

An hour later, they were joined by a small group of expatriates. Alan recognised some of the faces from the parties they had been to and guessed them to be the stranded U.N. staff. They were then whisked away by two helicopters, leaving three others at the port. *We are the last foreigners left in Ndombazu,* Alan realised as he watched the choppers depart.

"Hey, you got a Miss Lorna here?" A burly marine interrupted their silence.

"Yes, that's me," Lorna piped up.

The soldier nodded and addressed his walkie-talkie. "This is Falcon Golf calling Eagle Delta. How do you copy? Over."

"Yeah, Falcon Golf, this is Eagle Delta," crackled the reply. "I copy ya loud and clear. Over."

"Yessir, I got Miss Lima Oscar located at the onward transfers point. Over."

"This is Eagle Delta for Falcon Golf. Tell the subject to remain at her location. Over and out."

"Falcon Golf out." The soldier then turned to Lorna. "There's someone asking to see you, ma'am."

A minute later, another soldier arrived, followed by a middle-aged Rastafarian with greying dreadlocks and a short, trimmed beard. His looks were striking yet incongruous—twinkling brown eyes, hair pulled back into a ponytail, pressed but faded Hawaiian shirt, khaki combats, and sandals. His skin was lighter than the typical Kugombwalan—perhaps a mixed-race local businessman, Alan guessed.

"Roy!" Lorna called out in surprise and then ran over to hug him. It was a long embrace. Did Lorna have a secret boyfriend in Ndombazu? She'd kept that quiet.

"Lorna!" The man smiled. "How's your life? I didn't want you to leave without saying goodbye." He spoke with a strong Caribbean accent.

"Oh, Roy." A few tears rolled down Lorna's cheek. "I thought I'd never see you again."

"I almost did not make it past these American boys, who thought I was one of the locals. But I thank God for the British government, who gave me a passport many years ago, which I used to get in. Anyway, before I forget, here's a letter for my sister in London. Can you post it to her when you get home?"

Alan got up from where he was sitting to take a stroll outside. It disconcerted him to observe the obvious affection between Lorna and her lover, for it highlighted his more difficult relationship with Mandy. To distract his thoughts, he walked to the harbour edge in the hope of spotting bright tropical fish, but the water was empty apart from spiny sea urchins clinging to the sides of the jetty.

He looked out across the ocean. A growing bub-bub-bub-bub-bub staccato signalled the return of the two helicopters approaching from the horizon. They flew to a point over the harbour before undertaking a rapid helical descent—at times visible, at times disappearing behind the harbour office. The helicopters proceeded to a position some ten metres above the landing pad surface, briefly hovering in a mid-air halt while buffeted by the strong winds coming off the ocean, before making a slower and more controlled final descent. The distant bub-bub-bub-bub-bub had now evolved into an aggressive whump-thwack that bombarded his eardrums with the passing of each rotor blade. Alan was then struck by the deflected downdraft as each helicopter eased itself onto the tarmac surface of the harbour, blasting the puddles out to sea. The rear door of each helicopter was open, framing a marine manning a machine gun.

Alan felt a slap on his back. He turned to see the marine who had spoken to Lorna earlier.

"Okay, mister. That bird's for you." He was leading the others out of the airport terminal. "One at a time, guys, and mind your heads." He waved them towards one of the waiting helicopters, whose rotors were still spinning.

Roy turned to Lorna and embraced her again. "God bless you, my dear," he said and then turned to go but was stopped by the marine.

"Hey, dude, where's you going?"

"Why, back to this city where I live."

"Are you crazy? We've come to get the last foreigners outta here, and you wanna go back like it's some kind of Super Bowl tournament in there?"

Alan followed his colleagues in a half-crouch towards the helicopter. It was raining, and he was grateful for the shelter offered by the cabin once he got inside. He chose a place on a webbing seat opposite Lorna, fastened the seatbelt around his waist, and leant forwards to catch her ear.

"Who was that?" He had to shout to overcome the deafening roar from the chopper engines, which were spinning up sufficient speed and torque to take off.

"Father Roy." Her bellowed response was barely audible.

"Your boyfriend?"

"No." She smiled. "He's a Catholic priest from Jamaica who leads the church I sometimes attended here."

The ever louder engines made further conversation impossible. The marine who had arrived with the helicopter jumped in and gave a thumbs-up to the pilot. The rotor blades were then feathered and the engines strained to generate sufficient power to heave them out of the clutches of gravity. Then came the sudden increase in gravitational force as the helicopter broke free and pushed them upwards, juddering in the strong wind.

They had escaped Kugombwalan soil and now soared heavenwards, circling like a bird released from a cage, higher and higher into the freedom of the sky. They passed over the harbour office from which the last of the marines were now leaving, retreating in orderly fashion towards the remaining helicopters on the ground. They passed over an elderly man with a silver ponytail on a bike, cycling away from the office building, who stopped to wave. They continued corkscrewing up, circling back over the harbour shrinking below them. The last helicopter had now taken off, and Alan counted four other choppers in the convoy, all rising out of Ndombazu like flies disturbed off a rotting carcass.

He gazed back at the city disappearing out of sight below, dimming in the falling light of the approaching night and illuminated only by the fires of its burning buildings. In the short time it took the helicopter to gain altitude over the city, Alan jettisoned the stresses of the previous six months, the lifetime-long half-year of sheer madness that he was determined not to repeat. He was finally gone, and he would never return.

Kugombwala had gone berserk, so what would be the use of staying? And what benefit had come out of having been there? There had been a famine when he had arrived; MedRelief had saved the lives of numerous kids and some adults, but to what end? They might have rescued some of the men who were now roaming the streets of Ndombazu, armed to the teeth, perpetrating an orgy of rape, massacre, and looting. It was possible they had saved the lives of some of the women who happily joined the lynching of their fellow citizens for common theft, a crime they were probably guilty of themselves. They may even have rescued some of the little boys who now mutilated their fellow citizens at the checkpoints. Likewise, the little girls who giggled while they watched the dismembering of the corpses of people lynched for stealing a few pieces of cassava. They were all savages, utter savages. What was the point of saving their lives? The world was right to get out and leave the Kugombwalans to themselves. Why help them when they would turn upon each other at the earliest opportunity?

But then a thought arrived to disturb Alan's logic. All MedRelief had done was to prevent the Kugombwalans from dying, thereby cursing them to continue a desperate dog-eat-dog existence in a society so mutilated by civil war that it would be impossible to survive without becoming brutalised. He and the MedRelief team had been an alibi to mask the reality that the rest of the world was doing nothing for these people. They had applied a mere plaster on a suppurating wound that prevented others from having to see its unsightly mess without doing anything to heal the infection underneath.

The helicopter had by now gained sufficient altitude to be out of the danger of gunfire and had started on a direct trajectory to a waiting warship that was visible on the horizon. Alan watched the four other helicopters line up behind, all flying away as fast as they could from that cursed land. Kugombwala was now utterly abandoned by the international community, condemned to suffer its frightful fate.

For the first time since he had left the compound that morning, Alan remembered the local staff he had left behind. They, and the rest of the Kugombwalans, could not leave, and no one cared enough to help or even remain with them. Except for Lorna's crazy Rasta.

What was it that made him stay?

CHAPTER 6

BRITAIN

Chirp, chirp, warble . . .

Alan awoke to the sound of twittering birds and the sun streaming through the bedroom window. Mandy must have drawn back the curtains when she left. He vaguely remembered her getting up to go to work before he had fallen asleep again.

The downstairs clock started to chime the hour. Eight. Nine. Ten. Eleven—eleven o'clock again. It had been the same for a whole week now, ever since he had returned from Kugombwala. He was still exhausted, his body demanding extra sleep to recover from the accumulated stress of many months in a war zone.

But that was the past. Now, he was back in England. Spring was giving way to summer. The sun was warming the land with its gentle rays. Flowers were bursting forth in hedgerows and fields, while orchards were heavy with blossom. Fresh leaves were emerging on bushes and trees; insects buzzed with activity; and clouds scudded across a soft blue sky. Everything was alive, and everywhere, there was movement. Not the frenetic activity of the city, but an easy, relaxed, rural motion that celebrated the gift of life.

It felt so good to be alive, here in England, where life was worth living and full of opportunities and pleasures. It was bliss to wallow in such thoughts while lazing in bed, waiting for the clock to chime twelve times. And what comfort! Cushioned between a soft mattress and a thick duvet scented by Mandy's perfume.

Alan staggered out of bed sometime after noon and wandered down to the kitchen to prepare a large, cooked breakfast. He had lost a few kilos while in Kugombwala and now felt his appetite returning, allowing him to relish the scrumptious baked beans, fried egg, bacon, mushrooms, and tomatoes. British food beat Kugombwalan cuisine. In fact, everything was better in Britain. Why had he forsaken his native land? Never would he do so again, he vowed.

Thud.

The second delivery of post had landed through the letterbox.

Alan went to the front door to see if he had received any personal letters or postcards, but it was the usual bills and mailshots. He separated the business envelopes to look at later with Mandy. Normally, he would throw the junk mail away, but today, he decided to take a look, to delight in society's limitless material choices. After all, he had plenty of time and could afford to relax over a long breakfast. The sudden evacuation from Ndombazu had prevented him from telling his U.K. employer he would be returning, which suited him well for he deserved a break, given all he had been through. And he needed time to regain strength.

He made himself another mug of tea and popped two pieces of pre-sliced bread into the toaster. He was reminded of the dull bread they ate in Kugombwala. It was often full of tiny ants, who were the only ones who liked it, for it tasted bad and would crumble apart in protest at being sliced. Even something as humble as the great British slice of toast had been impossible to achieve out there. Not even wild horses could drag him back.

He sat down with the tea and toast and then turned his attention to the pile of junk mail. With the imminent arrival of summer, there were adverts for garden furniture, made from hardwood that came from the jungles of Africa. *Nothing wrong with that,* he countered the concerns of the environmental activists. *Those chairs and tables would be far better quality than the rickety contraptions they make out there.*

Next, he noticed the usual jewellery ads—gold earrings, silver bracelets, and diamond pendants. Perhaps he should buy Mandy a trinket to atone for his absence. She would certainly appreciate it, especially if he made a show of giving it to her.

Sandwiched between loose adverts for luxury goods, he was startled to see a picture of Megan cradling an African child in a pose reminiscent of the nativity—Megan and baby, like Mary and the infant Jesus. With the photo were the following words:

QUIDS PRO KIDS

A few pounds from your purse will put the pounds back on their bodies.

Support MedRelief. We'll feed Kugombwala's hungry children.

The text rankled. This was propaganda, peddling an exaggerated message of hope to entice people to surrender twenty pounds from annual salaries over a thousand times greater with the implicit promise that their paltry donation would right all the ills and suffering in Africa, thereby allowing the donor to keep the rest of their income with a clear conscience. He read on:

Help us to give them a future. Every little bit goes a long way.

What about the big bits of help that were even more needed? He was in no doubt that aid agencies did some good, but he was now aware that they unwittingly prevented more being done by refusing to proclaim the full scale of the problem out of fear it would negatively impact their fundraising. They had become sellers of quick-fix solutions, while not informing donors and politicians that vastly more help was needed to ensure real change.

He dropped the mailshot but could not let go of the thoughts that now flooded his mind. Surely, it was wrong for organisations like MedRelief to ask people to give money to Kugombwala when it had scant chance to help hungry kids because all the aid agencies had been forced to evacuate. He thought of the people who would react to Blair-Campbell's marketing, the good-natured souls who sent their meagre spare cash out of compassion and pity. Some were poor pensioners like his parents, who now supported the organisation, which meant he'd been part of a system that duped decent people into thinking that Africa's civil wars were getting sorted out because a bit of aid sometimes trickled through.

Alan picked up the mailshot and turned it over to see if there was anything else he could criticise. That was not hard, for it mentioned that MedRelief was organising a charity ball in London that was to be graced by the great and the good.

He crumpled up the paper in disgust at the thought of Blair-Campbell, Isabella, and the other snobby office girls delighting themselves over the opportunity to mix with high society. It was just an excuse for a posh party, a PR stunt for MedRelief that simultaneously gave the rich and powerful another reason to feel righteous about themselves, while doing nothing to help those in need. He imagined

London's socialites paying hundreds of pounds to attend such events, thinking they were being generous, while most of what they gave would go to expensive champagne and gourmet cuisine. Worse still were those with political influence, who would pretend to care by turning up on a free ticket, as if that was enough to help those in need.

The whole aid system stank. It made the super-rich feel good about giving a pittance of their wealth and allowed the powerful to get away with doing nothing, while fooling the masses to give up their spare cash under the false promise that it would solve the problem.

But the biggest fools, he realised, were the idiots like him who risked their lives to go out as aid workers—the self-indulgent idealists who thought their efforts would make a difference, especially those who did so for next to nothing. Perhaps that was why U.N. field staff accepted huge salaries without conscience for doing little for the people they were supposed to help. They had realised that they couldn't make a meaningful difference, however hard they tried, and regarded their massive pay as danger money, rather than a reward for excellence or achieving results. Good luck to them, successfully parasitising on an otherwise ineffective system.

A rising contempt for his earlier idealism welled up within him. He had considered himself a hero, going out into the quagmire of an African civil war to help the hungry, but now he could see he was a halfwit. That might explain the reception at his local pub when he got back, which was not the welcome he had expected for a returning warrior. His mates were happy to see him but were not interested in what he had done. Instead, they preferred to do what they did every evening—discuss the day's football results, chat up the barmaids, and brag about subjects where each could chip in with a contribution.

His embellished anecdotes of dodging gunfire in Kugombwala were therefore not welcome because his booze-and-banter partners were unable to compete with similar stories of their own. Maybe they also thought he was a moron for having risked his life for nothing?

His friends had further reason for not wishing to hear about his adventures, he now realised. He thought back to how they had reacted when he had departed for Ndombazu. Some of them had felt rejected by him for resigning the captaincy of the football team and for leaving them to go somewhere else and be with other people. He could now see he had given them a clear signal that they weren't important enough for him to want to stay, thereby betraying long-established friendships. It would take a while to regain their trust and to rebuild those relationships.

The only exception was Bobsy. He alone was fascinated by Alan's anecdotes and always wanted to hear more. He smiled at the thought of Bobsy's face lighting up, eyes wide with amazement, when he told him exaggerated stories about child soldiers, mortar attacks, and meeting militia leaders. His standing with Bobsy, which had always been high, was now reaching the level of worship.

By contrast, Mandy was showing him much less respect. There was a note on the table telling him to go to the supermarket to restock the larder. This was normally her job; he regarded supermarkets as being for women, the female equivalent of the pub, where the girls gathered to shop and gossip, their two favourite activities rolled into one. However, as he was home all day, it was almost understandable that he should help with the housework. But balancing that argument was the issue of their internal power tussle. Would caving in to her demand mean he would be expected to do all the shopping from now on? It was important for their relationship to show willing, but he didn't want to fall into the trap of being henpecked like Mandy's father.

Overriding those considerations was the thought that it would be fun to see a supermarket again after so many months in war-torn Ndombazu. He could then purchase the food he wanted to eat, rather than only consuming what Mandy cooked. *Good idea,* he concluded. He would go but only buy what he wanted, so she'd have to go herself to get what she wanted.

Smiling, Alan congratulated himself on having learned to compromise. Kugombwala had done him some good after all.

Alan closed the car door. The engine fired on turning the key, unlike the Land Rovers in Kugombwala, where you had to wait half a minute for the glow-plugs to heat the diesel before the engine could start. Everything in Africa had been a hassle, even such simple tasks as operating a well-maintained vehicle.

Instead of the normal route to the supermarket, he took a detour through the countryside to savour the scenery of his native Yorkshire. A short spring shower had rinsed the land so that it shone in the sunshine, framed by a rainbow glowing in the sky that smiled upon newborn lambs frolicking in the fields. He rolled down the window to catch the fresh air and turned up the volume to full whack, blasting his favourite thud-thud-thud car music into the open. The twisting country lanes demanded aggressive driving, and he threw the car into the bends, accelerating at speed out of the frequent corners. He felt exhilarated by the combination of the weather, the scenery, the music, and the joy of once again being able to drive a fast car on a smooth road. No risk of getting ambushed, no potholes, and no checkpoints.

He arrived at the out-of-town supermarket, parked, and pulled out a shopping trolley before entering the vast cavern crammed with consumer goods. It was an awesome sight—a kaleidoscope of enticing colours, hundreds of metres of shelves stacked with culinary choice. In the past, he would rush through on his occasional visits, going from point to point to gather what he wanted. But today, he wanted to bask in the amazing selection of offers, to sift through the sheer variety of food. He started with the vegetables, passing the breakfast cereals before reaching the cheeses. Oh, how he had missed cheese! The weekly delivery of cheddar in Kugombwala had been cut when the rebels had taken the airport, and he had gone without it for over a month. And now, he was faced with fifty different varieties. He wanted to sample them all, to savour the subtle varieties in taste. The problem was that his appetite had still not recovered from living for weeks on emergency rations. And even then, the amount he could eat would be limited by the size of his stomach.

If only he was fat, then he could really feast . . .

"All right, Al? Bet you're enjoying the sight of what you've been missing."

He turned around on hearing the voice he knew so well.

"Aye-up, Bobsy, you snack hunting as well?"

Bobsy's trolley was laden to the brim with large bottles of fizzy drinks and multi-coloured packets of crisps and sweets. Alan grinned at his friend's predictability. It was exactly the kind of junk he would expect big Bobsy to buy.

"No, mate, I'm doing the shopping for the special needs kids up at the home. One of them is having a birthday, so we're throwing a party."

"Special needs kids? Didn't know you was involved with the disabled."

"Actually, it was after you went to Africa to help them kids out there. Got me thinking, like. You know, there's you going off to help people what really needs it, and there's me doing nowt. I'd never done nothing to help anyone before, except me mates, but that was for favours. I mean, I never helped anyone who really needed it. Then, on Comic Relief day, there was this programme on the telly about them wanting volunteers for special needs kids, so I went along to the local centre to see if I could help out. I now go two nights a week. I really love it; the kids are ever so nice."

Alan's jaw dropped. Here was Bobsy, always the first to throw a punch against the supporters of rival football teams, now helping vulnerable children in his spare time—and apparently inspired by him going off to Kugombwala as an aid worker. Perhaps it had not been a total waste—at least not for Bobsy and his new fan club. It would be convenient to think that it had all been pointless, that there was no use at all assisting people in need, because that would mean there was no reason for doing so. But now he was not so sure; perhaps it did make a difference. It was a scary thought.

"Bert! Tea!" Yvonne Carter called out across the sunlit garden with its multitude of flowers and different leaf forms. It was her haven, where on warm days she basked in nature's beauty and calm; a strong contrast to the drab urban streets and many troubles outside.

"Cup's hot—mind you don't burn yourself." She poured out a mug for her husband once he had ambled over from the shed where he tended his ferrets. "You know Al's coming to lunch tomorrow."

"Great—I'll look forward to that!"

I disagree. She mentally fretted over how to deal with the coming confrontation. *He will have been hardened in the furnace of war,* she predicted, envisioning what it would mean. A simmering desire for violence. Coarse language. Magnified male-chauvinist behaviour.

Pent-up anger arose within her over how he had treated her beloved daughter—living with her without a marriage commitment, then abandoning her for many months, yet expecting he could return at any time and resume the relationship as if nothing had happened, while not even writing when he was away. *He's probably been carrying on with one of the nurses or some of the local women,* she imagined. Which was why she had urged Mandy to insist he take an AIDS test.

Al has to understand that his conduct has been totally unacceptable, Yvonne Carter concluded, *for otherwise, he will continue.* Firm boundaries would have to be imposed, with a clear message that they could not be crossed without consequences.

"Off with you!" she shooed a pesky wasp that had landed on the table. "We don't want you here."

Yap, yap, yap.

"I know, Arthur. There's a horrible man out there," Alan heard Mrs. Carter tell the barking dog behind the front door in a voice that was deliberately loud enough for him to hear. The door then opened to reveal her restraining the excited animal by the collar.

"Oh, hello, darling, lovely to see you," she addressed Mandy before turning to Alan. "I can tell you're back," she scolded. "You're late, as usual. Amanda was always on time while you were away."

Alan scowled in silence. It was always a struggle to hurry Mandy out of their house in reasonable time for the Sunday lunch ritual at the Carter home, and he often had to wait for her.

"I won't shake your hand," Mrs. Carter continued. "You probably picked up a few nasty diseases out there."

"Only Umbu-ungula," he lied. "It's highly infectious. Gave me a horrible green rash which itched for weeks on my—"

"Enough of that, Al," Mandy snapped. "Behave yourself and stop showing off." She became more easily irritated by him now, Alan realised. And she was more vicious with it, burdening him with an additional cost to maintaining their relationship.

"Hello, Alan, great to see you again." Mr. Carter had now arrived in the hall. His genial presence diffused the tension. "I can't wait to hear about your adventures."

"Not now, Bert," Mrs. Carter interjected. "You need to sit down, or the dinner will go cold."

"Of course, dear." He plodded over to his place at the table.

"No, not there, Bert."

"But it's where I always sit, dear."

"Not today, Bert," she rebuked. "You are at the end of the table."

"As you wish, dear."

"And you are at the other end, Al."

It took Alan a moment to work out her strategy. She usually sat at one end of the long table, opposite him. That meant she could talk to

Mandy or her husband at either side of her but never to him. It was an arrangement that suited them both.

Today was different, as she now placed herself in the middle, opposite Mandy, to control all conversation. This enabled her to talk to her daughter over the shorter width, creating a barrier between the two men. That would force them to remain silent unless she or Mandy spoke to them.

But Mr. Carter was so determined to hear about Alan's experiences in Kugombwala that he broke the unwritten rule of not talking over the two women.

Mrs. Carter became agitated. "Do you have to talk about that?" she demanded with exaggerated annoyance. "I'm trying to enjoy my meal, if you don't mind."

There was an awkward silence, but Mrs. Carter soon filled the gap by changing the topic to her son, Graham. Alan disliked Mandy's irritating little brother, who was the apple of his mother's eye. He had moved to London to earn more money, though Alan suspected it was also to get away from his mother. Graham's successes were Mrs. Carter's next favourite topic of conversation, after gossip about the people she knew.

"Graham's off to Milan this week to some big trade fair. It's all on expenses, so he's going to be living it up, I'm sure. They really like him, and they'll be upgrading his company car soon. Wouldn't surprise me if they make him a manager . . . "

Alan switched off his attention; it was the same vicarious boasting every time. Graham this, Graham that. Graham's wonderful girlfriend who—surprise, surprise—was never brought home to endure his mother. Graham's new flat. Graham's great job. It was as if she used Graham to make up for her own lack of success—a housewife with a monotonous life in a drab industrial town.

Or perhaps there was more to it than that, he considered, watching her scoff her roast beef and Yorkshire pudding, while she continued to bombard them with more of Graham's achievements. She was not the only person he knew who spent hours talking about their own successes or the achievements of their family. Many of his friends did that as well.

Perhaps there was a need to compliment those who did well, he pondered, in order to justify the Western material lifestyle? To celebrate society's collective selfishness by glorifying those who excelled in it. It was no coincidence that she, and many others, preferred to talk about that, instead of hearing about the suffering going on in other parts of the world. For to become aware of the unmet needs of others would expose the uncomfortable truth that success is no more than determined selfishness.

"Time to get up!"

Alan tried to groan himself awake, but sleep was stubborn.

"Come on, wake up." Mandy shook him. "I'm going to the office now, and you can't laze in bed all day."

"Right, love," Alan mumbled.

"Will you call your boss about going back to work?"

"I don't think so . . . "

"Why not?" Mandy's aggressive tone indicated that her mother had put her up to it. It was no coincidence that this confrontation came after the visit to the Carter home the day before. This would have been one of the subjects of the kitchen conversations about him, while the women did the washing up.

"Well, I need to think a bit."

"Think about what?"

"You know, about what I'm going to do with my life and that kind of thing."

"What you're going to do with your life? What's there to think about, Al? You've got to return to work, so we can pay the mortgage and get that new kitchen we saw at the showroom—the one with the solid oak doors. I also want to go to Tenerife this summer. Betty from the office went there last year, and she says it was brilliant."

"Aye, love. But ain't that a bit materialistic? You know, money, home comforts, holidays." *Life was also about other things,* he thought.

"Materialistic? What's wrong with that? It's what everybody else is doing, and it don't harm no one. I don't know what's got into you, Alan Swales. You're really strange now with your funny ideas. You're not yourself anymore."

Mandy was right. He had changed, despite his best efforts to revert to his old self. Yet no matter how hard he tried, he could not recapture the carefreeness of his earlier character, due to an inexplicable sensation that was troubling him deep inside.

It reminded him of the unease that had precipitated his departure for Kugombwala. Back then, he had thought his problem was boredom with an easy life that had never tasted the thrill of adventure. But now he had cured that by experiencing more excitement than most people encounter in a lifetime. Plus, he had acquired the additional achievement of surviving a war zone—the ultimate rite of passage to manhood.

No, this new feeling was different. Something was wrong, but he could not make out what it was. It was not the need to be a hero, for he was now released from that ambition and more than happy to be back in a world of physical security. Having been confined for many months to a walled compound, he appreciated the freedom to walk out of his front door to the street outside where there was no risk of getting shot or kidnapped. He was thankful to have escaped the constant onslaught of biting insects, and he relished the taste of disease-free water that gushed from the taps. And what a joy to have electricity twenty-four hours a day. Life was good here in Britain, he acknowledged. Very good.

Yet for him, it lacked something. He now recognised that he had not felt that way in Kugombwala—out there, he had somehow felt fulfilled, despite the hardships and danger. What was it about being in that vicious war that had given him an unexpected inner satisfaction, which he had failed to recognise at the time?

After Mandy had gone to work, Alan was left to himself in the house. Her departure left a vacuum in the building that he was not aware of having experienced before, although he reflected it was rare for him to be alone at home without her. He had always been off first for work and came back after her, timing his return to ensure she had enough time to run around with the hoover and prepare his meal ready before he got back. It had also been the norm for him to go out with his mates a couple of evenings a week, leaving her with only the TV and telephone for company.

But now it was he who was alone, with a whole day ahead of him. He planned to go jogging, after a quick check of the sports channel. There was only golf, which he found dull, so his attention wandered to the room itself.

His interest in interior design was limited to the layout of pubs, so he had left it to Mandy to choose the decor, using the opportunity to create a conflict and then allowing her to win, in exchange for her conceding on another issue on which they had disagreed. Hence, the flowery wallpaper with the fussy friezes, the curtains with the frilly edges, and the large-patterned carpet. If he had had his own way, he would have painted his football team's colours on the wall and built a bar in the corner.

As he stared around the room, he noticed for the first time that everything he could see was superficial, hiding what was behind, above, or underneath. He thought back to his room in Kugombwala—the bare cement floor; the concrete walls tinted with the thinnest coat of white paint. Those walls had been, unashamedly, *walls*. But here in his own home, everything was masked. The brickwork was shrouded, first with plasterboard and then with a layer of multi-coloured paper, transforming the walls into smooth, flat screens of small, pink roses scattered on a pale green background. Likewise, the plaster ceiling was hidden by patterned polystyrene tiles, while the wooden floor was covered by underlay and then a thick carpet. There was a deliberate attempt to cushion or mask everything against a hard and rough reality.

Following that thought process through, he came to see that it was not just in this room but also everywhere and in everything that people in Britain were cushioning themselves. Protected by insurance policies and shielded by social security against the full sharpness of disaster, disease, disability, destitution, and death, thus avoiding the calamities that the Kugombwalans encountered every day.

For them, life was not in the slightest padded but undeniably difficult. Yet there was one benefit to living in such a cruel environment—you felt alive. Was it due to the contrast between living, while surrounded by the dead and dying? Or because life presented greater challenges, which had to be overcome to not succumb to the ever-present risk of annihilation? Alan remembered the kick he got from forging order out of almost insurmountable chaos. Helping Keith battle with the generator to squeeze electricity out of it. Dealing with dangerous warlords and militia groups—and surviving.

Life in Kugombwala had been an infinitely varied adventure and had demanded the utmost of him. He had relished the opportunity to overcome difficult challenges and the consequent bonds of respect forged with his colleagues, even those he did not like. By contrast, his future in England would be dull—an easy and predictable existence that would be suffocated by a hum-drum and self-focussed lifestyle. There was no challenge to life here, except to earn and consume more. Was that what he wanted?

Click-click.

The sound of a key in the lock. Mandy returning from work.

Would she still be angry?

"Hi, Al," she said in her lovely, bubbly voice.

"Ay-up, love."

She gave him a longer squeeze than normal, a sign of her desire to be conciliatory. Perhaps she felt some remorse for having been so harsh that morning?

They combined supper with watching a film while snuggled up to one another on the sofa. This was how it had been when they had first moved in together, enjoying each other's physical proximity. She even ignored the phone when it rang three times in quick succession at eight o'clock. It comforted him to note that Mandy was not completely under the thumb of her domineering mother.

After the film ended, they went up to bed. They were back to their standard evening routine from the time before he had left, saying little to one another all evening, with the television providing convenient cover for the absence of conversation during dinner. Alan noticed that their relationship had become a mime, performed by two actors convincing themselves the other was unaware it was make-believe, an act that was easy to sustain because their bond was predominantly physical, performed for the conviviality of company and the practicality of a partnership to get through life. But there was little depth to their relationship. Mandy could just as well have been one of the other girls he knew.

He now saw that their union was maintained by mutual self-interest—each doing just enough to ensure the other still wanted to stay in the relationship but both monitoring how much the other had put in to calculate how much they owed to keep the balance, which meant they were continuously scheming against one another, masked by the pretence of being in love, while hoping the other did not discover the subterfuge.

Their symbiotic selfishness was reinforced by reciprocal lying, Alan realised. For not only was he lying to Mandy but also to himself. Could he live with those lies for the rest of his life?

Another self-lie was also disturbing him, which had been exposed on the American warship just after he had been evacuated. There had been an obligatory session with a psychologist, referred to by the Yanks as a shrink. The U.S. military wanted to check whether he was traumatised by his experiences in Kugombwala.

He had never before been to see a psychologist. In Britain, it was commonly accepted they were only for nutters—and Americans, which had made him really scared, as he had feared the psycho-path-ologist was going to look right into him and expose his darkest secrets. He shuddered at the memory of the incident that had taken place a fortnight earlier:

"Hey, Alan, I'm Major Mercedes Espinoza." She was a handsome, raven-haired woman, primly dressed in a white, tropical uniform. Huge, round glasses magnified glittering green eyes, a pair of lasers that threatened to drill into the depths of his soul.

"So, tell me," she started, "what were you doing in Kugombwala?"

"I was the logistician-administrator."

"No, I know that. What I mean is, what were you there for?"

"To help the Kugombwalan people." That was the MedRelief byline. He had heard it so often that he now assumed it for himself.

"Don't play games with me, Alan."

His heart fluttered faster, for she had straightaway discovered his first fib. What other secrets would she uncover?

"That was not your real reason for going out to Africa. What were you running away from? Were you abused as a kid?"

"No." He was relieved to be able to tell the truth.

"Just been through a nasty divorce?"

"No, I'm still with my girlfriend."

"Okay, I get it. She beats you up."

He almost blacked out. It was one of his deepest fears—the frying pan, with Mandy at one end of it, bashing, thrashing in wild anger. It had only happened a few times and had left him with a paranoid fear that their secret would one day get out. The social stigma of being an abused male, weak in front of his woman, not fighting back and overpowering her like a real man. His standing with his mates would collapse if they ever found out.

"It's okay." She correctly read his hesitation to answer. "It happens to lots of guys." She paused to let him dwell a moment in his darkness. And then she was back on the attack. "So, we've established you were running away from yourself and your girlfriend, but why did you go to Kugombwala? I mean, it's no paradise. Did you do it for the money?"

"No, I was a volunteer without pay."

"So, you are also working for the British government?"

"What do you mean?" What a strange question.

"Forget it," she said. "It's nothing."

So, this was both a psychological debriefing and intelligence-gathering exercise, Alan realised. What should he do? Should he play-act the answers she wanted?

"I went for the adventure," he tried.

"Okay, tell me more."

"Because I was bored at home."

"Uh-huh."

"I also thought it would be a bit of a laugh."

"Go on."

"And I wanted to be a hero."

"Oh, don't give me that, Alan. You went out to try to save the world, to do penance for your guilt at being abused by your girlfriend."

"No, that's . . . " He was about to defend himself but realised that confession was the only way to end the interrogation. "I think you're right," he said with a serious face but without meaning it.

Alan couldn't shake the feeling that something the psychologist had said had resonated with him, something he had not been aware of before. It was about him trying to save the world, though not for the Freudian reasons she had postulated. There was another reason, though he couldn't figure out what it was, which increased his discomfort.

Or did he know, deep down, but was lying to himself that he did not?

He woke with a start, though it was not to the rattle of machine gun fire that had often interrupted his sleep in Kugombwala. Alan had become so accustomed to waking to the noise of war that there was now something abnormal about the sensation of waking up to silence, without the accompaniment of fear.

It took him a few moments to remember he was back in his own bedroom in Britain, a long, long way from Africa. The bed was soft, and he was snuggled under a duvet, rather than sweating on top of soaked sheets in the tropical heat of downtown Ndombazu. The mattress sloped to one side under Mandy's weight. His thoughts turned to her, so close they were almost touching. Yet she was over three thousand miles away, separated not by physical distance but by his six months in the Kugombwalan civil war. He'd left behind something of himself out there, which he would never get back.

Alan recalled the previous Friday night when he and Mandy had gone out with a group of friends to one of the local nightclubs. The disc jockey had played many old favourites associated with the various stages in his youth. Those songs would normally have kindled memories of carefree teenage years, as they seemed to do for his friends and Mandy, who were clearly enjoying themselves as they bounced around on the dance floor. But it had been different for him that night. Surrounded by all those happy people, he had been inexplicably reminded of the suffering and pain in Kugombwala, causing him to slip into deep melancholy.

Yes, he'd left something of himself behind. Was it that part of him able to experience intense joy and happiness? If so, would it forever separate him from everyone else in Britain?

It was time to move on and bury Kugombwala in deep memory. To do that, he needed to fill his current life with activity, including a return to work.

Alan had yet to tell his former boss that he was back in Britain, as he had wanted to recuperate without the burden of the nine-to-five routine. But it was now time for him to end his break and discuss a date for the return to his desk.

He drove over to the factory, which was located in a modern industrial estate on the outskirts of a nearby city. It was a journey he had done over a thousand times on his daily commutes, weaving through the labyrinth of service lanes, warehouses, and office blocks. There were few people about, as most workers were shut inside the buildings, many of which had no windows. That gave a cold and sterile feel to the place, and Alan's pulse quickened as he approached his old works. When he finally saw it again, he recalled the sinking feeling he'd experienced every time he walked up to the entrance to start the working day. There was something forbidding about the sight of his old treadmill. Did he want to turn himself in to more years of daily imprisonment?

Growing doubt forced him to pull over to the kerb at a distance from the factory. He needed time to think. Work had often been boring. Worse still, his workmates were dull—a collection of ageing, self-centred moaners. No, he couldn't go back. He needed change, renewal, to be with a dynamic group of people in a decent working environment, while doing something useful for the world. None of those needs were met by his existing workplace.

That decided it. He turned the car around and went home, stopping to buy a bundle of newspapers and engineering magazines. He spent the following hours going through the job adverts to see what was on offer. To relieve the tedium of looking at unenticing vacancies, he flicked through the main content of the engineering magazines.

Ndombazu! There, in a full, double-page colour photo, was a street scene he recognised. A large title read:

Action Men. Our Heroes Who Help Africa.

It was an article about a British aid agency he had met in Kugombwala during the time of the U.N. intervention. His memory took him back to that day.

"Hey, Al, check out those trucks." Dave whistled on entering the U.N. compound. "Ex-army Bedfords. I love the yellow colour."

"They look like Lego lorries!" Alan joked, yet impressed by the meaty machines that bristled with equipment. Sand ladders, shovels, picks, and extra jerry cans of fuel were strapped to their sides. HF and VHF radio antennae sprouted from the cab, while multiple spare tyres were attached to the rear tailgate.

"It's all show." Dave laughed. "Looks good on camera, but who needs sand ladders in a jungle? Most of that gear's going to get nicked when they're not looking because it's not bolted down. Anyway, let's find out who they are."

Two men in khaki boiler suits were crouched beside a wheel. The word "TruckAngels" was written in large lettering on their backs.

"Hey, guys," Dave started. "You new here?"

They stood up, hands closed into fists. One of them spoke, without smiling. "Yeah, mate, arrived yesterday. Drove over the Sahara Desert."

"So, what's TruckAngels?"

"We're a group of former paratroopers doing logistics support to relief operations during crises."

"Who's funding you?"

"The U.K. government. They've seconded us to the U.N."

After an awkward conversation, Alan and Dave returned to their Land Rover. "They're just boys with flashy toys doing a glorified overland trucking expedition at somebody else's expense," Dave said. "Total amateurs . . . "

Alan turned the page, where his eyes were drawn to the pull quote:

"We're professionals. And we've got what it takes to get the job done."

The article featured a gung-ho interview with the founder of TruckAngels and projected a different story to the one Alan knew.

"Yeah, yeah, you arrogant show-off . . . " he spoke aloud to the empty room. Where was the mention of them being just two weeks in Kugombwala before withdrawing with the U.N. forces? Or that it would have been far cheaper to hire a few local lorries and drivers, instead of using expensive TruckAngels to deliver food to the outskirts of Ndombazu? "You're a bunch of con artists."

Alan was annoyed by the article's insinuation that Africa's wars and crises could be solved by a few ex-army boys rolling in with fancy equipment. That message seemed convincing on shiny magazine paper, but he knew from experience that patronising and self-promoting aid workers like the TruckAngels team were not the solution to the world's complex humanitarian crises.

Furthermore, the article presented another subliminal self-serving lie—that a small group of former British soldiers could sort out Africa's problems because the Africans were too useless to do so themselves. It was far from reality.

He thought of his local staff: MacJosiah's brilliance as a mechanic; loyal, level-headed MacJohn, who had become a good friend; and his happy gang of workers who could be a challenge to motivate but who, nonetheless, did a good job and were fun to work with. They were decent people and remarkably honest given their difficult circumstances. It was amazing how much humour and joy were in them, despite the hard knocks they received in life. He missed them. What had happened to them after he left?

It was impossible to know because Kugombwala was no longer headline news, and the fate of its many million inhabitants was considered by the British media to be far less important than its self-righteous opinions, the banality of national politics, and the gutter-level gossip about the lives of the celebrities.

With repeated frustration, Alan watched the TV news every evening, hoping to catch a reportage that remained ever elusive. After days without success, he resorted to buying the broadsheet newspapers. Here, he eventually found what he was looking for in a bulletin that read:

Rebels Seize Capital

Bakiboko forces claim to be in full control of Ndombazu, the troubled capital of Kugombwala. The city is reported to be under martial law.

That was it. Weeks of fighting, looting, and suffering compressed into twenty-seven words on page eight, a grudging epitaph for thousands of dead people that was too brief to have any effect as a distress signal to an indifferent world.

Alan tried to imagine how it would be for the citizens of Ndombazu caught in that combat—the fear, the uncertainty, the feeling of utter abandonment. The faces of his staff as they said farewell reappeared before him, and he struggled to swallow, amazed that he, Alan Swales, always so distanced and cool, had become so unexpectedly emotional. Something was wrong.

And then it struck him that the worst possible thing had happened. He had lost what he had always considered to be his fundamental right—to be able to turn away from somebody else's problem. But now, he could no longer ignore the fate of the Kugombwalans because—he struggled to admit it to himself—he cared about them.

NDOMBAZU

"Double-Oscar-Seven, this can be Zulu-Three."

Colonel MacEdwin Mfaume-Simbwa pressed the transmit button on his walkie-talkie. "Go ahead," he told the platoon commander.

"Building can be clean."

"All rooms checked for booby traps?"

"Yes, sir."

"Well done, Zulu-Three. Hold your location."

The colonel clipped the walkie-talkie onto his belt and armed his assault rifle. "Guards! Get into mobile formation," he ordered his personal protection squad who took up new positions around him as they advanced into the liberated battlefield.

He was almost oblivious to the corpses scattered along the empty street; for they were too fresh to stink, and he was now accustomed to such sights. But the many markers of death magnified his sense of being alive with a macabre boost of Darwinian euphoria—enhanced by the awareness his troops had conducted most of the killings.

Smoke still emanated from the Kugombwalan Ministry of Defence, where two child soldiers saluted as he approached the entrance. Inside was chaos: papers strewn everywhere, rubble from ricocheting bullets, and yet more corpses who included some of his own worphan warriors. *Too bad*, he mentally dismissed their sacrifice, as it was pointless to cry over spilled blood.

He knew the building from having served in the army under the former government, so he made straight for the minister's office. After entering, he desecrated the pictures of the previous incumbent, which elevated his ecstasy. Victory at last! He had conquered his enemies, thereby earning the right to assert dominion over Kugombwala's territory and people, albeit with his fellow commanders, for it had been necessary to side with a larger rebel group to seize power. Their leader would become president, while the colonel was promised a top government or army post, as well as the right to retain the rank he had conferred on himself when he had defected as a captain to command his own rebel force.

"Sir?" Zulu-Three spoke. "Journalist from BBC can be outside."

The colonel stamped on a large cockroach, annoyed at the interruption to his sweet moment of triumph. Yet he realised it heralded his new reality, for the obscurity of fighting a remote bush war was over; he and his fellow commanders would now be subjected to media attention, thereby opening another battlefront in the ongoing struggle to secure their supremacy.

"Ah, Cassandra, I recognise you from TV." He put on a gentle, disarming smile after exiting the building "I have always esteemed your intrepid and perspicacious reporting." Flattery for accomplishment rather than allurement was a sure way to win a woman over.

"Oh, thanks." His charm and impeccable English caught her off-guard, together with the charisma of raw, military power.

He interrupted her: "I'm sure you'll appreciate that I'm *frightfully* busy given the current circumstances, so perhaps we could meet later?"

"Er, yes, but I've just got a few quick questions for the news."

"Of course, let me start with a short word." He was in total control—as always. "Camera ready? Let's roll . . . Today marks the start of a new chapter for Kugombwala. We the people have ridden ourselves of the chains of totalitarian oppression and injustice, so we have placed the Kugombwalan Liberation Front at the helm of our nation to guide us into a bright new future of peace, democracy, free-market development, and respect for human rights. Tribalism will be abolished, and all citizens abroad are urged to return to rebuild our country—you will get your confiscated property back. Welcome home."

He paused to signify the end of the statement. "Great to meet you, Cassandra. Perhaps we could do dinner one evening?"

"Sure." She still looked bewildered. "But a few questions—"

"I'll be in contact. Do excuse me—urgent matters to attend to."

He did a sharp about-turn back into the building, laughing to himself over the nonsense he had sputtered. But the topic caused him to reflect. Winning the war was just the start; the challenge was now to keep a firm grip on power—which meant meeting his supporter's payback demands, such as granting contracts to their multinational corporations, mirroring their votes at the United Nations General Assembly, or conducting proxy wars in Kugombwala's neighbouring countries if they opposed his backers. That latter requirement would provide a win-win solution to the impending need to demobilise his delinquent child soldiers; they were too damaged to cope with normal civilian life without turning to crime, so it would be better to despatch them across the border to wreak havoc outside Kugombwala.

But the biggest difficulty would be to prevent uprisings or fair elections. The pretence of democracy would not fool the populace, many of whom belonged to a tribe that was hostile to him and his rebel colleagues. That group represented a potent threat to the Kugombwalan Liberation Front's hold on power. He would need to find a creative—or, should he say, *destructive*—solution to that problem.

BRICKDALE, BRITAIN

TWO WEEKS LATER

Ring-ring, ring-ring, ring-ring . . .

Alan rushed over to the hallway where he had installed the landline phone far from any chairs, in an attempt to control Mandy's calls. By not being able to get comfortable, he hoped she would spend less time on the blower.

"Hi, Al," said a recognisable voice. "It's Lorna."

"Lorna, hi! How's life?" He was pleased to hear from her again; a link to his time in Kugombwala had been reestablished.

"Quite fine, Al. I'm at the MedRelief London office, preparing to go back to Ndombazu next week."

"Wow, you're braver than me."

"Actually, the security situation has improved a lot, as the new rebel group in charge are well-disciplined and in full control of the city. They've disarmed all the militias, so you don't see any more guns on the street; and there is no longer risk of being kidnapped. The crime rate is reported to have dropped, and you don't get hassled by soldiers."

"Sounds too good to be true."

"I agree, but this is firsthand from Jules and Dave, who went over a few days ago. They have established a good contact with the new authorities, who want us back to help rebuild the health infrastructure."

"That's great to hear, Lorna. Thanks for letting me know—"

"Yes, but the update is not the reason why I'm calling. It's also to find out if you are available."

"Don't let my girlfriend hear you asking that!"

"I know you haven't put yourself down on the availability list, which is why MedRelief hasn't considered asking you. But I decided to give you a call, anyway, on the off-chance you might change your mind about never going back. I liked working with you, Al. You were one of the best log-admins I've worked with."

"Thanks."

"And the people here in the office were impressed by your quick thinking when you advanced the salaries to the staff at the Ndombazu base at the last minute."

"That wasn't what they said when I got back. I got a roasting when I handed in the accounts."

"Yes, but they've changed their minds now. With the exception of the vehicles that were requisitioned by the rebels, Jules and Dave found everything in perfect order at the base because the guards had continued to come to work and protected the place from looters throughout the time we were away. Everyone now realises that only happened because you acquired their loyalty with the salary advances."

"I don't know what possessed me to do that." Alan had forgotten about the incident. But it was one of the few times he had ever done anything for the benefit of others, while risking his career and reputation.

"So, what do you think? Can I entice you to join us out there? As you will be on your second mission, MedRelief will pay you five hundred pounds a month. It's not a lot, but better than nothing."

"I'll give it serious thought, Lorna. When would they want me to go?"

"I think it would be within the next two weeks. Shall I tell Isabella that I've spoken to you and that you are interested?"

"Aye, do that," he said, bewildered by the direction and evolution of their conversation.

"Might be a good idea if you called Isabella as well."

"Right, I will."

"Take care, Al. See you in Ndombazu!"

Alan smiled at her confidence as he put down the receiver. She knew him well, he thought, basking in the glow of being appreciated for the first time since his return to Britain.

Lorna's call gave him a lot to think about, spurred by a memory from his first weeks in Kugombwala, which now kept resurfacing:

It used to happen every morning. He and MacJohn would drive in a MedRelief Land Rover to the U.N. security meeting, guarded by the Indian army military escort. The long line of vehicles would hurtle through the streets of Ndombazu, drawing crowds of local kids to the spectacle, including many who were former patients at the MedRelief feeding centre. The children would raise their thumbs as he drove by and would shout in unison, "MedRelief—good! United Nations, go away!"

There was no doubt. Humanitarian aid was worthwhile, after all.

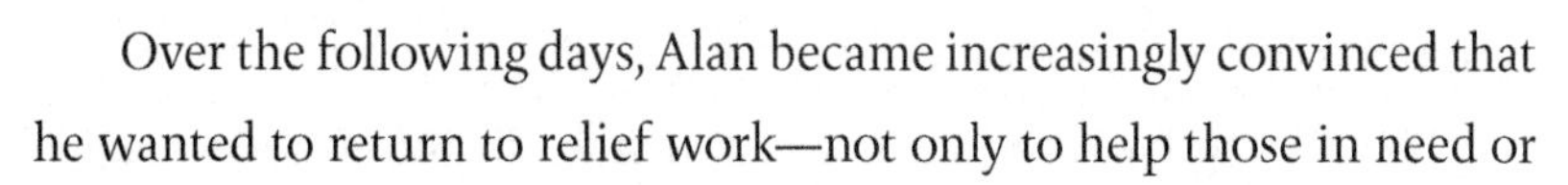

Over the following days, Alan became increasingly convinced that he wanted to return to relief work—not only to help those in need or to be with his local colleagues again. There was an extra reason.

He needed another dose of high-adrenaline adventure, which reminded him of the MedRelief expat team's frequent conversations about their fear of becoming disaster junkies. He now understood their concern, for he was craving another fix. Despite the hardships he had been through, his intense time in Kugombwala had been exotic, interesting, unpredictable, and exciting. Britain, by contrast, was boring.

Lorna had told him that Ndombazu was safe, yet he was aware the situation could change. It might become even more dangerous than his last trip, and unlike when he first went out, he was now familiar with the huge risks faced by aid workers in war zones of suffering serious physical harm or mental trauma.

Next, there was his career. His employers would not grant him another leave of absence, so going out again meant saying goodbye to his job. Whilst it would not be difficult to find alternative employment, he knew that the longer he stayed abroad doing humanitarian aid, the harder it would become to secure work in Britain.

Finally, there was Mandy. She would perceive a second stint in Kugombwala as a slap in the face. Could he get her to understand why he needed to go out again without it being seen as a personal insult? It would not be easy because of Mandy's inability—or unwillingness—to understand him.

He had previously regarded their personality differences to be complementary, but now they indicated mutual incompatibility. Though he loved her bubbly manner, her chat consisted of comment rather than conversation, contrasting with his need for a companion with whom he could share doubts and concerns. That required an intimacy beyond exchanging superficial opinions and compliments. Yet when he had opened up to her about his difficult experiences in Kugombwala, she had reacted like a frightened animal, whining that she didn't understand why he was "telling her about Africa again."

Alan recognised he had never made the conscious decision to choose Mandy to be his life partner. Their bonding had been a steady process fuelled by the prevailing propaganda of Hollywood and the music industry, which falsely promised everlasting love as the guaranteed reward for consummated romance. Starting with a kiss behind the bicycle shed at school when he was sixteen and she still fifteen, Mandy had soon succumbed to his intense pressure to partake in illicit afternoon trysts while her parents were out at work.

And so, their relationship had evolved over the ensuing years, until it had seemed natural that they would move in together. That development of their growing interdependence seemed set to continue, despite their diminishing feelings for one another—and would one day have spurred them to get married in the fake hope that it would be the magic formula to re-inject the lost zest into their partnership, followed by having kids as the next desperate attempt to live happily ever after. They would subsequently have found themselves chained together, unwilling to separate for fear of hurting their children.

Mandy might then have refused physical contact, to punish him for no longer being someone she loved. To satisfy an emotional emptiness, he might then have started an affair. Hating one another, they would then have bickered until death or divorce released them from the mutual torment of the irritations and unmet needs of their unhappy union. It was a tragic life pattern that Alan recognised in its various stages in many of the couples he knew—Mr. and Mrs. Carter, the next-door neighbours, and some of his friends.

Could he and Mandy continue together without a huge amount of hard work, self-sacrifice, and compromise? That might exclude a second trip to Kugombwala, he realised, feeling trapped by the dilemma of choosing between his own desires and those of his partner.

Yet he had to put his needs first, he decided, to stay true to himself. Self-honesty was surely a key foundation for a happy relationship.

"Aye," he said.

How was he going to tell her? How would she react?

"Good," he added.

Was this the right moment?

"Sure," he stated.

Why did it have to be so difficult? Alan dreaded the imminent confrontation that would immediately polarise them.

"I'm with you," he nodded.

"What do you mean?" Mandy's annoyed tone sharpened his senses.

"Er . . . just like you say."

"You're not listening, are you?"

"Yes, I was."

"Well, what was I talking about?"

"Er . . . about . . . er . . . " He racked his brain, desperate to find a word that his subconscious might have extracted from her monologue and deposited in his short-term memory. But it was empty, having blocked all incoming noise to focus his thoughts.

"You see, it's just like I say, you often ignore me." She sounded upset.

It was the wrong moment to break the news about returning to Kugombwala, as he was now bombarded by a diatribe about him not loving her, which doubled his desire to go.

Alan felt giddy as he boarded the intercontinental flight to Nairobi. Mandy's ice-cold reaction to the news that he was going back to Kugombwala clung to his mind.

"Well, I suppose you'd better just go then," she had said, leaving him even more uncertain about where they stood as a couple.

Memories flooded back to the previous time he had done this, some six months before. It was the same kind of plane, to the same destination, with the same passengers anticipating a safari adventure—but he had changed. He had been green then, taking a journey into the unknown, not knowing what he was doing. But this time was different, for he now understood what he would be facing. What kind of fool was he, knowingly propelling himself back into a potential war zone?

A few minutes later, the plane roared down the runway and then relinquished contact with the ground. He stared out of the window, watching the houses of west London shrink as the aircraft climbed into the clouds. *Bye-bye, Britain,* he thought, *will I ever see you again?* He felt a foreboding sense that things were not going to be easy in Kugombwala, which suffused him with sadness for stubbornly sticking with his decision to go.

He turned to the seat pocket in front of him to divert his attention from his own predicament. There was a glossy magazine, printed on thick, shiny paper with a variety of articles ranging from the benefits of timeshare flats on the Spanish Riviera to an appraisal of Etruscan art. These were interspersed with advertisements for luxury goods, but he glanced at them with only the vaguest interest in the projected lifestyles of the international jet set. It was all so false, promoting a self-centred existence in pursuit of ever-greater extremes of materialism and consumerism, while ignoring the suffering of the billions who lived in abject poverty.

"What would you like to drink, sir?" an attentative stewardess interrupted his thoughts. "Ice? And something with your meal?"

She brought his supper and came by regularly to inquire if there was anything else he needed, pampering him like a condemned prisoner granted his last wishes before an imminent execution.

Alan scanned the arrivals screen at Nairobi's main airport to identify the carousel that would deliver his sports bag.

"Please, you excuse me?" A voice behind caused him to turn around. It was a young Asian woman, he guessed from Singapore or South Korea. She continued, "I have message for you."

"You what?" Alan was taken aback.

"I was reading Bible while waiting for my suitcase when one verse stand out. God say to me it is for person here who is going to troubled place. Holy Spirit lead me to you."

Alan gasped. How could she have known that he—among the hundreds of passengers waiting for their bags—was destined for a war zone? Most of the other travellers had come for a wildlife or beach holiday or were returning from abroad. There was nothing from his looks or luggage to indicate he was not doing likewise.

"The text," she said while opening the book in her hand, "is from Joshua, chapter one, verse nine. It says, *'Do not be afraid; do not be discouraged, for the LORD your God will be with you wherever you go.'*"

"But I'm not religious . . . " Alan mumbled in bewilderment.

"Sorry if it is not for you." She did a deferential bow before backing away.

Alan stared as she disappeared into the crowd, while her words lingered in his mind. They perturbed him with the notion he had received a direct message from a supernatural Source, which challenged his ardent atheism. Did the God of the Bible really exist?

No, his rational scepticism countered. *That story about going to a troubled place is what they always say to make you believe them. It's just a coincidence that it could be true.*

Kahiga was waiting for him when he exited the terminal and took Alan to Nairobi's second airport, which was crowded with small private and commercial aircraft. After undergoing customs and passport formalities, they crossed the tarmac to a tiny, two-seater Cessna plane. It seemed flimsy and vulnerable compared to the huge Hercules transporter in which he had made the same flight some six months earlier.

"Goodbye, Alan." Kahiga shook his hand as they parted company. "Kugombwala is a troubled place, so may God protect you and be with you wherever you go."

Whoa, that's weird. Alan's eyes widened on recognising the same words he had received an hour earlier from a total stranger—and their potential implication. Were paranormal forces operating in his life? If so, was it a warning to avoid imminent danger? He was also moved by Kahiga's concern for his welfare that had prompted the blessing. Overcome by multiple emotions, he was unable to reply, managing only a slight smile before turning away to clamber onto the wing and into the cockpit. Kahiga was already walking away when he looked back to wave goodbye as the plane taxied onto the runway. He was now left alone to face the fate that awaited him.

The loud drone of the Cessna's engines prevented conversation, and Alan felt a strange detachment from the pilot sitting in front of him, his imagined ferryman taking him across the River Styx. He tried to forget his situation by studying the unfolding landscape below, only to see civilisation ebb away as the clusters of buildings, the thin ribbons of roads, and the farmlands became ever sparser, giving way to a grassy wilderness dotted with trees.

A relentless sun burned him through the Perspex window that had become hot to the touch. The sun was also scorching the ground below—a vast, waterless plain interrupted by occasional inselbergs cloaked with forest. It was a magnificent landscape, and yet there was a forbidding harshness to the immensity of it, a dry loneliness that welcomed nobody. A far cry from the soft, rolling, green hills of Yorkshire.

After crossing the savannah for an hour, he saw a range of mountains looming ahead in the distance, surrounded by mist and darkened by a blanket of black cloud. The plane continued towards the hills and then slammed into the wall of cloud above them, plunging itself into darkness as if night was falling. He peered down through the gloom. Through occasional gaps in the clouds, he caught sight of what looked like broccoli, which he realised to be the tops of rainforest trees. They were over Kugombwala now.

The clouds became ever thicker. Lightning arced between them, illuminating in bursts the enfolding fog and filling the cabin with blinding light. Deafening thunderclaps followed, penetrating his earmuffs—a celestial reception into a war zone.

The aircraft was suddenly tossed downwards by turbulence, creating a negative gravitational force in his stomach, then hurled upwards, briefly paralysing him as his body was rammed into the seat. Would the plane withstand the violent onslaught? He craved reassurance from the motionless pilot—his ferryman—sitting in front of him, but his seat straps and the headphones covering the man's ears made communication impossible. The thought crossed Alan's mind that he wasn't meant to get to Kugombwala—that cosmic forces were trying to stop him by casting him down upon that ocean of trees, where the aircraft would be swallowed up by the vast forest, so that his body would never be found. He thought of his parents, of all they had done for him—their great hopes for him and his future that would be dashed by the news that he was last seen getting into a plane that took off for Kugombwala and then disappeared without a trace.

The aeroplane came to a halt at the end of the runway. The engine was switched off, and the propellers slowed to silence while Alan sat numbed in his seat for what seemed an age. Had he really made it through the storm, or was it an illusion of the afterlife? The pilot turned towards him, and he expected to see a skeleton in a hooded cloak but was relieved to see a normal human face.

"Hey, you okay?" asked the pilot in a strong South African accent. "Ag, man, thet was sure some storm. Didn't think we were going to make it through thet one."

The voice and the face looking at him seemed real enough, and yet Alan could not dispel the thought that he had crossed over to the underworld and had now reached the land of the dead.

CHAPTER 7

"Passport!"

Alan required a moment to orientate himself. He was still sitting in the plane, half-dazed from the flight. A soldier had marched up to the aircraft, dressed in crisp combat fatigues, shiny sunglasses, and bright red wellington boots. Alan was reminded of the footwear of the search-and-destroy squad he and Dave had seen just before their evacuation from Ndombazu.

"Show me passport!" the soldier barked again, tapping on the window.

Alan opened the hatch and proffered the document, which was snatched from his hand. The soldier studied it, grunted, returned it, and walked off. Alan frowned, remembering how polite the Indian and Pakistani peacekeepers had been when they had run the airport. Back then, he had travelled freely in and out of Kugombwala without ever having to show any papers. But the U.N. troops had long gone and with them, his VIP status.

To his horror, Alan then noticed he was not in Ndombazu International Airport. They had landed somewhere else and were now on a dirt runway in a cleared strip of bush, empty but for a pile of fuel drums and a tin shack. He was about to panic over having arrived in the wrong war zone when he saw a car with a MedRelief flag parked beyond the shed.

He exited the plane and approached the vehicle, concerned it was not a standard MedRelief Land Rover but a beat-up banger with a few MedRelief stickers clumsily attached to the spaces between the bullet holes. Neither did he recognise the driver, standing beside the car. Was he still alive? Or was this a post-death dream experience, where things appeared normal and yet everything had changed?

He had only reached halfway to the car when a voice called him over from the shack.

"White man, where you can go?" It was the same rude soldier who had accosted him earlier.

"I'm going to meet my driver."

"First pass here; do immigration."

He entered the shack. It was stifling hot, for the sun's heat was soaked into the corrugated sheeting and radiated inwards. There was no furniture, apart from a beer-crate stool and an oil drum that served as a table.

"Give me passport one more time," the soldier ordered. "Where from?" he then demanded, flicking through the pages.

"Britain."

"Name?"

"Alan Swales."

"Date and place of birth?"

Alan supplied the necessary details.

"Where visa?"

"No visa." They had never required a visa before. That had not been necessary when there was no need to show your passport to get into the country.

"You give me one hundred dollars."

"A hundred dollars?" Alan exclaimed. "I'm not paying that!"

"Pay visa fee, or I can arrest you for illegal entry."

Alan had no choice. He pulled out a hundred-dollar bill from his money belt. The soldier shoved it into his pocket and leafed through his passport in search of a clean page. He then tipped the fuel barrel and pulled out an inkpad and rubber stamp from underneath it, demonstrating that the drum doubled as both desk and filing cabinet. The soldier rammed the rubber stamp down hard onto the inkpad before bashing it onto a page in the passport. He then tried to write a few words but failed to get the ink to flow from his pen, even with a lick of spit.

"Give me pen." He pointed to a biro protruding from Alan's shirt pocket.

Alan handed it to the soldier, who wrote the date above the stamp, and then returned the passport, while slipping the pen into his curly hair. *You thief,* Alan thought, but decided against pursuing the matter, as it was unwise to confront an armed soldier over such an insignificant item. He took some consolation in the words on the stamp in his passport: *Ndonbazu Arport*. That meant he must be in the right place, even if the new guys could not spell and the surroundings appeared to have undergone a radical transformation.

"Can I have a receipt?" MedRelief would refuse to reimburse him unless he had one. He suspected the rule to be motivated by Blair-Campbell's push to save money—get the staff to pay their own expenses.

"Wait! It can be coming."

With obvious irritation, the soldier reached up and retrieved a small booklet that had been squeezed between a rafter and the corrugated iron roof. Alan was surprised to see a printed receipt ledger bearing a new coat of arms for Kugombwala. To his further amazement, the soldier wrote out a receipt for the full one hundred dollars, went to the doorway, and called out in the local language. Another soldier appeared and, without a word, countersigned the receipt. The first soldier then tore off a carbon copy and handed it to Alan.

"You here before," the second soldier said.

Was it a question or a statement?

"Yes." Alan felt an unexplained unease that the soldier might already know the answer. There was no evidence in his passport to indicate his previous stay in Kugombwala.

"At the hospital?"

"Yes."

"Logistics and admin manager?"

"Yes." How did he know so much?

"At the time of AfriBat?"

"Yes."

"Okay, you can go."

Alan was relieved to leave the heat of the shack. He was drenched with sweat, both from the heat and from the tension of the minor interrogation.

"Alan Swales," a voice called out from behind him.

Oh no, he thought, *what now?*

"Your pen. You forgot your pen."

Alan studied the passing landscape as they drove towards Ndombazu, hoping to recognise familiar landmarks. He wanted further confirmation that he was in Kugombwala and, therefore, still alive.

"Old airport can be spoiled." MacCharlie, the new driver, seemed to read his thoughts. "Bad fighting. Runway broken."

So, that was the reason for landing at the bush airstrip.

"Kugombwala Liberation Front win big battle," MacCharlie continued. "Bakiboko people can be in charge. This country very different now."

"Is it any better?"

"Yes, war finish. No more fighting. No more looting."

Alan relaxed at the prospect of peace and security. That promised a new and better experience in Kugombwala.

Was this Ndombazu? Alan's concern was rekindled on entering the outskirts of the city. It seemed a different place and from another time. He had the eerie feeling of being in an old monochrome film as he viewed the streets from the moving car, for the battles of the previous weeks had drained all colour from the urban landscape that was scorched black by fire and dusted white with ash. A perceptible reek of smoke hung in the air.

Ndombazu had taken a heavy pounding since his departure a month earlier. The previously regular shapes and smooth surfaces of the downtown areas were now disfigured by multiple orders of shell and shrapnel damage, as if the buildings had been subjected to a complex mathematical equation that converted straight lines and flat planes into rough, fractal forms. Twisted strands of steel reinforcement rods sprouted from dead buildings, while concrete rubble covered the streets like mould. Burned-out cars lined the roads; and the gaping wounds of missing roofs, windows, and doors heightened the sense of empty destruction. Nothing stirred among the ruins, save for a few stray dogs and the great birds that launched into the air as the vehicle passed by.

"Where is everyone?" he asked MacCharlie.

"Inside. Away from main roads. People can still be afraid."

So much for peace and security. Alan frowned. It looked worse than before.

They drove on in silence, taking a route he did not know. After a while, the road merged into known territory, and he started to recognise familiar, yet altered landmarks, corrupted by wanton looting and war damage. Towards the hospital, the driver unexpectedly turned into a side street before stopping in front of a large, metal gate.

"New office," MacCharlie told him. "Old place spoiled. Too many bombs."

An ugly, concrete blockhouse loomed ahead, appearing to offer little possibility of becoming a home. It looked even more like a prison than the previous MedRelief base, but a few honks on the horn caused the gates to open, revealing familiar faces that triggered fond memories.

"Alan! Welcome!" The guards cheered and raised their thumbs on recognising him in the car. They and the waiting drivers ran up to the Land Rover, immersing him in a rousing reunion. It finally felt right to have come back.

"Oh, no, not you again."

"Yes, Paula, I've returned to annoy you." He had to accept that conflict was inevitable in Kugombwala, even though the war was over. Working with his old colleagues meant the same personal challenges as before but also provided comforting continuity in a city that had suffered so much change.

Yet there were signs of hope. The security situation in Ndombazu had improved for aid workers, as the new soldiers no longer demanded "presents" at the checkpoints. Instead, they avoided all communication with foreigners; even eye contact was impossible as they wore reflective shades. After stopping a vehicle, they would motion the driver to open the rear doors, so they could check the vehicle's contents. The cars would be thoroughly examined, but nothing was ever taken. They were always in groups of three, and Alan never recognised the same face twice, not even after repeated visits to the same checkpoint.

There were other welcome changes. Corpses no longer littered the streets and weapons were only observed with the soldiers. Though occasional gunfire could still be heard, especially at night.

"Criminals," MacJohn told Alan. "Too many now."

"Doing armed robberies?"

"Yes. But also killing for revenge and to remove rivals. Kugombwalans can be very bad people."

"Why is that?" Alan was surprised that the end of war would lead to rampant murder, rather than reconciliation and goodwill.

"It is the devil and his demons; they can trick people to do evil things." MacJohn often refered to his religious beliefs. Like many of his compatriots, he assigned a supernatural cause to all events to introduce certainty into their chaotic lives. "Satan wants to destroy us, but Jesus will conquer him in the end. That is why we must be on God's side."

"I'm staying out of that conflict as I'm a neutral humanitarian," Alan joked to deflect attention from his atheism. It was one of MacJohn's favourite discussion topics.

"That cannot be possible, Alan. You are either with or against."

"Is that how it is between you and the new government?" He tried to change the subject. "Are you supporting them or fighting them?"

"They are bandits!" MacJohn spat. "But I cannot counter them, so I must back them. It is the same for everyone here."

"What about MacGarry?" The driver and several of the logistics staff had not returned to their former workplace despite the end of the war. "Is he away because of the Liberation Front?"

"Yes, he is a Watumbwa."

"What's that?"

"The people of the former president."

African tribal rivalry, Alan told himself. Together with corruption, it was often cited by Western media as the cause of the continent's problems.

"So, where is MacGarry now?"

"Far away. With his own people on the plateau. The Liberation Front chased them out of the city during the war."

Alan felt for the Kugombwalans. Life was difficult when neutrality was not an option.

An impression of normality soon returned to the city. Shops reopened, and the inhabitants emerged back into the streets and markets. Rubble was cleared and small repairs made to buildings. Foreign embassies re-opened. The nighttime curfew was lifted, and it was deemed safe to drive around downtown Ndombazu after dark.

"I've just been to a productive meeting with the Liberation Front leadership," Jules enthused at supper one evening. "The new British ambassador introduced me to the president, General MacVictor Bakigoma, who led the forces that took this city. He was really welcoming and approachable and wants aid agencies and the churches to lead the rebuilding and running of the country."

"In other words, we pay for providing essential services to the people," Paula scoffed, "so that the president and his cronies can keep the income from taxes and bilateral aid, which they can then stash in their private Swiss bank accounts or buy property in London and Paris."

"Stop being so sceptical, Paula." Jules sighed with obvious exasperation. "Look, I've met General Bakigoma, while you haven't. I know what he's like. He's courteous and humble, not a paranoid, power-hungry despot. He goes about unarmed, without bodyguards. He talked openly about his desire for peace and stability—"

"That's what all dictators say. But it's the usual doublespeak for wanting to remain in charge without being challenged. I bet he promised free and fair elections?"

"As a matter of fact, he did."

"There you go. Another lying politician duping the international community by saying what they want to hear."

"Paula." Jules spoke in a reprimanding tone. "You're being cynical because you enjoy scorning everyone. You always put people down because you don't like anyone to succeed."

Alan smiled in mental agreement. He was enjoying the confrontation between his two least favourite team members.

Jules continued, "You should be grateful that General Bakigoma and his soldiers have ended a nasty civil war and put this country on the right course to democracy and development. Shame on you, Paula, for thinking otherwise. The new government needs support, not criticism."

Jules' backing for the "Conqueror of Kugombwala," as he was also known, was outmatched by the local staff. They praised their military messiah, which seemed to be the only topic that could wake them out of the torpor that had set in after the war. Even MacHenry, the hospital administrator, usually careful to avoid an opinion, had become an open supporter.

"I will soon be working for the Liberation Front," he told Alan. "They had a big meeting at the stadium yesterday. General Bakigoma promised us all jobs. You white people can go home now—we don't need you anymore. Give us your money, and we will do the job ourselves," he sneered in a tone that repeated what he had heard at the meeting.

With MacObadiah, the cook, it was a similar sentiment. "Alan?" he chirped in his squeaky voice, beckoning him over as he passed by the kitchen. "Please, I can tell you something small. The problems for Kugombwala can now be finished. The big general—he go make Kugombwala into great nation. Oh, he very good man. And strong, so much strong."

While Alan was making one of his regular inspection rounds at the hospital, he chanced upon the construction crew singing a Liberation Front song while digging a trench. It seemed like a contagious fever had infected everyone with the need to publicly demonstrate their pious loyalty towards the new regime.

It was no surprise when the posters appeared. Spreading faster than a cholera epidemic, the photocopied sheets depicting a crude portrait of the new leader mushroomed throughout the city and into the MedRelief compound. In a flash, the icons to foster idol worship were everywhere. Multiple copies appeared in the corridors and wards of the hospital, on the trees, and even in MacHenry's office, which caused Alan to suspect him as one source of the poster production and accounted for the increased consumption of toner by the photocopier.

The portraits revealed little about the appearance of General Bakigoma, beyond that he was an African with a beard, who wore reflective sunglasses and a Che Guevara-style military beret. More was revealed a few days later, during a visit to the new Kugombwalan government's NGO liaison office. This was located in a former ministry building close to the old parliament in a neighbourhood of crumbling colonial edifices that had once been surrounded by elegant avenues and manicured gardens.

"How come we've never been here before?" Alan asked MacNed.

"Old Watumbwa area. Not safe at time of United Nations. Too much shooting."

"And when AfriBat was here?"

"They can keep everybody away—to do private looting."

Times had changed, and the new Kugombwalan regime was asserting its authority by reoccupying the old government buildings. Signs of activity were everywhere, with orderly Bakiboko troops positioned outside the offices, while gangs of workmen went about removing debris and making repairs.

They drove along the grand independence avenue that led up to the parliament building, past the bases of the vandalised statues of the territory's former colonial governors. The monuments were arranged in chronological order, their dates and names still visible on the stone plinths, although little else remained. Half a leg here, a foot there, while one statue had somehow maintained its torso. Alan noted the years as they went by, recording the tenure of each governor: 1886-1903, 1903-1911, 1911-1914 . . . The series continued into the 1960s, followed by three brand new bases, made of concrete rather than stone. Simple gravestone-shaped slabs topped the first two; both displayed a real bullet embedded into the cement.

MacNed chuckled. "MacZechariah Tengulu and MacDavid Oliohu, our late presidents. And this one," he continued, "can be our new leader."

There was a complete statue on the third and furthest base, roughly carved from wood, depicting a large and well-built man in combat fatigues with beard, sunglasses, and military beret. The figure reminded Alan of the heroic socialist sculptures that had adorned East Europe during the recent communist era.

"General MacVictor Bakigoma, third president of Kugombwala." MacNed beamed. "He can be a too much great man."

Outside the parliament building, a group of labourers were cutting the grass, swinging a local version of a scythe shaped like a golf club. It was comforting to see the new leadership of the country was serious about its responsibilities, even to the minute detail of keeping the lawns kempt. The fresh pride in the appearance of the capital city might have seemed vain for such a poor country, but it was a welcome development from the utter disrespect that had been shown earlier, when everything had been dismantled, damaged, or destroyed. And the desire to establish continuity with the past in the form of new statues could be interpreted as a sign of hope for a stable future.

It was now sufficiently safe for the MedRelief team to explore the city's downtown nightspots, yet it was soon apparent that this was not unchartered territory, for most of the drinking holes and dance venues were already known to Dave. Wherever they went, they encountered women who giggled coquettish greetings to "Dev" with a knowing look that something had once passed between them.

"Hey, MacUlla," he hailed a former flame. "What happened? I thought you had left with one of the AfriBat officers."

"No, he cannot want me to be his wife." She looked down, reminded of the rejection.

"So, what are you doing now?"

"I can work at a new club. Bongobazu. It is for the Bakiboko soldiers."

"Sounds interesting. I should check it out."

"Yes, you will like it; there can be so many girls. But be careful," she added. "It can be dangerous."

"There's a new joint in town," Dave announced the following Friday. "Rumoured to be the hottest club in Ndombazu with loads of talent. Anyone coming with me tonight?"

"Count me in, mate," Alan answered.

"Me, too," Megan added.

"I can't, as I'm having dinner with some U.N. people." Jules often went alone to exclusive get-togethers with other senior expats, to which the rest of the MedRelief team were never invited.

"Thanks, Dave, I'll give it a miss, as I've got paperwork to catch up on." Lorna presented her usual excuse to hide her dislike of nightclubs.

"Can't wait." Megan could hardly contain herself. "I haven't partied in ages."

"Not since last weekend," Paula sneered, before moaning about being on night duty. Meanwhile, Keith muttered something incomprehensible that no one tried to understand.

The MedRelief party crew set off that evening with one of the drivers who doubled as guard for the vehicle while they were at the club. Although they only knew of Bongobazu's rough location, it did not prove difficult to find, in spite of being situated down a series of side streets. On reaching the area, they were guided by the loud thump-thump of deep bass notes emanating from a serious amplification system.

"Oh, wow, that's tidy," Megan exclaimed as they arrived at a building from which a kaleidoscope of flashing lights emanated. "It's a former church!"

Dave laughed. "That would give Bongobazu at least three stars in a tourist guide to Ndombazu." He then became serious as they stepped out of the car. "Three rules, folks: don't leave without telling me; don't get into a fight; and if you do, don't expect me to help you out."

They walked through the big, open church doors and into a packed congregation of revellers. Bongobazu was right up Dave's street. Half the clientele were vicious, surly-looking fighters who reacted positively to his large, mercenary-soldier-like presence. The other half of the clientele, who were probably employees rather than guests, consisted of stunning girls of a quality that exceeded the catwalks of the best fashion houses in the West. They warmed to Dave's admiring glances and quirky jokes. Within seconds of entering, he immersed himself in a sea of ready admirers, slapping the men's backs and embracing the girls.

Left to themselves, Alan and Megan located some empty seats and were soon joined by opportunists looking for free beers and a passport out of Kugombwala. Megan was surrounded by four confident youths who attempted to chat her up with imitation American ghetto slang, while Alan was accosted by three competing dusky beauties. They passed the evening teasing one another: the girls fighting to achieve an ever-greater intimacy, while Alan struggled to hold them off, thoroughly enjoying himself. It was a bizarre situation, he acknowledged. He had expected Ndombazu to be a war zone, yet instead found himself in the middle of one of the world's hottest flesh markets, like a sultan in his harem. That thought, combined with the vibrant beat of Kugombwalan music and the stroboscopic lights, made him giddy with pleasure. A broad grin broke out across his face as he scanned the room for further talent.

His eyes were drawn to the revolving glitter ball that scattered beams of projected, coloured light. The silvered sphere hung in front of a photo of the new president in the church apse, where there would once have been a crucifix. Beneath, like a priest at the altar, the disc jockey tended the music console, dressed entirely in black leather with wrap-around shades and an immense amount of gold jewellery. Alan laughed at this parody of a church service—the glitter ball was like an idol dedicated to sensual pleasure, he mused. How ironic it would be for religious people like Lorna to see this, a once-holy church now reverberating to the beat of a hundred dancing whores.

Just then, an inexplicable unease came over him, an impression that arose from nowhere, meaning something was not right. Baffled, he was forced to the logical conclusion that it indicated something was wrong. But it didn't make sense. He wasn't doing anything bad. He was not stealing anything, nor was he harming anyone. So why this sudden, intense feeling? His failure to find an answer could not dispel the negative sensation.

Maybe the problem was him, perhaps, because he could not see what was amiss. But that line of thought posed an even more difficult question: who defined right and wrong? He did not know. His mother had tried to teach him that it was wrong to hurt anyone, but he did not always agree with her simplistic moral views. They did not apply to the fans of rival football clubs whom he and Bobsy beat up after the Saturday matches; it was commonly understood they were asking for a kicking because they supported incompetent teams. He and Bobsy were surely doing society a favour by punishing such idiots.

He tried another approach by thinking back to earlier times in his life when he had felt guilty for wrongdoing. He recalled an incident when he had been caught shoplifting as a teenager. But on reflection, he realised that it had not been guilt, but fear, that had predominated. He had been scared of the punishment and public shaming that he was due, rather than feeling any remorse for nicking the cigarettes. After all, he had not stolen from anyone, only from a supermarket chain, which in any case was making so much profit that they would not notice a missing item. Besides, they would recover the loss through insurance or claim it against tax.

It was many years before Alan realised shoplifting was wrong because it went against the common good, but he had not felt any remorse for doing it. So, why was he now feeling a strong sense of wrong here in Bongobazu? He had been in many nightclubs and had never experienced that sensation in any of the others.

His survival instinct told him he had to get out, so he went to tell Dave that he was going.

"Leaving already, Al? We've only just arrived!"

"Aye, but all of a sudden, I'm not feeling good. Might be a bout of malaria coming on."

"Okay, see you later."

Released, Alan emerged from the crazed crowd and into the cool, still air outside the nightclub. The nasty feeling immediately evaporated, which perplexed him even more as to what it was about.

That sense of something being wrong returned to Alan a few days later.

MedRelief had started some projects in a large makeshift camp called Mulabo, located beside an army garrison a short distance beyond the outskirts of Ndombazu. The camp residents had been displaced from their homes by fighting in the interior of Kugombwala and were now shrivelled by hunger and debilitated by disease.

Jules and Lorna decided to set up a primary healthcare and nutrition programme to assist them. Alan was tasked with establishing a programme for water and sanitation—*watsan* in aid worker lingo—which meant constructing latrines and providing clean, running water.

The way to the camp was through a populated area of the city, crowded with small, cinder-block shacks separated by rubbish-filled lanes. A main road cut through the mess, but being the only open area in the neighbourhood, it had become stifled by market stalls that encroached onto the highway. Thousands of people milled about, constricting the road so that vehicles were restricted to a walking pace, to the advantage of the street hawkers who could then hassle the occupants of the passing cars to buy their wares. It was a vibrant place, full of the energy and vitality of African commerce; but despite this, Alan always felt uneasy being hemmed in and effectively trapped in the midst of a large crowd, for he could not forget the lynch mob he had seen tearing a thief to pieces. *Best to avoid the masses,* he thought, recalling the gang-thuggery of his fellow football fans in Britain.

One day, the mood of the crowd was noticeably different. There was tension in the air. Or was it excitement? Alan's heart started to thump, as the usual banter of market bartering was gradually drowned by shrieks and cheers. And then singing. A mighty chorus rose up as the whole community joined to sing the Liberation Front song, praising General MacVictor Bakigoma. A river of people flowed into the throng, leaping and dancing with joy. Young men bearing banners with revolutionary slogans and portraits of their great leader passed about them, carrying the bystanders along. All road traffic ground to a halt, and it felt like an army of ants was overrunning them.

"What's going on?" Alan asked MacCharlie.

"New recruits. For the Liberation Front."

"But I thought the war was over."

"It can be new start," the driver declared, reinforcing Alan's sense of unease.

"Lots of new names on the payroll," Alan remarked to Lorna as they checked through the monthly salary sheet.

"Yes, we have taken on additional staff for the clinic, feeding centre, and watsan team at Mulabo."

"I know, but I meant at the hospital."

"That's because a third of them have still not shown up since we got back, so we had to take on replacements."

"A third? That's a lot. Were many killed during the fighting?"

"No, I don't think so. From what I've heard, a few were, but I think most of the missing staff fled the city and are staying away."

"How come they haven't come back?" Alan was reminded of McGarry's ongoing absence. "The war's over in this part of the country. You'd think it would be safe now to return."

"Yes, strange, isn't it?" Lorna looked puzzled.

"Do you know what happened in Ndombazu while we were away?"

"I don't. No one at the hospital wants to talk about it."

"Same with the drivers and the logistics team. Silence all around." Alan frowned. "Why don't they trust us enough to tell us? Seems like they are scared of something."

Rattle, rattle, rattle.

Dave shook the iron gate to attract the attention of the occupants.

"Yes?" A young man peeped over the top. He seemed suspicious—and annoyed.

"Hey, Boss Man. I'm from MedRelief, and we're looking for a house to rent."

"Go away!"

After hurrying out of earshot, Alan commented, "Our neighbours are far from friendly!" It had been the fifth rude rejection of their attempt to find a better place for a base.

"That's because the guys we spoke to are soldiers in civilian clothes." Dave raised an eyebrow. "They've been billeted in the houses around us. We're living in the middle of a military garrison."

Slap!

Alan lifted his hand to reveal a satisfying splodge of blood, mixed with flattened mosquito. It had been in the process of feeding off his forearm.

There were predators everywhere in Kugombwala, he realised, noticing a gecko on the ceiling above him. They were not always easy to spot, merging into the background as they lay in wait to gobble up passing insects.

Alan's attention was wandering while listening to Keith, who was droning on about the drivers and the damage they did to the vehicles. The topic bored him, though he felt obliged to offer an occasional grunt of agreement during an otherwise one-sided conversation. That courtesy would prevent Keith noticing that Alan's mind was now focussed elsewhere.

On the wall behind Keith's head, another gecko had spied a fly. With great patience, it remained completely still, watching, waiting to make a move.

The fly twitched, unaware of the big, beady eyes staring at it.

The gecko gained a few centimetres on the fly while it looked the other way.

"Can I ask you something, Al?" Megan interrupted his thoughts. Keith had finished his diatribe against the drivers and had got up to go, leaving the two of them alone at the dining table. She must have been waiting for this moment.

"Best not to ask, Megan. You might be disappointed by the answer."

She laughed. "Oh, you are funny. I love it when you tease me."

He braced himself for the coming question, whatever it might be.

"Your girlfriend has left you, hasn't she?" The gecko made another sprint towards the fly.

"That's news to me, Megan. Where did you get that idea from?"

"You haven't received a card from her since you got back."

Alan's pulse quickened. First, from the reminder of an issue that had been subconsciously troubling him. Second, with the realisation that Megan was watching his every move, waiting to pounce at the right moment.

"She's not so good at writing." He fumbled for something to say, for it was true he had not heard from Mandy since his return.

"Yes, but she used to send you those cards every week." Megan grinned. "The ones with the silly teddy bears on them—ah, you're blushing! See, I can tease you, too . . . "

Alan had disliked the sentimental images with the accompanying inane pre-printed poetry, but now that he was receiving nothing from Mandy, he longed to receive those soppy cards again. They had been tangible proof that he was not ignored or forgotten. "They're not my style, Megan," he said, trying to sound unconcerned. "So, my girlfriend has agreed not to send them anymore. Anyway, I've got to go; the logistics team are waiting for me."

He quickly stood up, causing the fly to buzz off, leaving a disappointed gecko behind. But it continued to watch, still waiting for the next opportunity.

It's weird that Mandy hasn't written. The thought plagued Alan's mind as he stared at the passing streets on the way back from the weekly aid agency coordination meeting. There were always new sights to observe in the fast-changing city: fresh-painted billboards pronouncing the achievements of the Kugombwalan Liberation Front, a group of street urchins gathering litter under the watchful eye of a policeman, and a procession of prisoners in pink outfits accompanied by red-booted soldiers. *Good on the government for restoring law and order.* Alan smiled at the signs of social progress. *It's high time for justice to be done.*

A hunch then hit him. *Maybe Mandy is not writing in order to punish me.* This thought led to a question he could not answer: how long might that sentence of silence last?

Dave interrupted his ponderings. "What do you think of the new U.N. guy who did most of the talking this morning?"

"Definitely out of place in Kugombwala; he should be wearing a pith helmet instead of a United Nations baseball cap."

Born fifty years too late, Nelson Merriweather had missed out on the bygone era of the British Empire. The winds of change that had blown across Africa had thus pushed him to the U.N. as the natural successor of the Colonial Service, where he could practice the benign paternalism that he perceived to be his calling.

"What's his job here?" Alan struggled to map the roles of the many new faces who had arrived in Kugombwala following the end of the war.

"He's the protection officer for IDPs—Internally Displaced Persons—those people from the interior who are in the camps around the city."

"And what does that entail?"

"He's supposed to represent their interests. But don't expect a lot from him." Dave flicked a cigarette butt out of the window. "He's a typical bureaucrat, which means he's got his position because he is loyal and ineffective and, therefore, won't threaten anyone higher up the hierarchy."

"I thought those no-hopers were sent here because no one else wants to be in Kugombwala?"

"Nah, there are plenty of ambitious careerists clamouring for lucrative roles in lousy places like this. Not only because of the hardship allowances but also as a stepping stone to a plum position in one of the U.N. headquarters. They're all hungry for the huge salaries, pensions, and other benefits paid out from the bounteous U.N. cake to its permanent staff."

That cake was less generously apportioned to those who were supposed to be the reason for the U.N.'s presence. Although they were labelled as beneficiaries, the displaced people were lucky if they received a few crumbs from the United Nations' banqueting table, for the U.N. in Ndombazu was in the process of scaling back its outputs.

"Our donor governments," Merriweather explained at the next meeting in a tone that demonstrated his full support for the infallible wisdom of his superiors, "have decided to cut back the funding for the General Food Distribution, in order to encourage the IDPs to develop their own resilience mechanisms. We are not helping them by giving them food handouts. Instead, we are fostering a false—and unsustainable—reliance on our assistance, which is ultimately harmful to them. These people must learn to fend for themselves."

An aid agency representative spoke up. "How can the people in the displaced camps survive without help? They've got no farmland of their own."

"Yeah," another agreed. "Even if they do venture beyond the confines of the camps, they risk stepping on landmines or running into rebels, wild animals, or whatever else is lurking in the surrounding forest."

A liaison officer for the Kugombwalan government stared the other NGO representatives into silence. "It is not a problem," he declared. "They can go into the city to hustle for work."

No one dared point out that the displaced people risked being robbed, raped, assaulted, or even killed at the Bakiboko checkpoints.

"Of course," Merriweather continued his message, "these things need to be done gradually to give the people time to adjust. Until now, they have been receiving a daily food ration of twenty-one hundred kilocalories, but we will stepwise reduce this as an incentive for them to find alternative sources of sustenance. Removing the obstructions to self-help will get them off the vicious circle of dependence."

I hope they remember to thank you, Alan was just about to say, when the sound of drumming started, as heavy droplets of rain hit the corrugated-iron roof above them—a high frequency staccato that momentarily stilled their conversation. Alan's thoughts turned to those IDPs who would now be getting soaked, as the rain bucketed onto them through the meagre resistance of their hovels. The U.N.'s response to their afflictions was to identify them as the root cause of their own troubles.

It was tough being at the bottom of the world heap, abandoned to die a slow death from semi-starvation or boredom in camps that had become dustbins for unwanted humanity.

Alan was grateful for his heavy boots, as they squelched through the thick, dubious mire of muddy Mulabo camp. The sanitary conditions were appalling, giving off a permanent stink of excrement and rot. It was a crowded place, into which the Bakiboko military had herded thousands of frightened civilians. Here, they could be more easily controlled, to minimise the potential threat they posed as a resource base for rival rebel groups. The poorest of the poor were ready recruits for a rebel movement—a supply of unemployed young men to become fighters, a bastion of unprotected women to provide sexual relief and cooking for rebel soldiers, and a multitude of children who could be coaxed into being gun-bearers and porters. Even the meagre amounts of food circulating in the camps could be taxed or stolen to feed a rebel army.

"How do you know your way around here?" he asked MacBill, who was one of the MedRelief extension workers. Their job was to go into the community to inform them about health and hygiene. It was a wonder he could find his way around the maze of almost identical shacks.

"Small-small problem, Alan, I can be coming here every day."

Alan was grateful to be with MacBill; he would not have felt safe wandering alone in an overcrowded camp filled with desperate people who only spoke their own Watumbwa language. So, he was surprised to spot a fellow foreigner deep in the bowels of the unhappy camp. She was turned away from him, but her long, straight hair and crisp, clean clothes made her stand out from the crowd. What was she doing there?

Then he saw the camera. A photojournalist. She was crouched outside one of the shelters, forcing her telephoto lens into the faces of a dispossessed family who were sitting inside. The usual retinue of Kugombwalan kids were standing around, watching the latest bizarre antics of the mysterious white race.

"Hey, this is awesome; these people are just so photogenic," the woman cooed, having somehow noticed his presence as he came closer. "I'm getting some great shots here. Their sufferin' is written right over their faces. It'll look great in black and white, hey." A snap-clunk sound announced the opening of the camera shutter and the movement of the internal mirror. She looked up at him. "Hey, I'm Rosalie Desjardins, freelance photographer. Which agency are you working for?"

"MedRelief. We are a British NGO. Are you American?"

Her eyes flashed daggers at him. "No, absolutely not," she retorted. "And I'm not Canadian either, in case that was your next guess. I'm Québécoise. Anyway, pleased to meet you." Snap-clunk. A passing old woman carrying a bucket of water on her head had been captured for posterity. "So, what is your agency doing round here? Feeding centres? Clinics?"

"Both."

"Mind if I take a peek?" Snap-clunk: a child with a football made from discarded plastic bags tied into a bundle.

"You'd better ask the medic in charge. My colleagues can be uptight about visitors treating the patients as disaster exhibits. Especially the nurse called Paula."

"Hey, easy man, no problem. I've done loads of health centres; I know the game." Snap-clunk: a boy with a snotty nose. "Besides," she added with a grin, "we're gonna make a deal: I get to take some pics, while your logo gets into the press. Crucial for fundraising, hey?"

Alan acknowledged she was right. Jules was forever going on about the need for MedRelief to be more visible and attract additional donor funds.

"Oh, hey, what amazing dignity." Snap-clunk: an old man with a wrinkled, prune-like face, wearing a frayed yachting blazer and little else.

Dignity. It was a word Alan often heard among the aid workers in Kugombwala. He remembered one of the coordination meetings where an overpaid U.N. bureaucrat had spoken about the need to protect the dignity of the victims of war. Yet another aid cliché.

"What's all this dignity business?" he asked Desjardins. "People keep going on about it, the dignity of the victims and all that. I can't see anything positive about suffering."

"Hard to explain. I guess it's kinda when these folks do their best to not show their misery, while trying to overcome the terrible situation they are in. To demonstrate they still have self-respect." Snap-clunk: a greeting from a crippled man crawling on his hands and knees.

"But doesn't that concept just give rich people an excuse not to help the poor because they are apparently coping with the situation they are in?"

"Yeah, you could look at it that way, but I see it as a way of generating compassion rather than pity. If we only showed pictures of starving kids, it would always portray the beneficiaries as helpless victims; and in the long run, people would stop giving because the need would be seen as endless and therefore unsolvable. They would ask why they should have to help people who can't help themselves." Snap-clunk: a woman cooking in a discarded can of cooking oil over an open fire. "People in the West might then claim that the starving are only hungry because they are too lazy to work and that charity handouts should be stopped to provide an incentive for them to learn to feed themselves. Compassion, however, is a more genuine form of giving, motivated by love rather than the pride that is behind pity."

"How can you be so sure of the donors' motives?"

"Man, just look at the results. People in Europe empty their wallets for the victims of war in the Balkans. Charity starts at home, doesn't it? But I don't think that's the reason; instead, it's because they more readily identify with European victims and, therefore, have more compassion for them. It's the same in North America; it's much easier to raise money for South and Central America than Africa. Unless you do kids, which always works." Snap-clunk: a cross-eyed child carrying his little sister.

"Say," she said, as they walked over to one of the clinics, "I've been doing disaster photography for a decade now. I've done the refugee camps in Thailand and spent years shooting the famines that stalked Ethiopia and the Sahel during the 1980s." Snap-clunk: a scrawny old woman with a bundle of sticks on her back. "I've seen plenty of poverty and hardship; I know the score. But I'm telling you, there's something that ain't right here, and I can't quite put my finger on it. It's kinda like the people here have given up. There's no joy, no smiling faces, no laughing children. That's not normal, even in such miserable places as this."

"Any idea why that is?"

"Dunno, but the militaries here are kinda weird. Definitely don't want any photos taken of them. Normally, a bit of female charm and a few cigarettes works wonders. You know, men are men. Pretentious pigs, love to have their photos taken, especially by a woman." Snap-clunk: a small girl with hair knotted up to form two small antennae. "Sometimes, I even give them a comb before taking the photo, to emphasise the joke. Usually, they love it. Managed to get some great shots of a rebel standing proud over the corpse of someone he had killed when I did Sudan a couple of years ago. Those photos sure did the trick back at home, sent shockwaves through the public, hey."

"Maybe these soldiers don't want to be identified?"

"That's kinda what I was thinking. You think they got something to hide?"

"I don't think so. Everything seems normal 'round here. The situation is a lot better than it used to be, even though this camp is nothing to write home about."

Letters to Mandy were becoming ever more difficult to compose. Beyond the safe topics of weather and wildlife, there was little he could tell her that might not be misunderstood by a mind that could be critical of his actions. But he felt the need to try.

Dear Mandy,

I hope you are doing fine. The rainy season is about to start, so we get a lot more showers now, which also means loads of mozzies. I've had an interesting week building pit latrines in an IDP camp at a place called Mulabo, just outside Ndombazu.

He crossed out IDP. Mandy would not understand what he meant. He inserted Internally Displaced Persons instead. No, that would not work either, as it was near-incomprehensible aid jargon. So, he wrote refugees, even though it was technically incorrect, as refugees were people who had crossed a border and been granted asylum.

Three sentences done. So far, so good. But what next? Details of the ventilation system that netted the flies that bred in the faeces? No, too dull and technical, so of no interest to her.

Another possibility was to write about the subjects she had mentioned in her last letter. But that was impossible, given that she had still not written since his return to Ndombazu.

The final option was to describe his uneasy feelings about the situation in Kugombwala, but his cultural upbringing excluded being too personal on paper. His letter was therefore postponed until a future date, when he hoped for more inspiration, which left him concerned about the disintegrating communication between them and his own failure to deal with it.

"Something's wrong with my walkie-talkie," Lorna handed the device to him while they mustered for the drive to Mulabo. "It's charged and switches on but doesn't work, even though it's on the right channel and the volume is turned up to max."

Alan took the handset and pressed the talk button. A series of bars were displayed, indicating it was sending a signal. "Seems fine, but can't communicate," he muttered, as his own walkie-talkie did not react. "Let me try with a different antenna."

He rummaged in his toolbox until he found a spare.

"Yup, that was the problem."

"So, it was okay except for a non-functioning antenna?" Lorna asked.

"Aye, the main unit works perfectly."

She laughed. "It's like the problem for many people—all seems fine with them but is not because they have no contact with God."

"What do you mean?"

"Well, a lot of people are unaware there is a God as they have no relationship with Him. Their spiritual antenna is broken."

Like me, he agreed. "So, how can they fix that?"

"Ah, that requires faith—you have to make the effort to trust and believe in God to enable communication to happen."

Interesting concept, Alan conceded. He was reminded of the message the young Asian woman had given him at Nairobi's international airport. Had it been necessary to transmit it via her because he himself was not receptive to the supernatural? It would make sense if he believed in that.

No thanks, that's not for me. He dismissed the thought. Life was difficult enough without adding another dimension of complexity.

"You're spending a lot of time at Mulabo." Megan's tone was accusatory. "You rarely come to the hospital now. You're seeing someone there, aren't you?"

"No, not at all." Alan's baffled reaction would have been hard to fake. "I've got a lot to do in the camp, managing the watsan projects." *And I'm doing my best to avoid you,* he mentally added, uncomfortable in the knowledge his movements were under continuous surveillance. It was an ominous development. *We are not in a relationship, yet she is already trying to control me.*

"They look great, MacFred, well done."

"Oh, thank you, Alan."

Some aspects of his job were too easy, Alan acknowledged, after inspecting a row of recently completed pit latrines. He felt uncomfortable with just showing up and looking around to sign off a project, compared with the construction crew, who had worked for days on it. He was tempted to justify his privileged position by pretending to be more expert than they through pointing out a few faults. But he couldn't bring himself to do that. It would demean their effort.

He followed MacFred, who was in charge of the water and sanitation projects in the camp, back through the maze of hovels to the feeding centre.

"Hi, Al!" Lorna was there, investigating the sorry state of the children. "How are the watsan projects going?"

"The toilets are done. MacFred is working on the last water distribution points. I'll check again tomorrow." Alan was always grateful for a reason to leave his stuffy office. He was enjoying his visits to Mulabo; it was a pleasant drive out of the city, and he liked walking among the people in the camp. He found great satisfaction from being directly involved in projects that eased the otherwise miserable condition of the beneficiaries. At last, he felt he was doing something worthwhile with his life.

"By the way, have you noticed anything unusual here?" Lorna then asked.

"First IDP camp I've ever been in, so it's all new to me."

"There are hardly any young men."

"I hadn't thought about that, but I see what you are saying. Why do you think that is?"

"Maybe they are with the rebels up on the plateau?"

"But why would the families of rebel soldiers flee to Ndombazu if their men are fighting the government? They would be putting themselves in the clutches of their opponents."

There was a pause, as Lorna thought how to answer. "Perhaps it's about distancing themselves from the fighting and its potential consequences."

"What do you mean?"

"By coming here, they may be telling the government they hold no allegiance to any of the rebel groups. It would be an act of submission, seeking the protection of a powerful enemy, to avoid their retribution."

"Nah, that's not it. They're coming to get a free meal." Alan found himself echoing Nelson Merriweather's sentiments.

"That's also possible, but I don't think it's the whole story, as there's not much food here. The kids are starving, and life is difficult. It makes me think I should include a retrospective mortality study with the malnutrition survey planned for next week. We can ask each household how many members were in their family when the civil war broke out last year compared to how many there are now and then ask them why family members have died or disappeared—and also why they have come here to Mulabo. It would tell us a lot about this war; demographic data doesn't lie."

"Will the Liberation Front authorities allow it?"

"They don't need to know."

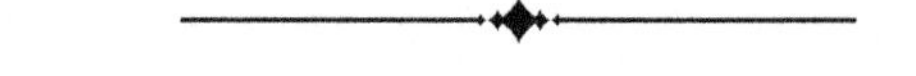

"Al, have you seen Dave?" Keith looked flustered.

"No, what's up?"

"There's a hand grenade in the vehicle inspection pit!"

"A grenade? How did it get there?"

"I don't know. Someone must have lobbed it in last night because it wasn't there yesterday afternoon."

"Wait! Let me get hold of Dave."

Alan brought out his walkie-talkie. "We urgently need you to come to the workshop," he told Dave.

"Can it wait? Over." He seemed busy. It was a mystery what he got up to all day, though it was not difficult to make a few guesses.

"It would be good if you could come quickly. Over."

"Okay. With you within half an hour. Over and out."

"Al out."

"Do you think it's a death threat?" Sweat trickled down Keith's brow, and his shirt was wet under the armpits. He looked scared.

"Could be, Keith. What have you been up to that we don't know about?"

"Nothing, really."

"Let's take a look."

They walked over to the workshop area that was the domain of Keith and his two assistant mechanics. This consisted of a shipping container that acted as the stores for spare parts, beside the carcass of a Land Rover mounted on blocks, which was stripped of components when required for the other vehicles. Next to it was the inspection pit. Alan crept to the edge of the concrete basin, wary of an imminent explosion. In the middle lay a hand grenade, drawing attention to itself like a lump of fresh, steaming dog dung.

Someone was trying to send a message. Who might that be? The mechanic assistants? The night watchmen? Or the Bakiboko? And to whom was the message intended? To Keith? To his assistant mechanics? Or to MedRelief? Any of those options were plausible. But what could the intended message be? A threat? A warning? And if so, about what?

Only one thing was clear: something was not right.

That strange feeling was back.

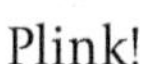

Plink!

A beetle had struck the lightbulb and fell dazed onto his book. It writhed about for a few seconds before regaining its feet. Then, with a whirr of its wings, it took off back towards the bulb.

Plink!

Alan looked up from the novel he was reading, amazed at the creatures's stupidity. Why was it trying to knock itself out?

It was not alone. The recent arrival of the rainy season had brought swarms of nocturnal insects that were attracted to the light over the terrace where he sat to relax after supper. Hundreds of flying forms were spinning about the electric bulb, producing a soft staccato as they repeatedly bumped into it. That sound was noticeable now that there was a lull from days of incessant rain that had drummed heavy droplets onto the city, superimposing a patchwork of small lakes and puddles upon the landscape.

Plink!

A large praying mantis fell to his feet, before relaunching towards the overhead luminescence.

Those insects are obsessed with light, Alan noted, watching even more knock themselves against the hot and hard surface of the bulb in an attempt to smash their way through the glass to reach the intense brightness of the burning filament. *What's going through their minds? he wondered. Why are they trying to get ever closer to the source of the light?* They risked killing themselves in their effort to merge with it.

He looked away into the all-smothering night. No other lights were visible in Ndombazu. Neither stars, nor moon—nothing but total blackness from a dense cloud-covered sky over a city shut down by permanent power cuts. He was glad he was not out there in that foreboding darkness.

The thought then crossed his mind that the insects were scared of that darkness. *Perhaps they are fleeing the night,* he hypothesised, perplexed by their willingness to die in order to unite with the light. Their mass self-sacrifice was evidenced by the scattering of critter corpses that young MacZak swept up every morning.

Maybe nature is trying to say something, Alan mused while watching a magnificent moth flutter about the bulb, creating a stroboscopic effect as it alternately shaded and revealed the light. *Light and dark, just like good and evil*—he recognised the parallel analogy. Were the insects trying to flee from evil rather than mere darkness? If so, what was the exact implication for him?

"I say, Alan, awful business about that Canadian photographer."

Nelson Merriweather handed him a cup of coffee. They had struck up an unlikely friendship through the bond of shared nationality. Plus, he was refreshingly open and direct, even if Alan did not always share his views. In that way, Merriweather was almost a Northerner, for you knew where you stood with him—unlike Jules, a typical, two-faced Londoner.

"I had rather hoped," Merriweather continued, "that the new government would put an end to extortion and petty crime. But I suppose there will always be a few bad apples in any bunch."

"Aye, do you know anything more about what happened?" Mention had been made at the U.N. coordination meeting about Rosalie Desjardins's camera being taken by soldiers while she was on her way to the airport to catch a flight out of Kugombwala. Fortunately, she was otherwise unharmed.

"The Liberation Front's U.N. liaison officer told me that they must have been off-duty soldiers at a bogus checkpoint. The army is conducting an investigation, and the culprits will be given a thorough thrashing when they are identified." Merriweather looked satisfied at the prospect of proper discipline being enforced.

"What else did they take?"

"All her films. Can't think what they wanted those for; most had already been exposed."

"Maybe they wanted to look at her pictures?"

"No, no, I really don't think they would want to do that. Think of the expense of developing all the films. They're hardly going to sell the images, are they?"

"Did they take anything else?"

"No. I was passed a copy of the incident report by the U.N. civilian military affairs officer, and nothing more is mentioned."

That was strange. If the soldiers had robbed Desjardins to line their own pockets, they would have also taken her money and other valuables.

"Seems to me the government might have ordered the soldiers to do it," Alan tried, "to remove her films."

"Nonsense!" Merriweather's condescending rebuke jarred. "Why on earth would the Liberation Front do that? She had full press accreditation, and there are other journalists in town who have not had their equipment and film removed. Besides, she had only taken photos of Mulabo camp. Hardly military-sensitive material."

Further discussion was pointless, Alan realised, as this would provoke Merriweather's natural predisposition to support government authority. But he thought back to what Desjardins had said in the camp about the soldiers refusing to be photographed. It now seemed the government did not want images of the ongoing suffering in the displaced persons camps to reach the Western media.

That was weird, for the Kugombwalan militia groups had previously done all they could to encourage as much aid as possible to reach the country, as it meant more resources for them to steal. The Liberation Front likewise had good reason to encourage more assistance, as the humanitarian organisations created jobs and provided services that the new Kugombwalan government would otherwise have to fund from their own meagre resources.

So, what was their motive for removing the films? It went contrary to all logic. For Alan, no amount of speculation could produce a satisfactory theory, except a strange sense that this incident was somehow linked to the many other events that contributed to his feeling of deep unease.

CHAPTER 8

Alan flicked away a section of a dried tube of mud that ran up the wall to the window frame. He had exposed a parallel world: a secret stream of termites—workers and soldiers—rushing back and forth along their hidden highway. Their self-made pipe allowed them to operate unnoticed, far beyond their underground nest, giving them unseen access to the wooden sill above.

Alan found he could push his finger through the paper-thin surface of the window surround. The insects had eaten away the timber underneath but had left the outer layer to screen themselves from potential predators. He punctured another place and then another. The frame was completely perished.

Now that he knew what to look for, he could see termite tracks everywhere—on all the trees and buildings, leading up to every wooden window and even to the roofs.

On the surface, the situation looked okay, but underneath, utter destruction was taking place.

The day had started bright, but dense clouds were now amassing on the horizon, looming ever higher in the sky as they approached. A tropical downpour was imminent.

MacJohn was refuelling the Land Rover, leaving Alan to wander around the petrol station to kill time. Africa was rich in detail, he observed, studying the discarded bits of metal that littered the margins of the forecourt. He could recognise some of the pieces—an old half-shaft, a connecting rod, some split rings, as well as others that defied easy identification. Keith would have loved the challenge.

He looked beyond the scrap to the scrubby vegetation that bordered the back of the petrol station. The land sloped down to a stream that flowed a revolting murky brown. Rubbish was strewn everywhere, and he could smell that this area was used as an open latrine by some of the city's poorer inhabitants. It was far from enticing, and yet an inexplicable urge came over him to go down to the creek. He took his first step forward into the minefield of human faeces.

"No, Alan, don't go there!" MacJohn, his ever-present guardian, called out from beside the vehicle.

"What's the problem?"

"Place can be very bad. Robbers."

"But there's no one here. It's empty."

"No, don't go. Not safe."

"But I'm not going far."

"Please, Alan. No go. For me. Please." The imploring tone in MacJohn's voice held him back, so he returned, disappointed not to have satisfied his curiosity, while also relieved to have avoided sewerage on his shoes.

They drove off as the first spats of rain hit the windscreen. The squall soon overtook the car, blanketing the vehicle in a protective shroud of pouring water that blurred their view of the mean streets of Ndombazu. There was now minimal risk of being stopped at a checkpoint, for Bakiboko fighters, like predatory cats, hated getting wet.

"So, what was all that about?" Alan's voice was barely audible above the background din of hammering rain.

"I'm sorry?" MacJohn had not understood the question.

"At the petrol station. Why didn't you want me to go down to the river?"

"That place—it can be full of dead people."

What was he going on about? Alan had not seen any corpses.

MacJohn reduced their speed to avoid skidding on the muddy roads, which had become quagmires of greasy clay. "You know the Bakiboko can be killing the Watumbwa?" he continued in a tone that was more statement than question. "They can bury some of them behind the petrol station."

"That's news to me." This was the first time any of the local staff had volunteered such information. "What have you been hearing?" he asked, while staring ahead at the miserable street. There was an unwritten rule that conversations of this nature were never face-to-face to reduce their crime to a careless slip of the tongue within earshot of an unsuspecting bystander, rather than the deliberate act of an informant.

"Last Saturday, fifty Watumbwa can be taken out of their homes and chopped in the village of Gagawaga. Women, children, old people. They kill everybody."

"How do you know?"

"My cousin can be married to one of the Bakiboko soldiers. He tell us what they are doing. Oh, it is bad-bad, my friend." His voice cracked with emotion, so Alan waited before probing further.

"Have there been other massacres?"

"Too much! Also, last week, they can attack Uliolugu. All the villages on the plateau, from Benikaka to Ngowezi, are deserted.

They want to kill all of them until the last one is dead." He continued to list a catalogue of atrocities, enough to fill a report for a human rights organisation.

How many of the other national staff had similar stories to tell? It dawned on Alan that everybody knew what was going on—everybody except the expatriate aid workers like himself. Yet little of the information that was public knowledge to the locals was able to diffuse to the foreigners, because they lived in a separate world, too remote from the Kugombwalan people to touch the soil upon which they had committed themselves to walk.

"They want to kill all of them, until the last one is dead . . . "

The words stuck in Alan's thoughts. But his mind retaliated by throwing back doubts. Could the situation in Kugombwala really be as bad as MacJohn claimed? Why would the Bakiboko want to exterminate the Watumbwa tribe? And even if they were trying to do so, then where was the evidence?

"Aw, come on, MacJohn," he chided. "Is there any proof for what you say?"

"I am telling you." MacJohn was emphatic. "The killings—it can be every day."

"But then we would have seen something."

"No, Alan, it can happen where they do not let you go—behind the checkpoints."

"But I thought the soldiers stop us passing because the areas beyond are full of bandits." The aid agencies accepted the imposed restriction, grateful that the army showed concern for their security.

MacJohn laughed. "That can be what they say, but it is the same soldiers who are the bandits—and the ones doing the killing."

Alan conceded that it was logical that access was being blocked for reasons other than the wellbeing of foreign NGOs, as Kugombwala's fighters had never before shown any sympathy for humanitarian relief. As rebels, they had previously been a perpetual menace for kidnapping aid workers and robbing food convoys.

But it was unlikely the alleged killings amounted to more than a story inflated from a few minor events, exaggerated out of all proportion to the original facts. Yet another tall tale from the endless Kugombwalan rumour mill.

He decided against asking more questions, for his time in Ndombazu had taught him not to show excess interest to the local staff about their sometimes-weird stories. Instead, he would discuss the issue with the expat team. But whom should he approach about such a sensitive subject?

Dave was the obvious candidate, as he often chatted to Bakiboko soldiers over beer in the bars. However, if he had heard any rumours, he would have voiced them at their weekly security meetings, as he always broadcast whatever whisper he had chanced upon. He sensed that it would be unwise to ask him, in case he blabbed the rumour back to the military.

Jules would be the next logical choice, but Alan felt uncomfortable about confiding anything to a boss who talked down to him. "Politics and security issues are none of your business—leave that to Dave and me," he could hear him saying.

He would have liked to ask Paula, as she had a keen nose for nasty smells, but that was out of the question, as they were no longer on speaking terms after a recent argument.

And there was no point raising the matter with Keith, as he wouldn't know anything. Besides, any verbal contact with him was a dangerous invitation for an unremitting monologue, so best avoided.

Maybe he should ask Megan. She was very observant. But he decided against it because it would be difficult to find a quiet moment with her that she would not misinterpret, in her ever-hopeful mind, as a romantic change of heart. He could predict what would happen next. She would find any pretext to share similar information in an attempt to build regular intimacy. What a relationship that would be, founded on rumours.

So, it was decided. He would ask Lorna. He could safely voice his concerns with her.

"Lorna, Lorna for Megan?" his walkie-talkie crackled.

"Yes, Megan, it's Lorna. Over."

"I need more infusions for the cholera centre. Any chance of you going to the main medical store soon? Over."

"I'm there now, so send two of the nurses with a list of what you need. Over."

At last, an opportunity to speak to Lorna alone, away from the other expats and away from the crowded hospital where there was always a queue for her attention. Alan walked over to the building, where he found her signing over boxes of syringes to two members of Megan's medical team. He waited in the background until they had left.

"Lorna," he started, "would you have heard anything about massacres on the plateau?"

"What have you been hearing?" She looked startled.

"Just a few stories from MacJohn."

Lorna took a deep breath. "Father Roy, my Jamaican priest friend, has also mentioned villages being attacked, but I thought he was overreacting to not being able to visit some of his parishes. There's been simmering conflict between the Bakiboko and the Watumbwa tribes for generations, and both sides like to accuse each other of atrocities like stealing livestock and kidnapping young women. My guess is that a few people have been killed, but it is probably no worse than in other years. Anyway, you cannot carry out mass killings without the U.N. and international community knowing about it. They would have reacted if it's really as bad as Father Roy and MacJohn say."

What a relief, Alan thought and let the matter drop from his mind.

Alan watched MacObadiah waddle over to the kitchen with a bulging plastic bag that was obviously heavy. A dribble of blood revealed what was inside—booty from his daily visit to the butcher. Hmmm, Alan noted, that much steak was normally never served. Maybe there was a scam going on to divert part of the expat food budget to pay for the meat consumed by MacObadiah and his mates.

Controlling the household expenses was Alan's responsibility, though he rarely checked the receipts returned by the cook, as he considered such small costs to be too trivial to spend valuable time on. Yet a suspected fiddle required action, so he did a quick inspection of the accounts. Nothing appeared amiss, for the amount spent on meat had been consistent over the previous weeks.

Oh well, he thought, *it must be roast for dinner.*

But it was stew for supper.

Something was cooking, Alan realised, as he chewed over the situation and the measly morsels of tender meat hidden among the vegetables. But he would have to wait until he got the receipts for that day's purchases to be sure.

A few days later, he received a chit from MacObadiah for just one kilo of meat, far less than the lump he had seen in the bag. That raised a new question. Had MedRelief paid for the entire joint or just part of it? The only way to find out was to check the food prices in the local market.

"MacWalter." He called one of the guards beside the main gate over to his office.

"Yes, Boss?"

"Can you go to the market for me? Find out the price of food. Cost of one kilo of carrots, one kilo of potatoes, one kilo of beef . . . " He listed many different items. "Ask for best price. For Food Security Survey."

"Okay, Boss." MacWalter was always eager for more interesting tasks than patrolling the perimeter wall. Alan wished he could go himself, but the market traders would inflate their prices for a white man.

Two hours later, MacWalter was back. There was a big discrepancy in the price of beef and pork—the actual prices were half those submitted by the cook.

It was time to share his suspicions.

"MacWalter." Alan looked him straight in the face. "Would MacObadiah be stealing some of the expat meat?"

A smile broke out on the guard's face. "That man can be very dangerous. He can give meat to one of the drivers so he no ask questions about where all the shopping goes."

"Has this been going on for a long time?"

"Ever since the meat price fall. I can think he always write the same amount, but when meat can be cheaper, he can buy more. Half for you. And half for him."

"Why is the meat price dropping?"

MacWalter paused, alerting Alan to a formulated response. "Other meat, it can be reaching the market. It can make meat price fall."

"Other meat? What other meat?"

"Man meat."

Alan gasped. "You mean . . . human meat?"

"Yes, that one. It is very sweet," he whispered, his eyes lighting up. And then he laughed in mockery of the obvious shock on Alan's face.

Yeah, yeah, very funny. Alan felt humiliated that MacWalter had pulled a fast one on him. To ask any more questions would reveal that he had fallen for the joke, so he let the subject drop.

Man meat. The thought of having tasted human flesh gnawed Alan's mind and caused his stomach to churn.

He first assumed MacWalter had been joking, but a horrible feeling haunted him because there was no other way to explain the fall in the price of meat. Only an abundant, new supply could do that.

Was this linked to the rumours of massacres in the interior? That would account for the sudden glut of meat in the market. It was a horrific thought, and it made him retch.

Worse still for him was the realisation that he might have feasted on his fellow humans. The victims of the killings, concealed in MacObadiah's stew . . .

A fresh wave of nausea washed over him at the thought that he had broken humanity's ultimate taboo, which distinguished the civilised from the savage—that he was now, albeit unwillingly, a cannibal.

Why had he come back to Kugombwala? He berated himself, revolted over what he might have done. And it was all his fault, for it would never have happened if he had stayed in Britain. He hated himself for having returned to this deranged land that defiled all who were in it.

The next day, Alan was surprised to see the clinic car returning to the compound during the morning, as it usually did not get back until evening. The team would barely have had time to get to Mulabo camp and back. A minute later, Lorna entered his office.

"What's up, Doc?"

"It's the checkpoint at kilometre thirteen. They won't let us through. There's been a rebel attack on the road, so it's not safe for us to pass."

There had been talk in town about a rebel group from the Watumbwa tribe that had risen up against Kugombwala's new government. They were reported to be vicious killers, so it was obvious to Alan that they—rather than the orderly Liberation Front soldiers—were responsible for the rumoured massacres. It was comforting to hear that unsecure areas had been cordoned off.

"Better wait until it's safe enough to go back."

"I know." Lorna frowned. "But I had hoped to train the team at Mulabo today in preparation for the coming malnutrition and retrospective mortality survey."

Every day over the next week, it was the same story. It was too dangerous to go beyond the outskirts of the Ndombazu. This was how it had been before they were evacuated, Alan remembered. Once again, they were confined to the city.

A perceptible tension hung in the air. Jules became concerned that the rise in rebel attacks might signal the start of a major counter-offensive on Ndombazu. The sense of peace and calm had evaporated, taking with it the fleeting hope for Kugombwala's future.

"Hello, Alan, how is your body today?"

The standard Kugombwalan greeting was timely, for Alan's stomach was still complaining about what it had digested many days earlier. He had not touched meat since then and was giving serious consideration to becoming a vegetarian.

"Not so good, MacAbraham; it's maybe something I've eaten." He was grimly aware of the huge understatement.

"My sincerest commiserations." The old man spoke perfect English. "Perhaps it would help if you could be induced to vomit it out? I can prepare some special herbs."

"Thanks, but it was a few days ago, so it's too late."

The gardener had once lectured in plant sciences at the University of Ndombazu, but the civil war had stalled his career, so he was now reduced to clipping hedges in the MedRelief compound. Alan noted the old man was also cultivating the small patches of fallow land around the ornamental plants to grow crops for himself without MedRelief's permission.

"You planting that cassava for me?" he asked with a wry smile.

"Not for you, for me."

The former professor surprised Alan with his straightforward response. Here, at last, was someone he could trust to give honest answers to his questions.

"MacAbraham, I've been hearing rumours about massacres," Alan started, giving minimal information to avoid influencing the reply.

"The streets are full of those stories, too." MacAbraham looked down at the ground as he spoke.

"Are they true?"

An awkward silence followed. MacAbraham lifted his head and looked straight into Alan's eyes. "They could be," he said. "I have been expecting this to happen for some years, as opportunists are stirring up old rivalries in this country."

"What's this story about man meat in the market?"

MacAbraham smiled. "It might look like human flesh, but it is just pork," he said, to Alan's intense relief. "The Watumbwa people keep many pigs, and they are being stolen during the fighting on the plateau, which means pork is now plentiful in the market. Some traders call it 'man meat' because it is not just pigs that are being killed—it is also their owners. So, the market people are using dark humour as a subtle protest against the killings of their fellow citizens. They know the meat they are selling is coming from pigs stolen from people who have been slaughtered in the fighting."

"Why has no one told us about what is happening? It sounds like major human rights abuses are going on."

The statement brought about an immediate change in MacAbraham's mood, and his face contorted with laughter. "You

Europeans are always talking about rights and values. Yet you don't understand how it is for others. The people who are being killed—the Watumbwa—are historically a slave people. Slaves don't have rights, and they know it. If you are born a slave, then you grow up believing you are inferior, and you know your fate is to get kicked around by everybody else—"

"Know your place in society," Alan butted in to make sure he was following MacAbraham's thoughts. That's how life was for the U.K.'s downtrodden masses during his grandparents' youth, he remembered them saying.

"Yes, but even though you don't expect any different, it doesn't stop you hating the way you get treated. As a slave, you get whipped and humiliated by your master; you despise him for it, but you keep your mouth shut and get on with life. Survival is all about working as little as possible without having to suffer the lash. You do what is necessary to make sure that at the end of each day, your body is not broken by either overwork or punishment, so that you can survive to the next."

"In that situation, you'd be desperate to break the chains of oppression."

"Indeed. Which is why all the while, you wait for that chance moment when you find a knife in your hand on a dark night as you come across the master drunk by the road. Then you use that brief opportunity to murder the one you hate."

"Quite right." Alan's Northern, working-class upbringing made it easy for him to sympathise with the oppressed.

"So, you see, that is why some of the Watumbwa have formed a new rebel movement against the Bakiboko and are making trouble."

"Okay, I understand that, but why don't other Watumbwa speak out?" He recalled his father's tales of union strikes and public protests.

"Alan, as a slave you never, ever complain about the way you are treated because you know it will only make life worse."

"Hold on. Why do you keep going on about slave people? Slavery was abolished a long time ago."

"Slavery is not just a legal state. It is also a state of mind . . . " MacAbraham paused to collect his thoughts. "Although the trade and ownership of slaves has long been abolished, you Europeans never set us Africans free. You replaced slavery with colonial servitude when you imposed your rule over us and took the best of our natural resources in exchange for providing us with elementary schooling and basic medical care. And then, when you left, you handed the control of our country to a small elite from our own people, who continued to subjugate us. We've never been fully freed; we've never been considered as equals; and we've never been valued as individuals.

"Our new masters, the Bakiboko, want to perpetuate that bondage. They will crush anyone who stands up to them. At the moment, they are setting an example with the Watumbwa, who were traditionally their slaves and who rebelled against their former masters after the country became independent. They represent the biggest potential threat to the Bakiboko's hold on power."

"Right, I now see why the Watumbwa don't protest here in Kugombwala, but why don't they complain to the United Nations?"

"Alan." MacAbraham was visibly frustrated. "They know it would be no use because the U.N. would not listen to them. That organisation has become a huge parasitic bureaucracy, staffed by ambitious sycophants who serve the world's ruling elite in exchange for huge salaries. Their talk of human rights is mere propaganda to make ordinary people think the United Nations is concerned about the poor and oppressed. But the reality is they don't care about the downtrodden people of Kugombwala—and especially not the Watumbwa—because slave people are too poor to outbid their rivals when it comes to securing the U.N.'s assistance and support."

Alan woke up in a sweat. The fan was silent and the air still.

Another power cut.

It was stifling hot in his room. He rolled over, seeking a dry area of mattress. But it was no use. Within minutes, the perspiration that poured from his neck and upper chest had saturated the rest of the bed. Sleep was now impossible.

He decided to get up and see if Keith needed a kick-start to go and fix the generator.

"Keith!" He banged on the door to be heard above the loud snoring. "Power cut."

"Oh, no" came the mumbled response. "Not again."

"Yes, again."

Alan walked outside, where it would be cooler. He breathed in deep to calm his irritation over Keith, who had failed to emerge and was probably asleep again. He was about to go inside to fetch him when a flashlight blinded him, fixing him like a rabbit in the headlights. Someone was approaching.

"Boss Man, power can be down." It was one of the guards, MacWalter.

"I know, and I've already told Keith."

"He can come?"

"Yeah, yeah, coming, coming." Keith bumbled past them towards the generator house.

"Need help, Keith?"

"No, I think I know the problem."

"Okay, I'm here if you change your mind." A rare, cloudless sky drew Alan's attention to an awe-inspiring array of stars that illuminated the night sky. *What happens up in the heavens?* he wondered before lowering his eyes to the dark silhouette of the compound wall. *And what's going on down here in Kugombwala?* His inability to answer those questions made him feel small and insignificant.

"Boss Man," MacWalter asked, "you can take tea?"

"Sure." It was going to be impossible to sleep, anyway, so a quick cuppa with the watchmen seemed like a good idea. It was a rare opportunity to spend time with them, which he knew they would appreciate, as he was their line manager.

He followed MacWalter to the main gate and through a small side door to the street outside, where there was a shelter for the three guards on duty. Alan sat down on a bench, while MacWalter fanned a small, charcoal fire to boil the kettle. The street was dark and silent, except for the sound of mosquitoes that honed in on a new target. *What a miserable job these night watchmen have,* Alan thought, swatting the exposed flesh of his ears, neck, ankles, and wrists. It must also be intensely dull, for almost nothing ever happened.

His attention was drawn to lights that traversed the end of the street. A convoy of trucks was driving past along the main road. That surprised him, for the government had imposed a nighttime curfew.

"What are those trucks?" he asked MacWalter.

"They can be from the prison. It can happen every night."

"Transporting prisoners?"

"Yes. Dead prisoners. Meat."

Heard that one before. He frowned. "Old joke, MacWalter."

"No, not funny. Prison now for killing people. They can bring bodies to the forest. For burning. Nothing left."

"How do you know?"

"Small-small talk."

Ndombazu was rife with rumours. But how to distinguish fact from fantasy?

"I'll join you when you try to go to Mulabo tomorrow," Alan told Lorna during a team meeting to coordinate vehicle movements. "It's been a fortnight since I last paid the day workers their salaries."

"Sure, but be prepared to be disappointed."

They left at the usual time the next morning. At the outskirts of Ndombazu, they passed three bored-looking Bakiboko soldiers sitting on beer crates, which might otherwise have been used to form a checkpoint. MacNed slowed down, expecting them to flag down the vehicle, but they showed no intention of stirring beyond the lugubrious movement of their eyes.

"Wow," Lorna remarked. "We got through that one without any problem. First time in a week."

The car jerked about on the rutted road, passing landmarks familiar from frequent earlier journeys to the IDP camp—a burnt-out armoured personnel carrier, an ant hill, the ruins of a roofless building, the wreck of a lorry, the charred trunk of a fallen tree. The waypoints were the same as ever, but the road was surprisingly empty of human traffic. Usually, a steady stream of people passed between the camp and Ndombazu, including traders bringing goods from the city and peasants carrying firewood to sell in the capital.

But today, there was nobody.

"I don't like the look of this," Alan murmured. "The road's empty."

"I was just thinking the same." Lorna spoke without taking her eyes off the track ahead. They lapsed back into mutual silence. No one in the car was in the mood for talking.

The sky darkened as they drove towards a blanket of black cloud that signalled approaching rain. The first droplets were soon bombarding the dusty surface of the empty road that unfolded before them, just as they reached the last corner, beyond which they would see the camp again. There had been a checkpoint here, but that had gone—a landmark that had disappeared.

They rounded the corner, and there it was. Or rather, it was not.

Nothing could have prepared him for the sight of the camp. It was utterly empty, devoid of all life but for the tattered scraps of plastic hanging from the frames of the stick-built shelters that fluttered in the breeze. He got out of the car and stood, staring. It was so unbelievable that he was stunned into inaction, except for a slight shaking of his head, his mouth wide open. No, no, this couldn't be real. But his eyes did not lie. The camp had been emptied, its inhabitants gone.

Where are they? Where have they fled? And why? Or has something else happened?

The questions hovered in his mind, stirring up the rumours he had been hearing the previous days.

He took a few careful steps forward, for although he had been here dozens of times, he was aware that he was now treading new ground. His sharpened senses noted the most minute details. It was like being in a slow-motion film, with double the time to appreciate the surroundings.

A scrunching sound caused him to look down. Spent bullet cartridges. Ten of them. Packed into the mud. He looked closer and found another. And another. He picked them up. They were fresh, for earth had yet to make its way into them. And they retained the distinct smell of ignited gunpowder.

For five minutes, he stood there, staring into the emptiness that engulfed him with the brass casings in his hand. And then, in the distance, at the other side of the camp where the clearing ended and the forest started, he spied movement. A party of people emerged, and through the tangled frames of huts that partly screened the view, he could make out about a dozen of them carrying digging hoes and accompanied by armed Bakiboko soldiers at each end of the line. The party had spotted them and were now stepping up their pace through the soft and slippery mud towards them.

"I don't like the look of this." Alan turned to MacNed, who was still in the car. "Let's go."

On the way back to the city, he considered saying something to break the silence, but his lips felt like they were glued together. Lorna was also uncharacteristically quiet.

They passed the landmarks in reverse sequence. It was like watching a favourite road movie being played backwards—the burned tree trunk, the wrecked lorry, the roofless building, the ant hill, the destroyed armoured personnel carrier. But rewinding the film could not erase the knowledge of how it finished, and he likewise could not return to

Ndombazu as if nothing had happened. For he had been to the end of that road and seen the destroyed camp at Mulabo; there was no longer any doubt in his mind about what was going on in Kugombwala—the Bakiboko soldiers were attacking Watumbwa civilians—which raised other questions. Why had they been chased out of the camp? What had happened to them afterwards? Had they been captured as slaves? Or, as MacJohn claimed, had they been massacred?

No, they couldn't have been killed, Alan reasoned. *There were no bodies.*

Unless . . .

The gruesome thoughts were back.

"Calm down, Al." Jules' tone was unmistakably dismissive. "A handful of bullet cartridges is hardly evidence for massive human rights abuse. I've fired more rounds on a single grouse shoot."

"But the camp's been emptied—"

"Yes, by Watumbwa rebels. The Liberation Front reported that at the press conference I went to this morning. Fortunately, there were only a few casualties."

"Right . . ." Alan felt bewildered by the information that conflicted with his own eyewitness impressions.

"You have to learn to put things into perspective, Al. We don't bother the U.N. Security Council every time we see a wisp of gun smoke."

"Lorna, where on earth have you been?" Jules grilled her as soon as she arrived at supper. "I've been calling you for hours. We've been worried that something might have happened to you."

"I'm sorry, Jules. I switched off my walkie-talkie. But I did tell MacRobert in the radio room where I was."

"That may be, but we had an emergency at the obstetrics ward, and you should have been there. Luckily, we were able to cope."

"As I said, I'm really sorry, but I needed time out."

"You're supposed to be on call at all times."

"I'm fully aware of that, Jules."

"Then where were you?"

"If you have to know, I was at confession."

"A whole afternoon is a long time to spend alone with a priest," Paula scoffed. "I suppose he will also have to say a few 'Hail Marys' . . . "

"I don't like what you are insinuating, and I don't need to hear this," Lorna snapped before doing an about-turn and walking out, leaving her food untouched.

"What's up?" Al was puzzled. "It's not like Lorna to be so easily upset."

"I think it's about Mulabo," Megan answered. "There's talk among the national staff that the camp was emptied to prevent the malnutrition and retrospective mortality survey that we were planning to do. They claim the Bakiboko were against it because of what it would have revealed."

"Such as?"

"Statistical proof that kids are dying at abnormally high rates. It would have been bad for the new government's image abroad. That's apparently also why they took the Canadian journalist's camera and films . . . "

"Sounds like a wild Kugombwalan rumour to me," Dave retorted, "given that it was Watumbwa rebels who cleared the camp."

"It's just anti-Bakiboko propaganda, spread by the losing side," Paula added. "But what's all this got to do with Lorna being so pious?"

"Don't you see?" Megan looked 'round at her colleagues. "It was Lorna's idea to do that survey, so she's blaming herself for the consequences. She thinks the camp would not have been attacked if she hadn't planned to question the residents. She didn't ask for permission from the authorities to do that, and she reckons the Liberation Front got wind of what she was up to and so made sure it didn't happen."

"That's ridiculous," Dave said. "She should pull herself together and stop being over-sensitive. There's no need to believe every story we hear."

"The soldiers in town say there's been fighting on the plateau," Dave informed the team a few days later. "Watumbwa rebels are attacking civilians, so the road will be closed while the army conducts its counterinsurgency operations to catch the killers."

"Shouldn't we be there to help the wounded?" Megan asked. "I mean, isn't that what we're here for?"

"That's what MedRelief's fundraising material claims." Paula smirked.

"We obviously won't try to reach them until it's safe to go there." Dave was firm. "No point risking our lives, for we can't help anyone if we get killed. That's also why the army has closed off the area—for our own protection. The Liberation Front high command have assured me they will let us through, as soon as they sort out the security situation."

"And that's the reason I'm going to Nairobi next week," Jules added. "The U.K. government is interested in supporting the clinics we used to run on the plateau, once we get access. I will be meeting our development minister at the embassy."

"Funny how the Foreign Office all of a sudden wants to fund a project when there's a bit of fighting around," Paula said. "Makes you wonder whether we are here to gather soft intelligence for them . . . "

Weeks passed waiting for the road that led to the plateau to open. Then one day, the checkpoints stopped being obstructive. Civilian vehicles were permitted to pass once they had been inspected and their intended route and purpose of journey approved.

"The U.N. monitoring team got a car up onto the plateau yesterday," Alan told Lorna after he had attended the morning inter-agency coordination meeting. "The road's now clear but only along the highway."

"That's great to hear. We should take this opportunity to go there, to see how the people are faring."

"Good idea."

"How about tomorrow? Can you come?"

"I'd like to, but I've got the monthly accounts to do."

"Please, Al. I know you're busy, but I'd like to have a male expat with me. With Jules at the meetings in London and Dave on holiday, that leaves just you or Keith . . . "

"Okay, I'll join you." He smiled. Lorna knew how to twist his arm.

"Fantastic. We'll leave at first light, to get the most out of the day and in case we get delayed at checkpoints or slowed by poor roads."

"We mustn't stay too long up there, though, as we have to be back in Ndombazu by nightfall. The U.N. security officer advises all expats to be off the plateau before it gets dark."

"Fine by me. I have no intention of getting caught in an ambush."

Alan scowled as he climbed in through the tailgate door. He hated sitting in the back. Lorna had taken the favoured front passenger seat, so he was relegated to one of the benches behind, which ran along both sides of the cabin. This forced him to face the other passengers on the opposite row, so he only saw a hazy outline of an ever-disappearing road when he turned his head to peer through the dusty rear window.

The dull drone of the engine, combined with an early start, sent him to sleep for the first part of the journey, but he was woken when they arrived at a checkpoint, where everyone had to get out and present identification documents while the vehicle was searched.

They were soon off again. Before long, the engine started to labour, signalling that they had reached the base of the plateau and were now mounting the escarpment edge. An hour later, they reached the top.

More checkpoint stops followed. At one of these, a fellow passenger opened the tailgate door to let in air, bringing in the smell of wood smoke. Alan got a glimpse of peasant farmers breaking down the mud walls of several huts and turning the soil around them. Two soldiers came into view, staring back at the Land Rover.

"Watumbwa rebels can raid this village," a fellow passenger, one of Lorna's medical team, told him. "Bakiboko soldiers now protect people. Very good!"

The situation seemed acceptable, given the circumstances. Alan had hoped for a more exciting and enlightening journey and now regretted coming, for it was claustrophobic in the cabin without the benefit of the passing view. It was even more boring than doing the accounts.

After another cramped hour, the vehicle stopped in a small town, and its occupants disembarked.

"This was one of the clinics we used to support." Lorna nodded towards a roofless cinderblock building. "And this is what has replaced it." In front sat a few traders offering a motley collection of expired medicines in dirty old packets, as well as an array of dried herbs, feathers, fur, and bones. "I will ask the local mayor for permission to do a medical survey, and I'm hoping the former clinic staff will appear once they hear we've arrived."

"Anything you want me to do?"

"Yes, could you walk around with one of the locals and get a feel for the place? I'd be interested to hear your impressions. We'll say you want to look at the local wells, to assess the water and sanitation situation."

"Sure."

A group of local officials soon showed up. MacNed spoke with them and then did the introductions.

"Alan, meet MacPete."

"How's the body, MacPete?"

"Oh, fine-fine, thank you, sir," said the little man with an infectious smile.

"MacPete can be a ten-house leader here," MacNed continued.

"What's that?"

"A member of the Kugombwalan Liberation Front's political wing in charge of a cell of ten houses." MacNed alluded to the classic Marxist method for monitoring the population.

It was a warning to be wary, for MacPete, despite his smile, was therefore part of a vast intelligence hierarchy. He might also be hungry to please his superiors with incriminating information . . .

Over the next hours, the eager official guided Alan around a labyrinth of narrow alleys between neat hedges and small huts. It was a pleasant but bland village, sprawled over a large area. Alan was glad to have a combined guard and guide, for he would have felt unsafe on his own and got lost among the small tracks. But he was also aware that MacPete was his minder, who decided where they went.

He was finally past the checkpoints and walking around on the plateau, yet he still saw almost nothing. It was like being in the back of the Land Rover with its dusty windows, his view limited to his immediate surroundings and his location controlled by someone else. He felt cocooned in a virtual capsule that hid all view of what was happening beyond.

After visiting twenty wells, Alan returned to the clinic. Lorna was sitting outside, examining a group of local people, so he kept back from disturbing her. MacNed was nowhere to be seen.

There was nothing to do except sit around and wait, which gave him time to think and forced him into another cocoon—that of his inner thoughts, where nobody else intruded. There, his mind regularly dwelt upon Mandy. Why hadn't she written to him? Her long silence indicated the chastisement was about more than his absence, which meant there had to be other reasons for the retribution. And it wasn't difficult to discern what they might be, given how much he had wronged her over the many years they had been together—from their first intercourse that she had not desired to his refusal to grant her marriage and children despite living with her. Their relationship had always been on his terms—until now.

His distant gaze returned to full focus and rested on Lorna, observing her interaction with the local people. The patients warmed to her gentle nature, as she stroked a crippled, old man on the arm and giggled with a mother.

Someone had once advised him to judge people by how they treated others, rather than how they treated him. By that meter, it was obvious Lorna was a kind person. Although she was not a stunner by the tastes of the tabloids, she emanated a beauty he had not noticed in anyone before, an invisible yet discernible radiance that originated from personality, rather than form or features.

Could he say the same of Mandy? She was certainly attractive, but her character was no better than many of the other women he knew. She was polite enough to other people, even towards Bobsy, whom she loathed. But she could also be nasty behind their backs, revealing a vicious streak inherited from her mother. *In her own way, she is just as bad as me,* Alan noted. It did not augur well for their future.

"Hi, Al, have you had a good day? Seen anything interesting?" Lorna had broken free from the crowd around her and walked over to him.

"Nothing unusual."

"That's a relief to hear. Puts a lid on the rumours, doesn't it?"

"I hope so."

"Anyway, I'm now ready to go back. I've sent someone to find MacNed. We're taking a patient who needs operating, so do you mind squeezing up in front with me? You've got narrow hips!"

"I'd be delighted." A seat with a windscreen view would ensure a more pleasant drive.

They crammed together on the passenger side of the vehicle between the gear stick and the door. Their enforced body contact inspired intimacy, while the noise of the engine, MacNed's music tapes, and the constant chatter of the nurses in the back meant they could speak without anyone in the vehicle following their conversation. After some time on small talk, Alan summoned the courage to pose the question he longed to ask.

"You're very religious, aren't you?"

It was an awkward topic to discuss among Brits, so best raised alone and ideally when not facing each other to avoid revealing facial expressions. During his schooldays, Alan, as an ardent atheist, had tormented the few kids who went to church, so he understood why some people preferred not to discuss their faith. Yet it seemed okay to ask Lorna; she was open about being a Christian, wearing a cross around her neck, and attending services when she had time on Sundays. Perhaps then, the fear to ask that question in public reflected his personal shame of showing an interest in the subject?

"Yes, I am." She stared ahead. "My parents are Christians, so that faith has always been a natural part of my life. It is hard for me to understand how it is for those who do not believe in God and Jesus. They are very real to me, and I pray to them at least twice every day. I know from experience that God answers prayer, though not always in the way I would expect, and it can take time for me to realise that it has happened."

So, Lorna was as superstitious as Megan with her pet crystal and the Kugombwalans with their witchcraft and fetishes. But Alan kept quiet while she continued to talk.

"Sometimes, I even sense God speaking to me, so my Christian faith means much more than just believing there is a God. It is also about having a relationship with God. I feel loved by Him, and I believe that God loves everyone and wants to have a relationship with each and every one of us, though not everyone knows that."

That was a new angle. The mention of love reminded Alan of various pop songs. He had always thought religion was about guilt and fear, which was why it was best avoided.

They had reached the edge of a village and were slowing for a checkpoint. Here were two soldiers, with cold, expressionless faces, hardened by cruelty and combat. Lorna's God surely did not love them—that was impossible to imagine. Ha! He'd found a flaw in her fine theory.

"You mean, God loves those guys, too?" They looked like real killers. For once, he was glad they were there, as they gave him the opportunity to challenge Lorna's silly religious views.

"Yes." There was sadness in her voice. "God loves us for who we are, even when we do wrong. But when we sin, it hurts Him, and that is one of the reasons He wants to develop a relationship with us—to show us a better way to lead our lives, so we can live without harming others and ourselves."

"He's not having much success with those guys, is He? I mean, they are clearly not saints." One of them had brought out a human skull for the benefit of the passengers and was showing off by holding a knife to it; the other waved them on.

Lorna remained silent while she considered how to answer. They sped away from the checkpoint, onwards over the undulating uplands of the plateau, though Alan's thoughts stayed with the soldiers. Why had that guy shown them the skull? Was he just posing, or was it a threat? There was something sinister about the Liberation Front troops. They were well-disciplined, and yet there was an underlying sense of violence about them.

"I think it is all about choice." Lorna interrupted his imaginings of the soldiers decapitating the original owner of the skull. "God allows us to do good or evil and gives us the option of whether or not to be in a relationship with Him."

"That don't make sense. Why doesn't your God have a relationship with everyone and show people how they should lead their lives? Then this world would surely be a better place."

They were driving through a burnt-out village, where the charred stumps of former mud walls were all that remained of the houses. The attack must have been recent, for the acrid stench of smoke still hung in the air, reminding him of the place they had stopped at on the way up. Some villagers were in the process of tearing down the buildings, guarded by soldiers.

What was going on here? Were the peasants willingly wiping the village off the map, or were they being forced to do so by the soldiers?

Lorna spoke again: "God has given us the gift of free will. That is what makes us different from just being advanced, pre-programmed robots. We can choose to do right or wrong. And we can decide whether to love God or not. The disadvantage for God is that free will includes the liberty to reject Him and to do wrong to others, which then hurts Him more."

Alan thought about the burned homes and the people who had lived in the village. It seemed illogical that there could be an all-powerful, loving God Who allowed such atrocities to happen, while simultaneously not liking what was going on. *Clear disproof for the existence of God,* he reasoned.

"God knows that healthy relationships can only be based on genuine love," Lorna continued, "which requires free will, for otherwise, it would be a forced love that would therefore be false."

They passed a barefooted, young woman in rags, carrying a large bunch of bananas on her head, followed by a Liberation Front soldier in crisp uniform and red wellington boots. Evidently, they were a couple, but were they also lovers? Or was she his cook and sex slave? It could even be a mutual partnership, the soldier providing protection in exchange for food and physical comforts.

What kind of love existed between Mandy and him? Sincere self-reflection revealed to Alan that it had started as lust on his part, to satisfy his teenage sexual urgings. Mandy's devotion while they first dated had then sustained his passion, fuelled by the elixir of amour that blinded him from seeing that he adored the experience instead of loving her as an individual. As that potion wore off, a calculated cynicism had taken over, and he was now aware that the advantages of staying together outweighed the disadvantages.

Had that caused her to do the same? Had she put up with him because of his status and popularity, combined with her fear of not having a partner? *I have abused her love instead of reciprocating it,* he recognised with remorse. *No wonder she has become more unpleasant, for I have only ever loved myself.*

That narcissism explained why he had never married Mandy. His apparent commitment to her was a sham, motivated by the comforts she provided plus the security of a fall-back option until he found someone better. Perhaps she felt the same, her loyalty towards him now corroded by the lack of a covenant between them, which meant she might one day dump him. The thought saddened him but also revealed a grain of genuine affection for her. He regretted that he hadn't tried to build their partnership on that love instead of running away.

His thoughts were interrupted by the sight of people fleeing in the distance, up on the hillside. Three women, two men, plus children. They made for some bushes and then disappeared from view.

"What's going on?" he asked. "Why are those people avoiding us?"

"I don't know," Lorna answered. "Perhaps they were scared by the approach of our car."

But they would have seen the MedRelief flag flying from the bonnet and realised they were a humanitarian agency. Why would the arrival of aid workers frighten them?

They continued until the next village, where they made a stop. Lorna wanted to find out what had happened to the MedRelief clinic that had once been there and whether any of the former staff were still around.

Alan sensed something was wrong the moment the engine was turned off. There was a deafening sound of cicadas, a shrill and constant buzzing shriek, as if a burglar alarm had gone off. The air was still and heavy, and uncharacteristically for Kugombwalans, no one came to greet them. Many of the windows of the houses were shuttered, and the doors closed. The few villagers at the marketplace were reluctant to speak to them, especially after some Liberation Front troops turned up.

Those soldiers seemed to be everywhere on the plateau. As soon as the vehicle stopped, they would materialise—insolent, threatening youths who demanded homage to their Kalashnikov power fetishes. Their presence made it impossible to ask the few locals they met about what was happening. It was clear something bad was afoot. And there was that feeling he couldn't explain, an ominous presence that made him feel uneasy.

It was like crawling around on a floor under a heavy rug in total darkness, not seeing where he was going, not knowing what was happening. And always weighed down, his movements restricted, and he vulnerable to whatever was lurking unseen in the shadows.

Dave returned from Nairobi the next day, bringing with him the mail pouch. Alan arrived at supper to find the team engrossed in their letters and Keith in his kit-car magazines.

"Surprise, surprise, Al, somebody's actually written to you." Paula smirked behind her stack of mail. Who sent her all those letters? Was it chain mail gossip? Or did she send them to herself?

He walked over to the table and picked up the envelope.

At last, he thought, recognising Mandy's writing.

He distanced himself from the group, to prevent them seeing the inevitable card with silly teddy bears. But there was no card. Just a short, handwritten note on cheap memo paper.

Al,

I've had enough. It's been terrible for me these last few months, what with you leaving me to live on my own, and now you don't even write to me. The gossip here is killing me. It would have been easier if you had told me you wanted to split up, instead of saying nothing and going out to enjoy yourself in Africa. Mum and I have put your things in your car and driven it over to your parents. I've changed the locks; Terry has moved in, and we are buying out your share of the mortgage.

Mandy

P.S. Don't try coming back or calling me. I never want to see or speak to you again.

A crushing sense of dejection and defeat descended upon Alan—not only because their relationship was over, for he had contemplated forcing that split himself, but also because there was the horrible feeling of being rejected, which brought home to him that he wasn't good enough for her to want to keep him. Though, he did not consider how it would have been for Mandy if, instead, it was he who had given her the boot.

Worse still was that she had cheated on him and thereby wronged him by collaborating with the man who had stolen his woman. It was also a coup for Mrs. Carter, he conjectured, convinced she had engineered the event by conniving once again to steer the course of his life. His attempt to regain control by going away had backfired because she had played her trump card to terminate his relationship with Mandy. *I hate you.* His spiteful mind conjured up an image of her.

Serves you right, the vision scolded back, using a favourite term for belittling her long-suffering husband. *You're no better yourself, Alan Swales. You were prepared to drop my daughter for that American woman who worked for the World Food Program.*

An unexpected pang of guilt struck him but was supplanted by anger for being humiliated. He was aware his family and friends would consider the breakup to be his fault and would mock his folly for going back to Ndombazu. And for what good? Doing the paperwork for a small hospital in the city, while the real needs were beyond their reach out in the countryside. MedRelief had now lost contact with the people they should be helping, the unseen victims of violence on the plateau. He and his colleagues were thereby failing as aid workers, which meant he was pointlessly destroying his life and career by coming to Kugombwala.

Bitter emotions engulfed him as his growing but suppressed unhappiness about the course of his life finally surfaced. Why had he come here? How could he have been so stupid to make that decision to return when he had known it might lead to disaster?

Alan retreated to his room. He needed time to himself, away from his bickering colleagues and their meaningless banter, to confront the wretchedness of his reality and to mourn the tragedy of his failed life.

As he looked back over the events that had led him to become an aid worker in Kugombwala, he became aware of an extraordinary set of coincidences that had forged his current calamity:

If Bobsy had not crashed his car, then he would never have asked him for a lift to the Industrial Engine exhibition . . .

If Mrs. Carter had not had her birthday that day, then he would not have accepted Bobsy's invitation . . .

If the exhibition hadn't been so tedious, then he would never have left the hall in search of a pub . . .

If that pub had owned a pool table or some slot machines, then he would not have read the discarded newspaper and seen the advert for the MedRelief job . . .

If he had not been so dissatisfied with his earlier existence in Britain, then he would never have been attracted to the thought of coming to Africa.

If, then . . . If, then.

Alan saw the story of his life simplified to a gigantic flowchart, with billions of possible outcomes. Yet of all these, far beyond the bounds of probability, he had ended up in the darkest pit on the planet, now ruled by a ruthless regime that had perfected the technique of unseen mass slaughter, while gaining international approval for their apparent good governance. Worst of all, it had been entirely his choice to return to Kugombwala—a fully informed, voluntary decision based on personal experience from his first mission that had indicated what he might be subjected to this second time. Why had he selected that foolhardy life sentence? What was going on?

A strange thought then struck him like a hammer blow to his head; it was meant to happen. A guiding hand was determining the events around him, creating a lifelong series of options to bring Alan Swales—through his own free volition—to where he was now. That immense and awesome power was in full control, yet was also so subtle that it was easy to ignore, unless sought for. Those thoughts led to one logical conclusion; there had to be a supernatural, divine presence. In other words, a god.

God! Alan's mind gasped at the realisation that it was the very Deity McJohn and Lorna had talked about and Who had sent words of comfort to him at Nairobi airport. Throughout his past, he had ridiculed such belief as simple superstition. But now, he was overwhelmingly aware—and therefore convinced—of the existence of the Almighty. The mist of his earlier mental confusion over that concept cleared, as he saw how the events of his life had been arranged to give him this opportunity to cross the threshold of ignorance and to thereby attain the one truth that really mattered—*that God is.* It was a staggering thought so vast, he felt his brain would explode with its magnitude.

Throughout that night, his mind blazed with unimaginable mental energy, as billions of neurons surged around his cranial cavity in complete harmony, continuously illuminating the Divine revelation. He knew he needed sleep, yet his brain refused to shut down, as if God were keeping the communication channel wide open. How utterly amazing! God had turned His face towards him, saturating him with the deep warmth of Divine affection.

The hours of night passed in an ecstatic state of raised consciousness. But as morning approached, he developed a sense of unease. Why was the Almighty Creator stooping down from His magnificence to contact him, a mere mortal among millions of others? Was some kind of response required on his part? If so, what form should that take? He dwelt on those questions but received no answers.

He then sensed these would come later, at the appointed time, and a deeper peace suffused him. The night dissipated into dawn, a new day, and the beginning to a new life that would now have a Divine dimension.

What, he wondered with a mixture of excitement and trepidation, *might that lead to next?*

CHAPTER 9

"Vermin!"

MacNathan pointed to the pile of rolled-up hospital tents. Alan straightaway spotted the dark rat droppings scattered over the white fabric and then noticed the pungent pong of stale urine as he approached. He looked around and saw additional evidence on the concrete floor.

"When did you last sweep here?" he asked.

"Friday."

There were a lot of droppings for one weekend. That meant loads of rats. It was clearly not a new development, he realised, with increasing irritation at his staff's incompetence—and in particular, his head storekeeper, MacSilas. It was no coincidence that the problem was pointed out now by MacNathan, the store's assistant who was in charge while MacSilas was on sick leave.

"Why did no one tell me before?" he asked, but he already knew the answer.

"MacSilas, he can make us sweep every day. I say many times to him, too much rats here. I can think he tell you."

But MacSilas had not informed him. Instead, he had swept away the evidence and kept silent, hoping the problem would disappear by itself. Meanwhile, the rats had continued to breed, thereby worsening the infestation.

"I can be thinking the vermin lives in those tents," MacNathan added.

That made sense, as there were many more droppings there than elsewhere. It was the perfect place for a nest, where they could chew chambers and tunnels in the folded fabric to hole it like Emmental cheese. Those same rats were raiding the adjacent food store, gnawing at the sacks of flour and milk powder, and then peeing on them, thereby spoiling the food they had not eaten. That explained why recent efforts to keep out those pests had failed—because they were already inside.

Alan hated those rats for the destruction and disease they caused. They had to be punished for ruining the tents and food, and they had to be prevented from doing so again—which meant they had to die.

"MacNathan, go fetch the logistics workers," he ordered. "Tell them to bring big sticks."

"Yes, Boss!" MacNathan laughed in eager anticipation of the hunt and scurried off to round up his colleagues.

MacNathan's departure gave Alan time to consider the task ahead. He thought back to his teenage years, when he and Bobsy had shot rats with air rifles at the rubbish tip. Those little beasts were sneaky, he remembered, for they ran fast and were quick to find boltholes. And they were stubborn, for they refused to die swiftly and so required plenty of pellets to persuade them.

The food store rats had to be systematically hunted down, one by one; otherwise, some would be overlooked, allowing them to escape and find alternative hiding places. A surviving male and female, or even a single pregnant mother, would multiply into ten more rats within weeks, and the infestation would start all over again. Any that got away would later return, knowing that the stores were full of food.

He had to wipe them out. The mission would fail if the rodents were not utterly annihilated.

A babble of loud, excited voices announced the arrival of the workers; this was going to be far more fun than their usual labours. They were so keen to get going that he had to stop them from disturbing the tents. Instead, he lined the gang in an arc around the pile, with clubs at the ready. MacNathan was then instructed to move the top tent very slowly.

As soon as he touched it, a rat leapt out, straight towards the waiting group of warriors. A flurry of falling batons came down upon the sprinting rodent, most missing, sometimes hitting. The workers whooped with joy at the fun of playing "Splat the Rat" for real. This was sport, teamwork, and competition combined, with each trying to deliver the final deathblow but also relying on the others to weaken the rat's resistance. After numerous thwacks, the rat was finally stopped in its tracks, its life smashed out of it.

They repeated the game of rat cricket many times that morning; after each round of slaughter, they returned to their starting positions, like a row of batsmen awaiting a ball. MacNathan was their bowler, disturbing the tents just enough to launch the next rat. To enhance the competition, Alan chalked up the scores on the wall, promising a crate of beer to the person who achieved the most kills. The game finished after they had played thirty-seven overs—all out, snuffed out, wiped out. The last was the queen rat. She was twice the size of the others and required much harder persuasion to die.

Three litters of helpless pups were then found in the tents and were despatched under the heel of Alan's boot. It was kindest to kill them straightaway, rather than let them starve a slow death.

The rat carcasses were then piled together in public display outside the building to celebrate the success of the morning's hunt that had cleansed the stores of vermin. He considered creating a funeral pyre to burn away all evidence that they had existed, but the workers asked if they could eat them, which Alan acknowledged would achieve the same result. He left them to barbecue their catch, while he went over to the MedRelief base for his own midday meal.

Rat was not on the menu, but he decided to serve the hunt as a topic for the lunchtime conversation. It would make a welcome change from the usual dull discussions about the hospital patients or Keith's status reports on repairs to the Land Rovers.

With the wisdom of hindsight, Alan realised he should have predicted the reactions to his account of the morning's events. Dave immediately interrupted with his own exaggerated tales, claiming to have once strangled twenty rats with his bare hands in half an hour. Then it was Paula's turn.

"You two are sick sadists," she spat. "Rats have got as much right to live as you. Why can't you leave them alone?"

"Because rats are pests," Alan retorted. Her standpoint surprised him. Did she believe what she was saying, or was she just itching for an argument? "The rats we killed this morning had ruined the tents, were eating the food, and were peeing all over it. We had no choice—either we eliminate them, or we allow them to continue to do a lot of damage."

"Why don't you keep them out? Why do you have to kill them?"

"Get real, Paula. They're not going to walk out nicely, are they? If we had tried to remove the tents, they would have all escaped at once and then hidden elsewhere in the stores. It would have been impossible to find them all without some running off to new hiding places."

"Then it's your fault for letting them get into the stores. Goes to show that you logisticians are not doing your job. And now you've murdered those poor rats to cover up your incompetence."

"Give us a break, Paula." Alan was getting agitated. "Rats are right difficult to prevent. Especially out here where our buildings are not made to block out rodents or to store food. Infestations are bound to happen sooner or later. And then you've got to go in and kill the critters. Only way to control them."

"You men are all the same." Paula scowled, now expanding her attack to half the human race. "Any excuse to justify killing."

"Reports are coming in of rebel atrocities on the plateau," Jules informed the team. "Two villages were attacked by Watumbwa insurgents a few days ago and burned to the ground. The army has seen signs of cannibalism on some of the corpses . . . "

"Urgh, those guys give me the creeps," Paula said. "I hope someone sorts them out soon."

"We can be confident of that." Jules smiled. "The U.K. government is now providing military aid to the army, while the Liberation Front's high command have promised to intensify their efforts to flush the rebels out of the bush and round them up. But for the meantime, they recommend for our security that we stick to the main road and be back here well before dark."

Alan guessed that the cannibalism rumour was war propaganda. It would be ideal cover for conducting military operations—create a nasty incident and say the other side was responsible, so the area could be sealed off and extra troops deployed without it seeming abnormal. Then blame the enemy for atrocities conducted out of sight by the army. "Conspiracy Theory Keith" would have called it a false-flag operation.

"How can we be sure it was the Watumbwa who did the killing?" Alan asked. "It could be the government soldiers, for all we know."

"Stop trying to be smart, Al." Jules huffed. "The army would not report their own atrocities. They are a highly disciplined and effective fighting force, rather than a rowdy rebel movement. You've got a real attitude problem with thoughts like that."

Alan regretted opening his big mouth. Discussion and debate were impossible with Jules, who regarded alternative opinions as insubordination, particularly from people who belonged to a lower social class.

"Yes, shut up, Al," Megan said, to his surprise. "Sometimes, you're so annoying,"

"Not just sometimes. All the time," Paula added.

"Sorry I spoke," Alan mumbled, taken aback by Megan's uncharacteristic outburst. What was her problem? Was she upset because he had refused her advances? Life would become unbearable if she ganged up with Paula, who persecuted him for the mere infraction of existing.

The last Land Rover swept into the compound. MacNed, MacJohn, and MacCharlie had now returned from the day's journeys, which was a cue for a chat break.

Beyond collegial conviviality, it was also an opportunity to debrief the drivers. The other expats, with the exception of Lorna, never told Alan what they experienced on their trips outside the city, which had left him in the dark about what was going on until he realised that an intelligence network was at his disposal. The drivers saw everything the expats saw and were happy to relay that information to him. But he had to be careful what he asked, for MacCharlie supported the Bakiboko.

"How's it going, lads?" he enquired as he approached them.

"Fine, Alan." MacNed was the first to respond. "Today I can bring white man to hospital."

"Yes, Jules is there."

"No, a sick one."

"What? A patient?"

"Yes."

"From where?"

"The plateau. He can be at a checkpoint. The Bakiboko soldiers tell me to take him. Too much sick."

It was incredible that expatriates still lived in that remote area. He might have some interesting stories and insights into the rumoured massacres.

"What's he doing up there?"

"He can say he works with monkeys. But that one is strange. The hair is long, like a woman." MacNed laughed at the thought, before adding, "And his clothes are dirty and too much spoiled."

"Maybe he can be an albino ape?" MacCharlie giggled.

"No, no, I cannot believe you." MacJohn joined the conversation. "A white girl-man in filthy rags? You are tricking me!"

It sounded strange, but then it clicked. "Is he a hippy?" Alan asked.

"Yes!" MacNed answered. "That word. Paula can use it."

"Was he barefoot?"

"Yes! He can be like a peasant!"

"No, my friend, you can fib me too much." MacJohn was overcome with cognitive dissonance at the thought of a new species of white man. He had hitherto only encountered neat, well-presented expats.

"Let's go and see him." Alan was equally intrigued—both to meet the hippy and to enjoy MacJohn's reaction.

They walked over to the hospital. A large crowd had gathered in the main ward, drawn by the spectacle of the shaggy sage sitting in a lotus position on a bed. Jules was listening to his chest through a stethoscope.

"Could you stop that chanting? I'm trying to conduct a medical examination."

"Hey . . . grease the peace, bro," the hippy responded in a pretentiously slow and ponderous tone.

"So, you were saying that you are called Dan Ryan, and you are from Sydney?"

"Truth is eternity, man. Lies are illusion."

"And you are a primatologist studying forest baboons in the interior. Who were you with?"

"With my siblings and cousins, the monkeys and mammals . . . "

"Please answer my questions properly! What have you been doing this last year during the war?"

"Smoking weed . . . it's what we all need."

Jules looked annoyed at the evasive answers. "So, tell me, what's happening on the plateau?"

"It's Africa being Africa—beautiful and sad, good and bad."

"And what's that supposed to mean?"

"Sweat and tears . . . to fill many years."

Jules tried a few times to rephrase his questions, but the answers were always the same cryptic poetry. Alan was enjoying watching Jules' increasing irritation at someone other than himself, safely hidden at the back of the sniggering crowd.

"What are you doing here, Al?"

He turned to face the familiar voice. "Oh, hi, Megan. MacJohn and I have come to see the new patient."

"Then I suggest you two leave, as you haven't got any business here. This is a hospital, you know, not a zoo."

Fair enough, he agreed. Megan was right about his motives, but it annoyed him that she was shooing him out, while doing nothing about the hundreds of Kugombwalans attending the free theatre.

It was about him, he realised, sensing she now despised him.

"How's Dan the Drugs Man?" Alan asked Lorna a few days later. She was the only person he could safely ask.

"Not good. He's riddled with parasites; and his body is on the verge of collapse from months of hunger, disease, and too much marijuana. We're giving him a thorough dose of antibiotics, antimalarials, antifungals, and de-worming medicine."

"He's sure to get a fresh kick out of all those chemicals."

Lorna ignored his attempt to be funny. "I'm worried about him, Al. He claims he can't remember what happened to him up on the plateau, and yet Paula says he often chants strange mantras about the jungle."

"Sounds normal for a hippy spaced-out on dope. Trying to be at one with nature."

"That's what I thought at first. But then this afternoon, I was examining the patient next to him, so I was forced to listen to his incantations. At first, I thought he was just repeating the words 'the primeval forest,' but he said it twice—'the primeval forest, the primeval forest'—and then a pause, and then the same phrase, over and over again."

"What's so strange about that?"

"I'm about to tell you. It sounds the same, but I thought I could detect a longer gap between the syllables at every second mention. Perhaps he was actually saying, 'the prime evil forest.'"

"Weird."

"Exactly! And it gets worse. I then asked him, 'Are you all right, Dan?' He stopped his babbling and looked straight at me with his piercing blue eyes. 'Earth and blood mixing,' he said. And then he resumed the primeval forest mantra."

"Scary."

"Very. I think he's really screwed up."

"Have you asked him about what happened to him?"

"Yes, but as I said before, he doesn't seem to remember. I suspect he's suffering from post-traumatic amnesia and getting occasional flashbacks that he tries to suppress. Paula says he has nightmares. He moans in his sleep and keeps waking up in the night, screaming."

"It's like I keep telling you. Something right bad is going on up there on the plateau."

"Oh, Al, don't start that up again," she implored.

Vrrooom, vrrooom, vrrooom.

It was still dark, but Alan could hear MacNed checking the Land Rover by pumping the accelerator to race the engine, without regard for the other expats who would have been asleep. He had risen extra early, as it was his turn to accompany the vehicle that was going to the plateau, which was due to depart at first light.

"Alan Swales?" A dapper, young Kugombwalan had appeared at the terrace, carrying an attaché case.

"Aye."

"I'm MacTrevor. From the Liberation Front NGO Liaison Office."

"Ah, yes, Jules said you would be joining us for part of the journey. Have you had breakfast?"

"Yes, thanks, but don't let me interrupt you."

Seems like a nice guy, Alan thought. *Well-spoken.*

"You're from Yorkshire, right?"

"Aye, that I am." Alan felt a warm pride well up within him, though it was illogical that a particular birthplace would automatically render him a better person.

"I was at Bradford University," MacTrevor continued. "Where's your hometown?"

"Brickdale."

"Wow, I've been there. I remember a pub called The Fighting Dogs."

"That's my local!"

"Is it? Small world. I've sipped the amber nectar there a few times."

That couldn't be right. Not with his skin colour. The landlord—and most of the clientele—did not welcome strangers, as signalled by the English flag on display in the window. Posh people in Britain preferred the Union Jack, with its connotations of the empire; but the predominantly white flag of St. George was the banner of white working-class tribal solidarity, the red cross symbolising their hot-blooded anger against everyone else, rather than Christ's crucifixion and His opposite message of forgiveness and reconciliation.

Alan knew it would be impossible for an African to hang out in The Fighting Dogs without being hounded out and him hearing about it. It was one of those pubs that went silent when intruded by outsiders, which included anyone who was not a regular. He recalled an incident when two local Pakistani lads had pushed their luck by coming in for a drink.

"Bobsy, will you say a word to the young gents?" the landlord muttered at the bar after they had bought drinks and sat down.

"Yeah, off you go, mate." An old man added his own xenophobic encouragement. "Them Asians got no place here. They should stick to their curry houses and corner shops."

The pub fell silent as Bobsy walked over to the table. All eyes were on him.

"Excuse me, lads, why did you call my pint a poof?" he demanded.

They looked up, surprised, having been silent since buying their drinks at the bar. "We didn't, mate," one of them replied meekly, looking away from the large presence looming over him.

"Are you calling me a liar?"

"No, mate."

"Then why did you insult my beer?"

They took the hint and immediately left, to the jeers of the rest of the pub.

Totally impossible, Alan mentally reconfirmed. *MacTrevor must be making it up. But why?*

"Time to go," he announced, having glanced up at the clock on the wall. They joined MacNed and the medical staff, who were waiting beside the vehicle.

"MacTrevor, meet Dr. MacTimothy." Alan did the introductions. "He is in charge of our field hospital on the plateau."

As per custom, Alan took the front passenger seat, which prevented further conversation with those in the back. Three hours later, they topped the plateau.

"Hey, Alan." MacTrevor tapped him on the shoulder. "I'll get out here, please. At the checkpoint."

MacNed brought the vehicle to a halt in front of the roadblock.

"See you, mate." MacTrevor got out and shook Alan's hand through the open window. "Thanks for the lift."

"Aye, any time." Alan smiled.

MacTrevor turned around and walked up to the soldiers. Both stamped to attention and saluted him.

What? Alan gasped. *He's not a civilian. He's a soldier.*

"Military intelligence." MacNed read his mind.

That explained the fib about The Fighting Dogs. MacTrevor was trying to be matey to gather information. Or was it a warning to him that they—the Liberation Front—knew everything about him, even down to the name of his regular watering hole in the U.K.?

He had to be careful not to get too paranoid.

A quarter of an hour later, they arrived at the field hospital.

It was immediately obvious that something was wrong, for nobody was about, except for a government soldier hanging around with a ten-year-old assistant in combat fatigues.

MacNed got out of the car and went over to speak to the soldier. He soon returned.

"The corporal, he can say patients all go home. He come by and find place empty, so he is watching to stop robbers."

It did not make sense. Patients and staff would not abandon a hospital unless forced to leave. Yet the tents were intact, and there was no sign of a skirmish. Alan decided to walk around the hospital to see for himself, hoping he might get an idea of what had happened.

He felt uncomfortable as soon as he opened the car door. Were just four eyes watching him, or were more militiamen spying on him from the forest?

"Alan, let us go back to Ndombazu." Dr. MacTimothy looked uncomfortable. "This place no good." Alan turned and looked at the doctor, who had remained in the Land Rover. He had a reputation among the MedRelief staff for being timid, yet he looked even more worried than usual. Prudency required Alan to take note of his Kugombwalan colleague's intuition.

"What do you think, MacNed? Is it safe to continue?"

"We can go, Boss, if you want." MacNed was irritatingly non-committal.

Alan thought for a moment. Opposing his own slight feeling of unease was the realisation that they still had supplies to deliver to the clinics in the villages further along the road. With the field hospital emptied, it was pointless to leave anything here. And having come this far, it would be a wasted journey if they went back without delivering anything.

He decided to carry on.

"Dr. MacTimothy, I think we should go to the clinics and deliver the supplies. Maybe the staff of the field hospital will have returned to work when we pass here on our way back."

"Boss, today can be a bad-luck day. Best to go home. We come again tomorrow."

It was awkward to be addressed with such deference by the doctor. Alan began to doubt his decision. He turned towards the soldier, who had come over to eavesdrop on their conversation.

"It okay to go?" He pointed in the direction away from Ndombazu.

"It can be okay," the soldier replied.

That settled it. They drove on.

The sky was heavy with thick clouds, threatening rain and even thunder. It felt uncannily dark, which added to Alan's increasing unease.

He couldn't shake the feeling he had made the wrong decision. But MedRelief had driven along this section of road yesterday and the day before. So, why should there be a problem today? Had he been infected by Dr. MacTimothy's timidity? Fear was becoming contagious in Kugombwala . . .

They passed a Bakiboko foot patrol—six well-armed soldiers walking in single file, one of them carrying a rocket-propelled grenade. Alan was, at first, comforted by the sight. Surely, no bandits would dare show their faces with such a heavy military presence in the area. On the other hand, were the extra soldiers deployed because there was a high risk of being attacked by rebels? Fear like a large worm writhed in his stomach.

Halfway to the clinic, they came to a beer crate checkpoint, where they were normally waved on by the usually silent soldiers. But today was different, for there was an officer in a crisp uniform who spoke good English and asked lots of questions. Who were they? Where were their I.D. papers? Where had they come from? Where were they going? What were they doing? Who had given them permission? Where were their authorisation papers? Was the vehicle registered? Where were the ownership documents? What were they carrying? Where was the packing list? To whom were the items intended?

The interrogation was directed at him. And as the officer spoke English, he could not hide behind the language barrier by using the driver as a shield, as he would otherwise have done. The soldier seemed suspicious, exploring every possible avenue for a reason to stop them or arrest them. He fired off the questions in rapid succession. Was it to affirm his authority and demonstrate his power over them, or was he actually interested in the answers? Was he on the hunt for something, or was he trying to hinder or block their progress?

Question after question, and so many queries of his own, yet no possibility to get any answers. Which led back to the big riddle: what was going on in Kugombwala? It was becoming ever more apparent that something bad was happening, something beyond his comprehension.

After two hours of interrogation and enforced waiting, they were permitted to proceed. Dave's rigorous security procedures had paid off, for they had copies in the car of every document that had been requested, including a forged letter from Queen Elizabeth granting NGO status to MedRelief.

Alan's shirt was soaked with sweat as they drove off, and he looked back to see the soldier speaking into a walkie-talkie. The sight injected him with a fresh dose of fear. He felt an incomprehensible dread of an unknown yet imminent consequence. But that fear was irrational, he told himself, for they had often travelled on this road, and on other occasions had seen soldiers talking to their VHS radios.

Yet an incessant inner voice was urging him to turn back. He looked at MacNed, whom he could see was also sweating. Was it the heat, or did he contend with the same concern? If so, it was amazing that he drove so well, negotiating obstacles without any apparent difficulty.

The horrible feeling mounted with each mile. Alan was now convinced they should not continue the journey, yet pride, as well as the prospect of being considered a coward by his colleagues, made him override his intuition.

And then it occurred to him that it might not be his own intuition, feelings, or even intellect driving his emotions. Maybe it was Divine instruction? Had God been telling him not to go beyond that last checkpoint? If so, it was an order he had failed to heed.

Did that then mean he was being assailed by the hitherto subconscious fear for the consequences of ignoring—and disobeying—God's command? He shuddered at the thought of what that might mean—that the Almighty had removed His protective hand . . .

It took fifteen minutes of such thoughts revolving around his head before he finally acted.

"MacNed, please stop," he ordered.

The vehicle came to a halt.

"What can be the problem?" the driver asked.

"I don't like this," Alan replied. "I don't think we should continue."

"Okay, Boss, as you want." MacNed showed no emotion. But it was a relief that he willingly obliged, without questioning the decision.

MacNed did a three-point turn, and then they were off again but in the other direction. The right direction. Back towards home.

“Very good!” Dr. MacTimothy piped up from the back.

Alan felt a burden lift off his shoulders, yet some anxiety remained. For they were far from Ndombazu, and there could still be dangers on the way. Despite this, it was comforting to be heading towards safety rather than uncertainty, regardless of the regular sight of heavily armed soldiers patrolling the road. They passed the same officer who had asked so many questions earlier and who waved them on after a short delay and demands to know why they had come back so soon. It all seemed so easy now.

They passed the field hospital, but still no staff were to be seen. Instead, there was a slight putrid smell.

A repeated thudding interrupted Alan’s thoughts. The sound decreased in frequency but became louder as the vehicle slowed to a stop by the side of the road.

“Puncture,” MacNed announced.

They had covered half the distance back to Ndombazu and were descending a series of hairpin bends down a forest-lined gorge on the edge of the plateau. It was a lonely spot; no villages or signs of human habitation anywhere, just rocky cliffs jutting through a forest-cloaked ravine. In any other country, it would have been a magnificent scene and a tourist attraction, but here they were exposed to possible sniper fire from the surrounding heights.

Alan joined MacNed by the side of the deflated tyre. “Have you found the hole?”

“No puncture. The valve, it can be spoiled.”

Alan crouched down to see for himself. The valve had indeed split, which was almost inevitable, as the MedRelief vehicles were fitted with inferior inner tubes from India, despite their reputation for not lasting.

There was no choice but to change the wheel, so MacNed retrieved the jack and started to pump it up under the axle to raise the tyre off the ground. But it failed to lift more than a centimetre because the cheap Chinese-made hoist refused to support the axle for longer than a few seconds. As they struggled to change the wheel, Alan cursed Blair-Campbell's meanness that was the ultimate cause of MedRelief operating with such poor equipment. MacNed was forced to search for suitable rocks to wedge up the axle, whilst increasing in stages the platform upon which the jack was mounted to lift the hub high enough to enable them to remove the damaged wheel and get the spare into place. It was excruciatingly slow work, and in the end, they resorted to excavating the soil under the wheel to gain sufficient space.

Only a few vehicles passed by, including the battered wreck of a lorry that made a lot of noise as it laboured up the road towards the plateau. Its cargo cheered as it passed—child soldiers in brand new uniforms, armed to the teeth with rocket-propelled grenades and assault rifles. The words *KILLER KIDS* had been painted onto the tailgate.

By the time they had finished, the sky was darkening with the onset of night, and mist was forming around the escarpment rim. The gorge was silent, yet Alan thought he could detect a distant whisper carried on the wind, sounding like a single word slowly repeated, yet too faint to discern. He walked away from the team who were burbling beside the vehicle, to prevent their conversation from disturbing his attempt to concentrate on the other noise he thought he was hearing.

Yet all he could hear was the same chilling silence.

So, was that unheard word just his imagination? Was he going mad?

And then it came again. Three recurring syllables, uttered over and over in a demonic whisper: "Genocide . . . genocide . . . genocide . . . "

As soon as the word sunk in, he sensed a distant, cackling laugh, and then the pseudo-sounds were gone. For a whole minute, Alan was transfixed with horror.

"Time to go, Boss," MacNed called from the car. Alan hurried over to hasten their escape, for this was no place to linger.

They drove down the gorge as twilight blackened into night, channelled by the road through a canyon of rainforest trees. They should never have tried to visit those clinics. Alan berated himself for disregarding the subconscious warnings from God. He thought back to that early afternoon when he had made the decision to carry on; he knew then it was the wrong thing to do, for he'd already had the premonition that something bad would happen. If only he had turned back straightaway, for the valve would then have failed once they were back in Ndombazu, which would not have been a problem. But instead, he had ignored his gut feeling, worried in part that his staff might think him a coward if he had ordered them to turn back. For that irrelevant—yet irreverent—act of pride, he would surely pay with his life and that of his colleagues, whose blood would be on his hands. This would be the day they died, ambushed on the dark road back to Ndombazu. It could have been so easily avoided.

After half an hour of driving between endless rows of trees, they noticed a faint glimmer in the distance. As they drew closer, the tree trunks lining the road appeared to glow, seemingly lit by a supernatural source.

"What's that light?" Alan broke the silence.

"I don't know." MacNed looked scared. "Not good to stop now. Bad place. Dangerous." He switched off the headlights and slowed the progress of the car towards the ghostly glow. "Harder for robbers to shoot us," he explained, causing Alan's fear to go into overdrive.

The road turned, and as they rounded the corner, they saw the source of the light. A vehicle was burning on the road ahead of them, engulfed in flames that illuminated the surrounding forest to produce reverse silhouettes of light on dark. A bitter smell of burning rubber filled the air, and from the fire billowed a thick cloud of smoke that closed the chasm between the trees on either side of the road, creating a wall of smoke that was lit white by the fire beneath.

The whole effect reminded Alan of a church—the rows of rainforest trees lining the road resembled gothic columns, leading to an apse created by the smoke wall. Yet there was an incongruity in the altar of the burning vehicle, as with the whole atmosphere surrounding the fire. He recalled the computer games he used to play, battling monsters in underground chambers lit by burning torches. Only this chamber was not lit by firebrands, but by a funeral pyre—a human sacrifice of the people who had been in that car.

MacNed brought their own vehicle to a halt, as the burning car seemed to block their onward exit.

"Can you get past?" Alan asked.

"I think so, but heat can be big problem. We must drive very fast to not get burned."

"Won't that be difficult with the smoke and with such a narrow space to get through?"

"Yes, we can maybe get stuck . . . "

This was a diabolical place. Alan trembled, unwillingly reminded of the cackling laugh that he had sensed at the edge of the escarpment. They couldn't go forwards; they couldn't go back, and they couldn't stay. And the thought that had haunted him all afternoon and evening was back—that he had fallen from grace, that God had removed His protective hand, abandoning his fate to the murderous men who stalked these woods. He was stricken by absolute terror, his heart thumping a staccato drumbeat on the inside of his rib cage. What if he should die now? What then? Would he go to Hell? To an underworld worse than this place of slaughter and torture? He looked ahead at the anti-church with its altar of burning humanity and froze at the thought that he might be at the entrance to Satan's abyss.

But it was too late to do anything, for MacNed was already accelerating at breakneck speed towards the inferno that would soon swallow them up. He shut his eyes in dreaded anticipation of the eternal damnation that was to come.

He felt a searing heat on the side of his face; the vehicle jolted over an obstacle; and then there was the sensation of coolness, as well as the calmer sound of the slowed motor. He opened his eyes to see darkness. He looked around; everyone was still there, still in the Land Rover. Beyond, disappearing into the distance, was the burning vehicle with its headlights still shining out, in spite of being on fire.

The relief was overwhelming, but there was still a way to go to Ndombazu. They had been spared for the moment, but was it presumptive to hope that they could return home unscathed? *Oh, Lord, deliver us from evil,* he prayed, over and over again, recalling the words from his primary school assemblies. *And forgive me for my sins.*

MacNed turned to look at him. "That was the old Mobile Five," he said, switching on the headlights again.

"What do you mean?" Alan was confused from having his thoughts interrupted.

"One of the cars that can be looted when the Bakiboko take Ndombazu." The drivers had an uncanny ability to recognise every vehicle they had ever driven. To Alan, it was just a Land Rover; but the drivers could spot the subtle differences in the shape of the bumpers, the radio antennae mountings, the roof rack, and other fittings that were unique to the vehicles shipped out by MedRelief.

They drove for an hour without incident. No one spoke, each silent in their own thoughts, as they stared at the few illuminated metres of endlessly unfolding road ahead. Now and then, a nightjar fluttered up from the track where it had sought to rest for the night on the sun-warmed sand.

Eventually, they reached a cluster of houses, where the vast darkness was punctured by a few pinpricks of light from the burning wicks of kerosene lamps. That meant people and, therefore, life.

In the middle of the village was a military checkpoint, the first since the villages on the plateau. They passed through with unexpected ease, perhaps because the soldiers were so surprised to see them still on the road at that time of the night. From there, it was plain-sailing back to the capital.

As his stress and worries began to ebb, Alan tried to make sense of the day's events—and of God's mysterious ways. What had He been saying and why? God had definitely told him to turn back when they were at the abandoned field hospital; Alan was in no doubt about that. But why the warning? Was it because the Almighty knew the valve would let out? Was He trying to return them to Ndombazu before the faulty inner-tube caused the wheel to go flat? Was it to prevent them from getting stuck on the plateau with a flat tyre that would cause them to return in the dark when they risked getting ambushed?

That was a possibility, he surmised.

And yet . . .

That explanation didn't work because he recognised that he had continued for part of the way against God's instructions. The valve had still let out, and the tyre had gone flat. Then they had struggled for so long with the faulty wheel that they were forced to finish the journey in the dark. Yet they had not been ambushed, unlike that other car. Why had it happened to that former MedRelief vehicle and not to the one he was in?

It was difficult to make sense of it.

Then the thought occurred to him that the attack had been on a vehicle exactly like theirs. Perhaps it had been intended for them?

A possible explanation struck him. The incident was not about a faulty valve. That was the wrong way to look at it. Instead, God may have been telling him to go back to avoid an ambush that was being set up for them on the way to the clinics where he intended to deliver the medicine.

Even though he'd initially ignored that instruction and continued the journey—Alan extrapolated his thinking—he'd fortunately decided to turn back before reaching the ambush point. When the officer at the village set up another ambush at the foot of the plateau, God intervened and caused the valve to fail, which prevented MedRelief's Land Rover from driving into the trap. Instead, the other vehicle fell prey to the attack that was meant for his car. How ironic that a vehicle looted by the Liberation Front—and likely full of their soldiers—had become the victim of an army ambush. Divine justice indeed . . .

He thought back with shame at how he had cursed the useless Chinese jack. Was that malfunctioning machinery another element of Divine intervention to slow down the changing of the wheel? If so, it was a sign that he had been forgiven for earlier refusing God's guidance. His life had been supernaturally spared by the Almighty through His amazing grace, which smothered disobedience with redeeming love.

Alan relaxed as the Land Rover rolled into the compound. *Safety at last.* Nothing could happen to him here.

Dave and Lorna emerged from the radio room to meet the vehicle.

"Great to have you guys back," Dave said. "We've been worried about you being out so late in the dark."

"It's been quite a day, Al," Lorna told him once they had gone inside. "Both with your vehicle breakdown and with Dan disappearing—"

"What? He's gone?"

"Yes. We didn't know until Paula did the ward rounds this morning. He wasn't at his bed, and the staff then told her he'd already left by the time they had arrived at work."

"We first thought he'd nipped out to buy more hash," Dave continued. "But he didn't return. When the nightshift crew came back on duty, we got conflicting stories about what had happened the previous night. They all said he just walked out, but the details didn't match—"

"MacAbigail then told me in private that some soldiers had come for him during the night," Lorna interrupted.

Alan knew only a few of the hospital staff by name, as he rarely had to deal with them, but he knew MacAbigail the head nurse. Definitely someone they could trust.

"Some of the other staff corroborated her story when we spoke to them one-to-one," Lorna continued. "It's alarming."

"Nah, no need to worry," Dave said. "I've called the government's NGO liaison office, and they spoke to the army. One unit is hot on the trail of a Watumbwa rebel group, disguised in uniform, that has infiltrated the city. The Bakiboko High Command have committed to catch them and to do a house-to-house search throughout Ndombazu to find Dan. They are an impressive bunch of guys." Dave smiled. "Highly professional."

"Al, I've got a favour to ask of you . . . "

"Aye, go ahead," Alan muttered without looking up. Hundreds of dollars had gone missing from the accounts—or was there a typing error in the balance sheet? He hated having the ultimate responsibility for the finances; it was easy to make a mistake, which would lead to the suspicion that he was pilfering funds if there was a shortfall.

Lorna closed the door and then sat down opposite him. "I'm concerned about my friend, Father Roy," she said in a hushed voice. "It's been a week since he went up to the plateau. He should have been back by now, but I haven't heard from him."

"What was he doing up there?"

"Trying to find out what's going on."

"That would be right risky! No wonder you're worried."

"Exactly. So, I'd like to go over to where he lives, but I don't want to take any of the drivers. The Liberation Front is bound to have spies among our national staff, so I daren't trust them, not even MacJohn. Would you mind coming with me, Al? I don't want to drive on my own, especially not through the rougher areas of town." After a short pause, she added, "I'm a bit scared."

The idea of driving into a bad neighbourhood did not appeal to Alan. Government informers were everywhere, and being seen in areas where they did not normally go would arouse the attention of the army. However, he did not want Lorna to go alone, and he was also intrigued to hear what the priest might have to say.

"All right, when do you want to leave?"

"Can we go now?"

"Better wait until after the drivers have gone home, otherwise people will wonder why we are taking a car without one of them. MacNed will be alone on duty tonight, so I'll find a reason for him to go on an errand."

"How did you get rid of MacNed?" Lorna asked as Alan started the vehicle.

"I hid the beers, so there were none in the fridge when Keith finished for the day."

"That must have annoyed him." Lorna smiled. "An evening without his pre-dinner drinks—he's going to moan about it throughout supper."

"Yes, you would think he'd suffered a major human rights violation. Anyway, as expected, he readily volunteered to take MacNed to replenish the stock."

They drove over to the main gate, which MacWalter opened.

"Oh, Alan, you are now a driver!" the guard exclaimed.

"Aye, a friend of Dr. Lorna urgently needs to see her. Medical problem."

"Okay, you can tell MacRobert?" He referred to the radio operator.

"Yes, I said we would be back before the curfew."

"Right, Boss!" He waved as they left the compound.

Lorna directed him along a series of main streets. After ten minutes, while driving through a mean area of metal-bashing workshops, he interrupted her chatter.

"Sorry, Lorna, but have you got your make-up bag with you?"

"Of course."

"Okay, get your mirror out but don't turn around. I think we are being followed."

"By the Mercedes with the smoked-glass windows?" she asked once she had pulled out her mirror.

"Yes, it's been hard on our tail these last five minutes."

"Can you shake it off?"

"That would be difficult. It's a lot faster and more manoeuvrable than a Land Rover."

"Who do you think it is?"

"Could be those military intelligence guys."

"Should we turn back?"

"Maybe."

He quickly weighed their options. The obvious was to return to the base, but he didn't like the thought that they would still be followed. He needed to lose his pursuers. But how to get away?

"Do a handbrake turn, mate," he heard Bobsy yell in his mind. It would be an option for most vehicles, Alan acknowledged, but impossible in a Land Rover, as its handbrake was not located on the rear wheels.

Then an idea emerged.

"Lorna, I'm going to try something, but you will have to do everything I say without question. And hold on tight. Are you in?"

"Yes," she answered meekly.

"Forget the Mercedes but use your mirror to watch the other traffic behind us. Tell me when a gap is coming."

"Okay."

He indicated to the side, drove off the road, and stopped the Land Rover on the sandy verge before applying the handbrake to counter the upward slope.

The Mercedes did the same.

With the engine running and the clutch depressed, he put the vehicle into low gear. "Now, open your door to make them think you are about to get out," he ordered Lorna, "but be ready to close it as soon as I tell you."

The bait worked. Opposite doors opened on the Mercedes, and two plain-clothes agents exited. They started walking towards the Land Rover.

"All clear behind," Lorna announced.

The timing was perfect, providing space to re-enter the road.

"Shut the door and hold on," he shouted as he slammed down the accelerator, while releasing both handbrake and clutch. The power from the Land Rover's massive engine surged to all four wheels, spraying his opponents with grit as the vehicle accelerated through the loose soil. The surprised soldiers hurried back to the Mercedes, but their attempted swift getaway ground the car's fast-spinning rear wheels into the dirt.

"They're stuck." Alan laughed at the retreating sight in his rear-view mirror of an agent struggling to push the car out of the soft sand. "But we had better get off this road in case they catch us up."

He rounded a bend, then turned into a side street and zigzagged through a maze of narrow lanes to the highway they had been on but at a distance ahead.

"No sign of the Mercedes," Lorna remarked. "What do you think? Shall we try to see Father Roy, anyway?"

"Aye. We've got this far; no point turning back now."

Lorna directed him to a neighbourhood of tumbledown colonial mansions succumbing to nature's relentless effort to reconquer lost territory. Palms sprouted through the perforated roofs of abandoned houses, while strangling figs grew out of cracks in walls that had grown black with mould. It was an area of Ndombazu that Alan had not known existed, an unloved and decaying memorial to a time Africa was trying to forget.

"Here." Lorna pointed to a rough, metal gate. Repeated horn beeps were required to make it open, revealing a decrepit, old man who looked as if he was long overdue a burial. He regarded Alan and Lorna with a lifeless gaze as they drove past.

"That's MacEbeneezer," said Lorna. "I don't know why they employ him. He's often drunk, or asleep, or both. He's the most ineffective guard I have ever come across." She called out, "Hello, MacEbeneezer. Is Father Roy at home?"

The simple grunt from the old man was impossible to decipher, but a motorbike and a pickup truck on the drive gave reason for hope. They got out of the vehicle and went over to the house. It was a low, concrete structure, built after Kugombwala had become independent and far humbler than the mansions surrounding it.

"Hallo-oh, Lorna," cooed an old woman from inside the house as she approached the door. "You are welcome. Father Lorenzo is here." She came out and greeted them in the traditional manner of a Kugombwalan servant.

"Hello, MacEsther." Lorna bowed as she took her hand. "Is Father Roy at home?"

"No, he is not here." MacEsther diverted her gaze in deference. "He is out at the moment. I think Father Lorenzo knows where he is. Please come inside, and I will fetch him."

Alan was surprised by the fluency of her English; her servile manner and wizened appearance were indicative of an uneducated peasant woman. But a closer look revealed a soft beauty that overcame wrinkles and broken teeth. She must once have been the envy of her village, some thirty years earlier when Kugombwala had also been full of hope for the future.

She invited them to take a seat on the uncomfortable armchairs in the lobby. There was little else in the room; a low table was draped with a cheap plastic cover printed with roses, on which stood a tacky vase containing artificial flowers, while the garish sky-blue walls were hung with gaudy biblical scenes that were so unrealistic as to seem superstitious. Was this the inevitable—and unenviable—fate of religious people? Condemned to a drab life devoid of the world's pleasures, while living in dull institutions with such tasteless decor?

"Roy shares this house with Father Lorenzo and Father José." Lorna interrupted his thoughts. "They are members of the same missionary order. They've been here for years. Ah, Father Lorenzo."

A stout, middle-aged South American had appeared, wearing frayed clothes and worn-out flip-flops. He gave Alan a firm handshake. His palms were hard, those of a man used to physical work.

"We go," he said. "To where Roy is. Shall we walk? Not far."

They took a narrow path between two plots opposite the house. The track opened out onto a wide space where a group of youths were playing football, refereed by a familiar figure with long dreadlocks tied back into a ponytail. After five minutes, Roy blew the half-time whistle and came over to join them.

"My man!" He gave Alan the traditional Kugombwalan triple handshake. "How's your life?"

"Okay, thanks."

"Lorna tells me you are the captain of your local football team. Do you want to referee the second half?"

"Sure. You got a red and yellow card to go with that whistle?"

"Yes, but I never need to use them. I've been coaching these boys for years, so they understand the rules. Both on and off the field."

The lads were in their late teens to early twenties and were vigorous players. Alan was struck by their willingness to accept his decisions, plus their polite personal thanks to him after the game was over. This would not have happened in Britain, he reckoned, remembering the ungrateful youth team he coached, as well as the verbal abuse that the teenaged Bobsy would heap upon the referee, particularly when declared offside just before a goal opportunity.

After the last of the youths had taken their leave, Alan joined Lorna and the two priests.

"Roy and Lorenzo got back yesterday," Lorna told him. "They took a back road out of Ndombazu and then turned off onto an abandoned logging track that goes up to the plateau, so they managed to skirt the army checkpoints. What's going on there is horrific."

"I've never seen anything like it." Roy's eyes radiated shock. "It's like a huge human abattoir—hundreds of corpses strewn out in streets and fields . . . " He paused, overcome with emotion. "Village after village has been totally destroyed."

"That place is so bad. Women and children, their skulls broken . . . " Lorenzo's face crumpled into a grimace of pain.

"For me, there's no doubt," Roy said. "It's genocide."

"Who's doing it?" Alan asked. "The government soldiers or the rebels?"

"The Bakiboko soldiers of the Liberation Front, for sure," Roy said. "We met three separate groups of survivors hiding in the forest, and their stories all match. The army is systematically massacring Watumbwa civilians on a huge scale and sending search-and-destroy squads into the forest to finish off anyone who escapes. We had a close shave when we almost stumbled upon one of them . . . "

"Did you take any photos?" Alan's heart beat faster at the news that confirmed his worst fears. The situation was even worse than he had suspected.

"Yes," Roy answered. "But it's too risky to get the films developed here or to talk to any journalists. So, I will go to Rome next week to alert the Vatican and inform the international media."

"Don't expect to be welcomed back in Kugombwala!"

"I don't. Lorenzo and José will also become Liberation Front targets when I go public, so all three of us must leave here for good. It's not been an easy decision as we've been here for decades."

"José is flying back to Argentina in a few days," Lorna added, "and we've agreed that I will refer Lorenzo to Nairobi for cancer treatment to reduce any suspicion that might arise from all three priests leaving the country at once."

"Won't that put you at risk?"

"I hope not . . . but I also have to do what I can." She fell silent, staring at the ground.

The pervading sense of gloom was deepened by the falling night. Alan's thoughts returned to their immediate situation.

"We've got to get back," he announced. "It's already late. The army will be suspicious if they see our vehicle at dusk; but if we leave any later, we'll be done for. Staying over is not an option, as the local staff will question why a vehicle is gone all night without a driver—and the Liberation Front will soon hear about it."

"You're right, Al." Lorna stood up. "We have to go now. Take care of yourselves, Roy and Lorenzo. I guess I won't be seeing you for a while, Roy." She gave him a hug.

"Goodbye, Lorna and Al. May God protect you both."

They walked back to the Land Rover without exchanging a word, for the topic on their minds was too dangerous to discuss in the street. Once inside the vehicle, Alan started the engine and switched on the headlights, which revealed the insects that flitted in the twilight air.

"What I don't understand"—he voiced an issue that was perplexing him—"is why God doesn't do anything to stop the massacres on the plateau."

Lorna swiped at a mosquito that was bothering her face. "It's because He has tasked us to deal with the evil in the world. Becoming a Christian is not just about getting saved from eternal punishment for our sins; it also comes with the duty to care for others—particularly for the poor, the suffering, and the downtrodden. That is why Roy, Lorenzo, and José are risking their lives to get the truth out about the massacres."

"Good on them, but it's not made any difference so far. Loads of innocent people have been killed. Doesn't God care about them?"

"I'm sure He does—" Lorna paused to consider her answer. "But it seems He has decided not to intervene for the moment. If He did, it would take away our own responsibility. The problem is not God; it is us. Too few Christians are doing anything to stop evil."

"Why's that?"

"I guess most of us are scared of confronting the dark side of the world." A mosquito-devouring bat was temporarily illuminated as it swooped down in front of the headlights. "I'm no better myself and now realise I deliberately ignored the indications of the killings that are happening around us. Like most people, I prefer the easy option of doing nothing. I thought I was okay because I'm an aid worker. But to God, that is not enough when there is so much evil around."

Lorna's words brought Alan's focus back to their current situation. His pulse now raced, for they were leaving the quiet suburb and were about to turn onto a busy main city street where there was a greater likelihood of checkpoints. It was the hour of the curfew, and he regretted having come.

They were waved through the first roadblock, but a soldier flagged them down at the next.

"Oh, no," Alan whispered. "We're in trouble." His mind raced to find a suitable excuse.

The soldier looked young, about twenty years old. His face seemed kind but for eyes that were dulled from having seen too much violence.

"Where you can go? Where Kugombwala driver? What you do? Where papers?" Suspicion, suspicion, and more suspicion. The dice was loaded against them from the start.

Alan started with the story he had told the radio operator. "The doctor and I had to attend a medical emergency—"

"Miss, you can be doctor?" the soldier interrupted.

"Yes." Lorna smiled. "At the hospital."

"Please," he implored. "My mama can be sick with malaria. Do you have medicine?"

"Here." Lorna opened her medical case. "Four pills now, two tomorrow and the day after." She wrote down the instructions and handed them with the tablets to the soldier. "Tell your mother to come and see me if she is not better after a five days."

"Thank you, Doctor," he clasped her hands and bowed. "May God bless you!"

Lorna turned to wave as they drove off. "Wasn't he sweet? They're not all bad, these Liberation Front soldiers. Their commanders must be forcing them to commit atrocities."

Genocide.[1] The word spoken by Roy bounced around Alan's brain as he lay in bed, trying to sleep. It meant much more than random massacres, he realised, amounting instead to carefully planned and executed killings, conducted on a massive scale by the Kugombwalan state.

1 From *Webster's College Dictionary*: Gen-o-cide (jen`a sid`) n. [< Greek genos, race, kind + -CIDE] The systematic killing of, or a program of action intended to destroy, a whole nation or ethnic group.

It was terrible to think about, so Alan tried to suppress the word from his mind, but it refused to go. If, as he suspected, it was true, then it required a response, an action, on his part. For to ignore it would be tantamount to complicity through the crime of uncaring apathy.

What should he do? He wished he had not placed himself in the impossible situation of having a burden of knowledge that needed to be shared yet was too dangerous to release.

His thoughts then moved on to God, Who had spared his life the week before and Who would be watching his every move, while knowing all his decisions. Whatever he did, he would have to account for his actions before the Almighty, at the hour when he would go on trial for his life's deeds.

Either way, he reasoned, it was clear he would suffer sooner or later; but the stark choice of who to fear for that was up to him. It was a toss-up between human injustice versus Divine justice—receiving retribution from the Liberation Front for standing up to their atrocities, against being punished by God for doing nothing. A dilemma he decided to postpone because Roy was soon going to speak out, which would alert the world to the massacres, and mobilise the international community into action. No point duplicating his effort.

The next day, it was Alan's turn to accompany MacJohn on the resupply run to the clinics on the plateau. It was his first trip since the week before when they had seen the former MedRelief car burn. He was not comfortable going, but it was difficult to refuse, as Paula and Megan had already undertaken the same journey earlier that week.

They set off at first light, at that tranquil time when the calm, night-cooled tropical air was first warmed by the gentle rays of the dawning sun. Cockerels crowed out their welcome to the coming day, while the inhabitants of the suburbs and villages commenced their morning chores at an unhurried pace.

By the time they had driven for an hour, the heat had become noticeable. Half an hour later, Alan's neck was bathed in sweat that the incoming air from the passenger window failed to evaporate. His back was soaked from the plastic seat, so he tried to sit forward to encourage some air movement but to little avail. He couldn't wait to get out of the car to dry off.

A sudden down-blast of cold air then heralded what was about to come. The trees around them shook violently, and the sky darkened as they came under the bombardment of heavy rain.

Alan wound up his window as liquid shrapnel was fired from the sky, blasting them from all angles and splashing off every surface. The tempest tore great branches from the trees and threw them down about them, while millions of small twigs and leaves were whipped up into the frenzied air. Explosions erupted from all sides as lighting struck again and again. A nearby tree took a direct hit, and for a moment, the entire ground around the vehicle was lit with intense, white, electrostatic light.

The terrifying spectacle continued for a whole hour while they cowered in the comparative safety of the stationary car. Water pushed its way through perished rubber seals, spraying them with mist, while huge drops of condensation gathered under the roof and dripped onto their heads. MacJohn prayed aloud that they would not be hit by lightning or a falling tree. It was easy to believe that the storm was a sign of celestial rage, as if the heavens were attempting to flush out the evil that was rampant upon the earth.

It struck him that the one true God was angry about what was happening in Kugombwala—an anger that he should heed. And fear.

Was this a warning to him?

They continued their journey once the rain had eased to a steady downpour. Torrents of water flowed down the road that led up towards the looming escarpment, faintly visible in the gaps between the trees as a distant, grey silhouette, blurred by low cloud. It was difficult driving, as the formerly hard-baked road was now wet and slippery as butter. MacJohn struggled to keep the vehicle going straight. Once, they had to winch the Land Rover out of the drainage ditch beside the track.

At the edge of the last clearing, close to the base of the plateau, he noticed the outlines of ten figures emerging out of the damp gloom, shrouded in camouflaged rainproof ponchos. In front of the soldiers lay a piece of board spiked with upturned nails. One of the soldiers flagged them down to halt before the spiny roadblock.

Alan shuddered. It was a new checkpoint, which had not been there before.

"Road closed. Not safe. You can turn back," the soldier ordered.

What was happening ahead? A mudslide? Military operations? Or more massacres?

"But we need to get through," Alan implored. "We have patients who require medicine. Villagers and displaced people."

"Ah," scoffed the soldier. "No need to worry about them." He made a gesture as if he was brushing an imaginary something away and then muttered, "Vermin."

CHAPTER 10

"Roman priests! They kill them!"

Alan looked up at MacZak, startled. "What do you mean?" But he had already guessed the answer. Roman priests meant Catholics—Father Roy and the two South Americans.

"The Latinos and the Rasta," MacZak confirmed, breathless from spreading the news around the compound. "Dead!"

Alan was dumbstruck. They were people he knew, albeit from a brief encounter. The killings were getting closer.

And there was further cause for concern. He had not anticipated that the priests might be murdered because he had assumed they were under God's protection. Just as he had been a week earlier, when his car had suffered a flat tyre on the plateau.

The assumption he was assured of Divine deliverance must be wrong, for God had not prevented the assassination of the priests, even though they were better people than he was. It was difficult to understand why this had been allowed to happen and kindled in him a deep disquiet about what the allegedly Almighty could or would do and not do. His newfound belief was under attack.

"How did it happen?"

"They can cut the heads." MacZak made slicing motions in front of his throat. "One, two, three."

"Who killed them? When did it happen? Where?"

"They can chop last night." MacZak appeared unwilling to donate more than one answer at a time.

"Who did it? Where?"

"In their house." MacZak pointed his chin in the general direction of the suburb. "The heads, they can put them on the doorstep."

Alan's face contorted in disgust before realising the murder might also be a message. "Who did it, MacZak? Who?"

The youngster paused. And then in a whisper, he uttered his answer. "They did—the Bakiboko."

News of the decapitated priests rattled the MedRelief team. Beyond the brutality of their murder, it reminded them that neither charity work, nor foreign nationality, conferred immunity from being killed in Kugombwala.

The news was hardest for Lorna because Father Roy had been a close friend. She withdrew to her room for the remainder of that day and did not appear at breakfast the next morning.

Alan hated the monthly administrative ordeal of creating payslips for MedRelief's local staff. It was a tedious task, as there were almost two hundred employees on the list, and every month required new names to be added, others deleted, holidays tallied, and pay deducted for days when people had not shown up to work.

This time, the job was going to be even more difficult because his brain wanted to be elsewhere, worrying about what was happening around him in Kugombwala's unseen shadows. He was plagued by the notion that all the local people knew about the mass killings on the plateau but preferred to stay silent and look the other way. It was easy to understand why, for it would be extremely dangerous to divulge or dig deeper into the truth, just as the priests had done. Yet it disturbed him to think that nobody else was willing to risk their lives to stop the evil from flourishing. *Has nobody here any backbone,* he asked himself and then fought to fend off the thought that he, too, had a responsibility.

Trying to focus on his duties, he studied the names on the sheet in front of him: MacEsdra Gulugulu, MacLeah Kilogi, MacSampson Ubofwa. He could not put a face to most of them, as they were hospital staff whom he rarely saw. It was the same with the alleged victims of the killings going on around him—they were featureless statistics. Roy and Lorenzo were the only ones he had ever met. Were the others real or mere rumour?

Alan forced himself to continue reading. MacNathan Mupanya, the assistant storekeeper; MacKevin Tembo, the leader of the maintenance gang; and then the names of the rest of the logistics crew, whose faces he knew but whose exact identities always eluded him. Eight names were in that group on the payroll. That was strange. Only seven came to work. What was going on?

He went to the office of MacQuentin, the purser, to inquire whether there might be a mistake.

"No, Alan, there have always been eight people. They each come every month to get their salaries. Each one of them."

Alan frowned. That meant either a ghost worker whose only effort was to turn up every month to get his pay or a scam by MacQuentin to extract extra money out of MedRelief. More research was needed, and perhaps a trap would have to be set to net everyone complicit in the scheme. He decided to take a coffee break to mull over the problem and devise a plan.

He went to the kitchen, poured himself a mug of coffee, and headed out to the terrace. A view of the ocean and the calming sight of the surf would straighten his thinking.

To his surprise, he saw Lorna sitting in one of the easy chairs, reading a magazine. Even more amazing was to see her smiling. She appeared relaxed, almost radiant.

"You okay?" he asked tentatively.

"Yes," she said. "Cried myself dry, but I'm better now. Have a seat."

He obliged. "How come you look so happy? I would have expected the opposite after all you've been through."

"Yes. It has been very hard. I wept for hours. I prayed to God, asking how He could allow Roy, Lorenzo, and José to die. For a long time, there was no answer." A sad expression crossed her face before she brightened up again. "Then, while I was praying this morning, I had a vision. I was at a place with stunning colours everywhere, the most beautiful scenery I have ever seen, and I realised I was looking into Paradise. In front of me was a large crowd of mostly young Africans, all about twenty years old, in long, white robes. They had lovely, serene faces; and from below my vantage point, three people appeared into view. I could only see the backs of their heads, but I sensed who they were. The people in the crowd reached out to greet the three newcomers, each introducing themselves.

"'Hello, I'm MacRebecca,' a beautiful young African girl said. 'You gave me food when I was hungry.' In that instant, the vision changed, and I saw a little child, starving and crying, and Father Lorenzo giving maize meal to her mother, a woman in rags." Tears rolled down Lorna's cheek as she spoke, but she kept smiling.

"I was then transported back to the same vantage point where I was looking into Paradise again, and this time, a young man introduced himself to the new arrivals. 'Hello, my name is MacElisha,' he said. 'You tried to stop those soldiers who were beating me.' Once again, the vision changed, and I saw a horrible scene of soldiers clubbing a teenager to death with the butts of their rifles and Father Roy being shoved away as he tried to intervene. And so, the vision continued, alternating between scenes of the welcome in Paradise and events in the lives of Roy, Lorenzo, and José at various moments when they had helped the poor and oppressed."

"Wow," was all Alan could think of saying.

"I was reminded of the words from the start of the Gospel of John: 'The light shines in the darkness, and the darkness has not overcome it.' I then saw a Figure wearing a crown, Who was walking through the crowd. I recognised it was Jesus, Who greeted and embraced Roy, Lorenzo, and José. The vision ended, and a tremendous sense of peace came over me." She wiped away her last tears. "Please keep this to yourself," she pleaded. "The others will think I've gone crazy."

"Sure, it's safe with me." Alan was bewildered by what he was hearing. Did God really communicate so clearly to Christians?

They sat together for a minute in their own silence, which amplified the ocean's anthem of eternal harmony.

"Do you often get such visions?" he then asked.

"No, only rarely. God has many different ways of communicating with us." She hesitated before continuing. "I also had this feeling that

I should go to the U.K. after the funeral has been held here for Roy, José, and Lorenzo on Sunday. Roy's sister lives in London, and I sense God wants me to visit her. Being a Catholic priest, Roy didn't have any children, but he was like a father to me, in the same way that I became a daughter to him."

"Will you be away for long?"

"About two weeks. It's a good time to go; we won't be going up to the plateau for a while now."

"I'm glad she's gone."

"I thought you got on with Lorna?"

"Only because I have to. But I can't stand that sickly sweet façade she puts on, with her doleful eyes and that simpering voice. She's a man-eater, you know."

"In what way?" Alan was taken aback by Megan's sudden outburst.

"She pretends to be a damsel-in-distress to lure you guys to do what she wants. I didn't realise you were into older women—"

"She's not that much older," he interrupted and then realised his mistake of not refuting Megan's other allegation. She would now be convinced he and Lorna were having an affair.

"I knew it; you're under her spell," she accused, her eyes seeming to glow green with jealousy. "You've stopped hanging around with us others after supper and instead only sit with her when you have those strange conversations."

"What conversations?"

"MacObadiah tells me you two talk Kugombwalan politics. He says you're anti-Bakiboko."

Alan gasped. It was easy to forget the local staff eavesdropped on everything the expats said within earshot. What he said to Megan might likewise be reported to the Liberation Front—the same people who had ordered the assassination of the priests.

He looked around to ensure they were not overheard. They were at the far end of the terrace, so he felt safe to gauge Megan's thoughts. "MacObadiah's wrong," he tried. "We've been talking about the rumours of massacres on the plateau."

"Oh, that is so typical of Lorna," Megan rebutted, "using a Watumbwa smear campaign against the Bakiboko to bait you with yet another concern."

"But what if it is true?"

"It's not."

"But maybe it is."

"Get real, Al. You sound like Keith with all his wacky theories."

Alan smarted from the accusation. She was implying he was as boring as Keith, referring to the mechanic's endless diatribes about the Americans never having landed on the moon and the assassination of John F. Kennedy by the CIA.

But it explained why it was impossible for people like Megan to recognise that genocide was taking place in Kugombwala. They regarded themselves as wise, which meant they ridiculed all rumours as conspiracy talk, thereby fooling themselves into failing to see the truth.

A full moon illuminated the white foam of the relentless surf, pounding the beach with a cyclical roar. Alan normally found it soothing, but it now suffused his troubled mind with deep melancholy as he pondered his difficult predicament. Following Lorna's departure, he was perhaps the only person among the remaining foreigners who dared acknowledge that people were being killed in huge numbers in Kugombwala.

He missed her company, aware now their friendship had developed deeper than any connection he had ever experienced with another woman and that she had become a pseudo-sister to him. By contrast, his relationships with the other MedRelief expats were deteriorating, as he withdrew into himself in response to not being able to trust his thoughts with them.

"Stop whingeing about the Watumbwa." Paula had rebuffed one of his attempts to raise the topic in the hope of finding a sympathetic ear with someone in the team.

He needed a new ally, someone unafraid to be outspoken with the truth.

"This, everyone, is my girlfriend, Anuka." Jules arrived late at the team meeting, accompanied by a stunning, young woman in a tight, leather miniskirt that allowed an uninterrupted view of her shapely legs. "She's just flown in from London and will be staying with us for a week to do some consultancy work."

"I thought our security rules forbade bringing partners," Paula whined.

"That's right." Jules looked irritated. "But Anuka's here in a professional capacity. MedRelief has asked her to make an ethical audit of our projects to meet donor requirements. Now, Anuka, tell the others about your task."

"Thanks, Juzu." She took over. "Great to meet you guys. I've heard so much about you and about the exciting things now happening in Kugombwala. I'm a professional gender consultant, and my job is to advise stakeholders on how to counter the prevailing global domination of straight, white-supremacist, male chauvinism. As a bisexual woman of mixed ethnic heritage, it's an issue I'm passionate about."

She claimed her background made it impossible for her to be racist, sexist, or homophobic because she belonged to the groups that were being oppressed by "primitive, patriarchal, Anglo-Saxon, elitist attitudes." Her reasoning implied that anyone with a less diverse ethnic identity than hers was intrinsically a rabid racist, while all men were chauvinists and all heterosexuals were homophobic.

Alan detected in himself a growing dislike of Anuka the more she preached her politically correct, virtue-signalling views. She continuously interrupted the meeting with critical remarks about their "patronising attitude" towards the beneficiaries and local staff. *Typical Londoner.* He frowned as he listened to her talking down to everyone.

After the exhaustive scrutiny of gender issues, Jules followed with an update on the murder of the priests.

"The police have learned they were killed by a hired hitman, so the army will now post a guard at each of our gates, as the Liberation Front's NGO liaison officer is concerned for our security. They are advising us to suspend all programmes on the plateau for the foreseeable future, until the security situation improves."

It was exactly what the Bakiboko wanted, to monitor the foreigners' movements and prevent them witnessing the army's dirty work. Alan hoped this would lead to a discussion about the rumoured massacres, but it did not.

At the end of the meeting, there was a point for any other business. Alan would normally have kept quiet but felt emboldened by Anuka's presence. He was certain of her support, as she claimed to stand up for the underdog.

"What about all this talk of massacres on the plateau? Ain't it time we say and do something about it?"

"Say and do something about what?"

He was, by now, accustomed to Anuka's many annoying comments but was taken aback by her aggressive tone. "About the mass slaughter of women and children," he replied indignantly, wondering why he had to clarify his question.

"I don't believe I'm hearing this. Africans are not savages, you know."

"That's not what I'm saying—"

"Well, that's what you are insinuating. Have you seen any killings? Have you got any evidence?"

"Those priests had—"

"Priests?" she interrupted. "Oh, get a grip on yourself, Al. Priests are the most bigoted child-molesters on the planet. All wars are due to religion, aren't they? Just look at the Crusades, Northern Ireland, and the Spanish Inquisition. Reality check, Al. Priests use their religious power to manipulate, dominate, and oppress the masses. So, you shouldn't believe what they say because they've got their own agenda to consolidate and extend their privileged paedophile lifestyles."

"It's not only the priests, Anuka. The local people are also talking about massacres on the Kugombwalan plateau."

"Which local people?" she demanded.

"Well . . . " Alan found himself on the defensive. "Some of our national staff."

"Who?"

"I can't say because they want to be anonymous."

"Sounds like you're making it up or falling for false rumours. You're letting yourself be swayed by Western hegemony's propaganda machine, which is obviously spreading malicious gossip here in Kugombwala to encourage the country's different people groups to fight against each other so that the neo-liberalist, military-industrial complex can profit from selling weapons to the warring factions. It's classic divide-and-rule and gives white supremacists the added satisfaction of watching a gladiatorial combat in Africa."

"I can't comment on international politics, Anuka, but it doesn't change what we've heard about the Watumbwa being killed."

"Who's 'we'?" Megan spat. "Speak for yourself!"

"Do stop going on about the Watumbwa," cut in Paula. "You're boring enough without repeating that story a million times."

"Yes, Al, give Africa a break," Anuka said. "This continent's moving forward and doesn't need neo-colonialists like you, who spread nasty rumours to satisfy their Caucasian superiority complex. Stop fantasising about Africans as murderous savages, who need 'civilising.'" She gave a visible imitation of speech marks with her fingers. "Here we are, in a country that has just ended a civil war and restored law and order. We are witnessing an African renaissance; yet small-minded people like you begrudge their success and are spreading dirty stories to tar this place with. Go back to little Britain and play out your empire fantasies in your own backyard."

"Oi, you leave him alone!" Alan almost fell off his chair to hear Paula coming to his defence. "You haven't even been here a day, and already, you're telling us what to do and think. You should just shut your face. You might be our head of mission's girlfriend, but that doesn't give you the right to order us about."

Jules quickly stepped in to prevent a major argument between the two Valkyries. "Paula, that's enough from you. One more word and you're sacked." He turned towards Alan. "As for the rumours of massacres, Al, you *must* stop talking about them. Without proof, they are just hearsay, and you could put our collective security at risk by slandering the state. Besides, MedRelief cannot consider the issue without concrete medical evidence."

"We need a drink, Al." Dave slapped him on the back. "I've had enough of being lectured like a delinquent teenager, so let's head into town where we can have our own opinions."

"I'm with you." Alan was as desperate to get away. "Where shall we go?"

"To the Africontinental Hotel. There's a cool, new crowd who meet in the bar there. I think you'll like them."

"Who are they?"

"Business people working for multinational oil and mining companies. Most of them have only recently arrived."

Dave's latest social group was a boisterous band of alpha males who were fattened by wealth or fittened by action. They strove to out-dominate each other with their bragging, banter, and Africa-bashing. This involved criticising Kugombwala for its bureaucracy and ever-failing facilities, as well as making fun of the local bar girls.

The business boys embodied the antithesis of the progressive ideals expounded by Anuka yet were welcomed by the Liberation Front authorities. Money and power were the only values that mattered in Kugombwala.

Knock, knock, knock.

Not again. Why couldn't he get any peace?

"Yes?" Alan answered in a deliberately irritated tone to signal he did not want to be disturbed.

"Alan?" The door opened, revealing MacZak, looking worried. "Police. They can want to meet you." The youngster then scarpered away down the corridor.

Two officers barged into the room and marched over to Alan's desk.

"Don't get up," one of them barked, arresting his attempt to raise himself from his chair. No hand was offered in greeting.

"Alan Swales," announced the other. "You are suspected of murder."

"What?" He was completely taken aback. And terrified. "That's ridiculous."

"What you say will be used against you in a court of law," the first said, mincing what he was thinking with words he had rehearsed for the occasion.

"What's all this about?" Alan could feel himself going into shock.

"The murder of three foreign priests!"

"They were killed by a hired hitman," the other added, "and we have reason to suspect that you ordered it." Fluent English indicated they were senior officers.

"That's rubbish! I hardly knew them," Alan retorted and then realised his mistake of admitting he had been in contact.

"So, tell us," the second officer said, "when did you meet them?"

"I . . . er . . . met Roy at the harbour," he stammered. "When MedRelief evacuated from Kugombwala."

"Stop tricking us, Alan Swales. We know that you also saw them on other occasions. Tell us about the last time."

"It was . . . just over a week ago." He realised he had to tell the truth. It was the best defence against false accusations to avoid self-incrimination through incoherent statements.

"Yes, we know." The second one smiled. "Just two days before they died."

"Why did you want to kill them?" the other followed.

"I didn't."

"Then why did you meet them?"

"I drove a friend who wanted to visit them to their house."

"Who was that?"

"Dr. Lorna." He felt like he was betraying her, so he was glad she was out of the country. "She works at the hospital here."

"Take us to see her. She must also be questioned."

"I can't. She's in England."

"Aha, she has fled the scene of the crime!"

"No. She's gone to comfort Father Roy's sister."

"So, the sister is also involved?"

"No, no." Alan felt exasperated. The questioning was going in a dangerous direction and would have been farcical if the matter had not been so serious. Regardless of what he said, they would twist it into a new accusation.

"How do you know she is innocent?" the policeman continued. "Is it because you ordered the assassinations?"

"No. I. Did. Not." Alan tried to sound firm without losing his temper.

"So, what did you and the priests talk about?"

"I hardly spoke to them. Father Roy asked me to referee a football match with some kids."

The two police officers exchanged glances; he must have confirmed what they already knew. They'd been interrogating the students. That was their source of information.

"And Dr. Lorna—did she speak with them?"

"Yes."

"About what?"

"I don't know." He now felt he could risk a lie. The students had all been on the playing field, so nobody—apart from Lorna and the priests—were witnesses to what was said between them. "In my country," he continued, "we don't ask people about private conversations."

"I hope you are telling the truth, Alan Swales," the older officer growled. "Do not try to deceive us because we will find out if you do."

"And then the consequences will be very serious," the other added. He glanced around the room. "Why is there no picture of the president in your office?"

"Er . . . I didn't know it was a legal requirement."

"It is a criminal offence to offend the Head of State. Refusing to display his photo would be a major insult to him."

"Okay," Alan answered submissively. "I will get one."

"My colleague will check the documents in your office, while I search your bedroom. You take me there."

Alan led the policeman down the corridor, reluctant to leave the other alone to rummage through his files. He was thankful he had not written down his thoughts.

"Do you have a camera?" the officer asked once they entered his room.

"Yes."

"Give it to me—and all your films. We will develop them to search for evidence."

Alan realised they suspected he had some of the photos taken by the priests. He would have to warn Lorna not to come back, for it would be too dangerous for her now in Kugombwala. But how to let her know without incurring further suspicion from the cops? A letter—even if smuggled out—could be intercepted, while all telephone calls would be tapped.

This must be a sign, Alan surmised, for him to get out before it was too late. Before Lorna returned, so he could warn her to stay away.

The policeman interrupted his thoughts. "In the meantime, you remain under suspicion of murder. You must surrender your passport to us, and you are forbidden from leaving the country until the investigation is over. The airport and border police have been notified, and any attempt to get away will be considered an admission of guilt."

Alan then understood that law was not always an instrument of justice. Instead, it could be a powerful tool of oppression.

Stop staring at me, Alan silently shouted at the portrait on the wall. The dictator's eyes followed his movements about the room, fomenting further paranoia.

He looked over his shoulder to ensure no one was looking through the window and then insulted the picture with a rude gesture.

Clack!

Terrified, Alan spun round towards the source of the sound.

"Cup of tea . . . " MacZak had opened the office door and was carrying a tray of refreshments. "Very good." He smiled on seeing the image. "Our great general! You can be like us now."

Definitely not, Alan repudiated in his mind, *because unlike you, I detest him.*

In Britain, it was normal to see images of loved ones in people's homes, ranging from religious figures to family members and national heroes such as Churchill and Nelson. He had done the same during his teens, he remembered, adorning his bedroom with photos of his favourite footballers, while Mandy's room was lined with pop star posters. Downstairs, her mother had decorated the lounge with portraits of the queen, together with porcelain commemorating the Silver Jubilee and recent royal weddings. Alan's initial verdict was to regard it as confirmation that she was a snob trying to climb the social ladder, though he later learned that Mrs. Carter truly loved the royal family.

MacZak was just like her, as he unconditionally adored his leader. And he wasn't alone; others among the local staff were equally entranced, though he was aware many Kugombwalans despised General MacVictor Bakigoma, particularly those belonging to tribes persecuted by him. So why was the dictator forcing everyone in Kugombwala to hang a photo of him in their homes and workplaces? The pervasive presence of his portrait would amplify his opponents' hatred.

How different they were from Britain's politicians, who—like celebrities—craved popularity, and even worship, from their supporters and fans. Why was Kugombwala's president encouraging animosity instead of affection?

It must be deliberate, he reasoned, *because the despot is no fool.*

Then it dawned on Alan that the intention was to amplify any hostility in order to generate a frustration that could not be redressed because its cause—the general himself—was too powerful to be retaliated against. That would create a deep fear of him among his oppressed opponents. Their need for psychological self-preservation would then subconsciously cope with the mortal terror by moulding it into a strange pseudo-love for the despot.

Through his ever-present image, the president was seeking to be idolised, while continuously reminding his enemies that they could neither harm him nor escape his watchful eye or power to punish them. His Machiavellian mission was to lord over loyal subjects as well as unwilling underlings through either love or fear. By doing so, he was appropriating different forms of worship from the entire population in Kugombwala by asserting his absolute authority over everybody under the dictum that he had the superhuman power to kill anyone he wished—and get away with it.

General MacVictor was not only slaughtering the Watumbwa out of hate or to crush an insurrection, Alan realised, but also to demonstrate—in defiance of the Almighty—that he had become a god.

"Huge party on Saturday," Dave announced, as they drove back from a U.N. coordination meeting.

"Where?"

"Some mansion on the beach, outside the city."

"Who's the host?"

"Dunno, maybe a politician, but we're definitely invited."

"How come?"

"It's thanks to the business boys, who've got good connections. They say the whole AfriContinental crowd are welcome. It's to do with a beauty pageant."

"Wow! Guaranteed hot chicks . . . "

"Yeah, so hot they'll be gagging for cool dudes like us, mate. But don't say anything to the others, as we're not allowed to leave Ndombazu after dark. Jules doesn't need to know where we'll be."

"Sure, the secret's safe with me. What's the plan for getting there?"

"Everyone meets first for a drink at the hotel, and then we drive over in a convoy, following someone who knows the way."

"Sounds like a laugh." Alan was desperate to lift his spirits.

"More than that, Al, it's a sign that we've made it. We're now members of this country's in-crowd. That could never happen to us in Britain because the toffs treat us like plebs."

"Keith will hate us." Dave laughed as the Land Rover rattled over rough roads emptied by the nighttime curfew. "This speed's gonna kill the shock absorbers."

"And the springs," Alan added, after a big bump bashed the axles into the chassis. The convoy's lead car set a fast pace for the others to follow, forcing them to charge round twisting bends, through large puddles, and into sudden potholes in a collective hubris of amateur rally driving.

The last buildings of Ndombazu fleeted past and were replaced by the high bushes of the coastal scrub. After half an hour of high-speed driving, they skidded to a halt in front of a magnificent seaside mansion, lit by powerful floodlights that flashed in tune to mega-woofers blasting the latest beats into the tropical night.

"Whoa, what a place. It's like a massive jukebox on the beach," Alan exclaimed.

"This is going to be an amazing party." Dave spoke for both of them.

The villa was protected by an ornate wall, against which were parked dozens of brand-new four-wheel-drive vehicles. All were top models with wide sand tyres, bumper-mounted winches, and smoked-glass windows, with a combined value of over a million dollars. A few soldiers lolled around, guarding the collection of mobile wealth.

They entered the sumptuous mansion, where everything was on an ostentatious scale: a vast reception suite, expensive tiled floors, air conditioners in each room, designer furniture and lighting, plus an enormous infinity pool that seemed to merge into the sea beyond. Somebody was making a lot of money in Kugombwala.

Hundreds of people had already gathered at the party, mostly from the nation's emerging elite, elegantly clad in the latest brand-name clothing. Some danced in front of a colossal quadraphonic stereo system on a terrace that overlooked the bay and the twinkling lights of distant Ndombazu.

Alan collected a drink at one of the four bars stacked with a global selection of spirits. A long trestle table sagged under the weight of an extravagant buffet, where he helped himself to food.

"Hello, my name is Wendy." A beautiful Kugombwalan woman in the queue beside him stroked his arm.

"Al." He greeted her with three kisses as per local custom. "How come you're not called MacWendy?"

"Traditional names are backward," she purred. "Kugombwala is moving forward. We are now modern and multicultural."

She worked for one of the ministries and was both friendly and forward. Soon, she was hugging and caressing him in a tremendous display of affection that he had long been missing. It was great to feel wanted again—her energetic and doting manner and her wonderful African scent of aromatic spices proved irresistible to Alan's one-track mind.

"I really love you, Al," she said between kisses after a delicious dinner.

Hold on a minute, his logic countered. *How can she love me so much when she has only known me for an hour?* Wendy was manipulating his carnal instincts and his need of affection. *No problem. Let her have what she wants.* He justified his own cravings. *What's wrong about fulfilling mutual desire?*

She led him by the hand to the main staircase that was monitored by a servant, who exchanged a few words with her in a local language as they passed. Unable to decipher what was said, Alan was alarmed by the allusion to a conspiracy, which made him feel he was being lured into a trap. *What am I letting myself in for?* he wondered, and then he realised that her seduction could snare him into a relationship he did not want. Consumating his current desires would beget consequences—binding him through *her* charms and *his* obligations to see her again. The same process he had experienced with Mandy would start all over again.

Don't worry about that, and do like Dave, an inner voice argued back. *Drop her after the night is over.* But another voice told him that would be wrong, for it would reduce Wendy to a disposable object—used and then binned like the convenience items of modern consumer culture. *Are you going to treat her like a prostitute?* his conscience asked.

They had reached the landing where Wendy tried various doors until she found one that was unlocked.

I'm near the point of no return, Alan realised, his heart agitated by both sensual excitement and the emotional stress of the struggle between hedonism and decorum.

"Wait, Wendy. This is going too fast." His foot was on the threshold.

"What is the matter? Am I not good enough for you?" Her grip tightened on his hand.

"No, it's not that . . . "

"Is it because I am an African woman?"

"No, no . . . I just don't think this is right."

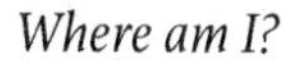

Where am I?

Alan awoke on an unfamiliar bed in an unrecognisable room. He was still in his clothes but had not over-heated, thanks to the air conditioner humming in the background.

It was already mid-morning, he realised, seeing the sun's steep rays on the floor.

What happened last night? Strange surroundings slowed his memory recall.

My wallet!

He instinctively reached for his pocket and was relieved to find his money still there. He now remembered that Wendy had departed after their disagreement, when he had locked her out of the room and seized the opportunity of a bed to crash out on. A huge meal, combined with drinks and the unwinding that came with absconding from a war zone, had sent his body into a much-needed deep sleep.

He ambled down the stairs to see servants and eager guests buzzing about a fine breakfast spread. He filled a plate and then went out to the terrace, where groups of people were sitting around the large swimming pool. A strong sea breeze cooled the air, adding the swishing tones of swaying palms to the soothing sound of the surf.

"Hey, Alan Swales!" a Kugombwalan called out. "Over here."

"Hiya, how are you doing?" Alan tried without success to match a face that was semi-masked by sunglasses. The man was in swimming shorts on a sun lounger beside some bikini-clad local women and a white businessman whom he recognised from the AfriContinental crowd.

"Come and join us, mate," the businessman added.

"Emmeline and Patricia are my sisters, and they want a European husband." The Kugombwalan laughed while introducing a couple of smiling young women. "I didn't know you hung out with this group, Alan. Forget what we talked about a few days ago; I'll make sure you get your passport and photos tomorrow."

"Thanks!" Alan was initially bewildered and then recognised him: one of the two policemen investigating the murder of the priests. *What a relief.* He sighed, a huge weight now lifted off his mind. He felt buoyant and optimistic—at long last, everything was turning out right.

A servant stopped to ask if anyone wanted coffee.

"Aye, mate, milk and one sugar."

This was paradise! Alan reclined on a sun lounger while exchanging pleasantries with the alluring women on each side. In front of him, the clear waters of the pool shimmered around exuberant bathers, framed by a stunning view of the tranquil ocean. The civil war, the problems at the hospital, and the rumours of genocide all evaporated from his mind.

More young Kugombwalans joined them for breakfast. They were the country's happening crowd, urbane and well-educated, with a refreshing knowledge of the West, which made it easy to converse with them. They were full of optimism for Kugombwala's future, given the plans to exploit the extensive mineral deposits in the interior. He chatted with a young diplomat called Oscar, who followed English football and who had studied in the U.S. He was involved in negotiations with the World Bank to secure major development loans and to encourage further foreign investment. Everyone gushed about "General Vic," whom they saw as an important source of stability for the country.

"You should stay here, Alan. We need people like you. Forget Britain; it's history. Kugombwala is the future. Life's gonna be great. Just look around you—what more do you need?"

Alan smiled. Oscar was right. This was a land of immense opportunities, especially if you had a bit of get-up-and-go.

"Hey, Al. Hey, Oscar. How's it going?" Dave was accompanied by a local girl in a skimpy swimsuit stretched over an opulent body.

Kugombwala's female population presented a further area of immense opportunity that Dave was already doing his best to exploit.

"All right, Emmeline?" Dave referred to the woman lying beside Alan. As usual, Dave seemed to know everyone. "Al, we've got to head back. Jules will be apoplectic, as we've been out all night with a vehicle." He laughed. Dave had little respect for Jules' authority.

With great reluctance, Alan bade farewell to his newfound friends and followed Dave through manicured gardens and over to the gates to the property.

Stepping outside brought him straightaway back into the real world beyond: five soldiers in characteristic red wellington boots stood outside, roughing up a ragged peasant who had ventured too close.

The two aid workers got into their vehicle and drove away from the island of illusion, back over rough tracks, passing people in tattered clothing who stumbled under the burden of firewood on their heads. Alan had become accustomed to such sights in Kugombwala, but the brief interlude in affluence temporarily removed his immunity from noticing the dire poverty he was now re-immersed in.

How easy it had been to forget the harsh reality of life in Kugombwala, while lying on a sun lounger with a beautiful girl at his side and attended to by servants. Sumptuous surroundings had fostered a desire to partake of luxury without questioning how it had been financed or how little was shared. Just like with Wendy, the seductive lure of sensual comfort blurred its costs and consequences.

What kind of Kugombwala were people like Oscar and the businessmen going to build with the profits from their mutual ambition of exploiting the nation's natural resources? All evidence pointed to a pact to prosper a pampered elite living off the backs of an enslaved population, assisted by international business that was greedy for a portion of Kugombwala's glittering wealth.

For the multinationals supporting the Liberation Front regime, it was a low-risk strategy. If a pressure group complained about their involvement in the country, they could sell their stake to buy innocence and even enhance their reputation by donating a tiny part of the proceeds to charity. For the Liberation Front cronies, an openness to foreign businesses purchased deaf ears in the international community if rumours of massacres ever seeped out of the country.

In short, Alan realised, it was a win-win deal for the Bakiboko and for business—an equation that excluded the oppressed Watumbwa.

"I've got a new job," Dave announced as Alan drove back. "With a Canadian mining company."

"You're leaving MedRelief?" Alan was surprised and saddened. Dave was now the only person in the MedRelief team whom he still considered a friend.

"Yeah, starting next week."

"Doing what?"

"Running supplies to a drill camp on the plateau."

"Good money?"

"Loads more than Blair-Campbell pays." Dave laughed. "But that's not the only reason I'm doing it. I've had enough of humanitarian aid, and I want to help build Kugombwala's economy. For me, it's the only way to bring peace."

"Won't the profits from the mine just line the pockets of the elite?" *And pay for ammunition for the army to kill more people,* Alan decided not to add.

"Sure, but some money will filter down to the people." Dave always found a positive angle. "It'll create jobs and improve infrastructure in a remote area where there are few other opportunities."

Just like the U.K., Alan remembered. His hometown had fallen on hard times during the bitter Miner's Strike of the mid-1980s, when the local colliery had closed. There were no other jobs available. It had been hard for the family thereafter, living off benefits while his grumpy father was forced to hang around at home with nothing to do except vent his anger on wife and kids. His parents had almost divorced as a result, pressed by poverty into a conflict that neither had wanted, while it had taken years for him to rebuild his relationship with his father.

"Another reason," Dave then added, "is that it could lead to a job in Canada. I don't want to go back to Britain."

"Why not?"

"The country's going down the hole. We're useless at everything now: this Land Rover is a load of junk compared to Japanese vehicles, and the Germans are better than us at football. There are no opportunities in the U.K., unless you're a toff or a smoked-salmon socialist."

"Like Jules and Anuka." Alan smirked. He had considered them an odd couple and had wondered what kept such apparently opposite people together. In addition to physical attraction, he realised, it was possibly a strategic yet subconscious alliance between old money and an upcoming intellectual elite that had conquered the moral high ground by bombarding the public with its politically correct dogma. That would explain the unlikely partnership between a modern demagogue prostituting principle to acquire prestige, with a scion of established privilege who recognised some power had to be shared to dilute ancestral guilt from exploiting colonial subjects and Britain's working class.

"Hey, Al, I think we're lost." Dave coughed. "Shouldn't we have reached the main road by now?"

"I was thinking the same. Trouble is, there are so many different tracks here. It's easy to take the wrong one."

"Just follow the deepest wheel ruts."

"That's what I've been doing."

"Oh, well, we'll end up somewhere, sooner or later. Let's enjoy the drive."

"But we'll be really late back. Shouldn't we call the base?"

"Dave, Dave for Jules," the car radio coincidentally crackled.

"Yes, Boss?" Dave took the handset.

"Where are you?"

"Somewhere outside the city."

"Where's somewhere?" Jules sounded annoyed.

"On the other side of the bay."

"What are you doing there?"

"Me and Al are going for a casual Sunday morning drive—"

"Going for a casual Sunday morning drive? Get back immediately—and that's an order!"

"Get lost, you stuck-up, self-important nob," Dave replied without pressing the talk button, so Jules couldn't hear. "I'm glad I've now got another job. You should join me, Al."

"Aye, maybe I should." Was this another sign that it was time to leave Kugombwala? It seemed so.

"Dave? Did you hear me?" Jules was back on the air.

"Sure, Boss, heard you loud and clear."

"I am expecting you back within an hour. If not, there will be serious consequences."

"Well copied, Dave out." He laughed after releasing the talk button. "Isn't life great, Al? No matter what happens, there's always a way out of trouble. Jules is going to discover that he's got no power over me. I can't wait to say that to his face and then tell him I'm leaving."

Alan stared straight ahead, imagining how Jules' anger would, in turn, be inflicted on him.

"Uh-oh! Army base ahead!"

They had rounded a bend, revealing a road that ran straight to the gates of a huge military compound.

"Shall we turn around?" Alan felt a shot of panic seize him.

"No," Dave was firm. "The guards will have seen us, and we mustn't do anything that seems suspicious—otherwise, they'll send vehicles or a helicopter after us. Our only option is to drive up to the gate and tell them we're lost. Park to the side of the sentry post," he then instructed. "Both of us should get out. Transparency is our best protection."

"Yes?" The soldier raised his rifle as they walked over. "What are you doing here? This can be forbidden military area."

"Hey, Boss, I'm Mr. Dave from MedRelief. We were trying to get to Ndombazu, but we have taken the wrong track. It is very confusing here. Can you tell us the way back?"

"Who are you? Where are your papers?" the soldier barked. "You can be spies."

Alan's stomach lurched. His passport was still with the police; this could be catastrophic.

"We are not spies." Dave remained calm. "I am a friend of Kugombwala and of Colonel MacBilly Ngumu."

"Who is he? I cannot know him."

"But you know the Anti-insurgency Brigade?"

"Yes, I can know that one."

"The colonel is in charge. He is my good friend . . . "

The soldier looked worried.

"Please call him. Tell him you are with Mr. Dave from MedRelief. Here is my passport. We were together at a party at the big house on the coast last night."

Visible droplets of sweat formed on the soldier's brow. "Wait," he said, before speaking to another soldier in a local language. He then departed with Dave's passport.

"Might as well take a seat in the shade." Dave nodded towards an empty bench by the wall.

Half an hour passed in idle chit-chat and casual observation of the comings and goings at the army base.

"Busy place," Dave remarked.

"Aye."

Both were careful not to say too much or to appear too inquisitive. How strange to be accused of spying, yet given a great opportunity to gather intelligence. Alan had noticed the words *KILLER KIDS* on a truck that had entered; it was the same one he had seen on the plateau, full of murderous child soldiers. And then his eyes were drawn to a jeep that zoomed out of the gate. There was no doubt about it—there were two Europeans inside . . .

"Mr. Dave?" The soldier was back with his passport. "Please, you can go. I can guide you to the main road."

"Isn't it great being part of the elite, Al? No one can touch us."

Dave was right. Privilege brought many benefits, including a peer group, lavish parties, legal and physical protection, as well as accelerated promotion and job opportunities. But it required giving unconditional support to other members of the establishment, even when it went against personal principles—a price he was not willing to pay.

"By the way, did you see those whiteys in that army jeep?" Alan could ask now that they were alone in the vehicle.

"Yeah, the British and American military attachés. I met them at the party last night. They're supervising a big programme to professionalise the army."

So, they and their governments must be assisting the killers, which, sadly, meant that Britain was not "Great," Alan reflected, dashing his hopes that the U.K. and U.S. might intervene to halt the genocide on the plateau.

That left no one else who could help, as those two countries controlled the U.N. and, therefore, the international community. Nothing happened without their approval.

"I'm off, Al." Dave had his bag slung over his shoulder. "I've just resigned from MedRelief."

"Wow, already? How did Jules take it?"

"Pulled the rug from under him; he wasn't expecting that. Anyway, I've got to run. There's a plane leaving soon for the mine."

"It's been great working with you, Dave."

"And you. Bye, Al."

"Bye, mate."

Five minutes later, Jules poked his head unannounced round Alan's door. "Al, I want you in my office." It was an order rather than a request.

"Sure." Alan got up from his desk and followed him, full of apprehension.

Jules stood by the door as he entered and closed it after him. "No need to sit down," he said sourly. "I've spoken to the London office, and we all agree you must leave MedRelief." He paused to allow the words to sink in. "As you know, I will not tolerate any insubordination. Your behaviour yesterday was a thorough disgrace, while your upstart opinions are a liability to the organisation's reputation and a serious threat to the team's security. I've just learned that you've already been under police investigation, for they returned your passport this morning. You will be leaving on the next scheduled flight."

So, this was it. The big decision had been made. His time in Kugombwala was finally over. Closure—at last—of this nasty chapter in his life.

The realisation triggered a wave of relief, followed by sadness that it had to end so badly. And then came an unexpected feeling of failure for having done nothing about the genocide that was taking place on the plateau. He'd had an opportunity to act, and he had flunked it because he had hesitated. He should have been more outspoken about his suspicions and done more to document the atrocities, but instead, he had missed the boat. Had he been waiting for that better opportunity which never came, or was he too much a coward to confront injustice?

If only he could have another chance.

"Furthermore," Jules continued, "you are immediately relieved of all of your duties. You have ten minutes to remove your things from your office and return your keys. MacQuentin will henceforth take over the administration until your replacement arrives, and from now on, you are not to visit the hospital or to discuss programme matters or politics with members of the team. Do I make myself clear?"

"Aye, as you wish." Alan shrugged. *Let him have his way.* He resigned himself to being powerless to alter the situation. All talk about "life being what you make it" was nonsense, he realised; those in authority always overrode your hopes and desires.

"Good afternoon, Alan." The gardener was clipping a bush near the doorway. "I am saddened to hear that you are leaving us. I will miss you, as well as our conversations."

"Thanks, MacAbraham."

News of the sacking had spread like wildfire around the MedRelief compound, adding to Alan's feeling of awkwardness and humiliation. Even though he was glad to be leaving Kugombwala, it was hard dealing with being fired; he now understood the full effect on his father of being made redundant. Worse still was the feeling of being an outcast among the expat team, which meant he now took his meals alone after they had eaten.

"When are you leaving?"

"I don't know. The next plane's full, so it'll be at least a week." *Of a living nightmare,* his mind continued, for he was confined to social isolation in an open prison with the added burden of boredom.

"Do you have time to help me pick some mangoes?"

"Aye," Alan answered lugubriously. "I've nothing else to do."

They walked across the compound to a tree near the generator house.

"We won't be overheard here," MacAbraham spoke just above the drone of the motor. "But you need to look like you are helping me. There are suspicious eyes everywhere." He brought a long pole to twist around the topmost twigs to dislodge the ripe fruit. "Catch the ones that fall," he ordered, giving Alan a large bag to hold out. "Why don't you stay with my family until you get a plane ticket?"

"That's good of you, but I don't want to be any trouble." Alan had lost all self-esteem; it was obvious no one wanted him. Not Mandy, not MedRelief, not even Megan.

"It is no problem. I live in a large house near the university, and we have a guest room."

"Thanks, MacAbraham, but I would feel like I'm imposing."

"Alan, me and my family would be delighted to have you to stay. We lived in Brighton for three years while I did my Ph.D., so we are used to being with Brits."

"Would it not be a security risk for you?"

"Yes, but it is manageable. Firstly, I am half Bakiboko, so under less suspicion than most others in the city. Secondly, my wife is Swiss, so the neighbours would think you are a relative. And thirdly, it is not yet a crime to host a foreigner. But it would be prudent to ensure that as few people as possible know where you are, for reasons I will explain. I will arrange for a car to pick you up."

"But the MedRelief staff will notice I am gone."

"Yes, MacObadiah and MacCharlie are both Bakiboko and spy for the regime. I suggest you tell everyone you will be staying at a small beach hotel—the one where my niece is the receptionist. I will instruct her to answer when Jules calls with details about your flight ticket. And if the military come looking for you, nobody will know where you are."

"What about the soldier outside the gate?"

"I will make sure he is distracted, so he doesn't see you leave."

Alan smiled for the first time that day. "Sounds good, MacAbraham, many thanks."

"Then we are agreed."

"Aye. What's the reason for being so careful?"

"You remember how you once asked me about the rumours of massacres on the plateau?"

"Yes."

"I am with a group who are trying to investigate the crimes. We may need some advice from you and even a little help, but it must always be your own choice to assist us. Don't let my hospitality influence that. You are most welcome, whatever you decide."

"Thanks again, MacAbraham." Alan's free will had been restored.

As he walked out of his room for the last time, Alan was filled with sadness and regret. It had been his home for many months: a retreat and a place of relative safety. The bare concrete chamber with its roughly built bed, table, and stool had been his sanctuary amidst the surrounding chaos. Now, he was leaving its protection.

He closed the door, slid the bolt into place, and snapped the padlock shut with the key attached. *Time to go.* The team didn't want him there, so there was no point saying fake goodbyes.

He turned towards the stairs that would take him down to the courtyard and from there to the main gate. He was still in the MedRelief building, but he had already made a mental exit. It was all over, and they would never see him again.

"Are you off already, Al?" To his horror, Paula stood at the end of the corridor.

"Aye. No point hanging around."

"Then I'm glad to see you before you go. I've been meaning to come and say I'm sorry about what has happened."

"Thanks, Paula."

"Goodbye, Al. If there's anything I can do to help you, then let me know. I really mean it."

She ain't such a bad lass, he conceded. *Just a bit scratchy at times.*

It was amazing how life could turn around within a day, Alan reflected as he lay in bed that night. An initially bleak situation of being sacked, unwanted, and ostracised had been transformed to staying in a real home with a kind family who welcomed his company.

It reinforced the surreal sense he now felt of being on his proper, destined life path. It was surely no coincidence that all flights were full for the following week, forcing him to stay in Kugombwala despite Jules' attempt to remove him from the country. Furthermore, fate—*or more likely God,* he corrected his thoughts—had brought him together with a local academic who was investigating the massacres and who needed his assistance, thereby giving him a chance—at last—to do something about the genocide.

Still, he'd be glad when the coming days were over. Adventure was sometimes best enjoyed in retrospect when safe beside the home fire.

CHAPTER 11

Night was falling in the forest, obscuring the mounds in a dusky haze. Yet, straightaway, he knew he had found what he was looking for.

Despite the fading twilight, he recognised them as graves—long mounds of freshly dug earth that interrupted the forest undergrowth. The heaps of clean soil might have appeared unremarkable but for the rank odour that clung to the mist wafting through the trees.

As he watched, he noticed a slight movement at the surface of the mounds. Soil began to roll down their sides as if something stirred within. Slowly, they lifted and broke open, birthing heads that rose to reveal bodies shrouded in stained rags, rising to their full height. Ten of them emerged from the mound in front of him; and beyond, twenty others sprouted from another earthen pile. In the distance, more and more human forms, barely distinguishable in the gloom. Without opening their eyes, they stretched out their arms towards him in synchronised supplication, murmuring a melancholic moan: "Justice . . . justice . . . give us justice . . . "

Alan woke, wet with sweat, yet relieved to find himself in the comforting reality of MacAbraham's guestroom. But the words had crossed into the woken world and continued to reverberate through his mind. They haunted him throughout that day with both the image of the dead demanding their killers be brought before a judge but also the question of what had caused him to experience that dream.

Was it his subconscious surfacing in the stillness of sleep? Or was there another, other-worldly, explanation? Were the spirits of the dead Watumbwa beseeching him? Might it even be a Divine message? He did not know. But he was alarmed about the increasing occurrence of the supernatural that now permeated his life and his difficulty to distinguish God's voice from the others. *I need to know Him better.* Alan resolved to get a Bible when he got back to Britain—and to read it.

"I have a dangerous task for you to consider," MacAbraham said at supper that night. "So, don't decide straightaway. Take time to think about it, and as I've said before, there's no obligation."

Alan sensed an invisible burden descend upon him. Was it in anticipation of the inevitable dilemma ahead or Divine warning to desist the wrong decision? "What did you have in mind?"

"I know a team of Kugombwalan human rights activists who are going to the plateau in two days' time . . . "

Rather them than me, Alan mentally responded.

"They will drive up an abandoned logging road to secretly access the massacre sites and record the atrocities, taking photos of any evidence. It would be good if you could join them."

"Right," he said to show he had heard, rather than signalling agreement. "But what can I contribute that the others cannot? I don't speak the local language."

"You would be a Western witness and can better convince the global media than an ordinary Kugombwalan, as our opinions are nowadays ignored by the international community. Everyone brands us as biased by tribal allegiances and animosities, whereas you would be a neutral voice."

"Aye, that's true." Alan was still undecided.

"It would be too risky to come back to Ndombazu after the trip, in case you get caught with films and documentation. As you will need to get the material out of Kugombwala, the plan is for you to sneak across the frontier on foot on the other side of the plateau. From there, you can make your way to a mission station. There are lots of them near the border; they will help you get to the capital."

"And then?"

"You go to the university and ask for the professor in charge of veterinary sciences. Leo Mwagumbi and I studied together in Moscow in the 1970s, and he is like a brother to me. He is the faculty's only senior academic, so you don't need to remember his name, only the department that he heads. Mention I sent you, and he will buy you a ticket back to Britain and clear any diplomatic obstacles from making an illegal entry into the country. He's got the right connections."

"Seems like a reasonably tight plan. Anything else I need to know?"

"Yes, you will be on your own. I cannot help if you get caught, and I obviously don't want the consequences to rebound onto me. I would need to organise another team to gather evidence of the killings, plus I have my family to care for."

"I understand." It would be a destiny decision, determining the direction of the rest of his life.

"You will know nothing about the others in the team until you meet them, to limit the potential consequences if you are stopped before the rendezvous. It's to protect them—and you."

"That makes sense."

"You will also need a cover story to explain how you first contacted them. Do you know the busy bar on the roundabout near the hospital?"

"You mean MacCats?"

"Yes, that one. We call it 'Maggots,' as it is associated with so much moral decay."

"I've been there a few times with Dave."

"Good. The others know the place, too, so all of you can describe it if you are caught and interrogated. Your story is you met them there by chance last night. After a long conversation, they suggested you accompany them to the plateau, to which you agreed."

"Okay, sounds plausible . . . "

The invisible burden of decision now felt heavier, enhanced by the obvious hazards and a strange feeling—which he could not shake—that he should go to the plateau.

His life had led to this very moment. Was that sufficient indication that he should go? If so, the choice was not whether he opted in with the team but whether he opted out. But he could only do that if there were good grounds to refuse.

So much could go wrong, and the consequences would be catastrophic. There was a high chance of encountering an army patrol on the plateau, who would grant no mercy for snooping on their bloody secrets. Then there was the risk of getting caught while making an illegal border crossing. Finally, the journey on foot would present yet further perils; they could get lost in the thick forest and run out of food and water or succumb to disease and wild animals.

He did a quick calculation of the potential costs versus the potential benefits and reached the conclusion that it would be utterly foolish to go. The chance of surviving the journey was minimal, coupled with a low likelihood of making any impact on international media with the information gathered.

Yet against all logic, the feeling clung stubbornly on that he should go. *Why was that?* he asked himself, hoping to find a dubious motive that would disqualify his inexplicable inner determination to join the team.

Was it to perform a daring deed to elevate himself to a hero—a modern-day David against a genocidal Goliath, fighting single-handedly against an entire army and government? No, for everlasting fame required an audience to see and record his deeds, while he would die in total obscurity in the forest.

Was it a consequence of his outrage over the killings, causing a desire to demonstrate to himself his defiance of an evil regime? Partly, but that would be an arrogant reason for risking his life because it was about a pointless personal statement, rather than trying to achieve a meaningful result.

Was it to assuage his anger at being unjustifiably sacked by MedRelief by proving he had been right about his suspicions of mass slaughter? That was certainly a motive but too weak to counter the heavy feeling of fear and foreboding.

He then realised another reason was driving his decision away from common sense and self-preservation. Somehow, he sensed that the risks, though real, were overridden by the absolute necessity for the task before him to succeed, however slight the odds. The world needed to know about the ongoing massacres on the plateau, and it seemed right to include a Westerner in the team to give the trip at least some chance of success, for the near-suicidal mission would otherwise be futile for the other members of the group, even if they came out alive.

Now the priests were dead, he was perhaps the only foreigner who was aware of the situation on the plateau, while caring enough to want to do something about it. If not him, then who?

The terrifying answer was indisputable: no one.

"A car will come at six tonight." MacAbraham got up from breakfast to go to work. "Take a shower just before, as it will be a while before you can do so again."

Alan's heart battered his ribcage, as if trying to escape the inevitable hail of bullets that would soon puncture his chest.

"Here is a list of things you need to take." MacAbraham handed him a sheet of paper. "The rest of your personal belongings can stay with me. I will hide them and bring them next week to the hotel where you were supposed to be staying. You should be out of the country by then, and I'll get my niece to call MedRelief with a request that they collect and return your bag to you in the U.K."

"Thanks." Alan was in no mood for talking. The anticipated dread sent him running to the bathroom all day. His body was instinctively aware of the limited opportunities for dignified discharge over the coming days and making sure nothing would be accidentally released if he were to be subjected to sudden shock. It was an ominous sign.

Tap. Tap-tap. Tap-tap-tap. Tap-tap-tap-tap.

Heavy droplets of rain hammered the vegetation outside, rapidly increasing in quantity. Alan shuddered, dreading the imminent departure from MacAbraham's house—his last refuge. From now on, he would face continuous uncertainty and danger in a tropical wilderness far from the comforts of civilisation.

He was reminded of the rainstorm that had engulfed the MedRelief vehicle at the petrol station many months earlier, when MacJohn first told him about the massacres. It had baptised him into a new life, opening his eyes to the scale by which those in power abused the downtrodden, as well as the lengths they went to conceal the consequent suffering. That spark of knowledge—which had grown to a blaze—was the impetus for him to take the coming journey into the unknown.

"The car's arrived," MacAbraham announced. "Thank goodness for the rain; no one will notice there's a white man under your poncho."

After saying farewell to the family, Alan grabbed his backpack and hurried through the deluge to the gate. A battered car waited beyond, its wipers battling against the torrent of water rinsing the windscreen. He struggled to open the passenger door, due to a damaged lock, and then jumped in, relieved to be out of the rain.

"Hello, Alan." A familiar face greeted him.

"MacJohn! What are you doing here?"

"I can help MacAbraham. He is my uncle. And I also came to say goodbye to you, my friend."

"Thanks!"

"It is me who can thank you. MacAbraham cannot say what you are doing, but I know it is to help Kugombwala. It brings us hope that some foreigners risk their lives to help us."

"Aye" was all he could say without becoming emotional. "Where are we going?"

"To the Crocodile brewery."

"For a beer?"

"No, no. Dry visit," he said, as they headed off through the sodden streets.

"My man!" Someone shook him out of sleep. "It can be time. Other workers come soon."

"Right," Alan groaned, unhappy to be awoken, after having finally fallen asleep during a restless night of near-insomnia. He would normally have attempted a consolation snooze, but the watchman stood waiting. It was still pitch-black outside; his torch illuminated a rusting metal desk, an office chair with missing seat padding, and a large, plastic crocodile.

"You can follow," the watchman ordered once he had pulled on his clothes, rolled up the mat, and packed his mosquito net into his backpack. "First can go toilet. Last time for long time," he said once they came to a door that failed to block the foul odour behind.

Steel stairs led them down to a large warehouse filled with beer crates, barely visible in the faint light. They rounded a stack to reveal a row of loaded lorries facing large, corrugated iron doors.

"It can be this one." The watchman pointed. "At the back."

He had been busy; a pile of crates had been removed from the rear, revealing a deep chasm in the middle, formed by removing crates and supporting the gap with sheet metal. "You can climb in."

"Okay." Alan obliged, crawling into the long space, grateful that a mattress was placed there for comfort.

The guard then reloaded the removed crates, burying him deep in beer.

"You fine?" the watchman asked once he had finished.

"Aye," Alan half-lied, in the claustrophobia of his pseudo-coffin.

"Not long now. Driver can come soon."

Chink-chink-chink-chink-chink-chink.

Thousands of clashing bottles disturbed his fitful slumbers.

Sudden stillness. The engine had been turned off.

Alan heard music from the cabin of the lorry. Was that deliberate to make sure there was always background noise to mask the sound of his breathing?

Where were they?

Voices.

Men.

Maybe a checkpoint. He must stay silent.

Clanking metal and then the rattle of a chain. The tailgate of the lorry being opened? Would they now remove the crates to reveal him?

Thud, thud. Footfalls on the flatbed.

Bump. The first crate removed.

Alan braced himself for impending disaster.

Pfffffffffttt. Someone opening a bottle. Pfffffffffttt. And another.

More voices. Happy banter.

Rattle, clunk. That must be the tailgate being closed.

Clack. The cabin door being shut?

Vroooooom. The engine started again.

Motion. Chink-chink-chink-chink-chink-chink.

MacAbraham is smart, Alan realised. A beer lorry was the perfect way to smuggle people past suspicious soldiers.

"Okay, my man, we can finish," he heard through the bottles.

The lorry had come to a halt, its pervasive engine noise silenced and the music turned off. He could hear birdsong between the driver's efforts to remove a row of crates.

Liberated, he emerged into bright sunlight.

"How your body?" the driver asked.

"The body good," Alan replied. *But sticky and dirty,* he mentally added, wiping some of the road dust off him.

He looked around. A continuous cement wall, about four metres high, ringed a large compound containing a collection of broken-down buses and lorries. It must be a maintenance depot in the bush, he guessed, given the tall trees that poked up behind the parapet. Nobody else was about, as it was the weekend.

"You can stay." The driver replaced the removed crates onto the truck. "Others come later. Not safe to go out, be behind old bus," he warned, as he climbed back into the cab and restarted the engine.

He soon exited through the gate, shutting it with a loud clang.

Alan was left feeling more alone than ever before.

An hour later, the gate opened, revealing a young Kugombwalan woman, in front of a twin-cab pickup, which drove into the compound. The driver and passenger—a couple in their late fifties—got out.

"Alan?" the man bellowed, once the younger woman had closed the gate. "We are friends of MacAbraham!"

"Hi." Alan felt safe to emerge from a broken-down bus.

"MacIsaac," the man introduced himself. "And this is my wife, MacRachel."

"Hello, Alan," she smiled. "It is very good of you to join us."

"And I'm MacSarah." The young woman had bounded over from the gate to join them.

"Good to meet you."

"We can continue introductions in the car," MacRachel interrupted. "Let's get going."

"Okay, it's safe to raise your head," MacRachel said after they had driven for ten minutes with Alan crouched in the footwell of the rear seat. "We are now on an old logging road. No locals or soldiers will spot us here."

"It's great to see where I'm going," Alan said, stretching. "First time since leaving Ndombazu this morning."

They were making slow progress on a rough track that wound through thick forest. MacIsaac worked hard at the wheel, steering the vehicle around the larger stumps in their path. The engine laboured to lift the vehicle over the branches and roots that littered the road, filling the interior with hot, dry air. Leaves, twigs, and an array of insects rained in through the open windows, released from the branches of the bushes that bashed the car's sides as it brushed past.

The action and noise muted conversation but Alan learned that MacRachel was a teacher-turned-journalist, while her husband owned a vehicle workshop. They were a tight pair, strong individuals harmoniously united by mutual respect and shared purpose.

"And what about you, MacSarah? What brings you here?"

"I'm a biologist. Before doing my Ph.D. in the U.S., I spent a few years studying forest baboons at a research station on the edge of the plateau near here, so I know this area like the back of my hand."

Their conversation was polite but detached, leaving Alan with the sense he would never be close to these people, with whom he was about to spend some of the most significant moments of his life.

"Stop!" MacSarah cried in a featureless area of forest, after four hours grinding up the slopes of the plateau. "I've just seen one of the lines."

MacIsaac brought the vehicle to a halt. MacSarah jumped out and backtracked a few paces.

Alan joined her, glad to get out of the hot confines of the car. To his amazement, a neat and narrow aisle stretched between the trees straight up the steep hillside before him. "What's this path for?"

"It's part of the grid of trails that the research station set up in the forest, so we could follow the monkeys we were studying and to prevent us getting lost."

"Is this our way onto the plateau?" MacRachel had joined them.

"No, this one requires a scramble higher up at the escarpment. There is another line further along that is easier."

"And the potential campsite you mentioned?"

"Also a bit further. About fifteen more minutes of driving, and then we turn onto a side track that goes to the base of a cliff where there is a freshwater spring."

"How come no one uses these roads?" Alan was puzzled by the absence of people and vehicles.

"It's because of the cliffs that line the top edge of the escarpment. They block the logging tracks from continuing onto the plateau, so they don't extend beyond the forest on these slopes. The locals don't use our primate grid either because of the difficulty of getting a bicycle up and down the cliff edges."

"How far did you say it was to the village?" MacRachel asked.

"About three hours by foot."

"Okay, let's go and set up camp and get ready for an early start tomorrow morning."

"Alan, can you remove the roof lining to get the tarpaulins and hammocks?" MacIsaac handed him a screwdriver whilst prising away the inside panel of a car door, revealing a hidden cache of food and cooking utensils.

The expedition had been meticulously planned, Alan noted, as he unloaded the smuggled camping equipment. It would have aroused intense suspicion if discovered at any of the numerous checkpoints outside Ndombazu.

They concealed the car with cut branches while MacRachel and MacSarah cooked on a small paraffin stove to avoid making smoke.

"Forest muffles sound," MacIsaac said once they started supper, "so it's safe to talk. No one else will be around this late in the day."

"And they would have to be close to hear us, as nature gets noisy at dusk." MacSarah referred to the choir of peeping treefrogs that surrounded them.

"Anyone for coffee?" MacRachel poured into plastic mugs. "It's decaffeinated, so won't stop sleep tonight. That's going to be difficult enough with our nerves on edge."

"Aye," Alan agreed, his head throbbing from the fight between deep fatigue and over-stimulation.

"Some words from Scripture should console us." MacIsaac pulled a Bible out of his bag. "It's good to remind ourselves why we are doing this dangerous task. You might be surprised, Alan, to learn that we are Bakiboko," the older man stroked his wife's arm. "MacRachel and I lived abroad during the civil war, but returned to Kugombwala when the Liberation Front took power. There were many new opportunities for our tribe, so I started a business while she got a job with a government-controlled newspaper. We were thriving and looked forward to a prosperous and happy future . . . "

"Until we heard about the three murdered priests." MacRachel took over. "Their deaths got us thinking because those foreigners had given their lives to serving the poor and oppressed here, while we ignored the horrors happening in our own country because it suited us to neither know nor act . . . "

"We called ourselves Christians, but we were hypocrites." Her husband nodded, looking at the ground. "Upstanding churchgoers whose response to knowing God was to seek His blessing rather than be His obedient servants."

MacRachel continued, "We had committed to follow Jesus, which means trying to live like Him in thanks for saving us from our sins, but apart from adhering to higher morals and donating to charity, we were little different from our neighbours. There was no evidence of the radical, life-changing faith that transforms lives compared to what they would otherwise be."

"In other words," MacIsaac added, "we were still living for ourselves, but doing a bit of Christianity to acquire the Lord's favour and to make us feel good. But we had not dedicated our lives to God—to quote the apostle Paul—by becoming living sacrifices. So, we repented for our selfishness that had sought personal success, comfort, and security, and we decided to devote our efforts to bring light to this dark world. Hence our attempt to expose the evil that is happening here."

"My love, the Bible verse . . . "

"Ah yes," MacIsaac opened the book. "MacSarah, will you read Isaiah, chapter one? He was a prophet at a time when the Israelites had turned away from God."

"Sure." She read out the passage.

MacIsaac then repeated the fourth verse: "'Woe to the sinful nation, a people whose guilt is great . . . They have forsaken the LORD . . . '" He looked at Alan. "That applies to us in Kugombwala, my friend, and it also applies to you in the West. We are all from countries that formerly followed God but have now turned away—and will be judged for it."

"I'm always struck by the next bit." MacRachel took the book and quoted from verses fifteen through seventeen: "'Your hands are full of blood! Wash and make yourselves clean. Take your evil deeds out of my sight; stop doing wrong. Learn to do right; seek justice. Defend the oppressed. Take up the cause of the fatherless; plead the case of the widow.'"

"Amen to that," MacIsaac concluded.

Night fell early under the thick tree canopy that filtered out most of the sunlight, forcing them to finish the evening's activities by torchlight.

"See the spiders?" MacSarah shone her torch into the darkness, illuminating myriad pin-prick pairs of multi-coloured light, reflected in the arachnids' eyes.

"Urgh, that's creepy." Alan reacted. "What are those glowing white blobs on the ground?"

"Luminescent fungi—and these are fireflies." She pointed to pearls of light that floated on the air around them.

"Wow, this forest is psychedelic. It even has a background beat!" He could just discern a distant bong-bong-bong sound.

They paused to listen.

"It's a drum," MacRachel said.

"I didn't think there were any villages here." MacIsaac instinctively turned off his torch.

"There aren't." MacSarah sounded worried.

"So, who's drumming here, deep in a forest and war zone?" MacRachel asked.

"Perhaps a lone witch doctor?" MacSarah offered.

"Or Watumbwa rebels," MacIsaac said.

No one commented as they continued to listen in total darkness, trying to fathom what the drumming might mean. Was it an exuberant burst of rhythm or a coded message?

They waited for many minutes, hoping that the haunting tones would stop, but they continued, an incessant bong-bong-bong, determined to last the night. There was something unnerving about that sound—perhaps a combination of its link to early humanity and the implicit threat in its mystery.

"Someone has no problem drawing attention to themselves," MacRachel said.

"It might even be from a military encampment," MacIsaac added. "And it's quite close . . . "

Drip.

Alan woke to an eerily still forest. A thick mist engulfed them, wetting trees that dribbled intermittent drops of condensation from their leaves.

MacSarah was already up, boiling water in a kettle. "This fog is a Godsend," she said. "The limited visibility will reduce the risk of being seen."

After breakfast, MacIsaac hid the camping gear under some bushes beside the cliff face and the car keys under a prominent rock. "If we get separated, then whoever gets back here can drive out. Even if the car is discovered, there will still be food and equipment to sustain the walk out."

MacSarah led the way, starting with the logging road, before reaching a primate observation trail. They continued on in single-file up the steep slope, past the cliff edge, and then onto the flat top of the plateau. They spoke infrequently to reduce the risk of being detected.

The silent walk provided fertile ground for Alan's brain to sprout a tangle of prickly thoughts that scratched at his mind. One of these imagined him before a court for what he was doing, wandering alone with three unarmed companions through a remote African rainforest infested with genocidal killers. In these trials, he would repeatedly play out the parts of prosecutor, defendant, jury, and judge. And always, he would reach the same verdict: he was utterly crazy for placing himself in such peril.

"Can you hear it?" MacRachel looked up. "Sounds like a plane."

They all stopped.

"Yes, for sure," her husband answered, as the distant droning noise got louder.

They all stared into the mist-shrouded canopy.

"It's circling above us," Alan noted. "Have we been discovered?"

"Impossible." MacIsaac shook his head. "They can't see us through thick cloud and trees."

"Then why is it flying around? It seems to be searching for something."

"It's surveying this area." MacIsaac paused to think. "Perhaps they are using infrared sensors to detect camp fires?"

"Does the Liberation Front have planes with such technology?" MacSarah asked.

"No. Another country must be helping them."

"Bootprints!" MacSarah crouched down to examine the path. "Wellingtons. Looks like five individuals, judging by the different sizes and print patterns."

"Are they recent?" MacRachel asked.

"I'd say from yesterday."

"I thought no one was using the primate grid?"

"That's what I had hoped, but I'm wrong. These are soldier tracks, which means we have to be extra careful."

"Could be a patrol," MacIsaac cut in. "One of the Liberation Front death squads on the lookout for survivors fleeing the killings."

"That would explain why so few displaced people ever escape the plateau," MacRachel said. "The survivors from the massacres are being located, intercepted, and eliminated—"

"To make sure no one lives to tell the tale." MacIsaac finished her sentence.

MacRachel was adamant. "All the more reason why we should continue."

"The cloud's lifted." MacRachel halted where the path reached the edge of a large forest clearing and opened onto overgrown farmland.

MacIsaac brought out binoculars. "I don't see anyone," he said, scanning the valley before them. "What about you, MacSarah?"

"Looks fine to me," she agreed. "The village is behind the mango trees a kilometre ahead, where some of our workers lived before the war. Most of the inhabitants, including many of my team members, were massacred when the Liberation Front captured this area."

"How do we get there?"

"Follow the path that starts at the opposite end of this field."

"Alan and I will go while MacSarah and MacIsaac should stay to keep watch in case anyone shows up." MacRachel squeezed her husband's hand. "There's no reason for them to risk their lives unnecessarily; only one Kugombwalan and one Westerner need to see the evidence of the atrocities."

"Right." Alan obeyed out of obligation rather than desire. His legs felt like jelly.

After fifteen minutes, he and MacRachel reached the former village, now reduced to a collection of abandoned buildings where grass grew tall in doorways. Roofless walls, burned and broken, provided the sole reminder that here, once, had been homes and a lively human community. But its earlier activity was now supplanted by an uncanny, pervasive stillness, as if nature was paying respect to the dead by lowering her voice to the hushed whisper of the wind.

They ventured into the shattered settlement without exchanging a word. Each step was now a cautious tread, careful of what it might find underfoot, fearful of disturbing the silence. With trepidation, they entered the ruined houses that had become blank tombstones for an unwanted people to search for visible evidence that they had been exterminated. But there was nothing tangible that could be meaningfully photographed, despite the feeling that a great horror had taken place—an oppressive claustrophobia that defied the sky that gaped through roofless shells. With it came an urge to get out, to leave, to run.

At the end of the street was a small church, a more substantial structure than the other buildings in the village, that had better resisted the destruction wrought by war and weather. Its pointed stained-glass windows and brick bell tower, reminiscent of distant Europe's gothic edifices, appeared incongruous in the abandoned jungle clearing.

Cracked steps led up to the church entrance. Alan had become separated from MacRachel and so approached the building alone. On reaching the stairs, he sensed an invisible barrier, as if the air was more viscous here, trying to keep him out. But an overwhelming need to witness, to find evidence, and to expose the truth spurred him to overcome the obstacle. With great effort, he pushed his way through and up the steps into the hollow vacuum of the church.

The oppressive feeling was stronger here: an empty space surrounded by pockmarked cement walls bearing the scars of automatic gunfire, a floor discoloured with uncertain stains, a lingering whiff of something that had rotted, and an inaudible presence of screams long silenced. It only required a few seconds to take in the scene before he could no longer bear being there. He turned to go, and then something attracted his attention above the door through which he had come. A pitted line etched by the bullets from a machine gun arced across the wall towards and through a statue of the crucified Christ.

Someone had deliberately shot Jesus, just like the Roman soldier who had stabbed the Messiah with a spear to make sure he was dead.

A chill ran down Alan's spine, following a sudden, supernatural revelation that the Kugombwalan civil war was more than a mere human conflict—it was part of an apocalyptic struggle between good and evil. He had intruded into the arena of the ultimate conflict, where the powers of darkness strove to extinguish the forces of light.

Something jumped on his shoulders, heavy, like a big dog.

Turning in fright, he saw nothing, triggering instant panic. For it was still there, now clutching stronger, with what felt like strong feet pushing on his back.

Terrified, Alan fled the church as fast as he could and then kept running, trying to escape. But it was futile; despite his efforts, it clung stubbornly on.

"Get off!" he shouted into the air, as he twisted, turned, and dodged in his desperate attempt to shake it off.

"What's the matter?" MacRachel rushed out from one of the buildings.

Only then did the evil presence depart.

Back in the relative safety of the forest and reunited with the others, Alan's thoughts dwelt on the villagers who had sought sanctuary in the church, where he sensed they had been massacred. They had turned to God in humble submission of their need for His protection, and yet, they had been slaughtered.

Why hadn't God prevented or stopped the massacre? Why were the murderers allowed to kill so many innocent people? Was it because the evil presence was stronger than the Almighty? He hoped not, for the eternal consequences would be horrific beyond all imagination.

It then occurred to him that God might nonetheless have protected the victims by allowing them to perish, to rescue them from a vicious world with its pervasive oppression, suffering, and distress. Death, he realised, can be a mercy.

"Ow!" MacSarah gasped, slapping her shin, while hopping about.

Alan was about to ask what was wrong when he felt a piercing pain on the top of his foot, followed by a sustained stab on the opposite ankle. Then another on his thigh. He looked down.

Giant ants swarmed over the ground, covering his boots and crawling up and over his trousers, going into every available gap in their frenzy to deliver yet more ant jabs. He tried to brush them off, but the biters clung on, so he leapt back along the path to a safe place away from the writhing mass of angry insects.

Once out of risk of further attack, he tried to remove the ants one by one, but their bodies broke easily, leaving the heads with their huge jaws still locked painfully into his skin. Additional effort was needed to extract them.

"Safari ants. We call them *siafu.*" MacSarah had joined him by now. "Come and see."

She led him to the forward edge of the torrent of fast-moving ants, which attacked every living thing in their path. A wave of frightened forest creatures attempted to scramble out of the way, but most were caught by the aggressive ants.

"Look at this huge centipede!" she pointed out. "It has a poisonous bite." But it was no match for the ants, who quickly overpowered it. Nearby, a large millipede had coiled up, secreting a venomous fluid in a desperate attempt to escape harm; but the ants soon overwhelmed it, biting so much that it was forced into writhing contortions that heralded its demise. "The small ones are workers—they don't bite as hard—and the big ones are soldiers." Her proximity caused the closest ants to turn towards her with jaws wide open, ready to attack. "*Siafu* try to kill everything they come across. They don't take prisoners."

MacIsaac snorted. "Just like the Liberation Front."

MacSarah stopped and then pointed to the ground. Mixed with the muddy soil were discarded belongings, the detritus of hunted humanity, which littered the path ahead. Here was evidence of an attack on a group of displaced people, who had been fleeing the plateau—buckets, a Bible, clothes, a foam mattress, plastic cups, a sack of maize . . . Their most precious possessions, their remaining symbols of identity, their last tools and food—all desperately jettisoned to escape imminent death.

From here on, those who had survived this strike would become an anonymous herd, rendered indistinguishable from one another by their sole remaining possessions—their soiled and tattered clothes.

The team continued along the trail, softly treading the soil to avoid being snared by additional human refuse. A kilometre further, the rank stench of rotting flesh forewarned them of further assaults on their senses.

First on the path was the carcass of a small child, its porcelain-white skull smashed by a blunt object and its body stripped to a skeleton by ants. *How could anyone do this?* Alan was sickened by the scene.

And then a suppressed memory surfaced in his mind. An incident he had long tried to forget.

Mandy was weeping. He had insisted on an abortion for their child, threatening to leave her if she didn't do the deed. Then more tears after her return from the clinic. Unconsolable sobbing that seemed to never cease.

And then anger.

A change had taken place in her, triggering the explosive outbursts, the hysterical screaming, the flailing frying pan.

She had never been like that before. But afterwards, something simmered within her, a deep resentment towards him, perhaps even a desire for vengeance. As if she needed to regularly inflict harm on him in return for the violence wreaked on her child.

Her child. Not his. Because he had rejected it through his demand to end its existence.

Alan regarded the remains of the infant in front of him, whose tiny bones would never grow to full size—a life cut short and thereby denied the opportunity to make a mark on the world. He had likewise erased the lifetime of good deeds that his child would have done and thereby denied the consequent benefits of those deeds for many people. *I am no better than the perpetrators of this genocide,* he grasped. They had murdered strangers, while he had obliterated his own offspring.

Alan surveyed the corpses that transformed the track into an open abattoir of slaughtered humanity. They lay one after the other into the distance, conjuring for him an image of generation after generation of the destroyed bloodline of his own descendants.

The horror caused him to vomit by the roadside, hating himself for what he had done and for who he was, while wishing he could somehow atone for his past and become a better person.

"Be strong, Alan. We need photos, and we haven't got much time," MacIsaac said, reminding him of his mission.

Alan took out his camera and proceeded to document the gruesome sight, body after body. Every further step had to be taken with care to avoid treading on or touching the human remains, which would have defiled him for being disrespectful towards the dead.

"Do you sense it?" MacIsaac asked. "The atmosphere?"

"Aye, there's a strange feeling here."

The sensation was difficult to describe—a silence devoid of menace, accompanied by the feeling they were not alone. Was it the spirits of the dead, hovering over their unburied earthly remains?

"Is it ghosts?" he asked, not sure of his conclusion, for the ambience was without the anguish or anger that he would have expected from the restless souls of murder victims. Instead, there was a surreal sense of peace, suffused with deep sadness.

"No." MacIsaac paused. "It is the Holy Spirit Who is here and is grieving—not only over the suffering and untimely deaths of these people but also in sadness over what the killers have done. You see, God loves them, too."

CLACK-CLACK-CLACK.

A rattle of gunfire.

Alan spun around to see a green tracer fly towards him. Bullets whistled past.

He instinctively hit the ground, covering his head with his hands. The shooting stopped and was followed by shouting from the road behind him. Close by, someone moaned.

"I'm hit," MacIsaac groaned. "Are you okay, my love?"

No response from MacRachel.

The shouting was getting nearer, but Alan dared not raise his head. There was a sound of rustling vegetation ahead of him and then a further clatter of gunfire from behind, plus more whistling bullets. The shouting sounded angrier.

Alan moved his head slightly to peer behind. Through the gap under his armpit, he could see part of MacIsaac's body and a puddle of blood seeping from underneath.

"Are you all right, MacIsaac?" he whispered.

"No, I'm bad" came the faint reply.

He could hear the sound of running; the flop, flop of wellington boots slapping alternately against calves and shins; and the reverberations of heavy footfalls on the ground.

Another loud burst of fire, this time from almost above him. A smell of gunpowder smoke. More shouting near where he lay.

Yet another burst of fire, followed by the rustle of vegetation. And then his spinal radar told him that guns were being pointed at his back.

His turn now.

He held his breath in anticipation of the shot that would rob him of his life.

"Get up, Priest." The order came from behind him. He hesitated, but a sharp kick in his side left no doubt the message was meant for him.

He got up slowly, holding his hands up in the way he had seen so many times in films. A quick glance revealed MacIsaac's corpse riddled with bullet holes. Beyond lay MacRachel with a fatal gunshot wound to her head. MacSarah had disappeared. She must have run off just after that first burst of fire. The second round of shots would then have been in response to her leaping into the forest. The third salvo must have been to despatch MacIsaac, the fourth, perhaps, into the forest where MacSarah had fled before sending a few soldiers to hunt her down. He hoped she would escape unscathed, comforted by the knowledge that she had the bush skills to survive in the forest.

"Who are you, white man?" one of the gunmen snarled. Six hardened and heavily armed serial killers all pointed their weapons at him.

"Alan Swales. I'm not a priest. I am an aid worker. And a B-British citizen," he stammered.

The soldier translated his answer to the rest of the group, causing an argument to erupt. There was much pointing at him, and he knew from their hostile stares he was the subject of the dispute.

God, he prayed, *have mercy on me. I need Your help now more than ever before. Please protect me from these people. And please preserve MacSarah's life.*

The quarrel continued, during which he studied the death squad who would soon be his executioners. They wore combat fatigues, together with the hallmark red wellington boots of the Liberation

Front troops. The soldiers were in their late teens or twenties—strong, muscular youths who had torn off their shirtsleeves to give freedom for shoulder muscles and biceps to bulge. Their leader wore a military beret, as well as a diverse collection of strange adornments that Alan guessed to be spirit charms or amulets. In addition to his rifle, he also had a pistol and a dagger in his belt.

After what seemed an interminable time of shouting at each other, the leader pulled out his knife and walked right up to him. Alan's blood coagulated inside, in anticipation of imminent stab wounds. The man thrust the dagger forwards while grabbing the bottom of his t-shirt, cutting off a strip of cloth before twisting him around. His arms were then yanked together behind his back, sending a bolt of pain to his shoulders, and his wrists bound tight against each other with the cloth. One of the others then searched him, taking his wallet, watch, camera, and passport, as well as his rucksack that had fallen to his side. Rough hands rasped his body, seeking possible weapons and more booty. The intrusion into his personal space brought home to him the full consequence of becoming a prisoner; he had now lost every form of liberty.

It's over, he thought. He was out of the game now, the tournament of life he had tried so hard to win and in which he was succeeding before he came to this cursed land. Even if they didn't kill him, he would spend his remaining days in captivity, subjected to continuous deprivation and abuse. Never again would he know happiness, for he was now one of the planet's uncountable millions of absolute victims, whose only hope was the grave.

Until then, death had been something to fear. But now, he craved it. *God,* he beseeched, again and again, *please forgive me for my many sins. Don't condemn me to stay any longer in this world of suffering and pain. Please terminate my existence straightaway; take me home, just like You did for MacRachel and MacIsaac.* He envied them their sudden release from their life sentences.

Yet, as he feared, there was no response, so his living nightmare continued. The soldiers pushed and shoved him for hours along forest tracks, while his shoulders and wrists shrieked in agony. Every time he started flagging, they kicked and beat him, adding further points of pain to an already overloaded body. He was hot, hurting, thirsty, confused, and scared, his body's constant complaints reinforcing his desire for his life to end. But for the moment, the soldiers had taken that choice from him.

After many exhausting and painful miles of struggle and stumble, the head of the column stopped and shouted into the forest. He received a distant call in reply. Soon afterwards, they passed a sentry before arriving at a rough encampment in a small clearing surrounded by the high walls of the forest. Three crude shacks, constructed of sticks and palm leaves, centred around a rising wisp of blue smoke that indicated the presence of other people. A teenage girl with frightened eyes emerged from one of the shacks and stared on impassively, clutching a broom and a dirty bolt of cloth around her body.

Alan was led to a row of large logs lying on the ground, arranged beside each other in parallel. Two of the central logs were removed, releasing a stench of human rot and excrement; and he was shoved into the gap, dropping a couple of metres into the dark hole. Contrary to his expectation, it was not a latrine pit, for it also contained humans, who were still alive.

There were about a dozen of them, zombie prisoners pre-interred in a dark tomb and already lifeless but for an occasional moan or groan from hunger, thirst, disease, and maltreatment.

For a while, none of them reacted to his presence, but after some time, one of them uttered, "My man?"

Alan looked up, trying to guess which of the forms had spoken. A youth opposite him repeated the words.

"Yes?" was all Alan could say, conscious the others were listening. How would his fellow prisoners treat him? As a threat? As a competitor for scarce resources? Or as a companion?

"What can be your name?" It was a question he had been asked hundreds of times, the standard school phrase learned by the kids of Kugombwala who would pester foreigners with it. But now, he was glad to be asked, for it meant he would no longer be anonymous to the other prisoners.

After answering, he returned the question.

"MacDaniel," the youth replied.

"You are Watumbwa?" Alan guessed.

"Yes, we can all be."

Confused from a day of seeing so many corpses, he asked, "Why have they not killed you?"

"The soldiers can kill all children and old people. But they keep some men for body clearing."

"What's that?"

"They can use us every day for finding dead people they killed before. We must burn the bodies in big fires, so the white people will not find them. When the job is finished, the Bakiboko can kill and burn us, too."

So, that was the story. The Liberation Front soldiers were systematically destroying all evidence of their genocidal acts by searching for the bones and cadavers of those they had killed and coercing their captives to gather and then incinerate every trace of the murdered Watumbwa people. That explained why there were no corpses in the village he had visited.

All that would remain from the massacres would be the memories of the soldiers who conducted the killings. The threat they posed as potential court witnesses would last only as long as they themselves were still alive and posed no risk to the Liberation Front's hold on power, for no one in the international community would believe the hearsay of ordinary Africans. Their accounts—if they were ever to escape Kugombwala's tight borders—could never be confirmed by physical evidence and would be dismissed as wild and fanciful rumours by an uncaring world that preferred to ignore what was happening in the killing fields of the distant Kugombwalan plateau.

"Where are the women?" Alan then asked, noticing there were none in the shared tomb.

"The older girls and young women can be in another pit," MacDaniel answered. Alan did not need to ask why they were being kept alive by the soldiers.

Shortly afterwards, a log was pulled back, and chunks of food were dropped onto the earthen floor, causing some of the hitherto lifeless prisoners to fight with each other over the few scraps in a gladiatorial battle to stay alive.

Alan did not join in, for he had lost the will to live. For him, there was no longer any hope. He had entered the abyss and was now in free fall, dropping ever further into a bottomless vortex of gloom and despair.

CHAPTER 12

NDOMBAZU

The soldier's knees trembled as he approached the mahogany door. He raised the back of his fist to below the brass sign, which read:

DIRECTOR OF MILITARY INTELLIGENCE

He paused and then rapped the door with his knuckles.

"One moment," came the annoyed response.

On the other side, Colonel MacEdwin Mfaume-Simbwa opened his desk drawer, revealing a jar containing dead flies. He strategically placed one on the paper in front of him.

"Enter," he ordered.

"U.K. Defence Adviser can be here to see you, sir!" The soldier saluted to a simultaneous swoosh-slap from the colonel's fly swat.

"Got the little bugger," he muttered before flicking the corpse over to the soldier's feet. Without looking up, he barked, "Send him in, and then shut the door."

The smiling Brit sauntered over. "Edwin, good to see you, old chap!"

"Gerard, thanks so much for coming at such short notice."

They embraced each other. Having many mutual friends cemented their close camaraderie.

"Do take a seat." The colonel offered as he sat down. "A potentially serious matter, Gerard. We've picked up a Brit snooping around on the plateau who might be one of your unofficial military observers."

"Good gracious, we wouldn't dream of spying on you—we're allies! Who is he?"

"Alan Swales, the former logistician-administrator from MedRelief."

"Oh, him. I hadn't expected that. I thought he was someone of no consequence."

"Yes, a common Northerner," the colonel sneered. "Our sources told us he was sacked last week for insubordination, but we had no intel on his subsequent whereabouts until an army patrol apprehended him during their routine security operations."

"And you haven't asked him?"

"His answers so far are cryptic, so I wanted to check with you first, in case he was one of yours, before authorising more pressure to be put on him."

"Quite understand. And you've asked the Americans?"

"Of course. He's nothing to do with them."

"Was he alone?"

"No, he was with a couple of local communists who were killed while trying to escape. We've got their cameras and developed the films. They were spying on our pre-prospecting activities with the intent to destabilise Kugombwala. That could have serious consequences for British companies like Anglo Imperial Petroleum that are working here."

"Oh, quite."

"So, we can deal with him as we see fit?"

"Do whatever you think is right, Edwin. Her Majesty's government will not intervene."

"Thanks, Gerard. I'll get the police to concoct a plausible story and report it to the embassy."

"Much appreciated, old chap. And I'll make sure no one on our staff makes a stink. Anyway, I've got to run; must get back to planning the prime minister's visit."

Gerard's a jolly decent fellow, for we understand each other, the colonel reflected after the military attaché had left. Their personal friendship strengthened his bond with Britain, which was predicated on him acquiescing to be a pliant client of a perfidious patron and its big American brother. He would have to render unswerving loyalty to U.K. and U.S. interests to pay for the privilege of life-long command over Kugombwala, but the superpowers would protect him from international prosecution for his war crimes. Not as a favour to him, but to hide their indirect involvement.

Yet one obstacle still had to be overcome to achieve his ambitions, the colonel reminded himself as he leant back in his chair. He smiled sardonically at the image of General MacVictor Bakigoma on the wall. *That will be me one day,* he told himself.

BRICKDALE
THREE DAYS LATER

Ding-dong.

Yap, yap, yap, yap.

"Be quiet, Arthur, and come here!" Yvonne Carter took the dog by the collar.

Mandy rose from the dining table and approached the front door that revealed a dark form behind the frosted glass. A black helmet was visible in the clear toplight window.

"It's a copper!" Mandy confirmed to her parents in the other room. She half opened the door. "Yes?"

"Good evening, ma'am. Are you Amanda Carter?"

"Yes, that's me."

"Is anyone at home with you?"

"Yes, hello, Officer, I'm Amanda's mother." Yvonne Carter joined her daughter at the door.

"Could we sit down somewhere?"

"Of course, do come into the lounge, Officer. Bert, take Arthur into the kitchen."

"Miss Carter, it's about your partner," the policeman started once Mr. Carter had returned and all were seated.

"What's happened?" Mandy voiced her family's concern for Terry, who was out on the evening shift.

"The Foreign Office has asked me to inform you that he's reported missing in Kugombwala."

"Oh, Al!" Mandy gasped. "Actually, we're no—"

"Do continue, Officer." Yvonne Carter put a firm hand on her daughter's arm, signalling her to be silent.

"His last known whereabouts was when he checked into a beach hotel a week ago, but he has not been seen since. All his luggage was still there, which the embassy will forward to you. The local police believe he was taken by a shark or swept out to sea while going for a swim."

"Al!" Mandy burst into tears. "It's all my fault," she sobbed.

"I'm sorry to have to bear this bad news." The policeman got up to go.

"Thank you, Officer." Yvonne Carter accompanied him out. "I'm sure Amanda will soon get over the shock."

To her surprise, she found herself smiling—not over Alan's demise, for she had no desire to be vindictive. Instead, she felt vindicated by the tragedy, which dispelled her inner disquiet over disliking him for breaking the social taboo against prioritising strangers above kith and kin, which he had done by becoming an overseas aid worker. She was now assured that her sentiment had been sensible rather than selfish, in order to protect Mandy's best interests. *I'm a good mother,* she told herself and her imagined spirit universe, *and a good person.*

She returned to the lounge to console her distraught daughter and steer her away from self-guilt. "Don't take it too hard, darling. Poor Al's untimely death shows you weren't meant to be together, and anyway, you were too good for him. Silly boy—I told him he shouldn't go and risk his life in Africa. If only he had listened to me. Isn't that so, Bert?"

"Of course, dear."

LONDON

THREE DAYS LATER

"Morning, darling." Isabella sat down at her desk and switched on her computer. "How was Ascot?"

"Terrific." Fiona smiled. "Sebastian got us into the Royal Enclosure. He's frightfully charming, you know."

"I simply can't wait for your wedding. Oh, do excuse me, the phone." She picked up the receiver, nervous that it might be a journalist enquiring about a missing aid-worker. "MedRelief. Isabella speaking."

"Hiya, I'm calling about becoming a logistician."

"Yes, who is it, please?"

"Robert Johnson, but just call me Bobsy."

KUGOMBWALAN PLATEAU

Dut-dut-dut.

Silence.

Dut-dut-dut again.

Some shouting.

And then another burst of gunfire.

Alan was restored to his full senses from semi-slumber. That horrible sound of a machine gun, heralding yet more death. It was pitch-black in their tomb, so it must still be night. What was happening?

After a few minutes, he heard the shuffling sound from someone walking on the logs over the pit. That meant trouble. More shuffling noises, and then a log came crashing down, hitting some of the other prisoners and releasing a cloud of dust into his eyes and nostrils. Instinctively, they all made for the sides of the chasm.

Another log came down. Were they being buried alive?

Then some shouting in a language he did not understand.

A faint glimmer of light now penetrated the pit from the opening created by the removed logs. Some of the prisoners congregated underneath the hole and then heaved someone up. Followed by another. And again another. It seemed like they all had to leave.

"Come," MacDaniel said. "We can go now."

A hand reached down and pulled him up, through and out of the hole. He felt an instant rush, as his eyes reached the edge of the pit and re-entered a hemisphere of sky. A recharge of light, space, and air. The heavens were lightening from the first rays of dawn with the beautiful bright morning star still visible. He crawled over the edge and stood up to join the other prisoners, who included a group of women. They all looked surprisingly relaxed and were chatting with each other. No guards were to be seen.

What was going on? He did not know, but despite the confusion, he had the strange sense he had been rescued from the abyss. It felt like he had been raised from the dead, yet it conflicted with the reality of being mustered for the massacre sites—or for a firing squad.

"What's happening, MacDaniel?" he asked once he, too, had been brought out of the pit.

"The prisoners can say the guards were drinking and then fight each other. Some can be killed, some wounded. See, only that one is left."

A figure in combat fatigues carrying a raised rifle appeared out of a hut and strode over to the group, shouting and gesticulating. The other prisoners started to move away from the pit.

"What is he saying? Is he going to shoot us?" Alan was confused but received no response as MacDaniel had drifted off, leaving him standing alone.

The soldier turned towards him, sending a shudder through Alan as violent eyes and lethal gun were directed towards him.

"White man. I can release you. Now go. With the people. Go! Now!" he ordered.

"Thanks, mate" was all Alan could think of saying as he trotted after the rest of the group to the edge of the clearing, half-expecting to be shot in the back, despite the soldier's command. They fled in single file along a narrow forest path and up a steep slope, putting both distance and altitude between them and the slave camp in the valley below.

Alan's physical condition was weakened by captivity. He struggled up the rise, out of breath, battling to lift his legs. His spirit wanted to maintain the momentum of his resurrection out of the pit, ascending further upwards to escape this troubled world. *God must have other plans,* Alan reasoned, for he was still alive. That was a miracle given his current circumstance, so there had to be a reason why his life had been spared.

CRACK!

The distant sound of a rifle shot rang through the air from the valley below.

"The soldier." MacDaniel turned towards him. "I can think he kill himself."

After a few difficult hours of stumbling along the rough forest track, they reached a stream. In front of them, there was a flash of movement, as if they had startled an animal. And then shouts from beyond the bushes on the other side of the bank—a woman's voice, fraught with fear and becoming more distant.

The leader of Alan's group called out before turning to address a young girl who was behind him. She pushed past to the head of the queue and then called out across the rivulet to the disappearing voice.

The distant woman called back.

"What's happening?" Alan asked MacDaniel.

"Outcast women. They can be living here because of smelling."

"Smelling?"

"Yes, body no good; always bad smell. Because too many soldiers can love them."

Alan was puzzled and then realised what MacDaniel meant. "Raped women?" he asked, remembering a conversation between Lorna and Megan about women who suffered fistulas from forced penetration, causing them to continuously secrete urine.

"Yes, their husbands no want them; their families no want them; their village no want them. So, they can come to live here, deep in the forest."

"To be safe?"

"No, not safe here. Soldiers can still be coming. But the women stay here because there is nowhere else for them."

The young girl from their group had crossed the stream and disappeared into the forest on the other side.

After some minutes, she re-emerged into view, together with another woman, who burst into laughter when she saw the incongruous sight of a white man in dirty, tattered clothes among the fleeing prisoners. The tension was broken.

The others in the group began to traverse the stream.

"Come." MacDaniel waded ahead. "This woman can be inviting us to her home."

Alan exhaled with glee as he poured the cup of warmed water over himself and worked a lather out of the tiny morsel of soap. It was invigorating to be clean again.

He took the piece of cloth that one of the women had provided for him, wrapped it around his waist, and stepped out from the crude, stick-lined cubicle to join the others sitting around an open fire. A large, clay bowl containing water was being warmed for the next person to take a shower.

"Your clothes." One of the women pointed to the stinking bundle at his feet. "I can go wash for you in river."

"Thanks!"

Five-star service, Alan acknowledged. He had not expected that in the remote jungle settlement. The outcast women had rallied to assist the ex-prisoners in an outstanding display of generosity, given their meagre resources.

"Food ready." One of them brought a battered aluminium bowl full of steaming cassava. He took a piece and bit into it. Soon afterwards, his hunger pangs disappeared. He then noticed that his skin had not itched for a while, ever since he had taken the shower. Life was improving.

It felt good to be free, washed, and fed—simple needs, so often taken for granted.

His fellow ex-prisoners sat around him, giggling together. *What sweet, gentle people they are,* he observed, his heart warming in love towards them. It was a wonder that they were still so positive, despite all they had suffered.

Sitting on a log, dressed in rags and chewing a bland lump of boiled cassava, he felt a curious elation. The sun shone its warmth on him, while the animals, birds, and insects of the forest sang choruses of praise to their Creator. Life was good. He grinned for the first time in many days.

Somehow, he knew all would go well now. MacDaniel had told him a woman from the outcast community would lead them by a jungle path across the border. From there, he merely had to follow MacAbraham's plan: make his way to a mission station, reach the capital, go to the university, and find the veterinary professor who would get him a ticket out.

He would soon be back in Britain. He eagerly anticipated the reunion with his family and friends, plus the opportunity to restart his life. He might even contact Mandy, he mused, to re-establish friendship or at least part from her on decent terms to ensure proper closure for their past relationship.

But despondency then descended on him over the awareness he would leave Kugombwala empty-handed, without photos, documentation, or any evidence of the killings. All he had was his own eyewitness accounts of an emptied village, of encountering corpses scattered along a track, and seeing two people shot by soldiers. Without actual images, people would think he was making it up, and besides, it was far too little material to mobilise the world's media. Which meant he would be unable to do anything to combat the horrors that would continue to crush the Watumbwa people.

Why, then, had God put him through the terrible experiences of the last few days? It all seemed so senseless, a wasted opportunity. MacRachel and MacIsaac's lives had been terminated, removing two decent people from the planet, who could have done a lot more good had they been allowed to live. MacSarah's fate was little better; she was probably now in exile, assuming she had survived in the forest. Both she and he would now be blighted by mental trauma from what they had witnessed and endured.

He was forced to acknowledge that nothing positive had come out of the perilous trip. Their efforts had been in vain—which meant they had failed. It was therefore time to admit defeat and surrender his personal battle against the forces of darkness. He sank into depression, thinking about the world's harsh reality that evil always wins because truth is ignored and lies keep it hidden, which means there will never be justice.

Accept it; don't waste effort trying to oppose it, an inner voice told him.

But another view arose to counter that: *at least they tried.* Like MacRachel, MacIsaac, and MacSarah, he had thereby maintained some personal integrity. Was that what it was about? Was that why he had to join the team to visit the plateau? Was God testing his character?

No, there had to be another reason. It couldn't be only about him. He needed to stop seeing everything from his own self-centred perspective.

He reflected on MacIsaac and MacRachel's renouncing of their comfortable lifestyle to serve God, which had resulted in nothing but their deaths. Obedience to the Almighty had cost them everything for no apparent gain, which he found impressive for its folly. *Maybe that is the crux of the matter,* he conjectured, before comprehending, *obeying God is more important that the results it might achieve.* That realisation inspired him to emulate MacIsaac and MacRachel's example, noting that they had offered their lives in response to Christ's gift of salvation through His sacrifice on the cross. *I, too,* Alan resolved, *will turn away from my selfish ways and dedicate my life to follow Jesus, whatever the cost.*

A thought then struck him like a thunderbolt from a cloudless sky about what he would do when he got back to the U.K. It occurred to him that he should find out the names of the perpetrators of this genocide in Kugombwala, together with those of their Western allies who had supported them, and reveal their identities and actions to the world. That information was surely out there, somewhere. There was no need for him to be a witness to the killings or to tell his own gruesome tales of seeing corpses. Combining everybody else's accounts would better demonstrate the facts than he could do with his limited personal experiences.

That might explain why he was leaving Kugombwala without any meaningful testimony—because he had to tell the whole story, not just his own. Once again, it was not about him.

And he should refrain from the arrogance of thinking he could bring the perpetrators to justice; that was impossible given that they and their allies controlled the world's media and legal systems. But he could deliver a message to the killers and their henchmen that their dark deeds would not remain forever hidden, which, by extension, indicated they would not escape eventual justice in the afterlife. It would be an urgent warning to them to turn from their wrongful ways while they were still alive before the time ran out for them to receive holy mercy—an exhortation for them to seek Divine forgiveness in anticipation of God's inevitable judgment on all humankind, when those who had failed to repent for their sins would suffer eternal punishment.

He was taken aback by the magnitude of those thoughts, quite unlike his own. How dare he imagine he could carry out such a daunting objective? Yet the concepts had been so clear and the idea so ambitious that he realised they must have come from God. He, Alan Swales, had been created to carry out this purpose, which was the Almighty's supreme will for his life.

How he would achieve his assignment was unknown to him, but he was convinced that God would show him what to do now that he had decided to serve Him. No doubt about that.

Despite that certainty, a new disquiet emerged that lingered in his mind, nagging him with a persistence he could not ignore. Why had God chosen him, Alan the Unsuitable, from amongst the billions of people on the planet, to do this particular task?

That question stubbornly resisted his attempts to find an answer, leaving him humbled by the privilege of Divine purpose.

Lead, Kindly Light, amidst th'encircling gloom,

Lead Thou me on!

The night is dark, and I am far from home;

Lead Thou me on!

Keep Thou my feet; I do not ask to see

The distant scene; one step enough for me.

John Henry Newman, 1833

ACKNOWLEDGMENTS

This book would have been impossible for me to create without much help from other people. Many thanks, therefore, for their time and input, including:

To my English teacher at Wadham School in Crewkerne, the late Eric John Williams, who taught me to love and appreciate literature and for instructing some of my writing skills.

To my friends and family who read earlier and less-polished versions of the novel, in whole or in part, and who all offered important advice, necessary criticism, and much-needed encouragement: Nana Cajus de Baez, Christopher Clarke, Susanna Booth, Mick Bellmooney, Bev Lloyd-Roberts, Julio Maffia, Ari Wegter, Geoffrey Clarke, Birgitte Clarke, Jane Clark, Sue Howe, Ian Blatchford, Sandie Wilson, Barbara Clarke, Ruth Clarke, Norbert Payne, Marcus Amery, Chris Moore, Niels Hahn, and Birgitte Riis Andersen.

To my editors, Bryony Sutherland and Katie Smith, who skilfully trimmed and tweaked the novel.

To my family and friends who co-financed this book through their generous support during the five years of 2014-2019 when the novel went through a massive rewrite: Lilian Clarke, Sally Slaughter, Birgitte and Geoffrey Clarke, and Mick Bellmooney. Thanks also to Claus Dantzer-Sørensen, Niels Hahn, Marcus Amery, Chris Moore, and Anne Catherine Færgemann for providing accommodation and office space during part of that time, and to Mette Wivel for the computer on which this novel was completed.

To Sean Devereux, Laurent Balas, and Esteban Sacco for their outstanding example of selfless Christian service in the war zones where I worked.

And to the LORD God for much Divine inspiration—which is not to say the book is perfect but to acknowledge God's guidance in what to write and what to omit and for giving me a wealth of personal experience that I have drawn upon to create this story. At times when I struggled with writer's block, I would meet someone who had the tale I needed; while on other occasions, I would speak to acquaintances and discover they had been through similar situations to those I had written about and were able to add important details I had omitted. Such encounters were surely not coincidental.

PUBLISHER'S NOTE

Ambassador International recognizes that this story contains elements that may be difficult for some readers. We believe that the Gospel can shine a light into the darkest recesses of the earth and that there is no one and nowhere that is beyond the saving work of Jesus Christ. The publishing of this material does not necessarily reflect the beliefs of Ambassador International but does portray the experiences of the author and will hopefully encourage the reader to seek out ways to help those less fortunate than themselves, as God has called us to "go into all the world and preach the Gospel to every creature" (Matt. 28:19). May we each be reminded of the atrocities that are being committed against our fellow human beings and stand up to fight against these injustices.

The author working as a logistican for Médecins Sans Frontières (Doctors Without Borders) in Goma, Congo/Zaire, December 1996.

ABOUT THE AUTHOR

Phil Clarke was born in Cornwall, U.K., in 1967 to a British father and a Danish mother. After an early childhood in Singapore and Hong Kong, he was brought up in Britain and educated at state schools in Crewkerne and Yeovil, followed by the universities of Birmingham and York, where he gained master's degrees in engineering and ecology. He spent most of the 1990s in Africa, both as a humanitarian aid worker and as a tropical forest researcher, about which he has written newspaper articles, scientific papers, and a textbook on the Coastal Forests of Eastern Africa. He then worked for almost a decade in Copenhagen as an executive director of Médecins Sans Frontières (Doctors Without Borders) before founding the war crimes investigation agency, Bloodhound.

Falling Night is Phil Clarke's debut novel, based on actual experiences by the author or his acquaintances in the various wars that took place in Africa during the 1990s but using fictional characters. Any similarity to real persons is coincidental and unintentional.

For more information about
AMBASSADOR INTERNATIONAL
please visit:

www.ambassador-international.com
@AmbassadorIntl
www.facebook.com/AmbassadorIntl

Thank you for reading this book. Please consider leaving us a review on your social media, favorite retailer's website, Goodreads or Bookbub, or our website.

Printed in Great Britain
by Amazon